The Venturers

Charles O. Goulet

Thanks, Marlene
Chas O Goulet
Oct 28, 2006

ISBN:1-894936-40-X
Saga Books/Authorship
sagabooks.net

Cover by RT

Chapter One — The Arrival — 1670

Pierre slipped his hand into Françoise's sturdy, firm one and squeezed it gently. She turned her tanned face toward him and smiled tentatively; her dark brown hair fell in shimmering cascades over her shoulders, and a hint of sadness, which Pierre did not miss, shadowed her hazel eyes.

"It's changed," he muttered.

"Well, it's different from the way I imagined it."

"Three years does make a difference, I suppose."

He stared at the tiny settlement on the south shore of the large bay that the three ships entered earlier that day. His piercing blue eyes rove over the low landscape before him; he too was disappointed by what he saw. The square, hewn-log fort looked dilapidated and forlorn, as if it was abandoned recently.

Françoise tugged at his arm and pointed to the left. A ship with its sails furled lay at anchor several hundred yards east of the log pier that jutted into the shore water before the fort palisade that rose immediately behind it.

"That's an English privateer, probably from Boston."

"Will they cause trouble?" she asked an intimation of anxiety in her voice.

"No, I don't think so," he replied confidently, but he was not sure. Since the Treaty of Breda of 1667, this ended the Second Dutch War and returned Acadia to France three years before, the New England governor, Sir William Temple of Boston, refused to cede authority to the French. The ship anchored in the bay, no doubt, was one of his.

Pierre noted its armament: It carried twenty-six 24-pounders, a formidable array for a ship which was not a warship. Although the gun ports were open, little activity took place on the decks of the alien ship.

The crew of their ship, the barque, "Le Cygne", scurried about as they brought it to anchor before the pier. The flap of sails being furled, the smell of tar from the treated lines, and the creak of the wooden blocks, reminded Pierre of the time he spent in France's Royal Navy.

"Will we be disembarking soon?" Françoise asked, the merriment of her personality returning to her voice.

"No hurry. I'm sure there will be a great deal of excitement among the others. Everyone's in a hurry to leave. It's been a long voyage, and like you, most of them aren't accustomed to sea life. So they will be in a hurry to go ashore. We will take our time and be more comfortable."

She nodded in agreement. The journey from Le Havre, the great seaport of France and her hometown, was not a pleasant one for her. She was seasick for the first half of the voyage, and it was only in the past two weeks that she returned to her customary cheerfulness and good health.

Pierre wrapped his right arm about her waist and drew her close. As he felt her warm tenderness and firm bosom press against him, a surge of passion and a quickening of his pulse excited him. His wife of just a few months awakened in him a lust, which was hard to satisfy on the crowded ship during the recent passage. He envisaged a private compartment ashore, and he pressed her tighter to him. She, sensing his arousal, pushed him away slightly, indicating that the time was inappropriate. His public display of affection and ardor embarrassed her. Although they were married only a few months, he understood her, so he dropped his arm.

Pierre noticed the wry smile of a sailor who was watching them. The man stared unabashedly at Françoise; his mocking gray eyes wandered over her ripe and pliant body. Pierre saw desire and lust; anger and jealousy surged through him.

The mate shouted to the man who turned back to the line that he was belaying. A nagging feeling of apprehension seized Pierre; with difficulty, he shook it off.

Françoise also became aware of the sailor's interest, and she whispered to Pierre, "I don't like that man. He's stared at me many times during the voyage…but he's not spoken to me. He acts as if he knows me, but he hasn't bothered me."

Pierre shrugged his shoulders. "Ah, he's just a woman-hungry sailor. He will find a willing woman ashore. Perhaps one of the native girls—for a colorful handkerchief—will satisfy his desires."

"You're a man of experience," she teased as she dug him sharply in the ribs with her elbow.

He was silent a moment, then replied, "When I was in the navy in the Antilles, most of the sailors found willing partners among the native girls. I'm sure there are many here as well."

"Were there many when you were last here?" she badgered, half seriously.

"We didn't get shore leave when I was here in '67."

"But maybe the girls came aboard," she persisted. She grew up in Le Havre, one of the largest seaports of France, where her father owned a tavern not far from the waterfront; she was not ignorant of the ways of sailors and seamen. She met Pierre in her father's tavern while he was serving with the French navy.

"If they did, I didn't partake of their pleasures."

She laughed; even though it was the truth, he was not sure she believed him.

Pierre recalled his first visit to Port Royal in the summer of 1667. His squadron, which was in the Caribbean on maneuvers against the English to protect French interests in the Antilles, was ordered back to France, and they sailed up the New England coast with a stop at Port Royal to provision.

The beauty of the surrounding countryside impressed him then. The small fort, before which they were now anchored, interested him. The English garrison—for it was occupied by the English then—kept it well maintained and in good repair.

He, as an ordinary sailor, was not allowed shore leave for fear of an incident. He loaded provisions, which the commander purchased from the few French farmers who stayed during the English occupation and who still cultivated the fertile sea marshes along the shores. They loaded vegetables and meats of various sorts. Since it was late in the summer, the gardens and crops were coming to maturity; Pierre was surprised at the quality and quantity of the produce. Although the colonists were under the English flag, they appeared contented and free. This surprised Pierre, for as a sailor he heard of the barbarity of the English and the atrocities they committed in the Antilles.

Around the fort he saw many Indians who, he noted, were friendlier to the French colonists than to the English traders and sailors, yet the peaceful serenity of the small colony affected him.

Françoise's voice brought him from his reverie. "Are you still tasting their charms?" she scolded.

"Enough, my love. We must get ready for our great adventure. Then I will taste your charms, my sweet."

She smiled coquettishly and slapped his face gently.

As they assembled and prepared their small pile of belongings for the move to shore, Pierre joked and helped his fellow passengers with their meager possessions. He knew all twenty-eight fellow adventurers by name, but he and Françoise were so wrapped up in each other that they made little attempt to get to know them intimately. Among there were two other young couples: Joseph and Marie Bergeron, Jacques and Louise Leblanc, and an older couple with three rambunctious children—a boy, about ten years old, and two girls, one about eight years old and the other, five years old. Françoise had told him, for one day she got into a conversation with the harried mother. The remainder of the passengers was men, some single, but most married, who left their families in France while they came out to establish a home for them. These he also knew by name, but other than that, he knew little about them.

The mother of the three children scurried about assembling their bundles, and then she grouped the children before her. They were quiet and subdued and appeared a little apprehensive of the situation into which they were thrust.

The mother called to her husband, "Albert, are you sure that you got all our things?"

"Adelaide, quiet down. Yes, I got everything. There's no need to be concerned. If I didn't get them this time, there will be time to get anything we missed later."

Pierre was glad the wife called her husband by name, for he had momentarily forgotten it. He approached the sturdily built peasant of about forty years of age and asked, "Sir, can I help?" His parents' teachings and his naval experience made him speak with deference to a person older than himself.

"No one calls me 'sir'. The name is Albert. Thanks for your offer. Perhaps you could hand the heavier bundles to me when I'm in the longboat. They're a little heavy for the wife and the boy."

"Certainly, Albert."

"You and your wife seem to be very young to come out to this new land."

"Well, I've just mustered out of the navy, where I served for four years, during the war against the Dutch and English."

"I was in the army," Albert interrupted.

"Did you see action?"

"No, I was lucky. My unit was always held in reserve. But we won't talk about war. The present's more interesting. What are your plans?"

"I hope to get a piece of land, as I was promised by our illustrious minister, Colbert. The land's good here, and I will prosper as a farmer."

"I, the same, Pierre."

Pierre was surprised the man knew his name, but, at the same time, he was flattered.

Albert continued, "I've been assured of a concession on the grant of land that's been set aside for Captain Grandfontaine. You know, I served under him in the war."

Pierre said, "I'm to get my own grant of land, but the details haven't been worked out yet. I have to see the captain as soon as possible to make the final arrangements."

"The captain's a fine person, and I'm sure there will be no problem. He's an honorable man. It was a pleasure to serve under him. All his officers and men liked him."

"I met him briefly before we boarded our ships at Le Havre. He seems to be an agreeable fellow."

As they conversed, they moved the baggage to the rail. Now, Albert crawled down the rope ladder to the gently bobbing boat that was held to the side of the ship by four roughly attired crewmen. Several people were already seated in the boat with their small accumulation of personal goods heaped about them.

Pierre took the youngest child by the arm and helped her descend the awkward ladder to the waiting arms of her father and one of the sailors who stood at the base of it. Each of the children dropped in turn into the swaying boat and was assigned a seat in the almost filled craft. Pierre then took Adelaide, the wife, by the arm and guided her down the rope ladder to the waiting arms of the men below. Just as the two men were about to grab her, an errant wave struck the boat, pushing it away from the side of the ship. The woman screeched and slid through the narrow opening between the boat and the ship. With a dull splash, she disappeared into the gray-blue waters.

For a moment, stunned silence enveloped the group as everyone watched the spot where she vanished. Then shouts and cries mingled as the people milled about waiting for the woman to surface.

Pierre stared at the area; if she did surface, she would be crushed between the ship and the heavy longboat. She would have to come up on the far side of the long boat, or at either end. If she did not, she would, at the least, be seriously injured. He saw a few accidents like that during his stint in the navy.

She needed help. He did not know if she could swim. Unlikely, he thought. Quickly he discarded his woolen shirt and heavy shoes, threw them to the deck beside Françoise, leaped to the rail, and plunged into the water before the bow of the longboat.

Although the cold surprised him, he allowed his dive to bring him deeply into the water. He could make out the dark outline of the longboat, and the hull of the ship shadowed the water making visibility difficult. Slowly he swam underwater to the spot where he thought she would be.

He searched for any sign of the woman, but all he saw was swirling gray water. He swam the length of the longboat using a powerful breaststroke. His lungs burned as he held his breath; they felt as if they were bursting; he would have to surface for air. He still did not see the woman.

As his head burst through the surface, he gasped in great heaving gulps. Several persons shouted to him at the same time, making it impossible to understand what they were saying. Finally, he heard Albert crying, "Where is she? Where's my Adelaide?"

Pierre ignored the commotion, pumped his lungs with air, doubled over, straightened his body vertically, and drew himself downward with powerful pulls of his arms. As he descended, he surveyed the area around him. Out of the corner of his eye, he noticed a flash of movement. He turned toward it. It had to be her. As he drew nearer, he could see the struggling antics of the woman. Her hands and legs were thrashing about, though feebly, and one hand was clawing at her throat while the other, her right, reached upward as if trying to draw the surface toward her. Her eyes were wide, staring wildly about. Bubbles streamed from her mouth, which seemed open in a scream. Her skirts billowed about her lower body like a tent flapping in a strong breeze. Pierre knew that she would be dangerous to approach.

He paused to decide how he would advance upon her. Slowly her movements became weaker, her eyes closed, her arms and legs stilled, and she drifted downward. Pierre swam toward her, coming at her from the rear. The bonnet she wore was awry, but her hair remained neatly coiled about her head. He could not grab her by the hair and haul her to the surface that way. He was still uncertain how he would grasp her. Although she appeared unconscious, he knew she might clutch at him, entangle him, and in her renewed struggles, endanger both their lives. He reached out and grabbed the neck of the loose bodice of her homespun dress. The material, which was coarse and strong, gave him a good grip.

She was unconscious and unlikely to impede him with any thrashing about. He started swimming to the surface, using a strong kicking stroke and drawing powerfully with his free left arm. Her weight and the drag of her heavy clothing made progress slow. His lungs ached. His vision blurred. His limbs weakened and wanted to quit moving. He seemed to be whirling in a maelstrom; demons were clutching at him and crying to him. He forced his mind to concentrate on what he must do. Every ounce of his strength, he poured into the struggle to reach the surface.

He looked upward. All he could see was darkness and shadow. He was disoriented; he could not decide in which direction the longboat might be. He noticed a brightening of his surroundings, although he was not sure whether he was imagining it or whether it was the surface.

Then his head popped through the suffocating water, and he gasped for air, looking back to see if his cargo was still with him. Water streamed down his face, and a piece of seaweed clung to his right ear, irritating him. The slimy taste of the water tingled his mouth. He shook his head sharply, like a dog, to remove the excess water from his hair and to dislodge the annoying plant.

Adelaide's face was still in the water so he changed his grip on her. He drew her across his breast and held her along his body, his right arm across her bosom, her back to him. She was quiet and still, and he saw that her lips were bluish-purple.

Someone shouted, but he could not tell from where it came. He treaded water slowly and breathed deeply as his faculties gradually returned to normal.

To his surprise, he surfaced near the stern of the ship, and out of sight of the persons in the longboat. Carefully he made his way to the south side of the ship into the sunlight.

The longboat moved out from the ship's side, and its crew was rowing in a tight circle out from the ship. They were ready to move toward the spot where he might surface.

Other swimmers were in the water, but he did not take time to count them. As he came from behind the stern, he shouted, “Here! Over here!”

Immediately a shout returned, and the crew of the longboat, with dexterity and speed, made for him. His strength was going fast, so he hoped they would arrive before he would have to release his burden.

Within moments, the boat arrived and clutching hands relieved him of the sodden body. Other hands helped him upward to clutch at the gunwale. His right hand contacted a thole pin that he grabbed tightly.

As they drew the limp body over the gunwale, Pierre shouted, “Hang her over the gunwale so her head is lower than the rest of her body. Let the water drain from her mouth. If you don't, she will not be able to breathe.”

They held her, head down, draped over the side of the boat. Water and mucous streamed from her open mouth.

Two sailors grabbed Pierre by each arm and hoisted him into the confusion of the longboat. Adelaide's children were huddled together, crying softly. The adults were grouped around the still form of the woman who was still half in the boat. All were offering advice as to how to revive the unconscious woman. Someone shouted, "Is she still alive?"

Albert, the husband, who was trying to clasp her in his arms, moaned in anguish, "My Adelaide, my love, you can't leave me now. I need you."

One of the sailors was pressing her upper torso as if pumping water from her. He tore the bodice of her dress as well as the cotton chemise that most women wore beneath their dresses. His rough hands wrapped around each side of her ribcage, and he squeezed her torso in and out. Slowly he moved his hands around to her breasts and massaged them firmly. At each compression, a stream of water and slime dribbled from her mouth.

To Pierre, some of the fondling of her breasts seemed unnecessary, and he looked into the sailor's face. It was the same man who was so intent on Françoise as they stood by the rail earlier. The man's face glowed and flushed, and he seemed to be enjoying what he was doing. Pierre was about to remonstrate at what he thought was improper behavior when Adelaide groaned, and her eyelids fluttered. The assembled spectators sighed with relief and then cheered. The sailor continued his ministration, slid his hand further into the bodice, and now rubbed vigorously. Someone pressed a cloth to her mouth to wipe away the water and saliva. She sputtered, coughed, and spewed forth more water and mucous. She struggled to rise, but the sailor held her down and continued squeezing her sides and breasts. The grin on his face disturbed Pierre.

Adelaide started to breathe in great gulping gasps, and she thrashed about as she struggled to rise from the awkward position in which she found herself. The sailor removed his hands from inside the bodice of her dress and stepped back. Other hands drew the woman fully within the boat and laid her on the bottom of it, her back propped against one of the seats. Her eyes opened, and she stared in fear. She looked wildly about, saw her husband and children, and made an attempt to reach them. Albert moved forward and clasped her within his arms. She closed her eyes and snuggled against his chest.

Pierre was upset by the way the sailor ministered to the woman, although no one else seemed concerned. They congratulated the sailor for his fine work and how he successfully revived the half-drowned woman. He smiled in acceptance, but Pierre thought that some of the smile was from the pleasure he derived from his massage of the helpless woman's breasts.

Later, after the excitement of the near drowning subsided, Pierre returned to the ship and helped Françoise prepare for their short trip to the mainland. As they waited for the longboat to return, he sat atop one of the duffels that held his clothes and breathed deeply to quiet his still pounding heart.

Françoise looked at him with admiration in her eyes. "That was a brave thing you did."

"Thanks, but I don't think it was very brave. I did it without thinking of the consequences. She needed help. I was glad that I was able to be of help."

"That sailor who pumped the water from her seemed to know what he was doing. Did he have to massage her breasts so hard?" she inquired in a tone that indicated she did not approve of what he did. "I was watching at the rail of the ship, and it seems to me he took great pleasure in working on that poor woman."

"I agree with you. I was thinking the same thing. He's the same fellow that you were complaining about earlier. He seems to have an eye for every woman."

"I think you're right. I will be careful when he's around."

"He's just another of the many dangers the we must watch for."

Gloom came to Françoise's face, and she whispered, "There are many dangers in this land. Falling into the sea is just one of them. Adelaide was lucky. She could have drowned."

"That's true, Françoise, but look out there. There's land to be used to make a man wealthy. The land's there for the taking—to be used to grow crops, to build houses, to establish homes, to increase the glory of France, to bring God to the savages, to prosper!"

She gazed north from the ship toward the land. She could see the longboat at the pier that jutted into the bay. People were unloading their possessions, and small piles of duffel and gear lay on the rough-hewn timbers. A short distance up the beach from the pier the gate to the small fort stood open. A gray patinaed palisade encircled the half dozen buildings that constituted the fort. Two enclosures jutted out at an angle from each corner of the palisade. Here, the logs that formed the walls were rotten in spots, and some leaned at a precarious angle. As a protective barrier, it left much to be desire.

She turned toward Pierre. "Do you think the fort will be able to protect us from an enemy?" she muttered scornfully.

"It needs repairs, but we will do that in the next few days."

"What if the English attack us now? That ship doesn't look very friendly—with its gun ports open."

"We're at peace with the English. They won't cause trouble. They're leaving. This land now belongs to France."

"What about the Indians? Will they be friendly? After all, it's their land."

"I've been told that they've always been friendly with the French. There's no reason to believe they won't be now."

"You may be right, Pierre, but I'm still afraid."

"I understand, Françoise. Everything is new and different. In a short time you will become accustomed to life here, and then you will love it." He made the statement with an assurance that he did not feel.

Coming as a colonist was a difficult decision. But he could not see a better life in his old home country. At fifteen, he joined the refurbished French navy and served aboard a brigantine, the "Defiance", which made a tour of duty in the Caribbean. During his service, he learned many things about the world and about the opportunities that awaited a person who was willing to take risks. He saw the sugar plantations of the Antilles, and the fortunes that were made by enterprising people. In the summer of 1667, when the squadron stopped at Port Royal, he liked the life the few colonists enjoyed at this tiny outpost. When the opportunity presented itself, he took advantage of it. Now he was here with his new wife to seek his fortune in the new land.

He gazed across the bay to where a man and a young boy worked in a field, which seemed planted to vegetables. They were hoeing the long rows, which he assumed were turnips, a popular plant with the colonists. They were easy to grow, required little care, and, as well, they were easy to store once they were harvested. They also provided a nutritious supplement to any kind of meat. He had in his luggage a package of seeds, which he would plant as soon as he obtained the final right to his land.

Pierre Marin was a sailor and fisherman, born in Harfleur, a small village a few miles east of the great port of Le Havre. All his life he helped his father on his fishing boat. Early in the morning, almost every day, since he was old enough to help, he accompanied his father as they sailed offshore in their small boat to cast their nets for herring and hake. The hours were long, the catch usually small, and the recompense for the arduous work was always meager. It did sustain the family, without luxuries, just the necessities.

His father was annoyed when he went away to the navy, his mother anxious, and his brothers and sisters missed him for the work that he did, and for the teasing that annoyed them.

He served out his contract, and then he was invited by Captain Hector de Grandfontaine to join him in Acadia. The idea intrigued him, and he convinced Françoise Chiasson, the seventeen-year-old daughter of the tavern keeper, Jean Chiasson, to be his wife and accompany him. Françoise was excited by the idea of going to a savage land to carve a home from the wilderness. Of course, she had no idea what the wilderness would be like. She thought it might be like the woods to the northeast of Le Havre. Now she seemed to regret her decision.

"Where are the women in the colony?" she asked, although he told her several times that the small colony had few women. Most of the colonists were men who planned to establish themselves, and then go back for their families if they were married, or else go back to France to find a wife to join them.

Patiently he explained. "Françoise, there aren't many French women here. Most of the women are Indians. But they don't live in the colony like the French women. They live in their own villages, which are usually far in the woods where they hunt animals for their food."

"Will we live in the woods too?"

"No, my dear, we will build a house not too far from the fort. We must stick together for protection—so we can help each other—if there's need."

"Oh, Pierre, it sounds so dangerous. Each time I think of it, I'm not sure I can bear it."

Pierre put his arm around her waist and drew her down beside him. "Dear, I know you will come to like this land. It will be our home and the home of our children. Maybe some of our brothers and sisters will come to join us."

She leaned her head against his shoulder and said nothing. Pierre was not sure he convinced her. He placed his arm around her shoulders and stroked her long flowing hair. She turned to him and kissed him gently on the cheek.

Several people milled about them, waiting impatiently for the long boat to return. Pierre noticed a young man leaning against the rail of the main deck near the ladder that was used to descend to the boat. Pierre saw him several times during the voyage, but he did not speak to him. The dark-haired, sturdily built young man was quiet and reserved and did not mingled much with the passengers. He was above average in height and build, with long sloping shoulders and muscles that bulged beneath his heavy linen shirt. He looks strong, Pierre thought.

The young man raised his head, noticed Pierre's gaze, and smiled shyly. Pierre returned the smile and hollered, "My friend, it's nice to have arrived."

"Yes," he nodded but said no more.

Pierre continued, "Are you one of Captain Hector's men?"

"No, I'm hoping to get a concession from Lieutenant Richard."

Pierre heard of Lieutenant Richard. He was one of Captain Hector d'Andigne de Grandfontaine's officers, and he, as an officer, was given a grant of land by the king. Lieutenant Richard arrived on an earlier ship to make preparations for the arrival of Captain Hector, the new governor of Acadia.

"I wish you luck, my friend."

The young man approached slowly, his right hand extended, and he said, "My name's Jacques Breton."

Pierre seized his hand and was surprised by the size and strength of the man's grip. "My name's Pierre Marin, and this is my wife, Françoise."

Jacques bowed slowly at the waist, and his tanned face turned a deeper color. Pierre noticed his embarrassment and smiled. Obviously he was uncomfortable in the company of females.

Hesitantly Jacques swept off his knitted stocking like headpiece and stammered, " It…It's v…very n…nice to meet you."

"Where are you from, Jacques?" Pierre asked.

"I was born on a farm outside Rouen, but the last years I've been working on the docks at Le Havre."

"Then you must know the Red Circle Tavern on Rue St. Etienne."

"I've heard of it, but I never went there. I was saving my sous to come to this land."

"Oh! Françoise's father owns it. I thought you might have seen her there. She helped her father a great deal."

Jacques stared down at the toe of his worn leather shoe and fidgeted uncomfortably.

"Well, Jacques, I'm sure we will be seeing more of you, and maybe we can be of help while you're getting established."

"Thank you." He turned away and returned to the rail as he saw the boat returning from the mainland.

Pierre turned to Françoise. "There are, you see, many agreeable people here. Jacques seems to be a very nice person, and I'm sure we will be seeing more of him."

Françoise smiled half-heartedly, the near-fatal accident and the behavior of the crude sailor still on her mind. "I hope you're right, Pierre."

"I know I'm right, my dear. You will see. Everything will turn out for the best."

"But if it doesn't, will you go back to France?"

The edge in her voice annoyed him, and, for a moment, he had misgivings. Would Françoise be difficult and badger him into returning to France before he had a chance to become prosperous in the New World?

He convinced her that their only hope of a brighter future lay in leaving the established society of France for the looser, freer society of the new continent. Yes, he painted a picture of opportunity and wealth, but he did not minimize the difficulties and dangers. They, after their marriage, talked for hours of the possibilities in the new land.

She was not unfamiliar with the promotion of the overseas colony, for a poster extolling its virtues was placed in her father's tavern. Colbert, the finance minister of the great and glorious king, Louis XIV, was promoting emigration, and assisting generously anyone who would leave his native land for the far, alien shores. Françoise was as excited as he, but now she seemed to be changing her mind.

Finally he answered her. "I will go back to France if I find I can't make a better life for us here. But first, we must try to make the best use of our chances here." For the first time he was irritated with his new wife, the sharpness of his voice shocked him.

She felt his anger but ignored it. "Will you promise me that, Pierre? Will you promise me that if we don't succeed here, you will go back to France?"

He hesitated. "I promise…but if I can't keep it…I shall feel that I'm cheating you, my sweet." Tenderness returned to his voice. He continued,

"We must do our best here, and you must help me. We must make a better life for our children, and we must start without doubts, Françoise. You must share my dream...be part of it...be convinced that we can accomplish it. I love you dearly, and I need you to make it worthwhile. Please be with me."

She nodded in agreement, but he felt it lacked conviction.

Chapter Two — The Fight

The trip from the ship to the pier took only a few minutes; loading and unloading the baggage and the passengers took longer than the quick row by the experienced sailors. On this trip Pierre, Françoise, and ten other passengers, including their new friend, Jacques Breton, filled the longboat to capacity. Since Adelaide's accident, quiet descended upon the group, and the trip was solemn and sober. Each person sat silent, engrossed in his or her own thoughts.

The six sailors rowed the heavy boat with skill and precision; it moved through the glistening steely waters with a faint swishing sound, the roiling sea gurgling as it passed the stern. The men bent their backs to the oars that creaked irritatingly against the oaken thole pins.

The steersman at the stern maneuvered the boat dexterously alongside the log pier, and two lines, one astern and another at the bow soon held it fast to the pier.

The passengers came to life; the two foremost sailors scurried up the short ladder to the platform to help the disembarking passengers. Quickly, the two men in the bow handed up the gear and duffel, and then the passengers climbed the ladder themselves.

It was Françoise and Pierre's turn to disembark. Pierre handed their few bags forward; these were passed to the waiting sailors who passed them up to those already ashore. Eager hands grabbed them and piled them on the crude dock.

Pierre grasped Françoise by the left arm and steadied her as she carefully made her way forward. One of the sailors extended his hand to help her to the bow. At that moment Pierre looked up. The sailor was smiling at Françoise in more than a friendly way. Pierre gritted his teeth as he recognized him. He was the same one who provided aid to Adelaide after her dunking in the bay. Pierre paused momentarily trying to control his emotions. But his anger refused to subside, although it leveled off, seething below the surface.

To Pierre, his solicitous manner was more than was necessary to aid a female passenger. He held her hand with more tenderness and solicitude than was warranted. His left hand came to her elbow and guided it caressingly, pushing gently against her torso, his fingers nudging gently against the lower part of her bosom.

As Françoise stepped upon the forward seat, he stepped before her and grasped her two hands. At that moment the boat rocked, and Françoise stumbled and fell gently forward into the sailor's arms. He grasped her firmly in his arms and held her against his chest, breaking her fall and setting her gently on the floorboards of the boat.

Françoise pushed him firmly away and looked up into his face. Recognition mirrored in her eyes, and they widened in surprise. Her cheeks reddened as she mumbled, "Thank you."

The sudden rocking of the boat threw Pierre off balance also, but his years around boats allowed him to recover quickly. No reason was apparent for the sudden rocking of the boat, and a grave suspicion entered his mind. Did the sailor cause it purposely, and at that precise moment to cause Françoise to lose her footing and tumble into his arms? His dislike for the man, which already developed, helped him to believe that that was what happened. His blood raced again, and his anger grew. He gnawed at his lower lip to suppress the retort that wanted to erupt from his mouth. He did not want to appear to be a jealous husband and make a spectacle of himself.

The sailor guided Françoise to the bow of the boat, placed her hand on a rung of the crude wooden ladder, and guided her other hand to one of the persons on the wharf who was reaching for it. Then he dropped his hands to her ankles and steered her feet to the ladder, all the while smiling lecherously. Once her feet were on the ladder, he slid his hands up the calves of her legs to her thighs, one remaining on her thigh, and the other gliding effortlessly up to her right buttock.

Françoise felt the pressure of his hand and knew that his help was not needed. Anger and resentment rose within her, and she hurried up the ladder to evade his exploring hands.

But his helping hands slid along her thighs and calves as she hurried upward, and she felt his right hand tighten around her right ankle as she reached the top of the pier. The sudden arresting of her upward flight surprised her; her awkward position on the ladder wrenched her loose from the grasp of the person at the top. Her left foot slipped from the wet rung, and she felt herself falling through space.

She cried out involuntarily, and whirled her hands, grasping at the air. She was falling backward clumsily when she felt strong arms about her, grasping her about the waist and torso. One hand held her left breast firmly, and she felt it squeezed tightly, so tightly that she gasped. She flailed her arms and tried to disentangle herself from the person who was holding her.

Pierre bellowed, "Get your filthy hands off my wife, you scum!"

Stunned silence followed, and Pierre seized Françoise by the left hand, drawing her to him. The strength of his anger pulled her swiftly past and behind him. He stood facing the crouching sailor, breathing heavily. For several moments the two men stared at each other. The sailor sneered and snarled, "What did you say?"

"I said, 'Keep your filthy hands off my wife!'"

"But you added something else, sir." He exaggerated the 'sir' from a word of respect to one of scorn.

"Yes, I did. I called you 'scum', for that's what you are. I've seen you now on three occasions use situations to paw helpless women. You're scum. You're filth."

"Sir, no one calls Jean Charlet such names without paying a penalty. You've accused me of coarse behavior when I'm only the victim of circumstances. You're a jealous man who sees wrong where there's none.

You stain my good reputation. I demand an apology, or I will seek satisfaction."

Pierre laughed sardonically. "You will get no apology from me. What I say is what I've seen, and I'm sure others have seen the same thing."

"What they've seen is a poor sailor who's come to the rescue of ladies in distress. That's all. Your jealousy has blinded you and made you see things that aren't so."

"You're a liar. Your behavior with Madam Doucet was despicable. The poor woman was helpless, and you intentionally played with her breasts."

The group on the pier and the passengers in the boat recovered from their initial shock and gathered around the two men. Murmurs of assent and dissent flowed through the shuffling group.

Pierre continued angrily, "And on two occasions, moments apart, you used your familiarity with boats and water to cause my wife to stumble into your arms. Then your hands, accidentally—I scornfully say 'accidentally'—groped and grasped her body. You're a lecher and a beast."

The stillness of the group tableaued into a scene like a painting; all waited in anticipation. The sailor whirled and agilely scurried up the ladder to the wharf. Once above the motionless group in the longboat, he snarled down at Pierre, "You whelping pup, come up here and repeat that accusation. Show me that you're as courageous as your mouth."

Françoise whispered to Pierre, "Don't fight. It's not that important."

Pierre ignored her and stared unblinking at the sailor. The man was taller, older, and heavier than Pierre was. He wore a pair of faded woolen pantaloons that extended to the knee, dirty and torn. His torso was covered by a worn, stained linen shirt. Around his head was a soiled and folded bandanna that held his unkempt hair from falling into his face. He wore no shoes, which was common with sailors as it allowed them to use their feet as well as their hands when working with the lines, halyards, and ropes around the ship. He was solid in build and well muscled, and stuck into the rope that he used as a belt was a short knife.

The cooling sweat of fear replaced Pierre's anger. He glowered up at the angry man and said calmly, "I don't want to fight you. I want an apology from you to my wife."

A raucous laugh escaped from between yellowed gaping teeth. "You ungrateful pup, I helped your wife. I've no reason to apologize. You owe me an apology. You started this fight with your foul mouth. You insulted me with your crude insinuations; you called me foul names; you besmeared my character; and now you want me to apologize. No, you young pup, it's Jean Charlet who requires redress."

Pierre's mouth went dry, and his chest tightened, squeezing the breath from his lungs. He did not want to fight, but he realized that he put himself into a precarious position by his anger and his name-calling.

He hoped that he could avoid a fight. As he sized up his opponent, he felt that his chances in a fight would be slim. The sailor looked as if he was in his share of altercations, and he knew how to handle himself. Pierre was in his share of fights as a youngster and as a sailor, but on those occasions his mates from his ship supported him. He knew that he could not back away from a fight in a cowardly way. If worse came to worse, he might have to accept defeat at the hands of this man. That would be better than avoiding a fight at the expense of his dignity. That he could not do, and he would not apologize.

"What I've said is true. You did not treat Madame Doucet properly. You took advantage of the situation. I'm sorry that I called you a disgusting name, but I'm not sorry about my accusation. It's true."

"I won't accept that apology. I will fight for my good name. Come up here and defend yourself, you worthless cur!"

Françoise seized his arm and pleaded, "Don't fight, Pierre. He's not worth bothering about."

Pierre shook his arm free and moved toward the ladder.

Murmurs and shouts came from the group. Pierre heard cheers of support, but he also heard jeers of opposition. The other sailors appeared to be supporting their mate, while the colonists seemed to be on his side.

His mind cleared; slowly and carefully he made his way to the deck of the raised pier. Those on the deck already formed a ring, and those on the boat hurried up the ladder to join the others.

Jean Charlet waited in a crouched position, his fists clenched, and his mouth twisted in a snarl. Pierre crouched to face him. As he did so, he heard Françoise cry, "Don't fight him, Pierre! You don't need to fight him. He's not worth it."

For a moment, Pierre was tempted to walk away, but he knew that his stature as a man would shrink. His self-esteem was at stake—not this dirty sailor's reputation—no, his own self-worth. He had to live with these people in the future. He had to live with himself. Even if he lost the fight, he could still face himself, but if he walked away, he was a coward.

Jean Charlet beckoned with fists that looked enormous to Pierre. They circled, eyeing each other furtively. Suddenly, Jean's right fist whipped out and caught Pierre on the point of the jaw. Fireworks exploded in his head, and he felt himself falling. His legs turned to rubber, and he sunk slowly to his hands and knees. He shook his head to dislodge the veil of grayness that covered his eyes. His ears rang as if a loud gong sounded inside his head. Far off he could hear people cheering and jeering. He shook his head a second time. His sight cleared; he was staring at the rough planks of the deck.

He tried to rise to his feet, and he felt an explosion against his ribcage on the right side. The force hurled him over onto his back, and the brilliant sunshine blinded him. He continued rolling until feet and legs blocked his way. He moaned and gasped for air; his lungs cried for it. His arms felt like lead weights, anchoring them to his sides.

He saw a shadow descending to his head, and instinctively he moved. He felt the swish as an object passed close to his ear. He scurried to his right and rolled to his feet.

His vision cleared, and he back-pedaled as his opponent, saliva dripping from his snarling mouth, rushed him. The hate in the man's eyes astounded him, and he realized that the man was about to kill him or maim him for life.

His senses cleared, and the scene before him became stark and sharp. He knew this was one fight he would have to win if he were to survive. Obviously the sailor was a better fighter than he was; he was bigger, heavier, and stronger; all the advantages seemed to be his. He struck the first blow, and it was a telling one. It hurt Pierre; it weakened him; it gave a decided advantage to the sailor.

The spectators were now vocal and excited. Their drab routine, for the second time this day, was enlivened by the unexpected, and they were enjoying it. The men tightened the circle, while the women were pushed to the rear.

Pierre could hear clearly the cheers and shouts of encouragement from the stimulated men. Some were for him, but many were for the sailor whom they felt was accused unjustly. Rough hands seized him and pushed him toward the expectant sailor.

He stumbled forward and ducked quickly as the man's right hand again shot forward. It whizzed over his head like the swish of a diving cormorant. At the same time, Pierre struck out clumsily with his right hand, and he felt a jolt as it hit the advancing fighter on the side of the head. The blow was a glancing one, but it opened a cut over the right cheekbone. Blood trickled from the corner of the cut and oozed slowly down the bronzed and stubbled cheek. Confidence and satisfaction filled Pierre, and he danced to his left, circling away from his charging opponent.

The man's left fist snaked out and caught Pierre along the left side of his ribcage. The blow was solid and hard. Pierre grunted as it forced the air out of his lungs in a sharp explosion. Involuntarily, Pierre doubled over in pain and shock. The sailor's right hand chopped around, and it crunched against Pierre's head behind his left ear.

Blackness engulfed him; the world seemed to end. Through a storm of black and blue roiling clouds, he heard a far off voice. It was the voice of an angel, pleading for him. "Please help him. Don't let that man hurt him any more."

The clouds rumbled in return, "He asked for it. He must accept his punishment. He was wrong!"

Again the angel pleaded. "No, he was right. That man's a beast. Someone had to show him for what he was—a lecher and a beast!"

Pain smothered him again. He felt sharp needles piercing the right side of his head. Darkness once more engulfed. The pain disappeared, and a stillness and peace descended upon him. But it lasted only a short time. The angel's voice penetrated the darkness; he could hear her pleading again. "He will be killed if you don't stop this. He's helpless; he can't defend himself; he will be killed." The angel's voice rang with urgency.

Another explosion of pain struck him, this time in his groin, and it rolled up through his body. He felt, rather than heard, a scream escape from his mouth. The blackness descended again, and, gratefully, peace and quiet engulfed him.

The voice of the devil stirred him. "He's mine. He deserves to be punished. I will ruin him."

The angel's voice interceded. "Please help him. He's a good man. He doesn't deserve this. He was only seeking justice."

And then it faded away.

Slowly reality returned, and pain, and fear, and anger.

Pierre lay on his back, and the first certainty was that the sun was shining brilliantly into his eyes. He closed them to protect them from the piercing rays. At first, he thought that the luminosity was the fires of hell and that the devil came for him. His head throbbed as waves of pain pulsed through his consciousness. He tried to move, but his muscles failed to respond. His whole body quivered, but it did not obey the commands of his brain.

Sounds came to his buzzing ears: the cacophony of many voices, the raucous squawk of gulls, the lap of waves against the shore, and the shuffle of feet on the rough deck. Then the angel's voice, which he now recognized as his wife's, penetrated to his mind. She was pleading. "Don't let this man hurt my husband any more. He will kill him. He's had his revenge. Don't you see that my husband's unconscious. He can't defend himself."

"It's his own fault. He made false accusations. Jean is not a bad man. He helped Madame Doucet when she was drowning, and your husband accused him of despicable behavior."

He heard other voices. "That sailor is a lecher. I saw what he did to Madame Doucet. He had no right to behave as he did."

"He was ungentlemanly with Françoise Marin. Pierre was right to call him to task. Pierre has suffered enough."

"This sailor has no right to continue beating him even when he's defeated."

Pierre groaned and rolled onto his stomach. His body ached in every muscle. He heard a snarl as his adversary advanced on him. "Woman, get out of my way so I may finish the job. This dog must be taught a lesson he will never forget. He can't accuse people if he's not able to prove his accusations."

"I won't let you strike my husband again. You will have to strike me first. If you do, then we will know what kind of man you are."

"This isn't your fight. Stay out of it. Women shouldn't interfere in the affairs of men." He seized her by the arm and hurled her aside.

Françoise shrilled, "You're scum—just as Pierre said!" She pressed forward; her left hand came to his face, and her fingernails burrowed into his right cheek, leaving three red streaks as they tore the flesh. A bellow thundered from his wide-stretched mouth, and spittle sprayed outward. His open right hand came up swiftly, and the slap reverberated through the excited crowd.

Anger and shock swept through the assembly. Men pushed and shoved; emotions heightened, and although no blows were struck, it would not be long before the single fight would become many.

Pierre struggled to his feet. The sound of his wife being struck gave him new strength; he snarled at his fearsome opponent, "You're a beast. You strike defenseless women. Come, try me again. I'm ready for you."

He did not feel the bravado that he exhibited, but he realized that he must divert the attention of the milling, shouting, emotional crowd that was increasing in size as people from the fort and those working nearby hurried not to miss the excitement that was taking place at the dock.

He staggered toward his enemy and pawed the air ineffectually. With an animal-like roar the aroused sailor stepped confidently toward Pierre, swinging his fists methodically and menacingly at Pierre's head. Pierre bobbed, weaved, and managed to avoid the blows that whistled past his ears. He smiled as he saw the blood streaming in numerous rivulets down his opponent's right cheek. It made his attractive face look evil and ugly. A feeling of exhilaration bolstered Pierre's courage and lifted his spirit. The blood, he saw, came from the cut that he inflicted and the scratches that Françoise administered. His head was clearing rapidly now, and he circled cautiously to the left, carrying his arms and fists high in front of him to protect his head.

Charlet, with his experience as a fighter, observed immediately the vulnerability of Pierre's torso and diverted his attack to the body. The first two punches, a left and a right, Pierre avoided by running away. But the third he could not avoid, as the charging Charlet caught up to him. His left fist thumped solidly into the right side of Pierre's ribcage. The pain shot through his chest, and he felt as if his heart burst. His mouth opened wide, and a cry of pain and anguish overrode the sounds of the boisterous crowd.

Pierre ducked low, more instinctively than consciously. The sailor's muscled abdomen appeared before him, and he moved forward butting into it as viciously as he could with his head. Like a battering ram it found the mark, and his opponent grunted in surprise; the air swooshed from his mouth; his eyes rolled in pain. The momentum of the collision forced both men to stagger.

Pierre swung his right fist in a short, sharp arc upward. He felt it strike solidly against some part of the man's anatomy, but he could not tell what. He felt his adversary quiver and stagger. He swung his left fist wildly, hoping that he would have as much luck with it as with his right. But it flailed harmlessly through the air.

Oaths, curses, and obscenities spewed from the twisted mouth of his enemy. Blood and mucous streamed from his mashed nose. His face was covered with bright red. He roared like an animal possessed. The savagery of the sailor's face made Pierre drop his guard for a moment.

The sailor's bare right foot kicked forward viciously, catching Pierre in the groin. A wave of nauseous pain spurted from his injured crotch, upward through his stomach. He retched, and sour, green stomach contents erupted from his mouth like from a fountain. He doubled over, grabbing with both hands at his lower abdomen. The pain convoluted through his lower body and he vomited again—this time green slime, foul smelling and sickening. He dropped to his knees and rolled his body back and forth, trying to ease the excruciating pain, oblivious to everything about him.

The next blow hit him directly below the right eye, and he felt skin and tissue splatter, and blood spurted from the mashed flesh of his nose, but he felt no pain. He fell forward onto the rough flooring and covered his head with his hands. His legs writhed in agony. The pain racked his body, and he wished for peaceful unconsciousness to relieve his agony. It would not come.

He could hear shouts and cries through his pain, but he could not distinguish individual voices. The noises were a jumble of sounds and cries—some male, others female.

He felt another blow strike the left side of his head. It was a glancing blow; it did not add to his comfort, but it did blur his vision further. He felt a hand grab his hair and lift his head. Something hit him on the left jawbone. He heard and felt no more.

Françoise rushed to her fallen husband. His face, the right side, was a mess of mashed flesh. The area below his eye was peeled of skin, and the crimson flesh glistened redly. Blood oozed from the damaged area, streaming down along his jawbone. A long cut ran along the ridge of his left jaw, and blood, bright and red, flowed freely from it down along his neck and onto the sweat-matted hair of his chest. His breath came in hollow gasps through his open, distended mouth. Vomit and spew covered his chin and upper chest.

She turned him onto his back and cradled his head in her lap. He groaned and moaned; his eyes fluttered open and shut, the whites showing. She wiped his face gently with the apron she wore over her hand-woven cotton and linen dress. As she did, she crooned softly and gently, rocking slowly back and forth.

She realized that Jean Charlet, the one responsible for her husband's condition, stood over her, cursing, swearing, and muttering further vengeance. She ignored him as she ministered to her fallen warrior. Finally, she glanced up at the snarling animal hovering, astonished at the malevolence in his face. It, too, was a heap of crimson. His right cheek streamed blood and his nose was a conglomerate of blood, mucous, tissue, and bone, broken and mashed by Pierre's lucky blow. His mouth was twisted into a vicious snarl that added to the ferocity of his appearance. He was frothing at the mouth and gibbering incoherently—curses, blasphemies, and deprecations. Françoise shivered and returned to her ministrations.

Pierre gasped, and his body convulsed in pain.

"Please, help me. My Pierre's hurt—hurt very bad." She looked around the milling crowd with imploring eyes. She called again. "My husband needs help. Will someone help me?"

The crowd murmured, but no one wanted to become involved. No one moved. No one came forward. Fear hung over the group like fog. It was so intense it smelled.

Françoise pleaded once more. "Please help me move my husband so I can take care of him."

"If anyone helps this man, he will have to deal with me. He doesn't deserve your help. He's a liar and a troublemaker. He deserved the beating I gave him. If someone comes to his aid, he will have to fight me."

"You're a beast. You've beaten him. Isn't that enough? Can't you leave him alone? He's been punished enough, although, God knows, he didn't deserve it. God will punish you, you wicked man."

"Shut up, you whore. I know you from your father's tavern in Le Havre. You're nothing but a tavern slut."

Françoise's eyes widened in recognition. That was why he was so familiar with her. He was a regular customer of her father's tavern.

She turned to the crowd. "This man is nothing but a troublemaker. Each time he came to my father's tavern he was involved in a fight. He always tried to compromise the girls, including me. Because we worked in the tavern, he decided we were all easy women. That's not the kind of tavern my father runs. It's a God-fearing, respectable establishment."

Mutters of approval came from the crowd.

"What she says isn't true; she's lying to protect her own reputation at my expense. You saw how I helped this morning, and you saw how I helped this woman when she almost fell overboard. She's a liar and troublemaker, like her husband."

His threatening pose did not make the crowd eager to interfere. They could see the result of his handiwork as Pierre still lay moaning and groaning in Françoise's arms.

Chapter Three — The Rescue

Pierre groaned and tried to move, but the pain paralyzed him. Although he was conscious, the effort of opening his eyes was more than he could bear.

A gasp from crowd forced him to open his eyes. Jacques Breton, his young acquaintance from the ship, approached his wife and him. A shocked look covered his bronzed face, and even his tan could not hide the pallor emphasized by his dark brown hair.

He looked down at Pierre, but he spoke to Françoise, "Madame, I would like to help you. What would you like me to do?"

An animal snarl hissed through the stillness that fell over the melee, and all eyes focused on the fuming assailant. Jacques turned slowly toward the offending sound and stared calmly at the agitated man; then he spoke softly, "Sir, I've no quarrel with you, and I don't wish one. I want to help my friends, nothing more. So leave me in peace." With that he deliberately turned his back on the enraged man and knelt to help the battered Pierre.

The crowd exclaimed as the raging sailor precipitated himself toward the kneeling Jacques. Instinctively Jacques hurled himself backward. The surprise move caught the advancing cyclone at its base, tripping him and hurling him violently to the log surface. Jacques scrambled to his feet, seized the shaken man by his loose shirt, and lifted him to his feet. The man's flailing fists beat a tattoo against Jacques's chest, but they were ineffectual as Jacques drew him close and hugged him tightly, so tightly that he crushed the air from his opponent. Jacques was not a fighter, but his size and strength made him a formidable adversary.

His childhood as the son of a peasant farmer on the seigneury of August Richard, Sieur de Barentin, and his youth as a stevedore on the docks of Le Havre developed his upper body, For his size, he was excessively strong. And on many occasions that strength kept him out of trouble.

Now he squeezed more tightly, and he watched as Jean Charlet's face purpled, and his eyes started to bulge; then he flung him away and turned to his fallen friend.

Jean was more enraged than ever, and he gasped deep breaths to recuperate. He lay for several moments, gathering his wits. With a roar, he rose to his feet and once more hurled himself at Jacques. This time he was more cautious, assumed a fighting stance, and called out, "I will do the same to you as I did to that liar and troublemaker."

Jacques rose slowly and deliberately. Without speaking he turned to face the cursing, wild fighter. Calmly he said, "Sir, I don't want to fight you. One of us will get hurt badly, and I don't want it to be me."

Jean laughed loudly and scornfully. "Are you thinking that you can defeat me, Jean Charlet, the best fighter aboard 'Le Cygne'? My friend, you jest."

He advanced on Jacques and struck out viciously with his left fist. Jacques right hand seized the extended wrist and twisted outward, rotating the wrist until bone and sinew would rotate no more. The suddenness of the maneuver caught the sailor flatfooted and the entire weight of his body fulcrumed against the imprisoned wrist. The strain was too much. A popping sound erupted as the elbow joint separated. A look of surprise and agony masked the bleeding face. He danced on tiptoes around the twisting stevedore.

Jacques pushed the screaming man away for a second time and calmly stated, "You've had enough. Now leave me in peace."

The pain and humiliation only made the defeated sailor more uncontrolled, and he kicked furiously at Jacques's groin, first with one foot and then the other. Jacques warded off the first blow with the side of his lower arm, and he calmly seized the other arcing foot and jerked forcefully. The sailor was lifted bodily from the deck and flew horizontally into the air. His body descended to the deck and thumped solidly driving the air from his lungs as if from a bellows. The fallen man lay on his back, stunned and unmoving.

Jacques, still holding the man's left ankle, dragged him to the edge of the wharf that faced directly into the bay. As he proceeded to the edge of the wharf, the crowd opened a passage for him.

Now shouts of encouragement issued. "Well done, Jacques!"

"The sailor needed a lesson."

"He's a bully!"

"He's a lecher!"

"God have mercy on him."

Jacques paid no attention to the fickle crowd who was now applauding him as a victor.

The dazed sailor wriggled feebly, moaned, and groaned. Jacques paid no heed.

The crowd continued to move back as he walked to the edge of the pier. At the edge, he looked down at the gray green water that swirled around the upright logs that supported the crude deck. Sunlight glinted on the rippling wavelets, and the peaceful scene belied the violence that transpired on the dock.

Jacques turned, seized the sailor's other ankle in his left hand, lifted, and whirled at the same time. Like a sack of baggage to be loaded aboard a waiting merchant ship, he flung the now stirring body out and away from the dock. With a cry, the sailor's body cart wheeled through the air, arced several feet high and descended to the sparkling water like a plummeting cormorant.

It struck with a splattering splash, rested on the surface for a moment, and then sank beneath the moving waters. Moments later, a dripping head popped to the surface, sputtering and thrashing about. And then the man calmed and moved quietly.

Jacques shouted at the floating, sputtering hulk, "Now don't bother me any more." He whirled and without a backward glance, he rejoined Pierre and Françoise.

By this time, Pierre, sufficiently recovered, rested on one knee, holding his battered head in his right hand. Françoise squatted on her knees before him, wiping his sweat and blood-covered face with the lower part of her gray linen apron.

Pierre still gasped for breath, spitting blood and mucous. Slowly his senses returned to normal. The crowd still watched Jean Charlet as he swam slowly to the longboat that was moored along the east side of the wharf. Two of the crew climbed down into the boat, and with outstretched hands they waited to rescue their fellow crewman. Jacques, Pierre, and Françoise were, for the moment, ignored and alone at the center of the pier.

Jacques glanced down at Pierre. "I guess there's not too much damage done. You look worse than you actually are." Jacques saw many fights along the waterfront, and he knew if the combatants could move and were active, usually little permanent damage occurred—minor cuts, bruises, and lots of blood.

Slowly Pierre rose to his feet. "Thank you, my friend," he mumbled. He staggered as he mouthed the words, and Jacques reached out with his large right hand to steady him by the shoulder.

"That was brave of you to come to our rescue," added Françoise.

"I waited too long. I should've put my nose in sooner. That man's not a nice person. You, Pierre…you were right. His behavior with women is evil. I'm afraid we haven't seen the last of that fellow. What did he say his name was?"

"Jean Charlet, I think, he said," answered Pierre.

Françoise interposed, "I remember him when he came to The Red Circle. It's funny, but I didn't recognize him until he mentioned it. It's true he only came in once in a while—I suppose between passages." She wrinkled her nose in distaste. "He was always in trouble. Fighting with the other sailors or bothering the girls who worked in the tavern. My father asked him on several occasions to leave, and each time there was a fracas."

"I don't know him, but I'm afraid you're right. We haven't seen the last of him," added Pierre.

At that moment, an angry shout interrupted their conversation. A curse and a cry of Pierre's name came from below the dock. The hatred in the voice startled Françoise, who clasped Pierre by the right arm.

"Ignore him, Pierre. If you ignore him, maybe he will forget about this fight."

"No, Françoise, he's not the kind of man who will ignore an affront."

"You're right, Pierre," said Jacques, "We can't let him think we're afraid of him. Find out what he has to say."

Pierre, between Françoise and Jacques, hobbled to the edge and gazed down. The longboat was now several yards from the shore, manned by its crew. Jean Charlet, bloodied and dripping water from his recent dunking, sat on the center seat, holding his damaged left arm with his right hand. Pain and anger wrinkled his rugged, though handsome face. He was still spitting water and saliva from his twisted mouth as curses and epithets issued forth.

He stared up at Pierre, lifted his right hand from his left arm, and waved a quivering index finger at the trio. For several moments no intelligible sounds came from his jerking mouth. Then a torrent of curses and obscenities erupted. Finally his invective diminished and he shouted, "I will get even with you. You will rue the day that you met Jean Charlet. You better learn to fight so next time we meet I will have the pleasure of a longer fight. I will destroy you little by little. I will make you suffer."

"You're right, Monsieur Charlet. I will be ready for you the next time we meet. Now I know the kind of fighter you are, so you will have no easy time of it next time. It will be my pleasure to give you the beating you deserve."

Pierre was surprised at his calmness as he returned the challenge that was flung to him. Although he did not feel the confidence and courage that he voiced, he hoped it would have the desired effect on the enraged sailor. But Pierre's words seemed only to increase his passion.

Sputtering and stammering, the sailor continued, "You're an innocent, my fine friend. I will tear you apart, limb by limb. I will have no mercy, and I will make sure that your ox friend is not around to come to your rescue. You can be sure of that!"

"The next time we meet I won't need my good friend. I will take care of you myself."

"As for your friend, I will deal with him as one deals with any ox. I will be fresh and ready for him. Monsieur Ox, your turn will come. So be prepared."

Jacques stared down at the impassioned, dripping sailor and began to laugh—a quiet subdued laugh.

This enraged the man more. He rose and seemed ready to throw himself into the water and storm toward the dock. Two of his companions reached for him and sat him down. They attempted to calm him, but he shook loose from them and waved the fist of his good arm at the group standing at the edge of the dock. He shouted, "I don't know your name, Monsieur Ox, but I will remember your face. When I'm through with it, it will not be the same as it is now. Then no one will recognize it."

Jacques laughed again and said quietly, "Charlet, we shall see—we shall see." He turned and walked away.

Jean Charlet turned his attention back to Pierre. "Your friend's strong, but that won't help him the next time we meet. Remember Jean Charlet—a man who never forgets an insult or a defeat. We've not settled this quarrel. What's your name? So I won't forget, and so I can let everyone know who will feel Jean Charlet's anger."

His insolence and sureness irritated Pierre. Without thinking, he blurted, "My name's Pierre Marin, and my friend's Jacques Breton. Neither of us is afraid of a cowardly lecher like you who takes advantage of weak and defenseless women."

"You will see that it's not weak and defenseless women I take care of—it's bold and mouth interferers and troublemakers. That's who I handle."

The sailors turned the boat around and rowed slowly out into the bay in the direction of the "Le Cygne". Still, as the distance widened, the angry sailor continued his harangue.

Pierre watched as the boat moved further and further from the shore. His heart beat rapidly, and a cold sweat covered his entire body. He was not sure whether it was from anger, fear, or weakness. Suddenly his knees lost their strength and began to buckle. If Françoise were not near to prop him up, he would sink to the deck.

She turned to him and asked, "Are you all right?"

For a moment, he stood tottering. "Yes, I will be all right. I felt weak for just an instant."

Jacques noted Pierre's faintness and rushed to his side, placing a sinewy arm around his waist. He said to Françoise, "We have to get him to bed so he can rest and get his strength back."

"Let's get him away from this crowd. Let's take him to the fort. Perhaps we can find a place for him there."

The tiny room in one of the buildings within the run-down fort was dark and cool. Little light penetrated to the interior of the building that formed one of the walls of the tiny log fort.

The fort was a quadrangle of buildings that formed the outer wall of it. Spaces between the buildings were filled with peeled-log palisades. All the buildings were two-story structures—the lower floors were use for living quarters while the upper levels were used for defense. Portholes throughout the outer walls accommodated defenders with weapons, whatever they might be—arquebuses, muskets, spears, bows and arrows, catapults—anything that could be used as a weapon.

Françoise and Jacques brought Pierre to a lower room in one of the buildings. They were not sure of the exact location of the room, as they hurried to follow one of the soldiers who led them to it. They helped Pierre to a crude mattress on the floor in the far right hand corner of the room. It was simply a tough canvas bag filled with hay or straw. Several patches on it indicated that probably mice or other rodents contemplated it as a home for their families. The room had a musty, long vacated smell about it.

Jacques went to the single window and threw open the unpainted shutter. The opening contained no glass; the afternoon sun filtered into the room. Jacques noticed that the room was on the north side of the quadrangle.

"I must find some water and some towels to clean Pierre," Françoise stated.

"I will stay with him while you're gone."

Pierre interjected, "I don't need anyone to stay with me. I'm not a child. And I'm not that hurt. A few minutes rest is all I need."

Françoise chided, "No, your wounds must be cleaned and tended to. We don't want you to be sick because of that fight. We have much to do."

"You're right. We do have much to do. Go. I will make sure this wild man's quiet until his wounds are looked after."

"Thank you again, Jacques. You've been most helpful. I won't be gone long." She slid through the door opening.

Jacques turned to Pierre, who lifted himself to a sitting position, and said, "Well, my friend Pierre, you're not a beautiful sight." He laughed. "You look as if you've been in a fight."

Pierre laughed half-heartedly. "You might say that. But I didn't do very well." He shook his head. "I guess I'm not much of a fighter."

"I think you're right. I have to show you a few tricks."

"Where did you learn to fight, Jacques?"

"On the waterfront one learned to defend one's self. I saw many fights, and I watched how the good fighters handled themselves; then I imitated them. We have to practice together. I'm afraid such knowledge will be necessary in this wild land."

"You sound like my wife, Jacques. What are your plans for this wild land—as you say?"

"Oh, I will get a concession from Lieutenant Richard who's been granted a seigneury here."

"Has it been arranged?"

"No, but Richard is the son of the Sieur de Barentin who owns the estate where my father's a tenant. He's an officer with Grandfontaine, the new governor who accompanied us."

"Ah, yes. I'm to get my concession from Captain Hector. The details haven't been arranged yet, so I have to see him as soon as he's settled in. I suppose that will be in the next day or two. You're alone?"

"Not for long. I'm betrothed to Marguerite Louise Hemard, who's already here. She's a servant with Lieutenant Richard's household."

"So you're soon to be married?"

"Yes, but there are a few details to be attended to."

"Ah, so you're in a hurry?" Pierre asked with twinkle in his eye.

Jacques ignored the question and continued, "Marguerite's a childhood friend. Her family's also a tenant on the Sieur's estate. My family and hers have been friends for many years. It was always thought we'd marry."

"Very convenient." Pierre laughed.

Again Jacques ignored Pierre's jesting remark.

"Monsieur le Cure at Barentin made the preliminary arrangement through the priest here, Father Molin, a Recollet, who has come to minister to the colony, which has been without a priest since the English were in charge."

"When will the wedding be?"

"Soon, I hope. I have to make arrangement with Father Molin. And, of course, with Marguerite."

"So Marguerite is waiting eagerly for her man?"

"I hope so. She came here in April, when the first ships left Le Havre. They've been here for at least a month."

"I didn't see her at the dock to welcome you. Nor was the lieutenant there. That's curious, isn't it?"

"Yes, Pierre. I was wondering about that myself. I didn't expect to see her, but I did expect the lieutenant to welcome the captain."

"So you plan to become a landholder here. You will become a great farmer for you've experience with the land if your family was a tenant for the Sieur de Barentin."

"I hope that life will be better here than it was in France. There was no opportunity to get ahead there. My father worked all his life as a tenant, and we were always poor."

"I know what you mean, Jacques. My father was a poor fisherman. He struggled all the time just to keep a bit of food on the table. He worked long hours in all kinds of weather, but couldn't get ahead. I worked with him, until I was fifteen years old. Then the great Colbert needed sailors in the navy. That sounded like a great adventure—a chance to travel and see new parts of the world. I contracted for three years and sailed the Atlantic. I was in the Caribbean, helping to keep an eye on the English. I never was in an engagement, but we did stop here in '67 after the peace was signed. I liked the land; it was so peaceful and pleasant, and it reminded me of back home."

"So you decided to return?"

"No, not at the time. Last year I met Captain Hector at The Red Circle, when I was courting Françoise, and he persuaded me to seek my fortune with him in this land called "Acadie". So here I am, with a new wife in a new land, and, I hope, a new future."

"That's interesting, Pierre. We're the same. Soon I will have a new wife, and some land, and I, also hope, a new future."

"Jacques, my friend, we must help each other to make that new future come true. I'm eager to meet your betrothed, and I'm sure that she and Françoise will be great friends."

"Oh, I hope they will. I hope our grants are not too far apart; then we can help each other more." He stopped and a pensive expression came to his hazel-brown eyes.

"What is it, Jacques?" Pierre asked as he noticed the change in his new friend.

"I've an important question to ask."

"Go ahead, Jacques. I will answer any question I can."

Jacques hesitated.

"Go ahead. Ask it."

"Do you…Do you think…that you and Françoise…could be witnesses to our marriage?"

Pierre laughed heartily.

The next two days were busy ones. The two other ships in the convoy arrived, anchored, and started disembarkation. Captain Hector d'Andigne de Grandfontaine arrived on the barque "The Fox", a small man-of-war of the French navy. His arrival was delayed because he stopped at several of the small fishing settlements along the south coast of the peninsula bordering the Atlantic Ocean. He felt it was necessary to make contact with the few French fishermen in order to get their support in the difficult days ahead.

The Treaty of Breda ceded Acadia back to the French after many years of control by the English who were represented by Colonel Thomas Temple, an important businessman and trader from the English colony of Boston, which was situated further south on the mainland. Temple established a profitable fur trading enterprise in Acadia. Thus he was in no hurry to have the French come in and take over his operation.

Captain Hector was pleased with the reception he received at the various settlements, and most of the French settlers were happy to see the land returned to French control. Although they was well treated by the Bostonian who seldom came to his domain, except to collect furs in the spring; they were pleased to see the French Crown take an interest in their welfare. They hoped that now "the damned English" would be pushed out of the lucrative fur trade, and that the Atlantic off the south coast would be theirs to monopolize. At the moment, the New England fishing fleet controlled these fisheries.

Grandfontaine's arrival at Port Royal was an occasion for celebration, and when the news of his arrival circulated through the small community, everyone was on hand to welcome him. As his longboat approached the shabby pier, all the small boats of the fishermen, the two other ships, and the canoes of the many Indians that were about escorted him to the shore. The established settlers and the newly arrived colonists gathered on the pier and along the shore to officially welcome him.

When he climbed the ladder leading to the deck, a cheer went up from the assembly. Once he reached the deck, an official welcoming party of Lieutenant Richard and Father Molin, the Recollet, who came out on the earlier ships, stepped forward to greet him.

Pierre, Françoise, and Jacques stood on the shore where the pier touched the land.

Pierre glanced at Françoise. "Captain Hector looks very handsome today."

Grandfontaine was a career soldier who served his country in various parts of the world. At one time, he served briefly at Quebec in New France, but most of his service was in Europe in the Dutch wars.

He was of medium height with a florid complexion. At age 52, he was a rotund man of ample girth accentuated by the white scarf that encircled his waist. His knee-length breeches held by lace-decorated garters were an immaculate white, his waistcoat, a brilliant royal blue with frogged buttons and gold epaulets. His hat, which he held in his left hand, was a matching blue, trimmed with a gold galloon. On his head he wore a powdered white wig with curls that descended past his shoulders. Compared to the remainder of the party, he was, indeed, a royal representative.

He strode regally toward the waiting Lieutenant Richard who looked drab in his unadorned blue uniform. He grasped the lieutenant firmly by the right hand and drew him into a warm embrace. Another cheer, louder and more enthusiastic than the first, burst from the crowd. Then he turned to the brown-robed priest and repeated the greeting. Again a roar went up from the crowd. The few English hangers-on and the small crowd of Indians appeared impressed.

A small guard of six soldiers surrounded the new governor, his officer, and the priest, as they walked slowly, and it seemed, cautiously, toward the fort that stood two hundred yards from the shore.

"That should impress the English," said Jacques.

"I think that was more to impress the Indians than the English. There aren't many English left to impress. They've all gone back to Boston."

"One of the soldiers told me that there's a small fort across the François Bay which is occupied by the English. They have to go. He thinks there may be trouble getting them to leave."

"I hope Captain Hector's force is strong enough. Fifty soldiers isn't a large army." Pierre was referring to the small force of the French army that accompanied the new governor.

"Maybe you will have to join the navy again," Jacques joked.

"I hope you're wrong, but you may be right. Every man—and even the women—may have to be soldiers in this land." He changed the subject quickly. "Have you been able to see your intended yet?"

"No, she's been too busy managing the lieutenant's household. I spoke to Father Molin, and he will be speaking to the lieutenant. Of course, there's the problem of Marguerite's contract. It's not yet up, and won't be for another year. I'm hoping an arrangement can be made with the lieutenant."

"I hope you're right. If the lieutenant wants to be difficult, I'm afraid the wedding will be postponed."

"I must see him as soon a possible. His seigneury is east of here, on the south side of this river, the Dauphin. I'd like to return with him when he's finished his business with the governor."

Françoise, who was quietly listening to the conversation, now interjected, "I haven't seen this beauty that you speak of so fondly."

"I haven't seen her either," Jacques responded, a note of sadness in his voice. "It almost seems they're trying to keep us apart."

"She wasn't with the lieutenant's party. I didn't see his wife and child," remarked Pierre.

"I heard they're at the fort. But I don't know where. I didn't see them arrive. The soldier to whom I was speaking said they arrived last night."

"That's curious," Pierre mumbled more to himself than to anyone in particular.

The governor and his small party entered the gate to the dilapidated fort; it was closed behind them. People returned to the busy activities that occupied them before the governor's grand entry.

Françoise gasped. Coming toward them was the dark figure of Jean Charlet, his left arm enclosed in a soiled cotton sling. He walked resolutely toward them, staring brazenly at Françoise. The three turned away to avoid a meeting.

"Stop! I want to speak to you."

Pierre hesitated. He did not want another confrontation with the seaman. He was not afraid, but he wished that the man would stay out of his life. Both Françoise and Jacques turned to face the oncoming man, so Pierre turned and waited as he approached. Neither of the trio spoke.

"I want to apologize for my stupidity of last Tuesday. I'm sorry I acted so badly."

The three stared at the sailor. Pierre was not sure if he was apologizing for his behavior toward the women or his defeat of Pierre in the fight.

Charlet continued, "I was out of sorts that day, and I let my anger make me act foolishly. I beg your pardon if my actions were offensive to you." He smiled at Françoise ingratiatingly.

He proffered his right hand to Pierre. Stunned, Pierre grasped it and shook it strongly. Pierre mumbled, "Accepted."

The sailor bent to Françoise, seized her right hand, and stooped to kiss it. He said, "Please forgive me, Madame. If I was offensive, I didn't mean to be. I was trying to be helpful."

The man's apparent sincerity confused Pierre. He could not convince himself that the sailor acted properly. Pierre was sure that his behavior with Adelaide Doucet exceeded the bounds of propriety. Perhaps he was hasty about the man's actions toward his wife. Maybe he was a bit jealous.

Françoise's reply to Charlet surprised and annoyed him.

"I accept your apology. It was my husband who took exception to your kind help when I stumbled in the boat."

Charlet straightened. "Jean Charlet at your service. Madame, if you ever need help and Jean Charlet is nearby, call, and I'm at your command."

Pierre could feel the blood rising to his face. The man's pretentiousness was insufferable. But, again, his doubts about the man preyed on his mind. His sense of justice and fairness piqued his conscience, and he smiled outwardly while he seethed inwardly.

Jean extended his hand toward Jacques. "I deserved to be treated the way you handled me. No hard feelings. Please, sir, accept my apology."

"I was a little more forceful than necessary. Anger can make a person do foolish things. I apologize to you."

"Jean Charlet accepts your apology, if you will accept mine."

"Done."

The two men shook hands vigorously.

"Thank you, Madame, and..." He paused, waiting for the two men to introduce themselves, even though he already knew their names.

Jacques stammered first, "I'm Jacques...Jacques Breton of Le Havre and Barentin."

"I'm pleased to meet you under these more pleasant circumstances."

Pierre recovered his composure and smiled woodenly. "My name's Pierre Marin...ex-sailor and now colonist of Acadia."

"You've a charming and beautiful wife, Monsieur Marin. I admired her each time I went to her father's tavern in Le Havre... The Red Circle, I believe."

"Thank you, Monsieur Charlet. You're right. She is charming and beautiful."

"Please call me Jean. I want to be your friend, not merely an acquaintance."

"If you wish, Jean." But he did not invite the sailor to call him Pierre.

"I hope I will be seeing all of you before I leave. It appears we will be sailing in a day or two. The governor's eager to proceed to Fort Pentagouet. He plans to make it his headquarters. Au revoir for now."

He waved his good hand in farewell and turned toward the wharf that was still a scene of much activity. The three watched him go with mixed feelings. Françoise was happy that the danger to Pierre and Jacques dissipated; she was flattered and exhilarated by his charm. His admiration made her forget her previous aversion to him. She was wrong about the man. Maybe he was not the libertine and rake that she believed him to be.

Jacques was the first to speak. "Maybe we were too hard on the man. That was courageous and noble of him to find us and to apologize like that."

Pierre was still skeptical. "A cod does not become a goldfish. I'm not convinced that he's sincere. I will still be careful with him. I don't trust him."

"But, Pierre, he was so sincere. I'm sure he meant well," Françoise said.

***

The next day she changed her mind.

The early afternoon sun glinted on the sparkling waters of the River Dauphin as it flowed southwestward into the Port Royal Basin. Françoise left the cramped quarters that were assigned to them in the ramshackle fort when Jacques and she helped Pierre after the fight with Jean Charlet.

The tiny room was their home since. Its dinginess depressed her, so at every opportunity she sought the outdoors. The weather, since their arrival, was ideal—sunshine and warm, pleasant breezes.

She walked slowly northward along the marshy shore of the slow flowing river toward five small log houses that were scattered haphazardly along it. These were the homes of settlers who chose to remain in Acadia while the English were in control. Each small home had a good size garden patch adjacent to it; she was admiring the lush growth and neat rows of flourishing vegetables when she heard footsteps approaching. She turned slowly to face them and tried to still the increased palpitation of her heart. The unexpected always quickened her heartbeat and shortened her breath. She was not yet accustomed to this wild country.

As she turned, an unfamiliar voice hailed her. "Good day, Françoise. Are you enjoying the fine weather and the pleasant countryside?"

Her hand went to her breast, and she whispered, "Monsieur Charlet, you frightened me." His familiarity did not lessen her heartbeat; her muscles tensed.

"I'm sorry about that, my dear. I didn't intend to frighten you. But you do look beautiful with a slight flush in your cheeks."

"Why, thank you, sir," she replied, hoping her lightness would relieve her tension.

He smiled at her. "It's nice to see you again. I was hoping I'd have the opportunity to further our acquaintance."

She did not like the way the conversation was going. His familiarity was disturbing. Her old impression of the man came flooding back. A chill seized her, and she trembled involuntarily.

He continued, "I've admired you since I first saw you in your father's tavern. Each time I look at you, my blood races, and I wish to touch you."

"Monsieur Charlet, you're a flatterer. But it's nice to be told that one's attractive. I know you tell that to all the women, but it's still nice."

A smile spread over his dark sun-bronzed face.

He's really a handsome devil, Françoise thought. No doubt he has a girl in every port.

His eyes roved from the top of her lace-trimmed bonnet to the inelegant leather shoes on her feet. A flush spread upward on her face as his eye moved downward from her broad forehead to her hazel eyes, framed with dark brown lashes. They followed her straight average size nose to her tightly pursed carmine lips. They descended slowly to the high neckline of her blouse. As they moved downward the seemed to strip away the linen bodice and the chemise she wore beneath it. Her breasts felt bare and exposed before his piercing eyes. She blushed brilliantly as she thought of her medium-size glands with their deep pink nipples. Many men scrutinized her in her father's tavern, but none made her feel as denuded as she felt now. The heat from her red face annoyed her, and she was angry with herself for losing control of her emotions. She was motionless as if mesmerized by his eyes that traveled lustfully down over her bosom, along her flat stomach to her lap.

Intentionally, his eyes gawked for a significant moment before they continued to her calf-length skirt and her stockinged ankles. Then they worked their way up again.

She struggled to regain control. She did not want this man to know how much he intimidated her; she stifled her embarrassment and anger. Her composure returned, and she gazed unemotionally into his face.

His knowing smile annoyed her, but she was not sure if she was angry with herself or with him. The spell broke when he said, "Françoise, you and I must get to know each other better." The direction of his thought could not be misunderstood.

She replied coldly, "I know you, Monsieur Charlet, as much as I want to."

He laughed deceptively. "My dear woman, is that the way to treat a man who's promised you his devotion and aid?"

"I appreciate your offer, but I won't accept it."

"Don't say that so hastily. One day you may regret it."

"I don't think so, Monsieur Charlet. The cost may be more than I'm willing to pay."

"The cost would be nothing. Simply a taste of your charms, my pretty one."

His boldness and effrontery shocked her; she could feel anger again, but this time without a doubt in her mind as to whom it was directed.

"Monsieur, you're stepping beyond the bounds of propriety."

Smoothly he replied, "What are the bounds of propriety when a man wishes to make love to an attractive and provocative woman?"

"I will never satisfy your wish, Monsieur Charlet. It's unthinkable that you should suggest such a sinful and degrading idea. I'm happily married and my husband is my only lover."

"Again I remind you, Françoise. Don't belittle the powers of Jean Charlet. I've conquered women more attractive and spirited than you, my dear."

She interrupted him. "You will never conquer Françoise Marin. Monsieur Charlet, you're the man my husband believes you to be—you are a lecher and a rake. Please leave me now. I don't want to talk to such an evil man as you. You're not my friend, nor are you my husband's friend."

He grinned evilly. "You're right, my dear Françoise. I'm not your friend, but I will be your lover. I will be your lover to punish your husband who's besmirched my character and embarrassed me publicly."

Her voice shrilled, "Leave me alone, you filthy, evil man. The Lord will punish you for your sinfulness. I will tell my husband of your lewdness."

"I will be civil and deny it. Only you and I will know for sure what I have said. I promise you I will make love to you—with or without your consent. When the opportunity arises, you will be my lover. I can feel your soft body in my arms now—embracing me and giving of yourself." His eyes roved over her body again.

"You're an animal. I won't listen to such thoughts any longer. You disgust and revolt me. I will scream and shout that you're molesting me."

"Who will believe you? I'm crippled, and I haven't come near you."

She turned and ran toward the fort.

Behind her she could hear his raucous laughter. As she hurried away, her revulsion increased. His last remarks repeated in her mind and frightened her. "I will make love to you—with or without your consent." His threat made her gasp from fear.

He was an evil, sinister man. He pretended to be sorry for the fight so that he could get close to her. He deceived her and convinced her that Pierre was wrong about him. She accepted his apology gullibly. Jacques Breton was deceived also. Pierre was the only one who was not fooled. He was right all along. The man was a rake, a lecher, and a libertine.

She slowed as she neared the fort. She would tell Pierre what happened. No, she must not do that. Pierre, in his anger, would find Jean Charlet and do something rash. He might even kill him. No, she could not tell Pierre. She could not tell Jacques. He probably would not believe her. He was taken in by Jean just as she was.

She stopped short. Why am I so foolish? He will be leaving soon. His ship will be going with the governor to Fort Pentagouet. She would probably never see him again. He was trying to frighten her. And that he succeeded in doing. She glanced back to see if he was following her, but he disappeared.

Chapter Four — Frustration

Two hours later, as Pierre and Françoise munched on their evening meal of fresh corn bread from the fort oven and strong cheddar cheese from the fort stores, washed down with cold water from the fort well, Pierre studied Françoise, and then smiled at her. They were seated on the straw mattress, the only other item in the room, other than their pile of belongings from the ship. Pierre said, "I hope to see Captain Hector tomorrow. Time's passing quickly, and I haven't been assigned my grant of land. I must have time to build a house and plant a garden...if we're to have adequate provisions for the winter."

"You're right, Pierre. If we're to stay here, we will need better accommodation than this. The rats and mice are more comfortable that we are. This room's small, dirty, and disgustingly infested with vermin."

"Patience, my dear Françoise. We can't rebuild Port Royal in a week. It will take many months, even years of hard work."

"That, I know. But if we're to rebuild it, we must get to work."

"First things first, my dear. I must see Grandfontaine and get my grant of land cleared up."

"What seems to be the trouble, Pierre? You were promised a concession here at Port Royal before we left France. Captain Hector said we'd have our own land as soon as we landed. That's almost a week ago, and we're no closer to that land than on the day we landed."

"I know, Françoise. There seems to be some trouble with the 'Seigneur of Port Royal', Alexandre Le Borgne. He has charters from the king that give him control of all the lands at Port Royal. He won't approve any new concessions until his claims are recognized. That's why Captain Hector's been so occupied these last days. He's been meeting with Le Borgne to arrive at some agreement."

"Who's this man, Le Borgne?"

"It's a very long story, but it seems that Alexandre's father was owed a great deal of money by Sieur d'Aulnay, an early seigneur of Port Royal before the English took over. Emmanuel Le Borgne tried to collect by acquiring Sieur d'Aulnay's charters when he died. In 1667, his son, Alexandre, was confirmed as the governor and proprietor of these lands. He didn't have much luck with the English who wouldn't give up control of the area. Now he's come to claim his grants. He has documents to prove his claim. So you see, that's the reason for the delay."

Françoise sighed deeply. "I'm tired of this needless waiting. Maybe we should forget about a home here and go back to France."

"We can't give up before we've started. I told you, Françoise, there'd be difficulties. This delay's only one of them, and it will probably be one of the lesser ones."

"That's what I'm afraid of, Pierre. I'm not sure I can handle this country. It's more than I imagined. I see the other colonists at work and it frightens me. They work like animals from dawn to dusk. Even the women work like draught animals hauling carts of hay, drawing water for the animals, hoeing and digging in the gardens. I don't think I'm strong enough to do that. I'm not a farm girl. I was raised in the city. The heaviest work that I've done is to deliver trays of wine and beer to the sailors and fishermen of Le Havre."

Pierre laughed. "You're a sturdy woman. That's why I married you. I knew I'd need a partner with a good body to help me work the land."

She swung her fist at him playfully and teased, "Is that the only reason you married me for my sturdy body to work the land?"

"It wasn't the only reason. Your sturdy body is fine for the production of children and for making love."

She swung her right fist at his head. He ducked and caught her wrist, twisting her beneath him. He kissed her on the cheek as she struggled to extricate herself from his grasp.

"No, Pierre, not now. I still have some thing I want to talk about."

Her confrontation with Jean Charlet came to mind. She was almost about to tell him; then she saw him lying bleeding and bruised on the deck of the pier. He still sported a purplish welt on his right cheek, and he walked with a limp from the kick to the groin that felled him. If she told him of the incident, she feared he would get involved in another fight. She feared the outcome of such an encounter.

Pierre raised himself on his elbow and stared at her. "Well, what is it you want to talk about?"

His brusque manner and the edge in his voice surprised her. She remained silent for several moments.

His voice became a little more intense. "What do you want to talk about?"

Homesickness and fear consumed her. Tears sprang to her eyes; heat flushed her cheeks. She flung her arms around his neck and cried, "I want to go home. I miss my mother and father. I miss my brothers and sisters. I miss the tavern and its people. I miss the city. I miss France." The tears spilled out, and she sobbed fitfully.

Stunned, Pierre stared at her for several seconds. Then his voice rose. "Françoise, this is foolish. We can't go back."

Between sobs, she mumbled, "Why not?"

"Because I made a promise to Captain Hector that I'd come and be a colonist because I haven't any money for the passage back. I spent it all on provisions…and equipment… and tools to work the land."

"I'm sure you could sell them to some of the others…some of the new colonists, or to some of those that are still here from before the coming of the English."

"Maybe I could do that, but I don't want to. I'm convinced this land will be lucky for us. We must stay and seek our fortune here. The land's prosperous. Look at the farms of those who stayed. They've many animals;

they've much produce, vegetables, fruits, wild berries. Some are traders with the Indians; there are many kinds of fish... and all are plentiful. No, Françoise, we won't go back to France. Only if we can't become prosperous here will we go back to France."

Quickly her tears ceased, and she straightened up. Her voice was shrill and angry, "I hate this place. I will never like it. I hate the people. They're dull…and stupid. They only know how to work."

Shocked, Pierre grabbed her by the shoulders and shook her gently at first, but with more ferocity as she continued to cry and scream words of recrimination. Finally her cries lessened, and her shrieks became mumbles. He drew her to his breast and stroked her cascading hair. She sobbed in muffled gasps; her shoulders quivered. He crooned softly. "I'm sorry, Françoise. I didn't mean to upset you."

For several more minutes she sobbed quietly as Pierre rocked her gently in his arms.

"I'm afraid, Pierre," she whispered. "I'm afraid of this land and these people."

He patted her shoulder. "I understand. But you will get over it."

But he did not really understand. He did not know about Jean Charlet.

The next morning, Pierre arranged a meeting with the governor. The captain took over the largest quarters in the ramshackle fort. His quarters were no more elegant than those of Pierre and Françoise, although they were larger with more furniture. The captain occupied two rooms; the inner room was used as his private chambers, while the outer was equipped as an office, a temporary one. Along the left side of the room, a long refectory table of crude construction served as a desk. When Pierre entered the room, a young soldier, one of the governor's aides, was busy writing on a document with a large quill pen.

Hat in hand, Pierre waited while the nattily attired captain rearranged some papers that he was working on. He was seated behind the table to the left of the young soldier who did not look up from his work.

"Good morning, Pierre. It's another beautiful day."

"It is, sir. And a good morning to you."

"I know why you're here, Pierre, and I'm sorry about the delay in getting you to your concession. I believe you're aware of the reason for that. Monsieur Le Borgne has been difficult to deal with. First, he doesn't want to acknowledge that I'm the supreme commander of all Acadia. He maintains he is. But his mandate is for certain lands, not the entire colony. I believe we've straightened that out, but there are still problems with the land grants. He has documents that do give him control of the lands, or, at least, most of the lands in the area. He's been quick to establish control. He's given a substantial grant to one of my officers, Auguste Richard, one of the sons of the Sieur de Barentin, near the city of Rouen. Richard has already taken possession of these lands and has even placed some of the new arrivals on concessions. Maybe you should come with me to Fort Pentagouet. I intend to make my headquarters there. And I will give you a large tract of land there."

For several moments, Pierre was speechless. His mind refused to think; his confusion was mirrored in his face. Finally he said, "Is there no way to get land here at Port Royal? I had built my hopes and dreams on establishing here. This is the largest settlement in the colony. It's well established with a church and a pastor, a mill to grind our grain, the Indians are friendly and helpful, the land's bountiful, and the sea abounds with fish. My wife will never agree to a grant in a more remote area."

"That's all true, Pierre, but I can't assure you of a grant of land here. My own position as a landholder here is tenuous, and my orders are to make my headquarters at Fort Pentagouet so I will be able to press France's right to the area."

"Sir, perhaps I can make other arrangements. Maybe I can make an agreement with Monsieur Le Borgne. My friend, Jacques Breton, has such an agreement."

Grandfontaine nodded his head solicitously. "Perhaps you can, Pierre, but I'd be most happy to have you accompany me to the fort to the west. I will need settlers too. And I intend to bring more colonists next spring. Think about it, Pierre. You'd be one of the first at Fort Pentagouet, and because of that I'd be very generous."

"Sir, I must discuss this with my wife. I will let you know my decision before the day is out."

Pierre bowed, turned, and left.

Outside the main gate of the fort, he spied his friend, Jacques, on the pier, helping one of the older inhabitants unload a shallop of several hogsheads of what, to Pierre, appeared to be flour.

Pierre waved and hallooed, "Good morning, Jacques. Could I speak to you for a moment?"

Jacques returned the greeting and walked toward Pierre. As they met, Pierre took Jacques by the arm and led him along a path that followed the shoreline north of the busy pier.

"Jacques, I'm having trouble with my concession. It seems the captain doesn't have a legal right to any of the lands here at Port Royal. The seigneur of Port Royal is Alexandre Le Borgne. If I want to stay here, I have to deal with Le Borgne. You've your concession from him. Did you find him a hard man to deal with? I've heard he's very firm about the dues that he exacts."

Jacques hesitated, as if gathering his thoughts. "I heard that too, Pierre, but he's been very generous with me. He's given me a concession two leagues up river on the north shore of the river. I haven't been to it yet, but I plan to go today, and I will also see Sieur Richard…to make arrangements for Marguerite. I haven't seen her yet. I think Monsieur Richard is being difficult."

Pierre, in his concern for his own plight, ignored the troubles of his friend and continued, "Do you think Sieur Richard will be granting more concessions on his seigneury?"

"He has a great deal of land that requires inhabitants. And his charter, I'm sure, requires that he place settlers on it."

"I have to see him. Maybe I will still find land here."

"Oh, that'd be nice. I'm sure that Marguerite would like Françoise to live here, even though they haven't met."

Pierre sensed that he ignored his friend's problems. "I'm sorry, Jacques. I was thinking so much about my problems that I forgot yours. How are the arrangements coming?"

"Not very well. I haven't seen her yet. Richard's been difficult. I know that all the arrangements have been made with the priest. When I spoke to Father Molin, he said he had made the marriage arrangements with Marguerite and that Monsieur Richard was favorably inclined, but not enthusiastic. He expects considerable remuneration for the balance of Marguerite's contract.

Pierre noticed with a grin that, in his excitement, Jacques made a longer speech than was his habit. "What do you plan to do, Jacques?"

"This afternoon I will go look at my concession, and then I will visit Seigneur Richard. I think he will be at the fort with Captain Grandfontaine."

"I've just come from the Captain, but I didn't see Lieutenant Richard there."

"I understand he spends most of his time on his seigneury. He's eager to make it a model for Port Royal."

"That's a good idea. Maybe I should see the lieutenant about a concession. He might be a good seigneur."

Jacques frowned. "Then on the other hand, he might be very demanding of his concessionaires."

Pierre and Jacques obtained the use of one of the shallops used by the colonist to fish in François Bay, the basin into which the Dauphin River flowed and along which most of the small farms were established. The fort was located on the south shore of the estuary, at a point where a small river joined the much larger Dauphin River. The tidal flats, which were plentiful here and provided most of the arable land, had a high knoll upon which the wooden fort was built many years before. Through neglect and lack of finances, it became little more than a pile of rotting timbers; as a defensible position, it was untenable.

With a favorable wind from the west, Pierre hoisted the mainsail and maneuvered the light boat upstream. Since the tide was flowing, it also pushed the boat at an exhilarating speed. Pierre gloried in the sense of freedom he felt as he manipulated the lines and tiller, trying to get the last knot from the fishing boat. It reminded him of the many trips he had taken with his father as they fished the estuary of the Seine River, back in France.

The steady breeze and the incoming tide made sailing an enjoyable experience, and even Jacques marveled at the speed and grace of the boat. Since he was not a sailor, he let Pierre handle the sails, the lines, and the tiller. He sat back and enjoyed the changing scenery along the wide river.

Swiftly, they proceeded northward to the point where the river narrowed significantly at the northern tip of the promontory on which Port Royal was located. The tidal flats, which were often flooded with the salt water of the bay, extended as far as the eye could see on either side of the river. At the point of the promontory, the river narrowed, and was called Detroit de Lisle. Here, woodlands descended from the hills to the shoreline.

Neither Pierre nor Jacques could make out the kinds of trees that made up the woodlands, but they were amazed at their size and density.

Jacques remarked, "Those trees will provide lumber and firewood." Pierre grunted in assent.

Once around the promontory, the wind lessened and their speed was reduced to a quiet sail. The river opened into a large bay, and again the tidal flats extended back to the wooded uplands. No habitations could they see. They were told at the fort that Lieutenant Richard was building a substantial house on the south shore of this wide section of the river. He built a small log shelter that was being used temporarily as a home. When the main building was finished, it would become a stable, a workshop, or a storehouse. The wind dropped, and they were becalmed. Pierre pointed to the oars as an invitation that Jacques should now do his share of the work. Although Jacques was not a sailor, he gained some experience around boats when he worked on the docks at Le Havre, so he knew how to row a boat. His strength soon had the sturdy boat skimming along the shoreline. At the extreme east end of the wide bay-like extension of the river, they could hear the sounds of construction—the tock-tock of a hammer as it sounded like a giant woodpecker, the buzzing of a saw like the quiet snoring of an old woman, the shouting of workmen like a hectoring wife. Soon they could see, as well as hear, the source of the activity.

Three boats were drawn up on the shore, half-hidden by the waving shore grasses. Pierre maneuvered the boat beside the others as Jacques, under Pierre's direction, continued his labor on the oars. A shout from one of the workmen announced their arrival, and all work ceased as four men came to the shore to greet them.

All were dressed in homespun breeches that came below the knee. A colorful sash encircled each waist and seemed to serve as a pocket as well as a belt. Various items were stuffed behind the sash: a hammer, a measure, and the ubiquitous white clay pipe. A loose linen shirt with wide sleeves and a narrow wristband, a wide neck opening some with a slit at the front, which was laced, was common to all. Two of the men wore broad brimmed felt hats, while the others wore knitted toques. Rivulets of sweat streaked each face that glistened from the moisture. The men were pleased at the respite from their labor.

As the prow of the boat nudged the shore, Jacques shipped the oars and made his way forward. Pierre followed him. One of the men, a small, wiry dark-skinned man who appeared to be in charge, extended his hand to Jacques and welcomed him with a smile. "I'm Lieutenant Auguste Richard, Sieur de Barentin. These are some of my concessionaires."

He did not introduce the men by name.

Jacques seized the extended hand and shook it firmly. "Lieutenant, you don't remember me? I'm Jacques Breton, from your father's seigneury at Barentin."

"To be sure. Now I remember you, Jacques. But I don't know your companion."

"This is Pierre Marin of Harfleur. He came on the same ship as me."

Pierre bowed at the waist and said, "A pleasure, sir. I have heard a great deal about you."

The man's lean face did not change expression. But the thin mustache beneath the aquiline nose and the wispy goatee on his narrow chin, both fashions of the day, wriggled in annoyance.

Pierre noticed and wondered why the man was annoyed. The moment passed and a tiny smile came to his angular features.

"Welcome," he stated curtly. Then he turned to the men, "Back to work. I've business with Breton, here."

The men bowed in greeting and turned to return to their work. Richard followed behind them, although at a slower pace, and Jacques followed him with Pierre in the rear. Halfway up the path, which led to a small clearing and a slight rise in the almost flat landscape, the lieutenant stopped and turned. "This is a good place to talk." Again a note of annoyance crept into his voice, and again Pierre noticed it. "Our business is private," he continued.

"I want my friend, Pierre, to be present."

"As you wish, Breton. You know I wasn't party to the arrangement that was made between my father, your father, and Marguerite's father. She's indentured for three years. There's still one year on that contract." The annoyance crept back into his voice.

"I'm aware of the contract, sir. But I was hoping some accommodation could be arranged."

"Do you wish to buy out the contract?"

"I don't have the money to do that. The little I have will be needed to develop my concession."

"What do you propose? My wife needs Marguerite's services. The work here is too much for her. She must have a servant. If you could find someone to replace her, I might consider letting her go."

For a moment Jacques was silent. He pondered the possibility of obtaining a replacement for Marguerite. He knew of some young girls in the settlement as he and Pierre admired the comeliness of some of them. The settlers who remained after the English takeover of 1654 were prolific, as many children and youths inhabited the colony. Half the population seemed to be below the age of twenty. Maybe he could make an arrangement with one of the originals to have his daughter complete the contract.

Richard's voice interrupted his thoughts. "Then again, perhaps we can make other arrangements."

"What was that, sir?"

"I was thinking that perhaps you might settle on my lands with your new wife. I need more settlers. If you settle on my grant, we might come to some agreement about the balance of your betroth's contract."

Jacques's face fell. He already signed an agreement to a grant of land from Alexandre Le Borgne, also known as Sieur de Belleisle. It was notarized as well. "I'm committed to a concession with Sieur Le Borgne."

"Well, in that case, I see only one solution. You and Marguerite will have to wait a year before you get married. She can fulfill her obligation to me; you can improve your land and build a house; and we shall all live happily ever after." His voice sounded triumphant.

Jacques looked defeated.

Pierre spoke. "Sir, perhaps there's another way. Suppose I agree to become your concessionaire in place of Jacques. I could replace Jacques and take on the obligations that you would exact of him for the balance of Mademoiselle Hemard's contract."

A smile brightened Jacques's face; a frown darkened Richard's face.

"That's a possibility. I'm in need of more concessionaires. My grant requires the development of my seigneury by placing people on the land, but I need good men. I know Jacques and his abilities. My father had high praise for the Breton family. What do I know about you? Your name is Pierre…?"

Pierre interjected quickly, "Pierre Marin. Of Harfleur. Fisherman's son. Lately of the French Royal Navy. Three years service."

"All very well. But what do you know about working the land. I need farmers, not sailors. No, I'm afraid I couldn't consider you as a suitable replacement for Jacques. That's out of the question."

The smile left Jacques's face.

But Pierre was not finished yet. He turned to Jacques. "Perhaps, then, I can assume your Le Borgne concession, and you can become contracted to Sieur Richard. Would you consider that idea, Monsieur Richard?"

"That sounds like an excellent idea, Pierre Marin. That's a suggestion I can agree to."

The smile returned to Jacques's face, and he turned to Pierre. "It will cost us money to make the transfer, but I will be happy to pay that cost. It will be a small amount, much less than Marguerite's contract."

"We have many details to work out. Let's go to the house. I'm sure Marguerite will be glad to see you. She talks of nothing else since Father Molin came to make the arrangements. She was pleased that her father agreed to the marriage."

"That's nice to hear. I haven't seen Marguerite for almost two years. I left the estate...with your father's blessing...to make my fortune on the docks of Le Havre." He laughed. "But that didn't turn out as I'd hoped."

"I know. We've heard the story many times from Marguerite. It seems she was fond of you even when you were children playing together on my father's estate. It's very nice when you can marry for love, rather than convenience." Sadness filled his voice, as if he was referring to his own situation.

Jacques did not know the circumstances of Richard's marital arrangement, but he heard the woman he married was a harridan and a shrew. Gossip from the servants and retainers of a lord were quick to laugh at any of the family's difficulties. They indicated that the match was made to assure the lands of the neighboring seigneur would become a part of the Richard seigneury, since the girl was an only child.

Jacques never met Auguste Richard's wife, so he did not know what kind of a woman she was. He wondered why they came to make their home in the Acadian wilderness. If she was the only child and the inheritor of her father's estate, it seemed peculiar for them to come to Acadia. He knew that Auguste Richard was not the firstborn in his family, and that, no doubt, was the reason he made the military his career. Career choices were limited for sons who were not the firstborn. The firstborn inherited the father's titles, positions, and properties, while other sons chose the church, the military, or government service.

They moved slowly up the path to the crude log structure, the home of a seigneur of Acadia. It was obvious the structure was hurriedly put together. The logs were piled horizontally one atop the other, notched at the corners to fit together tightly. The spaces between the logs were stuffed with grass and mud. The roof was steep and thatched with long marsh grasses that grew so abundantly on the tidal flats. Pierre noticed that the thatch was thick and neatly done, the job of an expert.

Two children were playing in the small clearing by the door. One was a young boy about four years old with tow hair, while the other was a chubby, brown-haired child about two years old, whom Pierre assumed was a girl because she was holding a stuffed doll in her arms. As the men approached, the children stopped their play and looked with blank curiosity at the strangers.

Pierre hoped that in a few weeks he and Françoise would have a similar home, temporary for now, something more elaborate and permanent in the future—a place to raise healthy, happy children.

Richard spoke to the children whose deadpan faces broke into joyful smiles. It was obvious that Richard loved the children, and they loved him. The change in their attitude was remarkable. Pierre noticed that, and his opinion of the father rose; a man who loved his children was a man to respect. That was a saying his father always used, and it came back to him now. He smiled as he thought about his father—a man who always loved his children and tried to make life easier for them. He hoped he could live up to his father's standard, and provide a better life for his children, and, perhaps, prosper in this new land.

That day most of the details of Pierre's grant and Jacques's new contract were worked out. The meeting with Marguerite was properly restrained. But it was obvious that she was pleased with the arrangements that her father, Jacques's father, and the elder Richard made. The smile on her face and the lilt in her voice indicated that.

Pierre was pleased that she was a handsome woman. Her coarse homespun dress could not hide the comeliness of her body. She was taller and slimmer than Françoise; angular was the first impression that Pierre got. Her features were angular; even her eyes were angular, and her nose was a bit sharp, but not unpleasantly so. This angularity extended to her shoulders and arms. The only part of her that relieved the impression of angles was her breasts, which were full and round. Pierre marveled that the slimness did not include her bosom; she was an attractive woman. He was happy for Jacques.

As the men discussed the final arrangements for the cancellation of the last year of her contract, she remained quietly in the background tending to her household duties while Richard's dark-haired wife joined the men at the crude table to help with the decisions. The final arrangement was that Jacques would receive a grant of land east of the seigneur's site. He would be required to work one day a week for the lieutenant as payment for the balance of Marguerite's contract. This was conditional on Pierre taking over Jacques's concession with Le Borgne, and they could see no problem with that, as such exchanges were commonplace.

Later the three men made a tour of the area of the tidal flat that would be Jacques's farm. The next day, they decided, they would meet with the notary to legalize their agreement.

The afternoon sun hid behind a bank of clouds coming from the east. A stiff easterly breeze accompanied the darkening overcast, and rain seemed a possibility. Pierre was happy about the shift in wind direction since it meant they were blessed with a favoring wind, a good omen to any sailor.

After they bid their adieus to the Richards, the two men crossed the broad section of the river to the north side to explore the land that Pierre hoped would be his. It was part of a large tidal flat directly across the Dauphin River, immediately north of the Richard seigneury. The land, when Jacques chose it, was the first in that locale so he had the opportunity to choose any piece that he wished. They noted the outlet of a small stream that ran through the thick marsh grasses so Pierre headed the shallop for the opening. As they approached the mouth of the stream it widened into a quiet bay. Pierre furled the sail and joined Jacques on a second pair of oars as they progressed up the languid stream. Waterfowl of all sorts—ducks, grebes, gulls, and herons, as well as a multitude of shorebirds—swam and fed in the quiet tidal waters.

The land itself was wet and flat, extending north for at least a league to the wooded uplands in the background. Sedges, reeds, and grasses covered the flats in profusion. The cacophony of the many bird voices made conversation difficult. As they rowed further upstream, the low water-inundated flats gave way to higher ground and the nature of the grasses changed from salt-water plants to fresh water grasses.

Pierre was pleased. He visualized earthen dikes to hold back the salt-water tides, exposing to the sun and rain the fertile higher ground. He saw that he would have to build dikes to keep back the salt water, and he would have to leave the land for a year or two so the salt would be washed from the soil by the rains. But he could also see the neat farm home, the barns, the stables, and the other outbuildings. His farm would be the best in Port Royal.

Since he was a fisherman, the river, the basin, and the sea would augment his farm produce. He would become prosperous, maybe even wealthy.

The more he saw of the land, the more excited he got at the prospect of acquiring it. The tiny stream led back to the uplands, draining the low hills to the north. These, he knew, were called North Mountains. They were covered with a variety of coniferous and deciduous trees—a mix of spruces, firs, oaks, hemlocks, and birch—which would provide the building materials needed for buildings, fences, and boats.

He was elated; his excitement was hard to contain. He was eager to return to the main settlement, to search out Le Borgne, to make the transfer immediately.

Jacques was happy that their problem was solved so easily. He had his land and Marguerite; Pierre was jubilant about the land he hoped to acquire. If no other obstacles presented themselves, everyone would be happy.

They hurried to the fort where Françoise waited for them.

Two days later, a rainy Monday morning, Pierre and Françoise held hands in the small church two leagues upstream from the fort. Father Molin, the Recollet pastor, in his brown cassock and white surplice, prepared to marry Jacques and Marguerite. They glowed from the vigorous cleaning they underwent in preparation for this eventful day in their lives. They were dressed in their best clothes, which, though spotlessly clean, were coarse and worn.

Jacques tied his dark shoulder-length hair at the back with a neat cord. His linen shirt fitted snugly over his muscled shoulders while the loose sleeves accentuated his strong arms. He wore a pair of faded gray breeches gathered below his knees; gray home-knitted stockings covered his ample calves, and a pair of worn leather slippers encased his wide, firm feet. He looked strong and healthy.

Madame Richard presented Marguerite with one of her gowns that she no longer found to her taste. Pierre found it very becoming. The bodice fitted snugly over Marguerite's ample breasts, emphasizing them. The mauve skirt billowed from the waist held out by several linen petticoats. The neckline and the tight three-quarter length sleeves were trimmed with a narrow band of delicate lace. The long skirt hid her feet so Pierre could not see what she wore on them.

They made a handsome couple as they waited quietly for the priest to begin the ceremony that would join them together for the rest of their earthly lives.

Only a few months ago, he and Françoise made the same vows that pledged their love forever. Until now he had no regrets; Françoise was all he hoped for—loving, understanding, agreeable—particularly loving. He heard of many wives who considered making love a wifely obligation rather than a pleasurable experience. With Françoise it was the latter as she seemed to enjoy making love as much as he did. This pleased him. The drone of the Latin prayers startled him, and he squeezed Françoise's hand.

Jacques stood at the right of his bride, his shoulders squared as the priest prepared to administer the rite of matrimony. Marguerite glanced up shyly and smiled timidly. Although she appeared self-possessed and forthright, Pierre saw that she was really shy and timid.

Father Molin lifted his eyes from the text, smiled at the two young people, and intoned in a flat, unemotional voice, "Jacques Breton, do you take Marguerite Hemard, here present, for your lawful wife according to the rite of our holy mother, the Church."

Flustered, Jacques did not reply. The priest urged, "Say 'I do'."

Jacques mumbled softly, "I do," and blushed in embarrassment. Pierre was not sure if it was because he became confused or from the realization that he was committing his life to another person. To Pierre's surprise, Marguerite's answer to the same question was strong and firm. Again, Jacques's face reddened, and he appeared flustered.

The priest continued, "Now join your right hands and say after me: I, Jacques Breton, take you, Marguerite Hemard, for my lawful wife, to have and to hold, from this day forward, for better, for worse, for richer, for poorer, in sickness and in health, until death do us part."

As Jacques solemnly repeated the vow, Pierre pressed Françoise's hand and smiled ardently. Her face reddened as she recalled their love making of that morning. Her flush excited Pierre, and he could feel his groin stirring. He squeezed her hand tighter; she understood the lust that was energizing him. She wriggled her hand to confirm that she understood.

The vow was repeated by Marguerite in the same strong voice as before while she gazed warmly into Jacques's hazel eyes. Her steady gaze agitated him, and he looked down sheepishly.

The priest intoned, "By the authority of the Church, I ratify and bless the bond of marriage you have contracted. In the name of the Father, and the Son, and the Holy Spirit, Amen. I call upon all of you here present to be witnesses of this holy union, which I have now blessed. Man must not separate what God has joined together. Go procreate, fill the land with children. You are now man and wife."

The lanky priest raised his right hand in the sign of the cross blessing and then turned to the altar.

Pierre extended his right hand and encircled Jacques's heavy shoulders with his left. He drew him forward in an embrace and touched cheeks on each side. Then he slapped Jacques vigorously on the back with his left hand. Jacques grinned from ear to ear, as if he pulled the coup of the year. Meanwhile, Françoise embraced and hugged the taller Marguerite, kissing her affectionately on either cheek. Both laughed joyously.

Pierre embraced Marguerite and bussed her soundly on either cheek. "Well, you're an old married woman now, Marguerite," he joked.

She responded in a mock angry tone, "Surely I'm not that old."

Jacques grinned shyly. "Time will tell, my dear."

She crimsoned, and then fluttered her eyes demurely.

Françoise broke the spell. "Come, Pierre. We must allow the newly weds some time to themselves."

At that moment, a young boy about ten years old entered the church door, genuflected, and came toward the small wedding party.

"Is Monsieur Pierre Marin here?"

"Here, lad," Pierre answered in a questioning tone.

"Sir, Captain Grandfontaine wants to see you. Immediately!"

A shadow of concern flitted across Pierre's face. A question came to his mind. What does Grandfontaine want? Is there trouble with the arrangements we made with the land? Saturday, when they signed the contracts, everything seemed in order. Le Borgne readily agreed to the transfer of grants. Of course, the idea of a transfer fee made the deal easy. After all, Le Borgne made two livres simply for agreeing to a new tenant.

Now it seemed urgent that the governor see him. "Tell the captain I will be there immediately.""

Jacques sounded worried. "I wonder what he wants? I hope there's no trouble with our arrangement."

Pierre tried to reassure Jacques. "Oh, I'm sure it has nothing to do with that." But he did not feel the confidence he tried to show.

"Françoise, I will go find out what the captain wants. You can escort this lusty couple to their quarters. Make sure they don't dally along the way. You heard what the padre said, 'Go procreate, fill the land with children.'"

With that, he turned, and without a backward glance, he left the church.

Chapter Five — The Request

Pierre stamped his heavy leather shoes to shake off the light mud that adhered to them. He brushed the droplets of rain from his coarse shirt and shook his broad-brimmed hat. Then he proceeded across the open central area of the fort to the door of Captain Grandfontaine's quarters. A soldier standing guard at the door nodded, and Pierre entered the small room that served as the captain's office. The same subordinate, who was working at the table that served as a desk, was again occupied with some paper work. The captain was not present.

"Pierre Marin to see Captain Grandfontaine."

The young corporal continued with what he was doing as if he did not hear.

Pierre repeated, "Pierre Marin to see the captain."

The young soldier grimaced and growled, "I heard you. Can't you see I'm busy?"

"I'm sorry, sir. I didn't mean to disturb you. I only wanted to let you know I'm here. At the captain's request."

"Well, then wait quietly. I heard you come in. Do you think I, Corporal Joybert, am deaf?"

"I'm sorry, sir. But the captain did make it sound urgent."

"The captain's always in a hurry. He expects to leave tomorrow, and there's still much to be done. He's always impatient."

Still grumbling, he rose and moved to a door at the rear of the small office. It led to the captain's personal quarters. Since it was a little after mid-forenoon, Pierre surmised that the appointed governor of the colony was enjoying his mid-morning beverage.

"Sir, there's a Pierre Marin here to see you." The corporal spoke through the slightly open door.

A strong, robust, bass voice issued from the opening. "Send the young man in immediately."

The scowling army officer jerked his head toward the opening as he swung the door wider. Pierre entered the room and glanced about. It was about the same size as the one Françoise and he occupied. A sturdy, but crude bed stood in the right hand corner of the room. To one side a small narrow table held a brass candleholder with a tallow candle, and a number of books lay haphazard beside it. The captain was seated at a larger table along the left wall. On it was several pottery dishes and a metal pot. From the pot, steam issued.

The captain pointed to another chair that was at the near end of the table and said, "Pierre, please join me in a cup of tea."

Pierre hesitated. He was concerned about the nature of his visit, and he preferred to find out why the captain summoned him so peremptorily. The captain's casualness now disturbed him more. "Sir, I'd be pleased to join you, but first, I'd like to know why you want to see me."

"Ah, Pierre, we can discuss that as we enjoy a bowl of tea. Joseph, please pour my guest a bowl of tea."

A middle-aged man with hair that was almost white moved from the darkness of the corner behind the door and quietly poured some amber fluid into the dun bowl that sat on the table before the unoccupied chair. Then he withdrew to the corner back to the three-legged stool upon which he had been sitting. Pierre assumed that he was Captain Grandfontaine's personal servant. Pierre nodded his head in thanks and sat down in the proffered chair.

Pierre tasted tea before, but it was not a regular beverage with him. Water, sometimes milk, but most of the time wine were the beverages that he was accustomed to. Tea was an expensive import that a lowly peasant like he could not afford. As well, on the few occasions that he tasted it, he was not impressed. Its acrid, bitter taste gagged him, and the first time he spit it out, but like now, it was a superior officer who offered it to him, so he was unable to refuse. He wanted to refuse now, but he felt that would be a demonstration of poor manners.

He lifted the steaming bowl to his lips and smelled the warm vapors. The sour-sweet smell offended his nostrils, and he grimaced slightly. He tilted the bowl slowly, allowing a small amount of the hot, steaming liquid to enter his mouth. He held it in his mouth for a few moments, testing its taste, and then he swallowed it quickly.

The stocky, slightly paunchy officer sipped contentedly from his bowl. He did not notice Pierre's discomfiture.

"Pierre, I've a problem. I need another personal servant. Joseph's a fine man and looks after my personal needs very well. But he's aging, and his health isn't as good as it once was. I don't want to replace him; I need someone to complement his services … temporarily."

Pierre was mystified. Surely the captain could not be thinking of him as a candidate for the position. The captain knew that Pierre came to the colony to acquire land and to settle here.

The captain, sensing his miscomprehension, continued, "In the next weeks, I will be going to Boston to obtain the official transfer of authority from the English governor, Sir Thomas Temple. I want, as my personal bodyguard, someone I can trust. That's why I'm asking you to accompany me on this voyage. We will be gone about a month."

Pierre remained speechless for several moments as he mulled over the significance of the officer's proposal. He liked the captain, for it was he who first proposed that Pierre try his fortune in this colony of Acadia. He met the captain in The Red Circle, Françoise's father's tavern in Le Havre. When the captain found out that Pierre was hoping to marry Françoise, the serving maid, he convinced Pierre of the opportunities of a young couple in a virgin land. Now the captain was offering him a position on his personal staff. This might open up further opportunities. Who could know?

"Sir, I will have to discuss this with my wife."

"You understand, Pierre, that your wife wouldn't be able to

accompany you."

Pierre never considered such a possibility. The import of this revelation struck him. How would Françoise consider staying alone at Port Royal? The idea of being away from her for several weeks did not appeal to him. Her warm, loving body close to his would be hard to leave behind. But the advantage of being closely associated with the governor seemed too good to let slip by. The contacts that he could make would, no doubt, be beneficial to their future. The prospect of visiting Boston again excited him. He knew that the English settlement was a flourishing, prosperous town, almost a city.

"I don't think my wife will like that."

"A man must do what he has to do. A wife must not stand in the way of her husband. Women cannot always be at their husbands' sides. Sometime it's necessary to leave them behind." A trace of annoyance filtered into his voice.

"Please, tell me more about this position. Why are you offering it to me?"

"Certainly, Pierre. I'm going to Boston on a difficult mission. This Thomas Temple has been contrary, and doesn't want to give up his position of governor. But his king has sent him orders to cede this territory to our majesty, King Louis. There may be trouble when I go to Boston to obtain the official documents. I will be taking all the soldiers I have. As you know, that's only fifty soldiers and five officers. They will be my main support, but I also like to have a personal bodyguard. When I looked over the possible candidates for the job, you were the only suitable one. You were a sailor with the Royal Navy for three years, so you have experience with arms... arquebuses, muskets, pistols...and ordnance. And you're not afraid of a fight, so I've heard."

No doubt he heard of Pierre's fight with the sailor, Jean Charlet, although his performance could hardly be a recommendation.

Grandfontaine continued, "I want someone I can trust and who will be absolutely loyal to me. I don't trust my officers with my personal safety, even though I know they're loyal to their country and king."

He paused, waiting for Pierre to make a comment. When Pierre remained silent, he said, "So you see, Pierre, I believe I can trust you, and I think you will be loyal. I will pay you well; your duties won't be heavy, although they may be dangerous. I will make available any opportunity to further your ambitions whether in the area of commerce, position, or land acquisition."

Pierre was speechless. The captain was suggesting some interesting possibilities—the fur trade, a government job, maybe even a seigneury. He was holding out some powerful enticements.

The July rain stopped, and the sun was shining when Pierre left the fort in search of Françoise. But the bright sunlight did not complement his mood. He dreaded the confrontation with Françoise, for that is what he feared it would be. How would she react to the fact that he intended to leave her here, alone, at Port Royal while he accompanied the governor on the remainder of his survey of the colony and his meeting with Sir Thomas Temple, the English ex-governor, who made his headquarters in Boston.

Grandfontaine's arguments and allurements convinced Pierre. The money he offered made the adventure attractive. He hoped Françoise would see it as the opportunity that he did.

As he trudged toward the pier, where he saw a group of people congregated, he wondered and planned how he would broach the subject to his wife. He also must make arrangements for her welfare while he was away.

Françoise was helping the Doucet family load their few belongings into a heavy shallop. Several bundles were already loaded into the small, though heavy, clinker-built boat, which was drawn up onto the shore beside the main pier. Several rough planks lay on the spongy marshland grass as a walkway to the boat.

Albert, the sturdy husband of the woman whom Pierre rescued from the waters of the estuary, was carefully loading the family's possessions into the boat. Adelaide, Françoise, and the three children carried the various bundles and articles to the boat, handed them to Albert who placed them carefully and securely in the bottom of the boat.

As Pierre approached, all greeted him joyfully. They seemed happy to be leaving. "I suppose you're off to your land," Pierre remarked, more to make conversation than to obtain information, for he heard that Doucet obtained a grant of land from Le Borgne west of the fort on the north side of the river on the inland side of the tidal flats immediately back of the narrow strip of marshland that fronted on the river. He heard that that land was higher and drier, but would require clearing of the underbrush, and later, the trees that grew in profusion. The advantage of this type of land was that it could be brought into production immediately—one did not have to wait until the salt leached out of it as the tides did not inundate it, except when they were higher than usual. The great height to which the tides rose in the basin and far up the Dauphin River—as much as thirty-five feet—amazed Pierre.

Albert laughed and wiped his forehead with the back of his hand. Still, sweat glistened on it. "Yes, I'm anxious to plant a few vegetables for the winter."

"That's a good idea, Albert. Maybe I will invite myself to your house for a good meal this winter. I hope you have a good crop."

"Oh, I will, Pierre. My wife has a way with plants. She can grow anything."

"Will you be staying on your land?"

"Of course! I will build a lean-to for now, and as soon as we've planted a garden, we will build a better shelter. I hope winter doesn't come too early."

"Which reminds me, I've something important to discuss with

Françoise? I will take her away for a few moments."

"By all means. She's been most helpful, and we thank her."

Françoise waved in acknowledgement and moved toward Pierre who put out his hand to her. Hand in hand, they turned and headed eastward along the small river, the Allain that drained into the larger Dauphin River. Its banks were low, and several shallops were drawn up on its shores on either side. Its mouth was used as a boat landing and repair basin. Three men were working, repairing one boat and building another. They waved to Françoise and Pierre as they went by. The two walked in silence, enjoying each other's company.

Soon they approached the beginning of a long dike bordering the north bank, following the turns and twists of the slow flowing river. The dike was about ten feet high, varying from fifteen to twenty feet wide at the base. It looked like a long mound of clay, and where it was repaired recently, the marsh grasses and the wild hay secured a foothold forming a carpet over the surface, in spots very dense.

Two days earlier, Pierre watched as four of the established settlers repaired a weak spot in this same dike. Its structure intrigued him. At low tide the men dug out the weak section and rebuilt it. They planted posts in five rows along the length of the dug out section. Then they laid logs horizontally between the line of posts, building the dike into a thick log wall. As they built it up, they filled the spaces between the logs with clay, when they could, or sod and heavy mud when the more desirable clay was unavailable. But what interested him the most was the ingenious sluices that allowed the water to drain from the land behind the dikes. These wooden passageways were fitted with heavy, solid, wooden gates that were hinged with wooden pins, horizontally, at the top. The water flowing from behind the dike pushed the gate open, but as the tide flowed in from the opposite direction, it pushed the gate shut and held the tide out.

Once, when his ship was docked at La Rochelle, he saw similar dikes. The nearby tidal flats were drained and dried in the same fashion. Of course, at that time, he did not investigated their operation as his shore leave was spent in more debilitating pursuits.

Françoise interrupted his thoughts. "What's the important business that you wanted to tell me?"

He paused, wondering how to start. Finally he decided the best approach was a direct one. "Françoise, I'm leaving tomorrow or the day after. I'm not sure which. Captain Grandfontaine has asked me to go with him to Fort Pentagouet, the fort on the Pentagouet River where he's been ordered to make his headquarters. Then we will go to Boston to meet the English governor, Thomas Temple."

He paused to observe her reaction. She frowned but said nothing. Her response surprised him. He expected opposition, and a vocal one at that. He knew she was not totally committed to settling in this new land. She was disappointed with the colony. It was not as developed as she thought it would be. Although it was in the hands of the English since 1654, she believed it would be more advanced that it was. Several dozen families were established, and the church was built, and now a priest came to serve them, but the colony was in poor condition. The fort was dilapidated and crumbling, the log chapel was run-down and neglected, the homes of many of the settlers were nothing more that crude shelters—even Le Borgne's house behind the fort, which was used by the English governor when he visited, was in need of repair.

Before she could object, he continued, "It will be a great opportunity to improve our standing in the colony."

She said nothing. Pierre was disconcerted and disturbed by her silence. Usually she was vocal about her thoughts and did not mind to let him know how she felt.

"The captain has made me an attractive offer of money, and he's hinted at other opportunities. I will only be gone a month. You, of course, will remain here. I will make arrangements for you to stay with one of the families here. I will miss you terribly, but, you know, it'd be too dangerous to take you with me. As well, the captain has made it clear that he doesn't want women along on the rest of the voyage. He doesn't anticipate trouble, but in this area, one can never be sure."

"Pierre, I won't stay here alone. We were to make a home here in this land. Now you want to run off and look for a fortune elsewhere."

Her opposition was now voiced. He hoped he could convince her of the wisdom of his decision. The thought of being forced to change his mind, and to tell the captain of a reversal of plans worried him. He knew that Françoise had a mind of her own and might challenge him. The first clue was when they were packing a fancy counterpane that a childhood friend gave her at their wedding. It was a beautiful piece of needlework, but totally impractical as an article of bedding. He tried to convince her that it was unneeded and would take up valuable space. She insisted, and the counterpane became part of her luggage.

"Françoise, look, it's only for a few weeks. The money will be useful to obtain supplies and equipment when we move to our land. The experience may be more important. The captain promised me many opportunities to improve my position. Don't you see, Françoise, this is a chance that I can't miss."

"What exactly has he promised you? What will your wages be?" A hint of anger edged her voice.

"He will pay me ten livres for my services during the entire trip. I will be his private servant."

He did not want to be more specific. If she knew that he was to be the captain's private bodyguard, she might object more strongly on the grounds that it was too dangerous. The captain assured him that he did not expect to require his services; it was just a precautionary measure that he was taking.

"He already has a private servant. I've seen the man waiting on the captain's least whim."

"He feels Joseph is getting too old to fulfill some duties satisfactorily."

"What kind of duties would that be?"

He did not know if she was suspicious of the nature of his duties, or if she was trying to use any excuse to deter him from going. "Joseph's not healthy—he's frail and weak. So the captain needs someone to look after his heavy baggage and such things."

She tried another tack. "What will I do while you're away?"

"Françoise, there's much to do here in the settlement. I'm sure it will be very easy to keep occupied. Many of the new arrivals will be busy getting their land and shelters ready for the coming winter. Maybe Marguerite and Jacques would be happy to have another pair of hands to help them on their concession."

"You're right, but what about our own land and shelter?"

"There will be plenty of time for that when I get back, and I will be able to employ the best tradesmen to help me."

She was not convinced, but he could see she was weakening. She grumbled, "You've thought of everything."

"I thought about it carefully before I agreed to the captain's proposition. I'm sure we won't be sorry if I take this job."

"I don't like it, Pierre. But this time I will let you have your way because I see you're convince this is good for us. I hope you're right."

Her sudden capitulation pleased him, and he drew her into his arms and kissed her fiercely. She responded passionately, and if it were possible he would have made love to her atop the dike. She sensed his lust and pushed him away playfully.

"We must prepare for your departure."

"And I must make arrangements for your lodgings while I'm gone."

"I think your pleasure is more important."

Only then did he gather the import of her words. He grinned and kissed her again. She grabbed his hand and led him quickly along the dike in the directions of their quarters in the fort. Pierre was pleased that he had such an understanding wife.

Spent, after their vigorous lovemaking, they relaxed in each other's arms. Only then did he comprehend the enormity of the decision he made. For several weeks he would be away for her seductive charms. The thought of leaving behind her firm and attractive body made him think again about the decision he made.

Before his marriage, he knew only one other woman, a young Negro prostitute in St. Christopher, when he was on shore leave after some naval maneuvers among the Antilles. The guilt of that sin haunted him for months until he confessed to the chaplain aboard his ship, a brigantine called "The Defiance." Of course, he never told Françoise of the incident. She kept herself for the man that would be her husband, according to the chastity teaching of the Roman Catholic Church. She was a virgin until their wedding night. Her sharp cry on his entry and the spot of blood on the bed confirmed that.

He drew her close, and the urges of passion stirred once more within him. He kissed her passionately, and she again responded to his persuasions. The thought of leaving her for several weeks gave him an energy that both surprised and stimulated him. She responded as if the separation would be unbearable and destitute. As he entered her, he whispered dreamily, "My darling, I love you more than the whole world."

She sighed unrestrained, "My love, I will miss you unbearably." She began to cry softly.

The afternoon shadows lengthened when Françoise roused herself from the troubled sleep into which she fell. The small room was dark, and she searched the pallet that was their sleeping accommodation, but Pierre had not returned. The somber aspect of the room, and its silence and emptiness made her sad and lonely.

For the next several weeks, while Pierre was away, she would awaken to a bed in which she was alone—in a strange place and a strange country. The magnitude of the situation engulfed her, and tears came to her eyes. Could she bare the fact that she would be left alone for long days among aliens and strangers? When they left France, the prospect of being alone without Pierre never entered her mind. She never considered that Pierre would not be at her side; no discussion of such a possibility happened. Now, the gravity of her agreement to let him go with Grandfontaine struck her.

Numerous questions revolved in her mind. Where would she be staying? She knew she could not stay in the fort, for it would be occupied by a company of ten soldiers that Grandfontaine planned to leave to work on the fort, readying it to defend the small colony. Even now she stayed clear of the soldiers because she knew how men behaved toward women. Her work in her father's tavern taught her many things about men who were always seeking the companionship to satisfy their lustful desires. She learned how to avoid or control the advances of such men, but then her father or one of his male employees whose main purpose was to maintain order and decorum in the tavern always protected her.

She wondered if Jean Charlet would be remaining behind at the fort. He frightened her, and she was sure his threat was not one she could ignore. She did not tell Pierre of the incident because she was sure he would not believe her. He would say she was imagining such things. Nevertheless, the thought of his presence stirred feelings she could not control, and a pall of fear descended upon her.

The newness of the land worried her. She had seen several Indians about the fort, but she kept her distance and avoided them. They seemed harmless enough—even friendly. They came and went silently, yet a few always lingered about the fort, although most of them seemed to spend their time at Monsieur Le Borgne's house north of the fort. She noticed on many occasions a flotilla of several bark boats, which Pierre said were called 'canoes', drawn up on the shore adjacent to the Le Borgne house.

She stood fascinated, the first time she saw a group of three canoes approach the small landing before the Le Borgne house. The swiftness and delicateness of the crafts struck her with wonder. The skill and precision of the paddlers as they maneuvered the canoes to shore delighted her, and she remarked to Pierre, "I wish I could handle one of those craft the way those women do."

He laughed and replied, "Well, darling, perhaps before the summer is over you may succeed in doing just that. There are few roads here so the river is our highway. I'm told those birch bark boats are the best means of transportation for these parts. They're even better than the shallops that the fishermen use. Notice how swift and maneuverable they are. And how light they are. Even the women have no trouble handling them."

Oh, how she wished she was back in France, amidst all the familiar things, instead of here, amidst all these strange things—the wilderness with its wildness and lack of civilization; the colony with its coarseness and lack of amenities; the people with their indifference and selfish concern for their own welfare; the natives with their strange customs and habits; and most of all, the lack of familiar persons—friends, relatives, and companions. She missed the hominess of the tavern and its adjacent living quarters, the babble of her brothers and sisters as they played or worked about the busy abode or in the inn. She yearned for the vexatious cry of her mother as she badgered and hectored the children to their chores. She longed to hear the satisfied grunts of he father as he surveyed his growing family and kept a watchful eye on his affairs—commercial and familial. The more she thought of the past, the sadder she became, and more tears coursed slowly down her cheeks.

Why did she agree to let Pierre go on this silly adventure? At the time, his arguments seemed so sensible and practical, but now they seemed selfish and unreasonable. He was abandoning her after just a few weeks of marriage. Was he already bored with her? Had she not satisfied his needs and desires? Was he searching for new excitement and stimulation? Had she not fulfilled her wifely duties adequately? Would he be looking at and for new women if he went to Boston with the captain? Oh, the very thought of it sent new streams down her already damp cheeks. A sense of abandonment filled her bosom, and a lump of tension throttled her. She gasped for breath and sobbed noisily until great heaves shook her whole body.

The darkness in the room deepened; she cried herself back to sleep.

Chapter Six — Departure

Pierre was away longer than he anticipated. The evening shadows deepened; sunset was upon the small community of Port Royal. First, he spoke to Captain Hector de Grandfontaine about the exact time of their departure. The captain planned to leave with the next ebb tide, which would be early on the morrow. Because the captain planned to leave so soon, Pierre knew he must act quickly; he must make arrangements for Françoise; he must gather his personal effects; he must move his other possessions to a safe place until his return; and he must make ready for his duties and responsibilities to the captain.

He asked the captain if he could suggest a place for Françoise.

The captain's reply heartened him. "Lieutenant Richard may need a servant now that Miss Hemard has married Jacques Breton."

Pierre borrowed a canoe and hurried to Richard's seigneury, but he was disappointed; Richard had already employed the services of one of the young daughters of Monsieur Bourgeois, a wealthy farmer of the small settlement. Monsieur Bourgeois was the personal surgeon of Monsieur d'Aulnay, an earlier seigneur of Acadia.

While in the vicinity, Pierre decided to visit Jacques and Marguerite who set up a camp further up the river on their concession. They were very busy. They established a temporary camp with a lean-to of small newly cut poles and a sailcloth covering. It made an adequate temporary shelter.

They greeted him fondly and joyfully and stopped their work to invite him into their humble abode. Pierre saw that already they were preparing to build a more permanent dwelling. They staked out the outline of their intended building, and a pile of logs about eight to ten inches in diameter was neatly arranged beside the staked out area. Pierre was surprised at the amount of work that they accomplished in a few days. Their industry and happiness brought a tinge of regret and discontent to him. Maybe Françoise was right: He was wasting his time and energy on a silly adventure with the captain.

"Well, Pierre, I hear that you're to accompany Grandfontaine to Boston."

"Yes, that's true, but it will depend on what arrangement I can make for Françoise. The captain won't take a woman on the trip. He thinks there may be trouble, and he doesn't want to be responsible for her welfare. I was hoping she might stay with Lieutenant Richard, and maybe work as his wife's servant, but he's already made other arrangements.

"Oh, I thought you'd be taking Françoise with you." A hint of rebuke crept into Marguerite's voice.

Pierre ignored it and continued, "That would be nice, but the captain's decided otherwise and there's not much I can do about that."

"You might stay here and work on your land."

Again Pierre ignored her remark and said, "I see you've been very busy. Soon you will have a house built and maybe some land ready for planting."

"Oh, we've seeded some vegetables already. That was the first thing we did, even before we built the lean-to." Pride brimmed Jacques's voice.

"You must be working night and day."

"It's already mid-July so our planting is late; so we hope for a late autumn."

Pierre laughed. "Jacques, you will be the best farmer in Port Royal. By fall, you will have a new house, a barn, and a harvest. You will be well on your way to being the most prosperous farmer here."

Jacques grinned but said nothing. Pierre perceived that that was exactly what Jacques intended to do.

An idea struck him.

"Jacques and Marguerite, would you consider having Françoise stay with you? She's a good worker, and certainly another pair of hands could be useful."

Marguerite answered for them. "That's a great idea. Why didn't I think of that? If Françoise would like to live with us until your return, we'd be overjoyed to have her. But I don't know how Jacques will be able to handle two women. He's got his hands full with one," she teased.

Jacques blushed, grinned, and said nothing.

"I'm sure Françoise will be delighted. She's been complaining a great deal about our quarters in the fort."

"Living here won't be better. The lean-to will be crowded; it's not bad when the weather's dry and pleasant, but conditions will be terrible when it rains, especially for sleeping."

Pierre could see that three persons in the small lean-to would be crowded. He could see that their privacy as newly-weds would be invaded, so he said, "I'm sorry. I wasn't thinking. You don't have room for anyone else. Newly-weds don't need a chaperone. It was foolish of me to suggest such an arrangement. You've been very kind to even think of allowing Françoise to stay with you. That, I appreciate greatly, but I will look for something else."

"I will not hear of it, Pierre. Françoise must stay with us. We will look after her, and she will be a great help to us. It's settled. If Françoise will come here, we will be happy to have her."

Pierre was about to remonstrate, but he appreciated Marguerite's sincerity, so he acquiesced silently.

Later, when he quietly entered their quarters at the fort, he was surprised to find Françoise asleep. Even in the deepening darkness he could see she had been crying, and he felt an urge to draw her into his arms and comfort her. As he bent to kiss her gently on the cheek, she stirred, moaned, and sensing a presence, sat up, startled.

A small cry of surprise escaped her lips, and her eyes opened wide in fear. Suddenly recognition came, and she flung her arms around his neck, throwing him off balance, tumbling him on the pallet beside her. She laughed joyously and kissed him wetly on the lips. He grabbed her and hurled her over and under him, kissing her vigorously in return. She gasped and struggled fiercely, but he held her firmly and smothered her with more kisses.

She squealed gleefully and kicked energetically. Her legs became entangled in her coarse skirt and petticoat, but she worked resolutely, finally freeing herself; she squirmed from beneath him and lay panting beside him.

"Where have you been so long?" she whispered. He rolled to his back and laughed. "Searching for another man for you while I'm gone."

She swung her left fist at him, striking him on the chest. "I need only one man, and that's you."

"Well, I hope so," he replied in mock seriousness, "but I've found someone who will satisfy your needs while I'm away."

She pouted. "And who might that be?"

"I've found an Indian family who are camped up the river. They've a fine lodge, and they've room for one more person in it. Mind you, you have to take your turn on the sleeping robes after the rest of the family have slept. There are only seven other persons in the lodge."

"That's fine. I will become a savage and teach you how to live in the woods."

He smiled. The thought of Françoise living with an Indian family made him laugh inwardly. She voiced her fear of Indians to him on several occasions. She was even afraid to get close to them. Their nakedness revolted her, and she found their fetid smell nauseating. He admitted to her that he found the smell of rancid grease with which they covered their hair and bodies a bit intolerable.

He drew her close and kissed her gently on the forehead. "You will live in a tent, but not with the Indians. Jacques and Marguerite insist you stay with them while I'm away. It's surprising the amount of progress they've made with their land. They've a large lean-to set up, they've planted a garden, and they've started work on a log house. They've done all this in the past few days. And they want you to come and live with them, my darling."

Silently, she digested the information, then turned and wistfully stared up into his face. "That's very nice. But I'd be happier if you stayed with me, and we went to our land and did what they've done."

"Darling, let's not quarrel now. This will be our last night together for at least a month. Please, it's decided. I will go, but I will miss you greatly. Tomorrow I leave, so let's make the most of tonight."

She clung to him desperately, and he held her gently in his arms. She began to cry softly. Pierre was annoyed. She would have to make accommodations. After all, he was only going with the captain to improve their situation. Could she not understand that? Why was she making it so difficult for him to leave? He was finding their prospective separation trying enough.

He turned toward her and gently shook her and tried to hide the irritation in his voice as he asked, "Françoise, why are you crying? Can't we be happy tonight, my last night with you for several weeks."

It was the wrong thing to say. She wrenched herself away and turned her back to him. The crying became noisy sobs, and her shoulders shook and heaved.

Irritation turned to anger, and Pierre fumed, "Why are you behaving this way? Why are you being difficult? I'm trying to improve our lot, and you're behaving like a spoiled child. You know I will be gone for only a few weeks, and that time can make all the difference to our success in this colony. Please look at the situation from my point of view, Françoise."

His anger did not soothe her. The effect was the opposite. She flung herself to face him. The tears stopped. Her sobs changed to fury. She raged, "You're only thinking of yourself. You don't care how I feel. You abandon me, and you think I should be happy about it. You place me in the care of strangers, and you don't ask me if I want to be with them."

Her fury and rebuke irritated him more. A woman should not question her husband. She should do what she was told to do. The man was responsible for the safety and welfare of his wife. He must assert his authority immediately.

"Françoise, you're being ridiculous. What I've done is for you. It's my responsibility to take care of you and to be sure that you're safe. I can't and I won't be asking your permission for every decision I make. You know that."

"You want to leave me so you can find another woman. You don't love me anymore."

The irrationality of her accusation infuriated him, and he shouted, "That's insane, my love. Where did you get such a foolish idea? You know I love you, and everything I'm doing is for our future—yours and mine."

"But your leaving isn't the way we planned it. You're not doing things the way we planned them. We planned to build a home in this new land, farm, raise animals, fruits, vegetables... and children. Now you want to run off to see the rest of the world in these parts. You want to consort with the English. You want to go to Boston, to become friendly with the English—and who knows what may happen there."

Pierre held his tongue and tried to regain control of his inflamed emotions. Shouting and bellowing would not help. Françoise was distraught enough. She did not seem to be thinking rationally. He remained silent as he calmed. Then he spoke quietly, "Please, Françoise, let's not quarrel. What's been done is done. I'm committed to go with the captain; you will stay Jacques and Marguerite for the next few weeks. You will be as helpful as possible, and when I return, we will build our home. I will have enough money to hire tradesmen to do the building, and we will have a nice home for the coming winter. If Jacques has a good crop, we shall buy some of his produce. If not, I will have money to buy provisions from the other settlers.

I'm told there's never a crop failure at Port Royal." He stopped for breath.

Françoise pouted, but she did not respond.

He continued, "We have all winter to improve our home, to hunt for food, to plan for the future, and to create children."

Her anger subsided, and she became subdued. She whispered, "I'm frightened with the thought that something might happen to you; I will be alone in this wild land. What will I do then?"

"Françoise, nothing will happen to me. We're at peace with the English. I'm going to Boston with the captain to obtain the formal papers from the English governor, Temple. It's just a formality. All the arrangements have been made. King Louis and Charles of England have agreed; control of Acadia is to revert back to France. We're going to Boston to make the final arrangements for the transfer of authority. Nothing will happen to me."

"If you're not back in one month, I shall make arrangements to return to France. I shall take one of the ships that will be returning in the autumn."

The finality of her statement jarred him. Her intensity frightened him. She seemed adamant; he was not sure she would go through with her threat. He was not sure that he knew her well enough to judge her determination. He stared at her incredulously and finally retorted, "If that's your wish, so be it. But I assure you I will be back by the end of August. I shall be back before any of the ships are ready to return to France."

"I will not spend the winter alone here. If you're not back by the time the first ship sets sail for home, I shall be on it." She was dry eyed now and intense. Her eyes shone brightly; her hands were clenched into tight balls. She glared at him, and the resistance showed in her body—it was rigid and taut.

Pierre was shocked at the magnitude of her recalcitrance. He could see he was getting nowhere. "Darling, I didn't think you'd be so opposed to my leaving. I'm sorry. I was only thinking of our future and what I thought would be best for us. I assumed that you'd see things the way I saw them. But now I see that I was mistaken. I can't avoid this trip now, but I promise I shall be back as soon as possible."

"If you're not back before the first ship leaves for France, I will not be here. I will be aboard the first ship for home." She spoke firmly and resolutely, and he was sure that she meant what she said. He hoped he would return to Port Royal before the first ship left for France.

The next morning dawned bright and clear with a brisk breeze from the southeast—a perfect day for departure from the Port Royal Basin. Pierre rose at sunrise to get his personal duffel stowed, and to arrange the storage of the gear and equipment that they brought with them on the ship. He managed to find a place in one of the fort storerooms, so, early, he stored it. At first light he rose, but he did not awakened Françoise. For several moments he stared at her sturdy body, and a longing for her seized him, yet he made no attempt to rouse her. He moved to stroke her tousled hair, decided against, turned, and left the small room.

Activity at the wharf indicated that soldiers and sailors were preparing to board the ship anchored in the estuary of the Dauphin River. With his duffel bag over his shoulder, he approached the noisy, motley crew.

"Has Captain Grandfontaine boarded yet?" he asked the young corporal who was trying to get some semblance of order from the milling group of soldiers.

"No," he growled, "but I'm sure he will be about soon. Captain Hector is a very early riser, and he likes punctuality."

"I'm Pierre Marin, the captain's new personal servant. I'd like permission to board the ship to see that everything's in order for the captain."

"That's already been done. Monsieur Joybert has already done that." Annoyance filled his voice.

"That's the military side of it. I'm the personal side. I'd like to board to make sure that all is to the captain's liking. I'd also like to see my own accommodation."

"As you please, Monsieur Marin. The next boat leaves in a few minutes. You can board as soon as the sailors say they're ready to leave."

"Thank you, Corporal." Pierre spoke to his receding back. The moving soldier made no sign that he heard.

Pierre was disgruntled that the encounter went so badly. He did not want to antagonize the soldiers under Captain Grandfontaine's command because he knew that their friendship and cooperation would be necessary, yet he understood the source of the young soldier's annoyance. The soldier, no doubt, knew why Pierre was aboard the ship, and thus, he felt the captain's lack of trust in his own men. They did not grasp, as did Pierre, that a civilian would have more freedom to move about the town of Boston than would a company of French troops.

Within half an hour, Pierre was aboard the warship that would transport the captain and his entourage to Boston and later to Fort Pentagouet, which was the most southern of the French forts, located on the Pentagouet, or, as the English called it, the Penobscot River.

The ship was one of the new brigantines with a complement of thirty culverins as its ordnance. It was similar to the ship on which Pierre served. The main deck was clean and uncluttered, and the poop was high with two small decks, the upper housed the captain's cabin while the shipmaster's cabin was immediately below. The fifty soldiers that were accompanying them would be billeted in the forecastle while the crew would be located below the gun deck in the fore part of the ship, as was customary on warships.

Pierre found everything to his satisfaction so he returned to shore to await Captain Grandfontaine's arrival. As well, he hoped to see Françoise before they departed.

He was relieved and surprised when he returned to shore to see

Françoise with Jacques and Marguerite waiting on the quay. They, as well as many settlers, came to bid farewell to the departing men. Pierre greeted the three warmly; he noticed that Françoise acted as if they never had their first quarrel. He put his arm around her shoulder, and she moved closer, almost imperceptibly. This he understood as a sign that she forgave him. He glanced down at her, smiling tentatively. She smiled back.

"We came to fetch Françoise," Jacques murmured.

"That's very kind of you, Jacques. I made arrangements for one of the soldiers who are staying here to take her to your place."

"We wanted to see the ship leave. It will be quiet here when the soldiers are gone. Is it true the governor will make his headquarters at Fort Pentagouet?"

"Yes. His orders are to set up at Fort Pentagouet. It's the fort the furthest south; it marks the boundary between the English and the French. I think it's to establish the boundary of French territory. The English, of course, want the boundary farther north and east."

"We have little protection here. Many pirates and privateers frequent these waters. So I'm told by Lieutenant Richard."

"The captain's leaving ten soldiers under the lieutenant. It will be their responsibility to protect the colony."

"That will be a difficult task," fumed Jacques. "The fort's almost useless. There are no cannons and the buildings and palisade are rotten."

"True, Jacques, but it will be up to the inhabitants here to do something about that. Grandfontaine has appointed Monsieur Le Borgne as deputy governor. Maybe he will manage something."

Jacques laughed. "I hear he's more interested in his trade than in the people."

Pierre laughed too. "Yes, I've heard that too."

A commotion among the milling people took place, and all eyes turned toward the entrance to the fort. A small group of people was heading toward the dock. At the center of the group was the stocky, portly figure of Captain Grandfontaine, dressed in a short-waisted doublet with slashed sleeves and a sash around his waist; long narrow breeches fastened with visible buttons, leather boots, and collar and cuffs edged with plain lace completed his costume. On his head he wore a broad-brimmed felt hat with a flat crown. A soft plume was stuck in the headband. All were a soft brown in color.

The remainder of his retinue consisted of Lieutenant Joybert, the officer that always appeared to be busy with paper work. Two soldiers marched stiffly on either side of the two officers, while the servant Joseph brought up the rear carrying a velvet valise with an ornate bronze handle. The group walked briskly to the pier where the gathered settlers opened a passageway to the ladder that led to the waiting boat.

They stopped at the edge of the pier, and Grandfontaine turned to the murmuring crowd. Then he spoke, "Friends and countrymen, it's a pleasure to see so many of you here to see us off. As you know, I'm sure, we're on our way to Boston to secure the legal release of this land for our most magnificent monarch, Louis XIV, king of France. He and his chief minister, Monsieur Colbert, have pledged to make Acadia an important colony. So I leave you now to do the king's bidding, but I will return soon to make sure that all your needs will be cared for."

A low rumble erupted from the small crowd. Pierre was not sure if it was of approbation or dissent. In any case, it was not enthusiastic.

He continued, "Due to the fact that Monsieur Le Borgne has vast holdings in the area through his connections with the late Monsieur La Tour, I've appointed him deputy governor in my absence."

Another murmur materialized from the crowd. Again Pierre was not sure if it was one of assent or dissent.

"My headquarters will be at Fort Pentagouet, on the mainland coast to the south at the mouth of a river of the same name. But I will be in close communication with you at this beautiful establishment."

At this, a ripple of laughter waved through the crowd and all eyes turned toward the dilapidated and crumbling fort. The irony of his remark caused several to snicker openly.

"Adieu, my friends, keep the peace and live happily." He turned and descended the ladder to the waiting boat.

***

Pierre stood on the main deck staring back to the pier where his wife and friends watched the ship as it lifted anchor, hoisted sail, and started slowly, at first, then more swiftly, when the brisk breeze filled first the tops and then the mains. He returned the wave of the receding figures and continued waving until they were no longer in sight. He stood at the rail for a long time after the ship was underway, unaware of the passing shore, gazing with unseeing eyes at the ridge of highland that extended along the north shore and which the locals called North Mountain.

He was unhappy with the way his last evening with Françoise went. Although she acted as if they had not quarreled and seemed to forgive him, he still sensed a barrier between them. She said nothing to forgive him although she kissed him tenderly and passionately before he boarded the boat that brought him to the ship. He, in turn, did not apologize for his anger of the previous evening.

As he stared at the shore, oblivious to the frenzied activity of the sailors as they got the ship underway, he thought of all the things he should have said to heal the breach that he felt so strongly. Unhappily, the opportunity was past, and he could only hope that he would be able to make amends when he returned. Within the month, he hoped.

He heard his name called; the spell was broken.

"Pierre, Pierre Marin, I'm happy you're aboard."

He turned to the sound of the voice. The handsome figure of Jean Charlet, his left elbow still wrapped in a tight, dirty bandage, nodded his head in greeting. He was securing a lifting line to a belaying pin with great dexterity; his injured elbow seemed to be causing no pain or lack of mobility. What was he doing on the “Achilles”? He crewed on the “Cygne”, the ship that brought Pierre from France.

Before Pierre could respond to the sailor's greeting, Jean said, “I see you're surprised to see me. I asked for a transfer. I was getting bored with the lack of activity at the fort. Not enough action for me. One of this ship's crew was sick, so Captain Georges was happy to accept my request. There will be more activity at Boston.” He grinned slyly. “It's bigger than Port Royal. There are more women.”

The sailor's glibness and his suggestive statement about women irritated Pierre. Although he apologized for the fight, Pierre still remembered the way he treated Adelaide Doucet as well as his suspicious behavior with Françoise. He still found it difficult to accept the sincerity of the man's apology.

“I'm pleased to meet you again, Jean,” he lied.

“I hope we have a fast trip to Boston. It will be nice to be in a town where there's a little activity.”

“The wind's favorable, my friend.”

“How's your beautiful wife?”

Pierre resented the reference to Françoise, but he answered civilly, “Did you see her on the quay as we were leaving?”

“Oh, yes, I did, but that's no indication of how well she is.”

His brashness irritated Pierre; a few moments passed as he sought to control his temper; then he replied, “She's well. I've left her with my friend, Jacques, and his new wife, Marguerite.”

Pierre purposely mentioned Jacques because he wanted to remind the inquisitive sailor of the trouncing he received at Jacques's hands.

Jean ignored the remark and added, “It must be difficult to leave such a handsome woman to go on a wild goose chase to an English town where you know no one.”

Pierre's irritation was mounting, yet he did not want to become involved in another fight with the handsome sailor whose only thoughts seemed to be about women. “You're right, but I know she will be waiting for me when I return.”

He did not feel the confidence he wished he could. Françoise's threat of the previous evening came back to him. Would she really leave him and sail back to France? She was resourceful enough to do that. Her experience in The Red Circle tavern gave her an independence and fortitude of few women her age. Her seventeenth birthday would not be until the 12th of October; she was mature beyond her years.

Jean's voice interrupted his worrisome thoughts. “It must be agreeable to have a woman waiting for you whenever you return home. I'm twenty-nine years old, and I've not found one woman I like to return home to. But I know many women I like to return to for a short visit.” He laughed quietly. "Some of them have been great lovers. Is you wife a good lover, Pierre?"

Pierre laughed. "The best!" He turned and walked aft to the steps leading to the poop deck.

During the next two days the favoring breeze held, and they made good progress toward Boston. On the evening of the second day they arrived off the entrance to Boston harbor. Since it was too late to enter the tricky harbor, the master decided to hove to and wait for the incoming tide on the morrow.

Pierre had two peaceful and restful days as the ship made its way down the coast. Only two minor incidents marred the otherwise quiet journey. On the first day out, as he lolled on the deck next to the railing, a shout of warning from up top startled him. A wooden pulley narrowly missed striking him on the head. It fell a yard from him, skittered across the deck into the scuppers and fell with a muffled splash into the rolling waves of the fast moving ship. Pierre thought it only a minor accident until the second incident. Then he thought more of it.

The second incident occurred that same evening as he was making his way from the captain's cabin down to the lower deck where he had a small sleeping area just off the shipmaster's well-furnished cabin. Earlier, he was invited to Captain Hector's cabin to discuss the forthcoming meeting with Temple. The captain requested his presence, and they talked at length about what might be expected at Boston and of what transpired since 1667 when the Treaty of Breda was signed.

Pierre was surprised to learn that Grandfontaine knew of his service with Mourillon Du Bourg who tried to acquire Acadia in the summer of 1668 for the West India Company, which was eager to resume control of Acadia. He informed Pierre that that was one of the reasons he chose Pierre to accompany him to Boston, even though on that occasion Pierre did not set foot in Boston town. The crew of the ship was forced to remain aboard while Du Bourg delivered to Temple the commission from the King of France and an order from the King of England to deliver up Acadia.

Pierre recalled the tenseness of the situation at that time. Temple refused to cede the territory to Du Bourg because he maintained that some of the territory specified in the order did not belong to Acadia but to Nova Scotia. While Du Bourg was detained by Governor Temple, the crew was confined the ship and closely guarded by several ships. Finally, a ship arrived from England with a letter from Charles II to Temple ordering him not to give up Acadia until he received further orders from England. Du Bourg was informed of this development and told to leave Boston immediately. To Pierre and the rest of the crew's relief, the ship was released and sailed without further incident to St. Christopher in the Antilles.

As the evening wore on, Pierre and the captain shared a bottle of fine Madeira; they discussed the possibility of a repeat of the incident of October 1668. Captain Hector informed Pierre that the situation had changed. Charles II of England had no doubts now to the claim of King Louis XIV.

A crescent moon brightened the clear skies, showing Pierre the way to his sleeping quarters. The wine made him light-headed, and he whistled softly as he slowly descended the stairs from the upper deck to the lower deck. As he stepped to the deck, he heard a soft swishing sound, followed by a dull thud. His giddiness made him careless and uncaring. Calmly he stared at the shiny knife imbedded in the railing six inches above his left hand.

The hilt of the knife still vibrated gently as he stared at it, fascinated. Slowly, he reached with his right hand and tugged the knife from the smooth worn surface of the railing. It was the ordinary, common hand knife that all sailors carried at their waist. The blade was about four inches long, and it had a cork handle. This one was well-worn but nicely balanced, and, like those of most sailors, it was sharp and pointed—a working knife that sailors used every day to cut lines, pry open jammed knots, or even cut them apart if necessary. It was balanced for throwing as the men used them to play numerous knife games, one of their main amusements. Of course, it was also used as a weapon.

Pierre studied it, realizing that it would be impossible to identify the owner. Too many similar knives were aboard. Why, one of his own was stowed somewhere in his duffel—one from the days of his service with the Royal Navy. His head cleared as he recognized the significance of what happened. Someone tried to kill him!

He stood entranced. Then he slowly surveyed the main deck before him. No movement except the roll of the ship and the ballooning of the sails as the ship moved gracefully southwest through the bright July night engaged his senses.

He could make out the figure of helmsman below him as he watched the whip staff, which was held in place by blocks and tackles. The knife did not come from that direction; it came from the main deck, probably from behind the main mast. It would provide cover for anyone waiting in the shadows, but no one was evident now.

Who would want to kill him, or injure him? The knife missed him by scant inches. A brisk breeze wafted, and the ship rolled and bounded gracefully. Maybe that affected the culprit's aim. The more he thought of it, the more confused he became. Jean Charlet was the only one who might have a reason to harm him. But that seemed unlikely. After all, Jean defeated him in the fight. He ought to be the one seeking revenge. He had no enemies aboard that he could think of. Well, he survived. Perhaps in the morning his head would be a little clearer, and he would be able to unravel the mystery.

He walked cautiously to the storage area beneath the stairs that was converted into his quarters for the trip. The conversion was simple—a hammock slung between two wall posts, the jumble of ropes, cloth, pulleys, buckets of tar, and sundry other pieces of nautical equipment pushed aside to make room for him.

Without removing his clothes, he flopped into the hammock and was soon asleep, the wine having made him sluggish and drowsy.

Next morning the weather changed. The brisk breeze that so favored them became light and a deep overcast of dull, gray clouds covered the sky, portending rain, although none fell.

Pierre rose early and breakfasted on cheese and hardtack. Then he went to the main deck. The ship's crew had it on course for the island-studded inlet to Boston harbor. As the ship proceeded westward around Pullen Point, Pierre scrutinized the land before him. Visibility was reduced to a few miles, but he could make out the contours of low hills and rising land to the west. Through the haze that covered the green and blue-green hills he could see many dwellings. The important men of the colony inhabited some of the many islands in Boston Bay. Impressive homes imposed their presence on the hazy, misty seascape.

The bay changed little from his visit of two years ago, and he tried to locate the spot at which his ship anchored during those tense, exciting days, but the islands all looked the same to him. In the center of the channel was a large island occupied by the first governor of the colony, John Winthrop, and now the island was know as Winthrop's Island. To the left was a smaller island with a stone structure; it was known as Castle Island. These were the only two islands that Pierre could identify; the others remained nameless.

Once past Winthrop's Island, the master hove to and dropped anchor. His white flag with the gold fleur de lys fluttered aft of the poop deck, plainly visible, as he waited official clearance to enter further into the harbor.

Pierre was astonished at the number of ships of every sort that crowded the basin. On a promontory that jutted far out into the basin he could see the buildings of a large town. Along the foreshore was a long quay and tied to it were numerous fishing vessels, large and small. The harbor was coming to life; many ships and boats scurried about like water bugs in search of food. Anchored on either side of the main pier were two English warships, each of about fifty guns. Boston made Port Royal look like a bad dream.

Unknown to Pierre, Grandfontaine joined him at the rail, and Pierre was startled by his voice as he said, "Doesn't this remind you of the harbor at Le Havre?"

The busy harbor did remind him of back home in France. True, Le Havre was larger, but he was not sure if it was busier. The English seemed to be in frenzy, with boats coming and going, with ships entering and leaving —sailboats, rowboats, scows, shallops, ketches, boats of every sort.

"Yes, in a way it does, but the English seem to do everything in a hurry."

"You're probably right. They don't take time to enjoy life. For them it's a very serious business. Even their religion is straitlaced and lacking in humor. They don't believe in sin and forgiveness. One must be free of sin at all times." He laughed heartily, as if he made a very funny joke.

Pierre did not see the humor in it and only smiled.

"Why, Pierre, you're as serious as the English."

"This will be the first time I meet an Englishman. I've heard a great deal about them, but I've never met one before."

"You will see, Pierre, they're all business. To them it's sinful not to take advantage of every opportunity to improve God's creation. And to make money."

"I thought the reason the English came here was to practice their religion without interference from their king and government."

"That's true, but it doesn't mean that they're not to make money as they practice their religion. They're very industrious; they've prospered here at Boston. They've created a settlement that's almost independent of England. As a matter of fact, they've surpluses of many commodities; that's why they're eager to trade with us or anybody who will provide them with the things they want. They want our furs, our fish, and our produce, and they will supply us with the goods we need, such as tools, pots and pans, clothes, shoes, and many things that take a long time to get from France. They can also provide us with sugar, molasses, and rum, and even slaves, which they get from the Antilles. You see all those ships, Pierre? That's why they're so prosperous. They control the shipping on the Atlantic. We must be competitive; we need a larger commercial navy."

Pierre frowned. "It's impressive. I was just thinking Port Royal will have to improve a great deal if it's to compete with this port."

"I don't think it ever will. You see, the English send all their dissenters away to form colonies, but our king will only allow Catholics to come to New France. That's why so many more English are in this land. They're coming for religious freedom while we're coming to convert the natives. We will never be as numerous as the English."

A worried look came over Pierre's face. Was Grandfontaine predicting the success of the English over the French? That could not be. God would take care of his faithful people; he would not allow infidels and heretics to triumph. "Do you think we have a chance to succeed over the English?"

"Only if King Louis changes his policies toward his colonies. He must send more colonists, more help, more soldiers, more missionaries, and then we will be able to survive against the English."

"He's promised all of that."

"Yes, that's true, and if he keeps his promise, we will have a chance."

An open rowboat manned by six men approached. Seated in the center was a tall lean man dressed in dark, somber clothing. He wore a pointed-crowned black hat with a broad brim that obscured the upper half of his face. Obviously, he was in charge, and he was dressed well enough to be an important official.

Grandfontaine waved his right hand, half in salutation, and half to indicate to Pierre that they would soon have official company. “He's probably an official from the governor. I'm sure we're expected, as the kings of England and France have made arrangements and given orders for the transfer.” He smiled at Pierre. “We must be prepared to greet our guest with appropriate pomp and dignity. We must impress these Englishmen.”

Chapter Seven — Hostility

“Chevalier de Grandfontaine, I'm pleased to welcome you to Boston. As the official representative of my king, it's my pleasure to extend the hospitality of Boston to you, the representative of your king.” This was spoken in impeccable French, which surprised Pierre who stood a few paces behind the captain's retinue. The small squad of six soldiers looked impressive in their marine blue doublets, their white breeches and leggings, with their shiny muskets at the ready.

The Bostonian mounted to the deck accompanied by two nondescript oarsmen from his boat. They did not act very military although they were both armed with battered, well-used muskets that they handled with nonchalance.

Pierre felt that if it came to using the weapons these colonials would give a good accounting of themselves. They seemed to know what they were doing while Grandfontaine's squad looked tentative and nervous.

The tall, lean Englishman in his somber dark clothes removed his high crowned hat, waved it with a flourish and bowed deeply at the waist.

“John Laverette, deputy governor, at your service.”

“Sir, it's a pleasure to meet you. I'm Hector d'Andigne, Chevalier de Grandfontaine, Governor of Acadia, representative of the great king of France, His Majesty Louis XIV. My mission here is to see Sir Thomas Temple, Governor of Nova Scotia.”

“I believe your visit is expected by Sir Thomas. I've taken the liberty to arrange quarters for you at the Cromwell Head, a local inn, which I hope you will find satisfactory.”

Pierre was surprised that Sir Thomas Temple had not come to greet the captain. To him, it seemed a slight. But he also knew that Sir Thomas was not happy to return Acadia to the French crown.

Grandfontaine stepped forward, grasped the Bostonian by the hand, and put his arm about his guest's shoulders in a friendly and intimate way. Then he moved his guest toward a small table that was set up on the deck. On it stood a decanter of amber liquid, and beside that were several shiny metal drinking vessels. The two men sat down, and old Joseph moved forward to fill two goblets, which he placed before the two men. They conversed in hushed tones so Pierre could not understand what was said, although he assumed it concerned the arrangements to finalize the transfer of jurisdiction.

The two armed men who accompanied the official stood indifferent and informal; one of them took out a dark brown wooden pipe, filled it, and placed it unlit into his mouth when he realized he had no way to light it.

Pierre watched the two men. They did not seem to be military men. They were too undisciplined. Both wore coarse homespun of great simplicity— knitted jerseys and nondescript gray-tan pantaloons with jagged leg openings, stockings which came to the knee, held up by a band which was tied around the leg below the knee; on their feet, sturdy, heavy, square-toed shoes. Around each waist was a narrow cloth belt, and stuck into the waistband of his pantaloons was the ubiquitous fisherman's knife. Their muskets were held casually in the crook of their arms.

Pierre smiled amicably, but neither returned his attempt to be friendly. Instead, he thought the serious planes of their faces turned into a scowl. So he sauntered over to the rail and gazed down at the boat that brought them. Four men leaned back comfortably against the gunwales, relaxed and indifferent. One noticed Pierre watching them and made a comment to his companions. Their heads lifted to stare up at Pierre. He nodded in acknowledgment, but the men smiled at each other and several comments passed between them. Their rudeness brought a flush to Pierre's face. The urge to hurl an epithet was difficult to control.

Pierre could not understand their seeming animosity. Their countries were at peace. He felt no rancor toward them. Why did they resent his presence here? Slowly his anger subsided, and he ignored their indifference.

Englishmen were difficult to understand, he decided. But he envied the apparent prosperity of the settlements scattered around the bay. The overcast still remained although it brightened, and he could see more clearly the numerous buildings of the small town that seemed to sit in the water of the blue-gray bay. He noted that behind the waterfront establishments a low hill with three peaks dominated the town and seemed as a beacon for the harbor and its quays. The hill, with its three peaks, he knew, was called "Trimontaine."

Pierre was eager to disembark and enter the town. Its size and wealth intrigued him. He envisioned the day when Port Royal would rival Boston. He could see a prosperous town along the banks of the Dauphin River, extending along the shores of the Port Royal Basin—a bustling harbor with many ships at the piers and wharves loading and unloading, while others waited in the protected basin for their turn at the docks. Behind he could see a formidable stone citadel that would protect the town and its inhabitants from the depredations of anyone foolish enough to attack. And he, Pierre Marin, would be an important wealthy man of the community with a beautiful seigneury, many storehouses filled with trade goods and produce, a charming family of many children, and his beautiful wife to encourage and love him.

In his dream, he could see Françoise dressed elegantly in the fashion of the day, brought all the way from Paris. Then he saw her as he left her three days before—pleasant, seeming to have forgotten their quarrel of the evening before.

Her threat of leaving him to return to France still disturbed him. Sadness filled him as he thought of the situation: he left with the uncertainty unresolved. He assumed that she made the threat in the heat of anger, but the doubt in his mind worried him and made him uneasy. He loved Françoise, and losing her would pain him greatly; yet if he could not make her happy, it would be better if she returned to France. Opportunities were scarce for a poor young fisherman and an ex-sailor in France. His fortune was in this New World. This town of Boston made him sure of that. If the English could prosper here, so could an ambitious Frenchman.

That evening, after Grandfontaine and his entourage were quartered at the inn, Pierre entered the taproom, intending to have a quiet mug of ale. The room reminded him of the tavern, The Red Circle, the one owned by Françoise's father. Three lead glass windows dominated the south wall making the room bright and cheery during the day. As evening came on, numerous candles were lit, illuminating the room with a soft, subdued glow.

Few candles were lit when Pierre entered the gloomy room; dusk started to descend on Boston. He found an unoccupied table near the center window along the south wall. He sat down and watched the activity in the room. Only half dozen patrons occupied the room, and most were engaged in eating their evening meal; very few seemed to be drinking.

As the proprietor approached, Pierre wondered how he would communicate with him. He could speak no English, and he doubted that the large man with the stooped shoulders and graying hair would be able to speak French. As he drew near, Pierre looked him over carefully. He was tall with a well-developed paunch and broad shoulders. He wore a dull colored linen shirt with a short waistcoat over it. His breeches were narrow and extended to the knees. He wore tight fitting stockings that emphasized his spindly legs. He walked with the characteristic rolling gait of a sailor, so Pierre assumed he must be an ex-sailor.

He stopped before Pierre and asked, "What would you like?"

Pierre did not understand what he said, but he surmised that he asked for his order.

Pierre replied in French, "Sir, I don't speak English. I would like a flagon of ale." He pointed to a flagon of ale on a nearby table.

To Pierre's astonishment, the older man replied in French, very English accented, but understandable, "Ah, my young friend, you're from the French ship. Most of us in Boston hope that we can be friends. Where are you from? I've heard the king of France has sent an envoy to take Acadia from Sir Thomas."

"We're here to arrange the transfer of authority of Acadia from Governor Temple to Governor Grandfontaine."

"The name's George Walker. I'm half owner of this inn. My partner's John Laverette, whom I think you met when you arrived.

"Yes, I met your partner. He seemed a very pleasant man."

"If there's money to be made, John can be very pleasant. He looks after the rooms, and I look after the tavern."

"That must be a fine arrangement."

"Yes, it is. I will get your ale." He turned and left.

Pierre mused. The man was affable and pleasant. His French,

though not cultured, was passable. Better than my English, he thought. As he waited, he studied the other patrons. To his left, seated at another window table and devouring a huge meal that seemed to be roast mutton and an assortment of vegetables was a small wiry man with thin white hair. Pierre estimated he was about sixty years old. He was interested in his food, and did not pay any attentions to the other patrons. Pierre doubted that the man even noticed him.

At a table before the large fireplace that dominated the west wall was a group of three men dressed in casual wear—simple, sturdy, short coats of a dark brown color. They wore knee breeches trimmed with a single ribbon bow at the knee, worsted hose, and square-toed shoes. Their apparel was so similar that Pierre thought they used the same tailor. They finished eating and were enjoying a mug of some beverage. Pierre could not tell what it was. They were engaged in an animated conversation. Their voices carried well, but Pierre could not understand what they were saying, although it sounded interesting.

Two rough-looking, bearded men about thirty years of age sat at a table in the center of the room. Two flagons occupied the center of the table, and they kept filling two earthenware mugs from them. Their conversation was animated but hushed—even conspiratorial, Pierre thought.

Four other tables of various sizes were unoccupied. This Friday night the first week of July was quiet and peaceful.

Shortly, the tapman, George, returned with a flagon of ale and an earthenware mug that he set before Pierre. Pierre placed a Spanish doubloon, which he received that afternoon from the captain, on the table before the man. The captain told him that the Spanish coin would be more acceptable than their French francs.

"You don't have any English money?"

"No, I was hoping to get some with this doubloon. That's all I have, except for some francs."

"I will take the doubloon. I will give you English crowns in exchange."

At that moment, three sailors entered the room, boisterous, and appearing as if they already spent some time at another tavern. Their behavior and language indicated they already had a bit to drink. They chose the table at the window to Pierre's right, and loudly called to the tapman.

They appeared to be regular customers of the inn, for George went over slowly with his rolling gait and spoke firmly but quietly.

A short, stocky man remonstrated loudly, and his two companions grabbed him by each arm and held him firmly to the sturdy wooden chair. He struggled weakly and then wilted.

Pierre watched with interest as the three sailors quieted; then one turned to him and asked a question which Pierre did not understand, but the tone of his voice did not seem friendly.

Pierre shrugged his shoulders and smiled at the three. He did not understand a word that was said and he did not want to provoke them.

The most boisterous of the three stood up and pointed his finger directly at Pierre. In a clipped, mocking voice he said, “Parlez-vous français, Monsieur?”

Pierre smiled and answered slowly, “Yes, I speak French, but, unfortunately, I don't speak English.”

The sailor did not reply to Pierre's comment, so Pierre decided that the few words the sailor said were all the French he knew.

The other sailors tried to make their companion sit down, but he would not. Although Pierre could not understand the words, the tone of voice and the manner of speaking let him know that the sailor was baiting and taunting him. His actions irritated Pierre, and he felt his face heat up as he forced himself to ignore the tipsy sailor. He turned to his mug and drank deeply; the sailor continued to rail at him. His companions, who, earlier, tried to constrain him, now joined him. Pierre felt the blood rushing to his face; he felt hot and uncomfortable. A thin film of perspiration suffused his face, and he felt the moisture in his armpits. With an effort, he controlled his urge to retort to the laughing, taunting group.

The short stocky one farthest across the table from him made gestures, inviting him to fight. The others laughed uproariously and encouraged their companion. He was about the same size as Pierre, perhaps a bit stockier, but Pierre felt that if it came to a fight he would be able to hold his own. He sized up the situation. He was in a strange town, alone, outnumbered, and he never was a fighter. He was involved in his share of fights, but usually they ended up indecisive, or he was bested to some degree. He did not want to fight, but if these drunken sailors forced him, he might not have an alternative.

As he continued to ignore their gestures and taunts, he watched them out of the corner of his eye. The instigator rose from his seat and sauntered over to Pierre's table. Without waiting for an invitation he sat in the chair across from Pierre. Then he waved his index finger beneath Pierre's nose and threatened him with a clenched left fist. Pierre stared at him in silence; then he smiled and tried to placate the angry man who continued to rant and wave his hands. Pierre could not understand what he was saying, but whatever it was, it was not friendly. Pierre's irritation mounted. Finally he grabbed the man's waving finger bringing it down to the table.

The man jerked his finger from Pierre's grasp and seized Pierre's wrist. Pierre was astonished at the power of the man's grasp, but he made no effort to release it. He still hoped to avoid a fight. By this time, the sailor's companions rose from their table and now surrounded him. He hoped they would take their friend back to their table and get on with their drinking. George, the tapman, had not returned with their ale, and Pierre wondered what was keeping him. He might be able to persuade the three to go about their business.

The tavern door opened, and a lone man entered. The squeaking of the neglected hinges held the group; all eyes turned to the door. The newcomer closed the door and stopped to let his eyes adjust to the gloom of the room. Then he swept the scene, taking it all in. Pierre recognized the tall figure of Jean Charlet, and he expelled a sigh of relief. Perhaps Jean could extricate him from his predicament.

Pierre called out, "Hello, Jean, would you care to join me? I seem to have some unfriendly friends."

Pierre half rose from his seat to greeted Jean. As he did so, the sailor confronting him pushed him firmly into the chair. Pierre exploded from the chair, and with both hands placed against the other's chest, he pushed forcibly. The quickness of the action surprised the man, and he stumbled back several paces. A scowl of fury masked his face, it reddened, and angry words flooded from his mouth.

Jean Charlet moved quickly from the door and placed himself between the combatants. By this time the barman returned. He placed the flagon and mugs that he was carrying on the nearby table and joined the scuffling men.

He shouted, "There will be no fighting in my establishment. I will have none of this. If you want to fight, there's plenty of room in the street."

Although Pierre could not understand what he said, he gathered from his tone that he was not pleased. Pierre was astounded when Jean spoke in English to the proprietor who quieted immediately.

Jean looked at Pierre and said, "I told him we'd finish this quarrel outside."

Pierre stared at him in disbelief. Jean did not help him; he made a fight imminent. Pierre said, "I've no quarrel with this man. Or with any man. I don't want to fight."

"Pierre, you don't have much choice. If we don't leave, George, here, will throw you out. And I assure you he's capable of doing it. He doesn't own this tavern because he's unable to control his patrons."

Pierre rankled at the injustice of the situation. He did not start the quarrel; he was the victim. Now he must accede to these sailors.

The tall, round-bellied man seized each combatant by the upper arm and squeezed firmly. His grip was vice-like, and Pierre's biceps hurt under the pressure. The other man grimaced and cursed as the large man directed them toward the door.

By now, the other patrons gathered around in curiosity, following as the noisy group moved across the room, between the tables, toward the door. One of the patrons held the door open, and the two were pushed out. They stumbled into the dusty street in the deepening dusk. Neither fell, but they struggled to keep their balance. They ended up facing each other, glaring.

Pierre turned to Jean. "Please tell this man that I don't want to fight."

Jean said something to the enraged sailor, and to Pierre's astonishment the man stepped toward him, shouting, cursing, and waving his fists more threatening than before.

Pierre stepped back, but the small crowd of spectators prevented him from moving far enough, and the angry sailor's right fist struck Pierre's left cheek. Tears blurred his eyes. He felt a stinging pain on his left cheekbone.

His heartbeat quickened, and his muscles trembled. His breath came in short, sharp gasps, and he blinked his eyes. He prepared to attack his adversary. Then he stopped short. He had nothing to gain from a fight. He had no reason to fight this Englishman, yet he could not see how he could avoid one. Whatever Jean Charlet said to the man did not soothe his feelings; Pierre could not understand why the man was so incensed and so eager to fight him.

Pierre raised his hands in front, open and unthreatening. Again he tried to show the sailor that he did not want to fight. His opponent advanced, both fists clenched, and he threatened to strike again. Pierre looked around to see what happened to Jean. He stepped aside and stood on the edge of the crowd that gathered.

Jean was shouting something to the sailor. Pierre could not understand what he was saying, but he appeared to be encouraging the other man to fight. Pierre was astounded; he hoped that Jean would help him avoid a fight. Instead, he seemed to be instigating one.

The sailor advanced, swinging his right hand at Pierre's head. Pierre was ready. He ducked under the blow. He could have struck his opponent a telling blow to the ribs exposed by the openness of his swing. He still hoped to avoid a fight so he stepped around the flailing fighter.

Then a sturdily built man of average height dressed in the uniform of a French lieutenant stepped between the two combatants. He shouted in French, "What's going on here?" The authority in his voice froze both men. The angry Englishman whirled to face this new threat and stiffened.

Pierre recognized the newcomer as Lieutenant St. Castin, one of the junior officers of the military detachment that accompanied Grandfontaine to Boston. He turned to the Englishman and said something in English. The sailor answered angrily. Then his mood slowly changed. The tone of his voice mellowed as he and the lieutenant conversed quietly for a few moments. Finally the sailor threw up his hands in disgust and joined his two companions at the edge of the still enlarging crowd.

Lieutenant St. Castin barked in French, "It's all over. There won't be a fight. Get about your business." He repeated the same in English. Slowly the crowd dispersed—some to their unfinished meals and drinks in the tavern, others walked in opposite directions down the narrow street. The three sailors did not re-enter the tavern but waddled their way northward in the deepening dusk.

"Monsieur Marin, how did you get yourself into such a mess?"

"Sir, I don't know. I was having a quiet ale when these three men taunted and badgered me, challenging me to a fight. I tried to avoid it and thought I had, when Jean Charlet, one of the sailors from our ship, came along. I was hoping he'd help me avoid a fight, but it seems he encouraged it."

The lieutenant laughed. "That Charlet has the reputation of being a troublemaker. Where's he now?"

"Well, sir, he seems to have disappeared."

"Come, let's finish that ale you started."

"A good idea, sir."

The officer extended his right hand. "I'm Jean Vincent d'Abbadie de St. Castin. Everyone calls me St. Castin."

"I'm Pierre Marin, in the personal employ of Captain Hector."

"Oh, I know who you are. There's been much discussion of your duties by the soldiers and the other officers under the captain's command."

"I'm pleased to meet you, Monsieur St. Castin. I know that you and the captain were very busy on the way over. This is a very opportune meeting for me. You saved me from an unfortunate fight, and for that I'm very grateful. Thank you."

As they talked, they entered the tavern and walked slowly to the table that Pierre occupied before the commotion.

George Walker came to the table. "I'm sorry about those ruffians. Those sailors from the homeland always cause us trouble. They never behave like the locals. They're always looking for trouble."

Pierre nodded. "Could you bring another mug for the lieutenant?"

"Certainly," he replied and left.

Pierre swung back to his companion. "I was impressed by the way you handled the situation out there, sir."

"Call me St. Castin. Well, it seems he thought you were one of the French sailors responsible for the death of his brother. One of his brothers was lost in an engagement with a French ship; he felt you were one of those responsible. Of course, he had too much to drink, which didn't help his thinking. And your friend, Jean, because he knew you didn't understand English, made sure the poor man believed the worse."

Pierre stared blankly at the lieutenant. "Do you mean to say the Jean wanted that sailor to fight with me?"

"So it seems. He told the sailor that you were the one who killed his brother. I guess he wanted to see you beaten. I heard about your altercation with him at Port Royal."

"But…but I didn't win that fight. As a matter of fact, I was badly beaten, and if it wasn't for my friend, Jacques Breton, it would have been worse."

"Well, Pierre, I fear he was seeking revenge. He badly dislocated his elbow which kept him in sickbay for several days."

"I know, but he apologized to me, and to Jacques. I thought it was all settled."

"I'm afraid you're wrong. He was waiting for the right moment.

Men like Jean Charlet never forgive. They're dangerous men. He will never forgive until he's evened the score. Remember that. You're his enemy. You've not seen the last of him."

Later, as Pierre lay in the narrow bed of his small room down the hall from the captain, he considered the events of the evening. He narrowly escaped a fight with three English sailors. It seemed they were not Bostonians but sailors from an English merchantman. They recognized him as a Frenchman, and even an ex-sailor. He knew his long association with the sea marked him as a sailor, but he did not think it was that obvious. Jean Charlet's duplicity annoyed him.

His job with Captain Hector was to avoid altercations and to protect the captain from that kind of confrontation. He was sure the captain would not be pleased with him for what happened, but Lieutenant St. Castin supported him. The young lieutenant, who was only eighteen, two years younger than he, impressed him. Over the flagon of ale they shared, they became friends.

Pierre learned that St. Castin was the son of Jean Jacques d'Abbadie de St. Castin. As a minor son, he chose to enter the army; at age thirteen he served at Quebec in New France as an ensign. There he served under Captain Grandfontaine. He returned to France in 1668 and rose quickly through the ranks to his present position. Now he served on the staff of Captain Hector de Grandfontaine, newly appointed governor of Acadia. His father made sure he obtained a good education, including some time in England, thus the reason he could speak the language.

Pierre liked the young, sturdily built, self-confident young man. Although he was only eighteen years old, he had the knowledge and experience of a much older person. An easy charm about him made him at home with everyone; he was affable and friendly with a disarming smile. He wore his uniform with ease and no pretensions. He treated everyone with respect and justice; Pierre soon perceived it was this quality that defused the situation earlier in the evening.

Pierre's thoughts turned to Jean Charlet. He still could not believe the man encouraged the fight between him and the English sailor. But the more he thought about it, the more it seemed that the lieutenant was right. Jean disappeared; they did not see him again that evening. As he thought about the man, he became angry. He decided to be careful in any future dealings he might have with him. He knew that Françoise disliked him, but she never discussed it with him. He doubted the incident on the boat was the only reason. Well, he would be careful. If the man was a troublemaker, as St. Castin insisted, then maybe he had not seen the last of him.

He wondered if the English sailors' animosity was a portend of the feelings of the people of Boston toward the French. He would find out tomorrow. He knew if that he was to do the job expected of him, he must learn more about these Englishmen from Boston. The innkeeper, George Walker, seemed friendly enough. The other patrons ignored St. Castin and him. Pierre was confused. Why did the sailors pick on him? Was it a coincidence? Or was planned? Maybe to discredit the French or, in particular, Captain Hector? He did not speak to the captain since their arrival because the captain was busy making arrangements to meet with Sir Thomas Temple. It appeared the ex-governor of Acadia, which he called Nova Scotia, was an important man in Boston.

It was Saturday, July 5, 1670. Tomorrow was the Lord's Day; in Boston it was a day of rest and worship. No business would be done on Sunday, so the earliest day they would meet with Sir Thomas would be Monday, the seventh. Tomorrow, after they attended service—for Pierre heard the Bostonians would be affronted if they did not devote some of the day to the worship of God—he would try to find out what was expected of him. He was concerned. He did not like the idea of worshipping God in the church of these Puritan heretics. If he accompanied the captain, he would be jeopardizing his soul; he would have to confess to a priest as soon as possible. Would he be able to avoid this occasion of sin? His pastor back in Harfleur warned him of the devil's ploys to capture his immortal soul.

He remembered Curé Dutertre with fondness. The white-haired old man was his mentor and teacher. Each morning, early, Pierre hurried to the parish church to serve Mass for the old priest, who was especially fond of Pierre, as he hoped that one day Pierre would become a priest. So he taught Pierre his Latin prayers and how to read and write some Latin, but mainly French. Pierre found the study of Latin difficult, but he learned how to read and write French easily.

He could still see the disappointed look on the old pastor's face when Pierre told him that he joined the French Royal Navy. The kindly priest blessed him, smiled sadly, and then he said, "Be a good boy, Pierre, and the Lord will look after you. Maybe some day you will become a priest. If you don't, then it's the Lord's will. God bless you."

That was in May 1665, and now here he was in 1670, married to a loving woman, far from France, on a strange continent, in a foreign town, and involved in something he hardly understood.

He prayed silently. He hoped his old mentor was right—that the Lord would look after him… and his wife. Having consigned his welfare to the Almighty, he rolled onto his left side and was soon fast asleep.

Chapter Eight — The Meeting

Monday, July 7, 1670 dawned bright and clear in the town of Boston, which was perched on a rocky peninsula that jutted northeastward into the island-studded bay on the east coast of North America. It was dominated by a triple-peaked upland that many people called a mountain, but which was only a large hill. The town, surrounded by tidal marshland, nestled at the foot of this hill. From its beginning, it developed into a dominant settlement on this northeast coast.

Captain Hector de Grandfontaine and his retinue of ten soldiers under Lieutenant St. Castin, and Pierre trudged slowly along the winding streets toward the residence of Sir Thomas Temple, Governor of Nova Scotia. Captain Hector marched at the head of the column while Pierre walked alongside on his left, just outside the double column of soldiers. The lieutenant brought up the rear. The group looked impressive in their royal blue tunics, white breeches, and white canvas leggings. Their chests were crossed with a double baldric. Each man carried a musket with a short, sharp bayonet stuck into the barrel.

The captain looked resplendent in his large-brimmed felt hat with a satin ribbon band. His blue satin doublet with a lace collar and a wide red taffeta sash around his waist accented his narrow satin trousers that fitted into his calf-high boots with high heels. His white lace-topped boot-hose emphasized his shiny boots. A straight, functional sword in a leather scabbard dangled from a leather belt beneath the sash.

Pierre looked out of place in his knee-length breeches, coarse homespun shirt, knitted hose, and rough, square-toed shoes. He did have a broad-brimmed, low-crowned felt hat that he was proud of since his father gave it to him when he left for New France. He knew that his father spent most of his savings to buy the hat, so he wore it with pride and satisfaction.

The small column elicited a fair amount of curiosity from the early risers of Boston. As they wound their way through the streets, a dozen or so youngsters followed behind them, while more adults stared in fascination as the colorful group headed north-west to the rural home of the wealthy trader and proprietor of the lands know as Nova Scotia.

Pierre knew that the captain was impatient and anxious to meet this man who, to this time, stymied France's effort to re-acquire the strategic territory. They spent the last two days arranging this meeting, and, again, Temple used every ruse to avoid the formal transfer of authority to the French crown. His excuse was that he was ill, too ill to receive the representative of the great Louis XIV in a proper and fitting manner. Several messengers made the trip between the inn and the governor's abode before the final arrangement.

While these negotiations were going on, Pierre was busy observing the people who came and went in the inn. Unobtrusively, he watched the men and women who were patrons, as well as the employees of the establishment. Nothing suspicious happened; Grandfontaine's fears for his personal safety seemed unfounded. He informed Pierre that he believed the ex-governor would take any means to retain control of the lucrative area of the northeast, which included the settlements of Port Royal, Fort Pentagouet, and the fishing ports on the south shore of the main peninsula of Acadia.

After a few minutes of brisk marching, the scattered houses and the landscape became rural in appearance. Soon the houses were those of wealthy farmers and merchants. Sir Thomas Temple's home was on a small peninsula that jutted into the estuary of the Charles River. The approach road wound through lowlands and entered his property from the south. A large wooden gate blocked access to the property, but no guards or sentries were on duty. Pierre ran ahead, opened the gate, and the company entered without breaking stride.

Captain Hector was annoyed because neither he nor Pierre could hire a carriage to bring him to see Sir Thomas in the style that befitted the representative of the king of France. The reason they could not hire a carriage was the shortage of such conveyances and the horses to draw them. Most people traveled on foot or their own carts—carriages were scarce. Very few were for hire because of little demand for such a service. The captain seemed surprised that a town the size of Boston could not provide such a service. Pierre could understand, for he could see that one would not find such a service in Port Royal. True, Boston was much larger and more progressive than Port Royal, but it was still a frontier town lacking the amenities of a town of similar size in Europe.

A winding road led from the gate to the front of a large frame house. The building was three stories; a long veranda ran the full length of the facade. Wooden columns held the roof of the gallery that was twelve feet in depth. The front entrance centered the south wall, and an ornate-carved oak door dominated it. The entire structure was painted white with green trim around the doors and windows. Pierre was impressed with the size and richness of the structure. It dominated the slight rise upon which it was located. Behind it, Pierre could see a number of lesser buildings that, he decided, were storehouses and barns.

As they approached, the door opened, and an elderly man with graying hair parted in the middle and drawn back, shouted, "Stop! The master cannot see you. He's too ill this morning to entertain anyone."

They stopped. Grandfontaine raised his hand and beckoned. The lieutenant came to the front of the column and stood beside the captain.

"What did he say?" he demanded. Grandfontaine possessed little knowledge of the English language. A scowl covered the captain's face. Although he did not understand the man's speech, he anticipated its message. His face darkened; annoyance showed in every movement of his body. Pierre got the message also: another delay.

Captain Hector insisted they be allowed to see Temple. Finally, they were ushered into the sitting room on the second floor. Pierre, along with Lieutenant St. Castin, was chosen to accompany the captain, although Pierre could see no reason why he should be present. Nevertheless, he was pleased at being asked.

The room was large and office-like. It faced south; two large windows let in the early morning light, illuminating the room brightly. Three men waited in the room. One, a large man in his late fifties, was seated in a great upholstered armchair. He was dressed expensively in a silk or satin shirt with lace collar and cuffs. His maroon velvet knee breeches were decorated with mauve ribbons. His strong, well-muscled legs were encased in fine white cotton stockings, and on his feet he wore sturdy leather shoes with square toes and ribbon ties. The two other men flanked him.

The one to his left was dressed in a similar manner, but over his flowing shirt, he wore a richly embroidered waistcoat. He was a younger man, his shoulder-length brown hair tied back with a narrow black ribbon. He stood waiting with a casual air. Pierre assumed he was an associate, probably a secretary.

The other man, about Pierre's age, cradled a musket in his arms. His clothing was more utilitarian than the other two. His dark, almost black, hair was cut short and square at ear length. He wore a simple cotton shirt and coarse brown knee-length breeches. His legs were covered with coarse knitted woolen socks, and he wore a pair of Indian moccasins on his feet. He probably was one of Sir Thomas's soldiers, Pierre surmised.

Sir Thomas indicated a straight-backed chair that was placed at an angle before him so the occupant would have to turn his head if he wished to look directly at the ex-governor. Silently, Captain Hector sat down and beckoned to Lieutenant St. Castin. The lieutenant followed and stood beside the captain to his right. Pierre stopped a few paces inside the door and waited.

Not a word was spoken. The silence was foreboding; the atmosphere within the room strained. Pierre felt the tension. His heartbeat quickened slightly.

Finally, the large florid man smiled and, in passable French, said, "Welcome to my humble home, Captain."

The captain returned his smile and replied carefully, "It's a pleasure to be here, Sir Thomas. I know it's not a pleasure for you because you are losing valuable lands and property, but I'm sure your sovereign will recompense you."

The smile disappeared, and a scowl replaced it. "I wish I could be sure of that, my good sir. King Charles is not my benefactor. He does not care a whit for my welfare. I've written him many letters concerning this arrangement, but he has little understanding or appreciation of the situation here. He is too concerned about the situation in England and Europe."

"That's unfortunate, sir."

Sir Thomas continued bitterly, "He's too taken with your glorious king. He admires and fears him too much. He cares little for his own country and his loyal subjects. It were better he hadn't returned to the throne."

"Sir, I can't help you with your quarrel with your king. I'm here to repossess the lands that belong to France. We've some arrangements to make. I want to sail as soon as possible so I may set up my headquarters. Let's get down to business."

"You're right. A number of issues have to be settled. The first is the indemnity that's to be paid for my property in Nova Scotia. I've many posts—both trading and fishing—for which I need reimbursement. My king has ordered me to return all authority to your king, but he doesn't say that I must lose my business and property. How will that be effected?"

"Sir, I've no authority to reimburse you for your losses. That's the responsibility of your king. My authority is to assume legal control of the lands of Acadia that extend from the Gaspé peninsula to the Kennebec River."

The older man reddened and sputtered. Finally, he managed to control himself and growled, "The Penobscot River is the southern boundary, not the Kennebec. You assume too much, my dear captain."

Captain Hector smiled. He struck an exposed nerve; the southern boundary of the territory was indeterminate. "I will be using Fort Pentagouet as my headquarters. We will not discuss the boundary now."

Anger returned to the older man's face. He reddened, and his breath came in long wheezing gasps. Pierre thought he was about to suffer a fit of apoplexy, but he quieted and said, "My deputy, Captain Richard Walker, is there now conducting my business. He's the man you will deal with. As you can see, I'm too ill to go with you and supervise the transition."

"Then it's agreed. Fort Pentagouet will be turned over to me by your deputy at the earliest convenience; that means as soon as I can leave Boston."

"Yes. But you must allow me to remove all my trade goods and personal property. You must make an inventory of all the forts and their accouterments so I can present an account to my king."

"That's fair. I will arrange to have an accounting made and presented to your man."

"Other matters need decisions. I've many fishing and trading vessels, and I've contacts with the Indians and the French settlers who've been my concessionaires for the past ten years. They need my goods and trade. I want access to them so I may supply their needs. I must use the fishing posts I've established along the south shore."

"That's not part of my order, sir. I'm to take possession of all lands and to allow trade with Frenchmen only. I can't allow you to retain trading privileges in Acadia."

Sir Thomas grinned slyly. "If you say nothing, your king will never know. If you don't agree, then I shall be forced to use my own means to save my enterprises."

To Pierre, the threat was obvious. He waited with bated breath for Captain Hector's reply. His answer might decide the future of the colony of Acadia. Pierre knew that the strength of Sir Thomas's forces exceeded that of Grandfontaine; three small ships—two armed merchantmen and one small warship with a hundred soldiers—was hardly a large force in comparison to the many ships and people that Pierre saw in this flourishing settlement of Boston. The French in Acadia were weak.

The vulnerability of the French colony and the strength of the English colony struck him. He concluded that the settlers of Port Royal and any of the other French communities in Acadia were at the mercy of the English. This perception sent a chill through him; he could see that it would be an advantage for the Acadians to remain on friendly terms with this vibrant, aggressive people. Temple exemplified the strength and resourcefulness of the Massachusetts colony.

The captain replied, "I don't want to use force, but if you force me to, then I shall do my duty. I'm sure we can come to a compromise."

"Don't misunderstand me. I've no intention of disobeying the orders of my king, but I must make the best deal I can. I must protect my interests—trade and territorial. I'm sure we can come to an understanding that will benefit both of us."

"Sir, I don't understand."

Temple's voice became impatient. "My good man, you're the new governor of Nova Scotia. You've authority over the land, the sea, and the people. You can give privileges, or you can take them away. You can issue licenses to fish…to trade. You can help me and yourself."

Pierre was astonished at the boldness of this worldly Englishman. But he perceived that what he said was true. The authority of the king was far away, and the governor of New France in Quebec had little communication with his deputy in Acadia. Grandfontaine, if he wished, could be the absolute authority in Port Royal and the other outports. If he wished, he could do as he pleased—he could turn a blind eye to the comings and goings of the English traders and fishermen. He could encourage them or discourage them. He could follow his orders strictly, or he could allow the English to continue business as they did for the past fifteen years. Pierre wondered which approach the captain would take.

"You're right. France is far away, and the communication between Fort Pentagouet and Quebec is uncertain. Perhaps we can come to a mutually agreeable arrangement. What do you have in mind?"

The large man leaned forward, grinning with satisfaction. Now the negotiations were going his way. "I'd like to continue my trade with the settlers at Port Royal and the other settlements, and I'd like to continue fishing on the banks east of the south shore. As well, I'd like to continue using the fishing posts along that same south shore."

"Sir, you ask for a great deal. How will that help me?"

"Captain, there's much money to be made in the trade with the Indians. You get the furs from them, and I will provide you and your people with the provisions they most need—sugar, molasses, tools, axes, spades, hoes—they're readily available here in Boston."

"And what will I receive from the fisheries?"

"For each shipload of fish—green or dried—I will give you five percent of its value. Of course, no one need know of this arrangement."

Pierre's was shocked. Would the captain agree to such an arrangement that was counter to the orders he received from the minister, or, at least, Pierre believed they were? He could see how such an arrangement would increase the price of these things to the inhabitants. The governor and the Bostonian would have a monopoly on the trade and the fishery.

"And if I don't agree, what will happen?"

"Well, I suppose other privateers and pirates will establish themselves on the south coast. The coastline is long, and there are many coves, bays, and inlets from which to operate. My people tell me that you have only three ships and very few soldiers with which to patrol and keep order."

Again, Pierre was surprised that the Englishman was so well informed. He knew more about the happenings in the French territory than did the captain. And he was using that information to his advantage. What he said was true: The captain had a meager force to maintain his authority over a vast region. Anger tightened Pierre's chest, yet he exulted at the opportunities that this new world presented to a bold and enterprising person. He could see that trading could be more profitable and less arduous than working on the land—building dikes, hoeing, seeding, and harvesting. Why, if a person managed properly, he could amass a fortune?

He looked around the room. Sir Thomas Temple had not done badly for himself. His associate appeared to be prosperous as well. He stared at the young man who stood at Sir Thomas's side, listening attentively to the discussion. He admired the man's fine clothing, and he became envious. Perhaps, if he could become involved in the trade and help the captain to supervise this agreement, he could share in the wealth that would come from it.

Grandfontaine spoke. "Perhaps we can do something about the fishing, but I fear it would be unseemly and impossible to do anything about the trade. My orders concerning the trade in furs are very specific. The West India Company has a monopoly, given by the king himself, on the fur trade. If I were to disobey that order, my very life would be endangered."

Sir Thomas wrinkled his nose. "Then we shall leave the matter of the fur trade, but we can make some covenant about the fishery. Suppose you allow my ships and fishermen access to the banks and fishing stations at

Canso, Mirliegueche, and a few lesser ones. You will be well rewarded, and no one will be the wiser. We will put that in a written agreement, but we will not mention your share of the agreement. That, we will put in a private contract between you and me, and these gentlemen can witness it." He waved his hand to encompass the entire group.

Grandfontaine nodded in agreement.

Pierre was disbelieving. The captain agreed to an arrangement that would benefit him but which would be detrimental to his French colonists. He sold the south bank fisheries to the Bostonians. Pierre was stunned. He could not believe that the captain made such a deal. A sense of betrayal and disappointment and, finally, anger swept over him. He could contain himself no longer. He stammered, "Captain, do you think that's a wise deal? Don't you think the people of Acadia will lose? We will be at the mercy of these Englishmen?"

His outburst startled both Captain Hector and Lieutenant St. Castin who stared at him in shocked silence. The three Englishmen stiffened, and their eyes turned to him. Several moments of ominous silence descended upon the group, making Pierre feel uncomfortable. His heart pounded, and heat rose to his cheeks.

The captain spoke softly, but his tone was edged with steel. "Pierre, this is none of your affair. When I want your advice, I will ask for it. Your purpose here is not to offer suggestions concerning the operation of the colony."

His tone was menacing and threatening. But Pierre continued, "Sir, this is not a good arrangement for the people of Acadia. The English will get all the fish…and the furs…because they are closer to the source. They have many ships. Sir, I don't think you should agree to such an arrangement."

Lieutenant St. Castin was signaling with his eyes. He was trying to catch Pierre's attention. To silence him.

The captain looked toward his host. "Excuse me, sir. I'd like to have a few private words with my young friend. May I use your hallway for a few moments?"

Temple nodded as Grandfontaine rose from his chair and moved toward Pierre. They proceeded out the door to the long hallway that ran down the center of the upper floor. Once in the hall with the door to the inner room closed, Grandfontaine swung around and face Pierre. "Pierre, this is an opportunity of a lifetime. You and I can make money, and besides, we have little choice. If we don't agree to his proposal, he will simply ignore us and go about his business without us. As he says, there are many isolated places from which he and his people can operate."

"I don't like him. I don't trust him. He has all the advantages; he owns all the ships, and he has many men working for him. I'm sure he will cheat us."

"Pierre that's always possible, but we've the kings of France and of England on our side. That's something he will have to keep in mind. We will always have that as a deterrent to any plans he might have to cheat us."

"But, sir, won't that arrangement hurt the colonists? Won't it be more costly and dangerous for them to deal with the Bostonians?"

"Pierre, they will do it anyway. They've been dealing with the English for the past sixteen years; they know what to expect and what they have to do."

Grandfontaine's logic could not be ignored; the governor was right. The West India Company would have no more concern for the colonists and fishermen than would Temple. The company's own welfare and profits would be of utmost importance.

"I'm sorry, sir, that I embarrassed you before the Englishman. But I was surprised and concerned about the people of the colony. I didn't think of all the possibilities."

"Then you agree? We should make a contract with Sir Thomas?"

"It still bothers me that we will be dealing with the English. It's hard to forget that a few years ago they were the enemy."

"You're right, Pierre. I've the same trouble, but we must remember that now they're our friends."

They returned to the bed-sitting room. As they entered, Sir Thomas asked, "Has your friend been convinced?"

"Yes," Grandfontaine answered curtly and did not elaborate.

"Well, then, let's get on with it." He motioned to his well-dressed companion who sat down at the desk, produced paper, a quill pen, and charcoal ink.

"First, a letter to Captain Walker. He will surrender the Penobscot fort to Sir Hector."

Pierre noticed that he elevated the captain by his use of the word 'Sir' and he wondered if it was accidental or intentional. He decided that it was intentional, for it seemed that Sir Thomas Temple was not a man to act without thought and planning.

Soon the meeting ended, and they returned to the inn.

Later that evening Pierre met St. Castin in the taproom. The discussion turned to the events of the morning.

"Well, Pierre, what do you think of the negotiations that took place this morning?"

"Lieutenant, I think it's a good deal for Grandfontaine, but I'm not so sure it's a good deal for France."

"Pierre, what's a good deal for Frenchmen is a good deal for France. Do you think Colbert or Louis is very concerned about your welfare? No, they're looking after their welfare, not yours or mine. We, Pierre, must take care of ourselves. This arrangement will give us a chance to live comfortably."

"How do you plan to take advantage of the situation?"

"I plan to become a trader. As an officer, I should have access to information that will make it profitable for me to deal with the Indians and the colonists."

"Do you think the captain will allow you to carry on such activities while you're under his command."

"He doesn't have much choice. You and I are witness to his contract. If he doesn't allow me to become involved in the trade, I will buy my contract and become an ordinary settler."

"You sound as if you've made up your mind about what you will do?"

"Yes. When I saw how profitable the trade has been for Temple, I discerned that one can make a fortune in this land if he chooses the right enterprises."

"So you don't think settling the land is the way to become prosperous?"

"I think there are easier ways to become prosperous? First, I will establish myself as a fur trader with the Indians, with the colonists, in produce and provisions, and with the fishermen, in fish. Then I will acquire land and build a comfortable seigneury."

"But that's not legal, sir. The company has the king's authority to trade and fish. They'd never allow you to operate as an independent trader."

"That's true, Pierre. But they will need the resources to stop me, and I don't think they have them. They will have enough trouble protecting themselves from the English. Grandfontaine's made some generous concessions to the Bostonian. Remember, he gave him the right to fish on our banks, and to use our shore stations. Technically, he refused him the right to trade in furs, but remember, for the past sixteen years the Indians have been dealing with him. It will be hard for us to change their habits."

What St. Castin said seemed to make sense to Pierre. He had not been in the new land long enough to understand all the intricacies of dealing with the English and the Indians, but St. Castin was stationed at Quebec for three years. Obviously, he kept his eyes and ears open and, as a result, acquired a great deal of knowledge about the working of the New France economy. Pierre enjoyed talking to the younger man, for it gave him a chance to learn about the situation in the New World.

They remained late in the tavern and discussed the future with enthusiasm. At times, Pierre angered at the cynicism of the young officer, but most of the time he agreed with his philosophy. It appeared that St. Castin had not yet formulated exact and sure plans for his future, but he dreamed of making a fortune in Acadia, not as a colonist, but as an opportunist. He planned to use his position as an officer to achieve his goals. To Pierre, he seemed to lack worthwhile values although he insisted that one of his goals was to Christianize the Indians and bring them to salvation.

As their discussion progressed, Pierre was mystified by the complexity of the man. One of his goals was to acquire a fortune, and he seemed to have no qualms about using any means at his disposal—even disobedience to his orders as an officer of the French army. He did, though, seem to have a religious and spiritual conscience.

"Have you any dealings with the Indians, Pierre?"

"No, Jean." St. Castin insisted that Pierre use his Christian name. "I met a few at Port Royal, but events happened too fast, and I had little time to associate with them. There were a few about the fort; I noticed that most seemed to congregate at Sieur Le Borgne's house."

"You're right, Pierre. Le Borgne, who's better known as "Belleisle", trades with them. Belleisle fancies himself the governor of Port Royal. Of course, he uses the fact that old Charles Latour was a creditor, owing him a great deal of money. As a result, he insists that all the land around Port Royal is part of his seigneury. I think there will be trouble with that man."

The last statement startled Pierre. After all, he just acquired his concession from Le Borgne, and now his newfound friend indicated he might have trouble with his seigneur.

"What do you mean, Jean? I'm one of his concessionaires. I signed the contract before we left."

"Well, Pierre, I'm afraid you will find Belleisle very insistent on all his dues and rents. He will try to recoup his losses by getting them from his concessionaires. And he's rather old-fashioned about the status of a seigneur to his tenants."

"How do you know all that?"

"It's a long story, Pierre. I've an old friend who served with me in Quebec who's now studying in the seminary at Quebec. He tells me that Belleisle and the priest at Port Royal...you know, Father Molin...are very good friends, and between them they control the colonists."

Pierre's eyes were beginning to open, and what he learned fascinated him, as well as angered him. He only hoped that St. Castin's assessment of the situation was wrong. He found Sieur Le Borgne or Belleisle pleasant and affable, even agreeable, when he and Jacques dealt with him. He readily agreed to the exchange of land from Jacques to him. Now he was wondering if he did the right thing.

"Do you really think he will be troublesome?"

"He seems to be a troublemaker, insisting on his way. Maybe I'm wrong. I certainly hope so. When he and Grandfontaine met, I found him very intransigent. He insisted on his way until the captain, in exasperation, gave in. The captain made him governor of Port Royal. I'm sure that's a mistake."

This did not reassure Pierre. "What sort of trouble do you anticipate, Jean?"

"I'm not sure. But I think if he's too hard on his tenants, they will rebel. You see, the English has allowed most of them to go about their business with little interference. For the past sixteen years, under Temple, no one bothered them about rents and dues. They've acted as if the land belongs to them, and suddenly Belleisle arrives and insists that he's the owner with a right to some of their produce, some of their time in labor, and all the other rights of a seigneur in France. After such freedom, for so long a time, I'm afraid if Belleisle insists, there will be a confrontation, and who knows what will happen. Father Molin, I'm sure, is on Belleisle's side, so that may be helpful since most of the people will listen to him. Their faith is still very strong, even after these many years without a pastor."

Pierre listened attentively as he sipped on his final mug of ale. It was getting late; they were the only customers in the gloomy room. Most of the candles were extinguished, and the tapman, George, dozed in a far corner of the room as he waited for them to leave.

"Where do the Indians fit in?" Pierre asked.

"Most of them have no love for the English, thanks to our missionaries. The Micmacs are our friends. Many of them have been converted and hold our priests in high regard. The Indians in Acadia are not like the Iroquois to the west. Since early times the Iroquois have been our enemies, but the Micmacs, the Abenaki, and the Malecites are our friends. I believe it's because we treat them as equals—with dignity and respect. Why, our glorious King Louis makes them French citizens if they become Catholics."

"You seem to like the Indians, Jean?"

"They're not dumb savages as the English seem to think. They're capable fighters and diplomats if they're given the chance. I find them interesting and fascinating."

"I hope I will be able to share the same feelings you have for them. You make me eager to return to Port Royal to begin my future."

Chapter Nine — A Profitable Friendship

The next morning Pierre arose early even though he went to bed late. One of Boston's frequent mists descended on the town; the bay was shrouded in a gray diaphanous veil; the sun tried to peep through the gauzy curtain, but without success.

Pierre entered the tavern that was quiet and deserted. He found a table near the fireplace where a cheery fire picked up his spirits. They were to leave Boston today, but if the weather did not improve, it was unlikely any pilot would want to direct them through the dangerous and intricate channel.

Pierre was eager to be on his way. He was in a hurry to get back to Port Royal and Françoise. He missed her greatly; his desire for her intensified with each hour that he was away. As well, he had much to do: he must build a house before the winter snows came; he must put up a supply of provisions to last the winter; he must learn more about the politics of the colony. Lieutenant St. Castin whetted his appetite. Now he was more curious than ever about the happenings in Acadia and New England. Since his arrival in Boston, he learned much about the interrelationship of the French colonies of New France to the English colonies of New England. The situation was complex—the animosity between the two people interwove with their need for each other. The confused ownership of the land did nothing to simplify the entire situation.

Pierre could now see how the earlier French settlers, who were under English rule for the past sixteen years, would find it difficult to come under the direct and close supervision of the French crown. The English interregnum was loose and perfunctory with the governor more interested in commerce than the development of the colony. He was beginning to understand that the commercial elements would not encourage the settlement of the land with permanent residents as they would be a detriment to the fur trade, and they might encourage the fishermen to take up permanent residence at the many fishing posts scattered along the coast. If that happened, the settlers would be more interested in their own prosperity than in the welfare of the royal favorites with their privileges and monopolies.

As Pierre sat gazing into the flickering flames contemplating his place in the scheme of the affairs of Acadia, the opening of the main door of the tavern interrupted his reverie. He glanced in the direction of the squeaking hinges. The identity of the man surprised him.

The newcomer stopped momentarily in the doorway, squinting to let his eyes adjust to the gloom within the room. Then he removed the dark, heavily embroidered cloak that protected him from the outdoor dampness. He was wearing a dark felt hat with a wide brim and a low crown. A large satin bow adorned the left side of the hat. From that distance, Pierre could not distinguish its color, but he thought it was a rich brown. The man wore a black wig with ringlets that came past his shoulders. Around his neck was a falling band of pure white lawn that was more like a cravat, now coming into fashion. His coat was of dark velvet, deep brown in color. The lapels were folded back revealing the scarlet taffeta lining that showed from the neck opening to the knees. The three-quarter length sleeves of the coat allowed the lace and ruffles of the shirtsleeves to extend beyond in snowy whiteness. A brilliant red satin vest peeped through the opening of the unbuttoned coat. The vest was shorter than the coat that came to his knees, showing the matching velvet breeches. Ribbons and bows at the knees accentuated his dark red stockings. On his feet he wore leather shoes with red heels and large leather bows over the instep. To complete his costume he draped a gallooned velvet baldric over his right shoulder extending to his waist on the left side. An ornate silver-handled sword in a fine leather scabbard dangled within easy reach of either hand. In his right hand he carried a simple cane with an unadorned globe handle. Pierre decided he looked dashing.

After the man established his bearing, he waved his caned right hand in a semi-greeting to Pierre. He was the same man Pierre saw the day before at the meeting with Sir Thomas Temple, the man that Pierre thought was Temple's secretary. No introductions were made, so Pierre did not know his name.

He came straight toward Pierre, making it obvious that Pierre was his point of interest. He spoke perfect French. "Good day, my good man. You're Pierre Marin, aren't you? In the employ of Captain Grandfontaine? I'm William Harvey, secretary to Sir Thomas Temple. You're just the man I want to see."

He extended his right hand, and Pierre rose to grip it. Although the man was of medium height and slight of build, his grip was firm and strong.

As Pierre indicated the chair across the table, he inquired, "You want to see me?" His voice could not hide his surprise. He could think of no reason why Temple's secretary would have business with him.

"Sir Thomas was impressed by the fact that the captain desired your presence at the negotiations yesterday."

The man's vernacular French impressed Pierre; it was so normal he did not noticed it until the man was comfortably seated across from him.

Harvey noticed the quizzical look on Pierre's face and explained, "You're surprised that I speak French? I was born and raised in France. My parents lived in La Rochelle for many years as the representative of the English East India Company; so you see, I learned French almost before I learned English. I was sent to England for my education, but I'm still very comfortable when I speak French. It was because of my facility with the language that Sir Thomas included me in his circle of associates."

Pierre nodded. It was most interesting to find so many Englishmen who could speak French. Then he remembered that many Englishmen were in France during the exile of the present king of England. It was even rumored that Charles II kept a French mistress, and that his wife was related to the French king, Louis XIV.

"What did you want to see me about?"

The Englishman leaned forward. He spoke so low that Pierre leaned forward too. "My business with you is private. Sir Thomas and I are looking for a gentleman of your standing to represent us at Port Royal. Although we are no longer the government, we still have many interests in the colony. Many of the settlers are our friends and want to remain so. We need someone to keep an eye on what is going on. We need someone to be available for our friends who may want to do business with us rather than the new governor…or his deputy, Belleisle. We think you're the man."

Pierre was astounded. He found it incomprehensible that the English would be prepared to effect a deal such as this with a poor ex-sailor from Normandy with a meager education—barely able to read and write French and even less Latin—and who could speak no English. He stared at the visitor, gathering his thoughts, before he replied. "Sir, you're asking me to become your associate to avoid the orders of the King of France? You know the governor has been given strict orders to make Acadia French…with French laws… with French commerce…for the French settlers that are already there… as well as the many who will be arriving shortly."

Harvey did not seem surprised at Pierre's rebuttal to his suggestion. He smiled, slowly settling back in the chair, toying with the shaft of his walking stick. Then he leaned forward again. His composure and sureness made Pierre uncomfortable. Before he could speak, George Walker entered the room and came over to the table.

"Good morning, gentlemen. You're very early this fine bright morning." He laughed at the irony of his greeting. "Boston is favoring us with one of its fine sunny days."

Both nodded their acknowledgment; Harvey spoke first, "A flagon of your best ale for my friend and me."

Pierre tried to remonstrate because he was still feeling the effects of the ale from the previous evening, but it was futile. Instead he said, "I'd like breakfast instead. What's your usual fare?"

"This morning it's beans and fried back pork."

Pierre nodded and said, "Mr. Harvey, would you join me?"

"No, I've already eaten."

George Walker turned to fill their order. Harvey took up where he left off. "If more settlers are coming, it will be a golden opportunity for you…both for you and for us. Look at it this way, Pierre. If you don't take this offer, you can be sure someone else will. France and England are far away. They don't understand the needs of the people here, and even if they did, I doubt they'd be concerned about them. If you consider carefully, you will see you will be offering a service to these poor people. You will be giving them an opportunity to sell their production, and you'd be a source of goods that they need."

Pierre was not sure he understood the arrangement the man had in mind. Up to now, he was vague and ambiguous. Pierre was confused. "I don't understand what you expect me to do?"

Harvey smiled his all-knowing smile. "It would be your job to acquire from the colonists of Port Royal all their surplus products—meat, wool, vegetables, pelts, hides, fish—anything that is over and above their needs. We will send a ship to get it, and we will supply you with sugar and molasses, tools and utensils, cloth and clothes, and anything else that might be needed in Port Royal. Since it will be cheaper than that supplied by the French, everyone will benefit."

Pierre nodded. What Harvey said was true. The English products were cheaper than those of the West India Company. That, he already discovered from the few transactions he completed with the French company. He hesitated. "I'd be in conflict with the interests and the wishes of my country. The king will consider me a traitor; the governor, a knave; and Belleisle, an enemy."

"That's possible, my good man. But to prosper, one must take some risks. After all, you came here to make a fortune for yourself. Coming out here was a risk. There's always danger for the adventurous."

"That sounds interesting, Monsieur Harvey, but what's in it for me?"

"I was waiting for that. You will receive ten percent of the profit. You will receive ten percent of all the trade that you acquire from your neighbors, as well as ten percent of anything that you sell to them. Your expenses should be very little. You will store what you buy, and we will take care of the shipping. We will send ships to a place that is suitable for both of us. Maybe even Port Royal. Our countries are on friendly terms so our ships should be welcome. My dear Pierre, it's nothing more than a business arrangement. We will all profit, and, I hope, handsomely."

Pierre was not totally convinced; he experienced fears and concerns. The arrangement seemed too facile. Harvey made it seem that he had little to do, and the profits would be rolling in. He made it sound so simple that Pierre felt sure there must be some pitfalls. Since Harvey approached him secretly, he wondered about the dangers he could not foresee. He wondered how Grandfontaine would view the deal. Would he think that Pierre deceived him? Was he avoiding the governor's authority? Was it legal? Would he or his wife be in danger? Harvey implied there was an element of risk, and what would that risk be? Would it be financial or physical? If he agreed to act for Sir Thomas and Mr. Harvey, would Françoise agree to such an adventure? Would he have time to look after his land as he was operating his business?

All these questions flitted through his mind as he stared into the intent face of the well-do and confident man. For a moment, Pierre was envious; he could see himself dressed in a similar fashion, and his wife dressed in the fashion of the day. The prospect pleased him, but still he hesitated. "Monsieur Harvey, I will consider your proposal. Many aspects intrigue me."

"Monsieur Marin, we can't wait long. You will have to decide quickly, or else we will look for someone else."

Pierre remained silent as he considered the ramifications of being involved with Sir Thomas and William Harvey.

Harvey frowned. "When can we expect to have your answer? We'd like to hear from you before you sail."

Pierre glanced out the window; the atmosphere was still gray and dismal. Visibility improved but he could see no more than half a mile. "I doubt we will be leaving today. I will give you my answer before the day is out. Will that be satisfactory?"

"Yes, I will await your reply with anticipation. I hope, Monsieur Marin, that you will join us."

Harvey rose, flung his velvet cape about his shoulders, and without a backward glance, left the tavern. Pierre was annoyed by the way the man left, almost rudely. He felt more a servant than a business associate. He made no sign of farewell; his departure was perfunctory and quick.

As he mulled over the events of the past few minutes, George Walker returned from the kitchen at the back of the inn carrying a heavy pottery plate filled with a generous serving of baked beans, two slabs of fat back pork, and a small loaf of bread. The aroma of the food made Pierre realize that he was famished. Saliva filled his mouth as he reached for his knife in its sheath. He dipped the blade into the beans and carefully licked them into his mouth. Then he smacked his lips in appreciation.

As he devoured the meal, he reviewed the offer Harvey made. It seemed like a providential opportunity—one of the reasons he gave Françoise for making the trip. Here, it landed in his lap. They sought him; he did not go looking for them. The more he thought of it, the more excited he got. If the venture went well, he would become a wealthy and important inhabitant of Acadia—his friends and fellow colonists would look up to him. His prestige would be great. He might be able to purchase a seigneury, and if he prospered greatly, he might even be able to purchase a lesser title—a knighthood, a barony.

All his hopes and dreams came flooding back. When he decided to accompany Captain Hector to Acadia, the possibility of improving his station in life was one of the enticements presented to him. Now he saw this proposal as the fulfillment of his aspirations.

He stopped daydreaming. He must look at the deal more objectively. Disadvantages and risks must exist, even grave dangers that Harvey did not mention. Why was he so secretive and conspiratorial? That suggested illegalities. Pierre knew that part of the transfer of authority was an agreement to allow the Bostonians rights off the south shore, and even in François Bay. As well, they would be allowed some shore stations. Boston ships could use Acadian ports, but they were not allowed to trade in furs. No mention was made about trade in other goods. Harvey mentioned pelts—he did not use the word 'furs' specifically, but everyone knew that pelts meant furs. No doubt he was thinking of trade in furs. Other than the fur trade, everything else seemed to be within the law. The Acadians could still obtain their necessary manufactured goods from Boston and the other English colonies along the mainland coast.

Maybe Grandfontaine would feel left out. If so, perhaps he would cause trouble. But the main obstacle would be Le Borgne de Belleisle, the man Grandfontaine appointed deputy governor of Port Royal. He was Pierre's seigneur with rights over him. The West India Company would not look kindly on his dealings with the English since they owned the monopoly on the fur trade and were deeply involved in the fisheries. All the risks would be his: he would accumulate the goods, store them, and prepare them for transshipment to Boston or wherever Temple and his associates decided. Would the profits be worth it? The more he thought of it, the more he felt he should have a greater share of those profits. He would have to meet Harvey again to improve the arrangement, or else it would not be worth the risks.

Lieutenant St. Castin entered the tavern and strode toward Pierre's table. "Good morning, Pierre. You're very early."

Their conversation of the previous evening came flooding back to Pierre's mind. Dare he discuss Harvey's plan with the lieutenant? "I expected to leave today, but it appears the weather won't co-operate. How are you this morning?"

"You're right. The captain has decided not to leave today. He's a few details he wants to clear up with Temple, and, of course, the weather hasn't co-operated."

Pierre tensed. What were the details with Temple that needed clearing up? Would they in any way affect his dealings with Harvey?

Before he could say anything, the lieutenant continued, "I noticed Monsieur Harvey leaving as I came in. Did you see him?"

Pierre was taken by surprise, and for a few moments, he was speechless. He was not sure if he should tell St. Castin about his discussion with the Englishman. Finally he replied, "Yes, as a matter of fact, he came to see me. Sit down. I will tell you about it." Pierre waited as the lieutenant chose a chair across from him, the same one that Harvey occupied a few minutes before. "He offered me a deal."

St. Castin leaned forward. But he said nothing.

"He wants me to act as his agent in Port Royal. He and Temple plan to continue trading with the people of Port Royal, and I would be their contact with the settlers. And I suppose, the Indians in the area."

St. Castin murmured, "Very interesting."

"I would obtain and store any goods that the habitants would have to trade, and they would get English goods from me. He's offered me ten percent of the value of the goods coming and going. What do you think, my friend?"

The lieutenant stroked his chin as he digested the information.

"What are the risks, Jean? Do you think I'd be antagonizing the governor if I were to become involved in the trade between Boston and

Acadia? Does Belleisle have a monopoly in Port Royal? What about the fur trade? Can an independent trade with the Indians without a license from the king?"

"Pierre, you ask some tricky questions. The king has not been too clear as to who has the right to trade in Acadia. There are many independents. Many of the fishermen who come to these coasts make more profit from their commerce other than fish. Especially in the north…in the gulf of St. Lawrence…Newfoundland…Tadoussac…Gaspé. I'm sure if one is discreet, he can deal profitably with the settlers, the Indians, and the English."

"You do think the deal has possibilities?"

"Let's just say if I was offered the same opportunity, I'd consider it. But I'd seek more of a return. Ten percent isn't enough. Many risks must be considered. Pirates are everywhere. We know that a number of pirates operate in this area—English, French, Dutch, and even a few from other countries such as Spain, Portugal. Who knows where else? I'd insist on fifteen percent both ways."

"You're right, Jean. The risks are great but the profits are substantial."

"You know, Pierre, if the opportunity arises, I will also become involved in the trade. Much money can be made. But I wouldn't like to be an agent for someone else. I'd begin my own enterprise. Some day, when my commission expires, I may join you in the business."

Pierre grinned. He noticed that St. Castin already assumed that he would accept the offer. "You're right, Jean. I think I will meet with Monsieur Harvey, and if he increases my share, I will be his agent."

St. Castin slapped him on the shoulder and laughed. "That's the spirit, Pierre. Nothing ventured, nothing gained. One must speculate to accumulate."

"Thanks, Jean, for the advice. You've helped me to make a decision. I will look for Harvey immediately and see if I can get better terms."

Pierre knew the meeting with Harvey would not be an easy one. The man was shrewd, and he would use every argument and ruse to get the best deal for himself.

Pierre located Harvey with difficulty, as he could not speak English. But after several false leads, he located the man supervising the loading of one of Temple's ships. Within the main cabin on the quarterdeck, he found Harvey busy working with bills of lading, receipts, and accounts. One of the sailors showed Pierre the way after he made known his purpose by means of signs and gestures. Pierre was happy when the sailor decided to refer him to a higher authority. Since the ship captain was not aboard, he took Pierre to Harvey's cabin.

Harvey greeted him enthusiastically, which pleased Pierre. His greeting erased some of the annoyance that he felt when Harvey left him earlier that morning. He decided Harvey's abruptness was perhaps due to his preoccupation with the business of the day.

"I assume you've considered my offer…and find it acceptable. I felt you'd see it my way."

"Sir, I've considered your offer, but I find it wanting. I'd be taking too many risks. Grandfontaine may not look with favor on such a deal; the deputy governor at Port Royal, Belleisle, will certainly oppose it—he expects to be the sole proprietor and trader; the French company will consider me a usurper; pirates abound and may attack me and any storehouses that I erect. I can't consider the deal unless I receive a greater share. I must have twenty percent on goods coming and going."

Harvey looked shocked. "My good man, that's impossible. We can't pay that much. Your risks are minimal; ours are great. We have all the risks that you will have, plus more. We've ships to maintain, markets to find, authorities to placate on this side of the Atlantic…and on the other. No, it's impossible. What I offered this morning is the most I can give."

"Then, sir, I don't think we can do business. I've considered carefully, and it's not worth my time, effort, and risk."

Pierre rose from the padded chair and headed toward the door. He took several steps before he was stopped by the older man's voice.

"Don't be hasty, my good man. Let's discuss this a little further. You must understand the position Sir Thomas is in. For the past years, King Charles has been wavering back and forth on the accession of Acadia to your king. First, he ordered Sir Thomas to leave Nova Scotia and to give up all the forts and post that he established, and then he changed his mind and can't decide what part of the area is Acadia. Now, he's decided all Nova Scotia is Acadia and has ordered Sir Thomas to leave. Sir Thomas has spent much of his own money establishing these posts and forts, and now he's to lose it. His losses will be great. For that reason, we can't accede to your demands. Twenty percent is too much, but maybe we can raise your share a bit. How about twelve percent?"

Pierre returned slowly, sat down, and said nothing for several moments. Harvey waited patiently.

"No, sir, that's not enough. But I will consider eighteen percent, plus all my needs at cost. Clothes for my wife, tools, and utensils for the kitchen—pots, pans, kettles, and dishes."

"Pierre, you ask too much. I can't agree to those terms. The very best I can offer is fifteen percent both ways. That's my final offer. No extras. Simply fifteen percent. That's it."

The finality in his voice did not escape Pierre. He hesitated. This was the moment of decision. He could accept it or forget it. He was sure he negotiated the best terms Harvey was prepared to offer.

"Agreed. Fifteen percent on all goods."

Chapter Ten — A Place of His Own

On July 10, the weather cleared so Grandfontaine and his entourage embarked. With a favoring wind they made good time to the mouth of the Penobscot River where Fort Pentagouet was located. Pierre was disappointed when he got his first view of the fort. It was not much better than the crumbling fort at Port Royal, no more than a palisaded trading post—small, lacking in armament, without room to house the small garrison that Grandfontaine planned to maintain.

Temple's deputy governor, Captain Richard Walker, received them in a matter fact manner, not cordially, nor discourteously, but he made it plain that he was not happy to turn the area over to the French. Together, Pierre and Walker's aide made a careful inventory of the fort and the stores that would remain behind so that Temple could make a claim to the King of England. Pierre's association with the young clerk appointed to work with him, Jonathan Hawkins, whose family was one of the mercantile entrepreneurs of Salem with ties to Acadia through its association with old Charles La Tour, helped him learn a smattering of English. As they worked at counting the accoutrements of the fort, they joked about Pierre's mispronunciation of English words. Pierre enjoyed his time at Fort Pentagouet.

A week later, a French fishing vessel on its return to France agreed to stop off at Port Royal to replenish its water and food supply, so Pierre made arrangements with the captain for passage. Because the winds were unfavorable, it took them six days to make the voyage to the Port Royal Basin. Pierre immediately obtained a shallop and sailed up the Dauphin River to Jacques's concession.

Fortunately, a west wind made his trip up the river quick and effortless. He made the three leagues up the river and around the narrows known as 'Detroit de Lisle' in two hours. As he passed Lieutenant Richard's headquarters, he noticed that the house, under construction, was finished, and there seemed to be little activity in the environs. Within minutes he could see Jacques's homestead, as the marshland was level and untreed. Protruding from the grasses on a knoll was a lean-to and beside it a rust-colored tent. Before the two shelters was a smoldering fire; from a distance he saw a wisp of blue-gray smoke dissipate in the brisk breeze.

From a hundred yards away he could hear the echoing sound of an ax biting into green wood. As he approached, he saw two female figures—one bent over a large three-legged, smoke-blackened pot on the outdoor fire. To the left, another worked on the carcass of some animal that hung from a pole tripod. They were so busy they did not see the fast approaching shallop. Once within shouting distance, Pierre hallooed, and both women raised their heads, startled. The woman at the cooking pot was the first to react; she rose quickly from her stooped position and cried, "Françoise, it's Pierre. He's back."

Before she could move, the other figure started running toward the crude pier that jutted from the edge of the riverbank. When Pierre landed, all three were waiting to secure the boat.

Pierre disembarked, and Françoise flung herself into his arms. She clung to him and smothered his face with kisses, her arms tightly encircling his neck. She sobbed, and tears streamed down her cheeks as she mumbled incoherently. He held her tightly, and lifted her off her feet. Through the thin linen dress he could feel the warmth of her body, stirring his blood. The firmness of her breasts pushed against his bare chest through his open shirt. He felt the pleasant smoothness of her body under his caressing hands, and the scent of her body tickled his nostrils. A surge of passion engulfed him; he tingled with desire. He could feel the heat in his groin, and he was sure she was aware of his lust. His mouth searched hers; his tongue moved entwining with hers. The strength of their passions surprised both. They were oblivious to all.

A voice interrupted them. "Hey, hey, you two! There will be time for that later." Jacques laughed.

The spell was broken, and they stepped apart. Françoise's face turned crimson as she stepped behind Pierre.

Pierre laughed and shouted, "How are you, my friend?" He flung his arms about his large-bodied friend and kissed him firmly on each cheek. Then he pushed him to arm length and surveyed him critically. "Well…married life hasn't been bad for you. You look better now than you did before. It agrees with you."

Before Jacques could answer, Marguerite stepped forward, her arms upraised. Pierre embraced her and kissed her on both cheeks. "It's nice to see you again. You're more beautiful than ever. Jacques must be treating you right." He winked and grinned slyly.

Marguerite got his implication and a slight blush came to her tanned cheeks. She turned to Jacques and smiled lovingly. "He's the finest and most tender husband that a woman could wish for."

Now it was Jacques's turn to blush, and he reddened perceptibly through his deep tan.

Marguerite seized Pierre by the hand and turned toward the campsite that was a hundred yards from the landing place. Françoise clung to his other arm and Jacques followed behind as they moved toward the fire.

"We're about to eat. You must tell us about your trip and all that happened," Marguerite said.

"I think I'd like to hear what has happened here. More has happened here than on my trip. Jacques, you've made much progress."

He surveyed the surroundings and was impressed by what he saw. A spacious log lean-to was constructed. It faced south with three walls; unpeeled logs leaned from a sturdy framework to form the room and the main wall; other logs leaned along each side of the main wall. The whole structure was covered with bark, and this was held in place by squares of sod cut from the nearby marshland. The open side faced the long fire. At one end stood a blackened, three-legged cooking pot, and a sapling framework extended the length of the fire to support pots and kettles. At the other end, two logs were set almost paralleled to each other, a skillet resting on them. A secondary fire could be lit between them or coals from the main fire could be pushed between them to heat the skillet.

Next to the log lean-to was the cotton tent. And beyond it was a pile of logs, neatly peeled and ranged in neat rows to dry.

Once they were seated around the fire, Marguerite brought out some tin plates and filled them from the pot that simmered beside the fire. It was a meat pie cooked in the manner of Acadia—a meat dish that could be cooked with chicken, rabbit, or pork, in fact, any meat that was available. It consisted of a layer of vegetables, usually turnips, followed by a layer of meat and onions and spices, particularly salt, which were then covered by a layer of coarse meal dough. These layers were repeated until the kettle was about three-quarters full, and this was allowed to cook over the fire for four or five hours. Marguerite was generous with her portions, glowing with pride as she handed Pierre his plate. "This is made with rabbits that Jacques snared in the woods. They're delicious."

The savory smell of the dish assailed Pierre's nose, and he realized that he had not eaten since early morning.

Jacques went into the lean-to and returned with a crockery jug with a wooden plug in its narrow neck.

"You must taste some of this special brew, Pierre. Charles Leblanc, one of the long-term settlers, gave me this as a wedding present. I've been saving it for an occasion. Try some." He removed the stopper and handed the jug to Pierre, who brought it to his nose and sniffed. It smelled different from any brew that he knew. A woodsy, turpentine aroma, sharp but not acrid tickled his nostrils. The smell of molasses mingled with the spruce tree odor.

Pierre looked at Jacques. "What is it?"

Jacques smiled. "Try it. Tell me how you like it. Then I will tell you what it is."

Pierre brought the spout to his mouth and tipped the jug tentatively. A trickle of the liquid entered his mouth. The coolness pleased him, and the sweetish, spicy taste encouraged him to tip the jug higher. He understood from the bite of the liquid that it contained alcohol. He took another swig and handed the jug back to Jacques. "Very good. Now what is it?"

"It's a concoction they make here. The recipe comes from the Indians. They call it spruce beer."

"You will have to get the recipe. We must make up a supply. I like it."

"It's not as good as French wine, but I understand it's more healthy. Leblanc told me it's good for gout, and it's a protection against scurvy."

"That's the more reason we must make a batch of this marvelous drink."

Jacques took a long drink and then handed the jug to Françoise. She took a swallow, wrinkled her nose, and handed it to Marguerite.

Pierre looked at his plate, sniffed, and said, "It smells good. You've been busy, Jacques. You've built a lean-to; you've a supply of logs, almost enough to build a house; your garden is growing well. You've made good progress."

"Françoise has been a great help. She and Marguerite have worked hard. They're responsible for the garden, and they've even helped me peel the logs that I got from the uplands. You're right. We've done much."

Françoise moved closer to Pierre on the short piece of log that they used as a seat. "Now we must go to work on our land. We must prepare for winter. It's already the middle of August and we've done nothing." She did not say it with reproach, but as a matter of fact.

"I will be able to hire someone to help me with the heavy work. Captain Hector was most generous. He paid me more than I was worth. Actually, I did little for him. The trip was uneventful. The Bostonians were, for the most part, very cordial and pleasant. I really didn't earn what I was paid. Has all gone well here?"

Silence ensued. Then Marguerite spoke lowly. "I think there will be trouble here. Sieur de Belleisle has been insisting that the settlers who were here during the English tenure owe him many dues. Most of them feel he's being unfair. They acknowledge he's their seigneur and that their land is part of his seigneury, but they don't think they owe him past dues. There's much anger. Even Father Molin's become involved. He sides with Belleisle, as he would like to collect tithes for the church. The censitaires aren't accustomed to such highhanded tactics. The English weren't interested in colonization; there was more profit in the fish and fur trade, so they allowed the French to do as they pleased. Belleisle is trying to change all that, and he's making everyone angry. I'm afraid there will be trouble."

Pierre turned to Françoise. "Has he bothered you?"

"No, he hasn't bothered the new people. It's the back dues that he's trying to collect."

Jacques enjoined, "He wants his dues, but he isn't in a hurry to give the people their rights. He hasn't provided them with a mill, nor has he said anything about roads between the various farms."

"He must have some supporters," Pierre said between swallows of meat pie.

Françoise muttered, "Yes, he has. Lieutenant Richard, who's also a seigneur, is on his side. Father Molin has preached about giving to Caesar what is Caesar's and to God what is God's. Some of the Indians who are Christians seem to be on Belleisle's side."

"This sounds rather serious. I'm sure Grandfontaine didn't think Le Borgne would create such uproar. He thought he'd maintain order, not create disorder."

Françoise continued, "Nothing serious has happened yet, but some tempers are rather frayed, and if Belleisle pushes them too much, he will have a serious situation on his hands. These Acadians are an independent lot. Some have already said they'd leave and start an new settlement elsewhere."

"Where would they go?"

Jacques answered, "To the head of François Bay. It seems several areas have marshlands as fertile as and more extensive than here."

The four fell silent as they concentrated on their food. Several minutes passed. Finally Françoise said, "Pierre, you haven't told us about your adventure. What's Boston like?"

Pierre chewed on his food deliberately; the others waited in anticipation. "It's a great town. More people live there than in all Acadia, maybe even than all New France. The people are friendly and want to remain involved in this settlement. They're not happy to lose Acadia as a colony. The English governor, Sir Thomas Temple, was disappointed with the agreement that our kings made. He accepts it, but he still wants to trade with us. He's so interested that he made arrangements with me to be his agent here."

Silence descended upon the group. They stared at Pierre as if he committed treason. The expressions on their faces showed their disapproval.

Françoise spoke first. "Pierre, there's enough trouble here. I'm sure Belleisle won't approve. He will cause a great deal of trouble."

"Perhaps. If I'd know what was happening here, I might not have accepted the deal or signed a contract. But I have, and I intend to keep my word."

"What have you agreed to?" Jacques asked.

"I've agreed to buy and sell goods on behalf of William Harvey, an associate of Sir Thomas Temple, ex-governor of Acadia. I will supply him with produce, meat, lumber, and even furs, if I'm able to obtain any. In turn, he will provide manufactured goods—tools, utensils, cloth and clothing, sugar, molasses, and anything else we find difficult to obtain from France."

Marguerite gasped. "That will put you in direct conflict with Belleisle and the West India Company. You will have nothing but trouble. I'm sure they won't let you operate in peace. They will defend their monopoly even if it's not in the best interests of the settlers."

"You're probably right. But I will try it and see what happens. I plan to build a storehouse and start operating slowly and carefully. I won't advertise my business, and I will be honest and fair with everyone."

Françoise interjected, "But first you must build a house and get ready for winter. The winters are cold and difficult. The older people told us that last winter was an especially cold one. Many people suffered from the cold and a shortage of food. We must be prepared, Pierre."

"You're right, Françoise. I intend to start building immediately."

Jacques smiled at Pierre. "I will help you."

Pierre grinned back. "And I will help you, Jacques. We should be able to start building your house immediately. Your materials are almost ready. While we're building yours, I will hire someone to cut logs for mine. Once they're peeled and dried somewhat, we will build mine."

"That sounds like a good idea, Pierre." Marguerite beamed.

Françoise smiled, but it was tentative. She was not as enthusiastic about the plan as the others.

Pierre noticed her lack of enthusiasm. "Something seems to be troubling you, Françoise. Don't you think it's a good idea?"

"Oh, helping them is a marvelous idea. I'm worried about the business that you've gotten yourself into."

"My dear, I was hoping your experience in your father's inn would help me in my dealings."

Françoise shrugged her shoulders. "I was hoping to get away from such dealings."

Pierre placed his arm about her shoulders and drew her close to him.

Jacques lifted the jug of spruce beer to his mouth and before drinking exclaimed, "To our health and our future." He took a long draught, and then handed it to Pierre.

Within the week, Pierre and Françoise set up their homestead with the tent borrowed from the Bretons. They kept to their plan, each day paddling across the wide river in the birch bark canoe that Pierre purchased from one of the Indians who frequented the fort and Sieur Belleisle's house north of the fort.

Although Pierre had little experience with a canoe, he soon found it was an easy craft to handle—swift and stable, maneuverable and surprisingly sturdy. He was even astonished when he discovered that Françoise could handle it. Its lightness and speed made it an ideal craft for women and children; as a result, it was the favorite craft on the river. Every settler owned one and used it incessantly.

The next week was a busy one. They set up camp, and Pierre made arrangements to have several of the men who were not too busy and who were eager to earn money, which was in short supply in the colony, go to the uplands bordering the marshlands of his concession to cut a supply of fir logs that grew abundantly to the north. Once cut, the logs were floated down to the lowlands in the small stream that flowed through his property.

While his logs accumulated, he helped Jacques raise the walls of his tiny home. Since it was late in the season, they built it in the style of the English, with peeled, but unsquared logs placed parallel, one atop the other, rather than the sturdier and aesthetically pleasing manner of the French, the logs set vertically. Later, they would build more substantial homes in that manner. For now, it was imperative to build before the approaching winter.

At the moment, the colony was quiet, although there was still much talk of the highhandedness of Sieur de Le Borgne de Belleisle and resentment against Father Molin, even though the men were busy building a new chapel upstream from Pierre and Jacques.

They were happy it was being built away from the fort and Belleisle's house. The location of the new church was not the choice of Father Molin who finally gave in to the wishes of his congregation. The chapel was being built far up the River Dauphin at a point where it narrowed perceptibly on a bend of the north shore. Pierre thought the site was well chosen, far enough from the fort to be uninfluenced by the deputy governor, at a point safe from the guns of enemy warships, on a height of land that made it safe from the periodic inundation of extremely high tides, and its aspect was striking. Françoise did not like the location because she felt it was too inaccessible, too far upstream, requiring a long trip against the current.

The following Sunday, August 17, was a cool, overcast day. After attending Mass in the morning, Pierre and Françoise spent the day with Jacques and Marguerite. The afternoon was a pleasant one. The two couples took their canoes and explored upstream from their concessions. They were frequently surprised at the abundance of fertile marshland that was still available. The river meandered for several leagues until it narrowed, the marshes becoming thin strips along its banks. At some places the forests of spruce and fir came to the edge of the flowing waters. As the river narrowed, its current became swifter; forcing the canoes against it became arduous. They enjoyed the abundance of wildlife—ducks, geese, and other water birds abounded; fish were everywhere; and deer, moose, and an occasional bear were seen as they came down to the river to drink.

After a late picnic lunch on the shore of a small stream that emptied into the river, they floated downstream back to the inhabited area at the mouth of the Dauphin River.

Pierre was excited about the availability of land for more settlers. He could foresee an extensive community of farms and homes of all sorts. He expressed the hope that the king would send more colonists to bring it to fruition.

Later that evening, as Pierre and Françoise lay in their bed on the rush-filled mattress with their woolen blanket, Pierre sighed contentedly and drew Françoise into his arms. "Françoise, I can see the day when the whole area will be peopled by contented farmers. The land is fertile; the grass is lush—perfect for herds of cattle, sheep, and swine. It's such a peaceful valley. I hope the peace between the English and French will be a lasting one. Then we can make this land into one of milk and honey."

"I hope you're right. And I also hope there will be peace among the Frenchmen who are here. Belleisle seems to be a difficult man—stubborn and irascible. Don't you think so?"

Pierre's thoughts were not on the difficulties that seemed caused by Belleisle. He was thinking of his future plans, so he ignored her question. "This week we will start the storehouse. I'm eager to begin trading with the people, and, maybe, even with the Indians, although they seem to have disposed of their furs for this year with Belleisle."

Françoise drew away. "Pierre, we must have a house before you think of building a storehouse."

"I plan to build a storehouse that we can live in for the present. Then when my trading business is established, I will build a proper home, a beautiful house that you can be proud of."

She bristled. "That's not what you promised me. You said the first thing you would do would be to build a house—like Marguerite's."

Pierre tried to draw her back into his arms, but she pushed away. "Darling, of course, we will have a house, a grand house. But for a while we will do with a building that can be used in a dual role—as a house and a storehouse. I can't be a trader without a place to store my goods."

Her voice was cold and brittle. "Pierre, I don't like the idea of you becoming a trader. We came here to settle on the land, to become farmers…like the Bretons. Now you're changing everything. I don't like it."

"But, sweetheart, it's an opportunity to become prosperous. We can be both. While we're developing the land, we can trade with the farmers and Indians. It's an opportunity we shouldn't miss."

Françoise clenched her fists, and her voice became shrill. "But you will neglect the land. You will be too busy with the trade. No dikes will be built, no animals will be raised, and no buildings—barns and granaries—will be built. You will be away from your family most of the time. I can see it all. Already you left me for a month while you were in Boston and Pentagouet. It will be like that most of the time. Pierre, I can't live like that. I need you, here, with me, living together, sharing life…love…work…and play. That's why I married you."

The bitterness in her voice saddened Pierre. He tried to reassure her. "Françoise, it won't be like that. What I want to do is for your benefit as well as mine. I feel it's an opportunity that's been given me. We will be important in the community; we may become wealthy and prosperous. I must try to succeed at this. Don't you understand?"

"No," she shouted, "I don't understand. I think that our love is more important than becoming prosperous and wealthy. A family that loves God and works for each other and does God's will is more important than all the money in the world."

"That's true, Françoise, but maybe it's God's will that we prosper and become wealthy. Maybe it's God's will that I become a trader as well as a farmer."

She was silent. Then her face crumpled, and tears streamed down her cheeks. "Oh, I'm so confused," she sobbed. "I'm not accustomed to this life. A tent is not my idea of a home. Cooking on an outdoor fire is not my idea of a kitchen. And when I'm alone, I'm frightened the whole time until you are with me. The wilderness and the loneliness horrify me. I fear the wild animals—the wolves, the bears, even the skunks."

Her outburst stunned him, and he reached to embrace her. She did not resist, and he wiped the tears from her cheeks with the back of his hand.

Then he pushed her long hair from her face and gently caressed her cheek. She placed her head on his chest as he stroked her hair and head lovingly. "I'm sorry, darling. I was inconsiderate. I didn't understand how you felt."

In the next weeks, he was very busy. He and Jacques worked long hours on their homes. Jacques's was built first as he possessed a good supply of logs. Slowly the building rose from the stone foundation that they situated on a small knoll far enough back from the river's edge to avoid inundation from the tidal bore. As the building rose, Marguerite became more excited about moving in. Françoise shared her joy although she was disappointed at the structure that Pierre was building. Pierre went ahead with the building of a storehouse that for the present would be their home.

One evening, as they shared the evening meal at Jacques's homestead, Marguerite turned to the three and announced quietly, "I've a small secret I'd like to share with you."

Jacques walked to her, and grinning foolishly, put his arms around her. He drew her close and kissed her fervently on the cheek.

"Jacques and I are going to become parents. I'm sure I'm pregnant."

Françoise stared, speechless. Then she rose and rushed to embrace Marguerite. "I'm happy for you and Jacques. This is marvelous news. Congratulations!"

Pierre noted wistfulness in her voice. He knew how eager she was to become pregnant. Each time they made love, she mentioned her desire for a child. He admitted he was excited about becoming a father, and he envied Jacques who stood proud and pleased beside his wife. Pierre rose from his seat beside the fire, extended his hand, and warmly shook Jacques's large, callused hand. "I'm pleased to congratulate you, Jacques. I must admit I was hoping to beat you, but I guess you're the champion lover."

Jacques grinned more. Then he replied, "I must give my wife all the credit. She made me a champion lover." He looked at her with shining eyes.

Marguerite lowered her eyes; a rosy tinge came to her cheeks. "That's not true. I only did my duty."

The days of summer turned into fall, and life became a routine of work. When he and Jacques could not work on their homes, they went hunting or fishing to get a store of meat for the coming winter. Jacques acquired a musket and became an excellent huntsman. Slowly their store of venison, moose meat, bear meat, and all sorts of birds grew. The women kept busy salting, pickling, and smoking game. Pierre, on the other hand, was the fisherman. Regularly they speared and netted fish that could not find their way back to the mainstream after the tide carried them past their weir. They constructed a sapling stage and dried the split carcasses in the fall sunshine. These they packed into hogsheads for future use.

Pierre was so busy it was several weeks before he noticed the change in Françoise. She was quiet and subdued, going about her work mechanically. She seldom spoke and only answered when spoken to. She smiled wanly, not caring about what was going on about her. Marguerite was the one who pointed it out to him. One day she asked Pierre if Françoise might not be pregnant; she was acting peculiarly.

"I don't think so. If she is, she hasn't said a word to me." He thought for a moment and said, "No, she's not pregnant. She just had her sickness. Maybe that's why she's not herself."

"I don't think so, Pierre. I've noticed something's wrong for a while now."

"I don't know what it is; she hasn't said anything to me. And it appears she hasn't said anything to you. I will ask her."

That evening, as they lay in bed, Pierre whispered in her ear, "I love you, my sweet Françoise."

She clung to him and kissed him frantically.

"What's the matter, my darling," he murmured as she embraced him more vigorously.

"I'm not a good wife!" she sobbed. "Marguerite's such a good wife. She's carrying Jacques's child. She's so capable. She knows how to do everything well. She can cook anything—breads, meats, pies…everything. She knows how to spin and weave and make clothes of all sorts. Her garden's a masterpiece. She keeps Jacques happy."

Pierre was amazed. Françoise was jealous of Marguerite. It never occurred to him that Françoise would compare herself to Marguerite. As he though of it, he could see how Françoise might feel inferior. Marguerite was a capable person. Her background was rural; she grew up on the same seigneury in Normandy as Jacques. Her experience was agricultural; thus the work that she now did was the kind that she knew, unlike Françoise who grew up in Le Havre in a sailor's tavern. She was not used to the farmer's life. Everything in Acadia was a new experience for her. No wonder she felt inferior to Marguerite.

"My darling," he soothed, "you shouldn't compare yourself to Marguerite. She spent all her life on a farm. She's familiar with the works that needs to be done. You came from the city, my dear, and you will need time to learn the crafts of the country. You're doing very well."

Her sobs turned to sniffle, but her body remained stiff and rigid. "Marguerite is so good at everything. She can prepare any animal for the pot or storehouse. She knows what to do with vegetables so they will keep for the winter. She knows how to prepare hides to make clothing and footwear. She knows everything." And she began to sob convulsively again.

Pierre patted her shoulder and held her tight. "Be patient, my dear. You will become as good as her. I didn't notice she was better than you. You've worked hard, maybe too hard. Maybe you're tired. We've been working very hard these past weeks. Perhaps we should slow down a bit."

She blubbered, "You see. That's what I mean. Marguerite's pregnant, and she's not tired. She does more that I do, and still she's strong at the end of the day, while I'm tired."

"My darling, you can't compare yourself to someone else. You're you. Be happy with that." He drew her close and kissed her passionately. She responded.

Chapter Eleven — The Indians

Fall arrived in a parade of colors. The sedges and the rushes along the banks of the river and streams turned to muted gold, while the hay fields retained their rich, verdant color. The uplands and hills sparkled with bright reds, yellows, browns, and oranges as the leaves of the assorted trees marched across the landscape. The weather remained pleasantly warm, allowing the farmers and the new colonists to continue their preparations for the snows that all predicted would come.

Pierre and Françoise moved into the solid structure that was a combined home and storehouse. It was divided into two sections. The first was the storeroom separated from the second by a solid log wall. Pierre felt it would be easier to heat the smaller of the two rooms, and, as well, most things that needed storage would keep better in an unheated environment.

Their home was small—a single room with a small fireplace of stones and mortar built by one of the craftsmen. It heated the room and was used for cooking. The furniture was meager—a small table, two stools, and a bunk along the inner wall that separated the storeroom from the living quarters. Window openings in the three outer walls were shuttered, as glass was in short supply. During the day they were opened to allow in light and fresh air. Since they were high up in the walls, it would be difficult to enter through them if the building was attacked; as well, they could be used as ports through which defenders could fire muskets and other weapons. It was sturdily and practically built, but it lacked the homeliness of Jacques and Marguerite's house.

When the Bretons moved into their new home, a grand feast was held. Most of the inhabitants of the colony were invited, and Jacques roasted a whole deer to feed the hungry visitors. Lieutenant Auguste Richard supplied the wine while Sieur Belleisle provided loaves of bread; others shared their produce—milk, butter, cheese, and vegetables from their bountiful gardens. The feast was a great success: Father Molin blessed the new house and Marguerite, as it was now apparent she was pregnant. Due to her height and slender build, her parturient condition was not too obvious, and the additional pounds relieved her bony, angular structure that gravidity brought her.

The mid-October sun was warm. After Sunday Mass most of the community rendezvoused at Jacques's homestead to properly initiate his home. The day before, Pierre and Françoise helped Jacques and Marguerite prepare for the invasion. The building was a bit larger than the structure Pierre built; it was constructed solely as a house with two fireplaces, one at each end of the building. A single door to the right of the fireplace opened into the combined kitchen-living room that was dominated by a large, sturdy table Jacques built. It stood before the fireplace, serving for eating as well as the preparation of food. Three sturdy, wooden chairs with woven seats were placed around it—one at each end and the other on the side away from the fireplace, but facing it. Two windows high up in the walls on either side of the room covered with sheepskin parchment and shutters with leather hinges at the top that could be opened to allow in light. A wall of saplings separated the sleeping quarters from the front room, while along the back wall was another smaller fireplace of stone and clay with a chimney of small logs plastered thickly with yellow clay reinforced with straw. It lacked the substance of the main fireplace, for it was to be used as an auxiliary when the temperature became very cold.

Françoise envied Marguerite's home, although she seldom mentioned her desire to have one like it to anyone.

The day went well; Marguerite was concerned that some difficulty might occur: Sieur Le Borgne, who preferred to be called Sieur de Belleisle, was still creating dissent within the community. Many of the inhabitants were still angry with him for his insistence on the rents and dues that he wanted to collect retroactively. Although some complied, the majority refused. As a result, he was harassing them and even threatening to dispossess them. To this time, he did nothing but rant and rave and stir up the people, but he managed to split the community into supporters and adversaries.

During the festivities, one of the soldiers from the fort brought news that a band of Indians arrived and were looking for Sieur de Belleisle. In a flourish, he left, and the mood of the feast became more relaxed and jovial.

Pierre remarked to Jacques, "It's too bad he has such an effect on the people."

"You're right. It worries me. If he doesn't change his attitude, there will be trouble."

"Let's not make more of him than he is. I'm sure Grandfontaine will do something before we have serious trouble."

"He did nothing when he was here in September. A delegation went to see him, but he dismissed their complaints as unwarranted."

"That's true, Jacques, but I fear he had too many things on his mind at the time. He was preoccupied with establishing his authority over the territory. I'm sure he will listen if this trouble comes to a head."

"Pierre, what do you think of all this?"

"I'm trying to be realistic. No doubt Belleisle has a legitimate claim to this seigneury, and as such, he has rights. He has rents and dues coming to him. But, his manner and attitude are highhanded. Trying to collect long past due rents isn't making him popular with the older settlers. I think he should forget the past and start afresh. He should befriend these people, not alienate them. His way is foolish."

"It's too bad Grandfontaine has orders to make his headquarters at Pentagouet. The people are here. This is where we need the authority of a fair and just man."

"Right, Jacques, but it appears Louis's more concerned with establishing a boundary between the English and his lands than in the welfare of a couple hundred peasants."

"What we need here, Pierre, is a leader, someone to whom the governor will listen. Someone who can get an audience with the governor."

Pierre felt uncomfortable. This was not the first time Jacques implied that he should become the spokesman for the community. He seemed to think Pierre would have a special influence since he accompanied Grandfontaine to Boston. Pierre tried to explain that the trip was so uneventful that he doubted he made any impression on the governor.

Two days later it happened.

Pierre and Jacques were putting the finishing touches on Pierre's building when they heard a halloo from the landing that Pierre built on the stream that flowed into the Dauphin River. A figure was pulling a small birch bark canoe onto the beach. At first Pierre could not recognize who it was; then he saw that it was Albert Doucet's ten-year-old son. Young Albert seemed very agitated and excited. A steady stream of words flowed from him as he approached them on the path.

Pierre hollered, "Whoa, slow down, young fellow. What's the matter?"

The sturdy boy gasped and almost choked on his words in his hurry to convey his message. "There's trouble at the fort. A man's been killed. Everyone's upset. You must come quickly."

Jacques grasped the boy by the shoulders. "Let's start over. What's happened? Who's been killed? Slow down. How did it happen?"

"My father sent me to get you. There's a commotion at the fort. An Indian was killed. There was a fight. Monsieur Le Borgne's slave…a black man…Rufus, has been injured and one of the braves that arrived two days ago is dead. It seems Rufus killed him. I don't know how the quarrel started, but now the Indians are very angry, and Monsieur Le Borgne fears trouble. So come quickly and bring your weapons."

"When did all this happen?" Pierre tried to keep his voice calm so the boy would settle down. He was obviously very frightened.

"Not long ago. I was there. I saw it happen, but I don't know why it happened."

"What did you see?"

The boy stopped and drew in a deep breath. "I was getting a bucket of water from the well when I heard an angry shout. It came from the path to Monsieur Belleisle's house."

"Who was it?" interjected Pierre. He was trying to restrain the boy's emotions.

"It was an Indian in war paint and waving a club. I think it was a tomahawk. He was shouting and waving it about. I think he was drunk because he seemed to stagger and wobble about. He swung at the black man who grabbed his weapon and jerked it from his hand. Then he flung it at the Indian. It hit him on the head, and he fell to the ground. By that time people rushed up to them, including other Indians. I ran too."

"Was that all that happened?"

"Yes…but the Indian was covered with blood. The tomahawk struck him on the side of the head…it caved in. He was dead. The Indians grabbed the black man and were going to kill him…but Father Molin was able to rescue him. Papa told me to get everyone to the fort. He fears more trouble because of this."

"All right, Albert. You go and tell the others. Jacques and I will go to the fort to see if we can help."

They helped the boy launch his canoe, and they followed in theirs, paddling down stream to the main channel. At the fort, they were surprised at the size of the crowd that milled about noisily. Most of the settlers already gathered. Twenty or so Indian braves and as many women and children formed a solid group to one side of the crowd. Belleisle, Father Molin, and a frightened, subdued black man held firmly by two men in motley soldier's livery faced them. Pierre recognized the two soldiers as Belleisle's men.

From the angry tone of the voices, Pierre could see that the problem was not resolved. Although his command of the Indian language was still limited, he could understand they wanted retribution for the life of one of their warriors. The Indian leader stood firmly in front of Belleisle and shook his fist angrily. In his right hand he held a shiny knife, and with his left, he pointed at the frightened black man.

"What's happening?" Pierre asked one of the men who stood at the edge of the crowd.

"The black man killed an Indian, and the Indians want him punished. They want Belleisle to turn him over to them so they can punish him properly."

"What does that mean?" inquired Jacques.

"No doubt the poor devil will be tortured for hours before being put to death."

"What will happen if Belleisle doesn't give him to the Indians?"

"I don't know. It would be an affront to the Indians. They might attack the whole settlement and kill many of us. They're few at the moment, but they are many who can gather and destroy us."

"What do you think should be done?"

"Why, give the slave to the Indians. Belleisle can get another slave."

The man's callousness unnerved Pierre. "Do you think that will help? I'm afraid the Indians would take that as a sign of weakness. Then we'd never be safe from them. No, I think we must try the man and punish him."

The other smiled. "You're new here. You don't know how an Indian thinks. He wants an eye for an eye, a tooth for a tooth. The black man is dead. If we try him, he must die. They will not be satisfied with less. If we give him to them, he will die also, and the manner won't be a pleasant one. I can see no way to save the poor fellow."

"What if we gave them many presents? Wouldn't that appease their anger?"

"I fear not. These are Micmacs. They're very cruel to their enemies. If he wasn't a slave, they might adopt him into their tribe in place of the dead warrior, but since he's a slave, he must die."

While this exchange was going on, the heated discussion between the Indians, Belleisle and Father Molin continued with little progress. The priest seemed to be acting as a mediator. The main spokesman for the Indians calmed, while his followers became more agitated. The Indian was tall and well built. His black, shiny hair fell in long braids that fell over his chest; each was interwoven with a moose hide thong, and several feathers of various birds were attached to the thongs. Two hawk feathers dangled at the end of each plait. His loincloth was a porcupine quill-decorated piece of deer hide held at the waist with a wide silk sash. On his feet he wore low-vamped moccasins. He stood grim and repeatedly pointed at the terrified black man whose eyes rolled in his head. It was obvious the black man did not understand what was going on, but he knew his life was at stake.

Finally, Belleisle shook his head in the affirmative, and Pierre knew that a decision was made. The two men holding the black man were directed by Belleisle to take the prisoner toward a small clump of trees east of the fort. The crowd, including the band of Indians, followed as the group made its way behind the leaders. Pierre did not understand what was happening; he wondered as he followed the clamorous crowd. Some were laughing and jeering, while others were angry and critical.

Pierre turned to Jacques. "What do you make of it?"

"I'm not sure, but I think they're going to punish the black man. They seem to have arrived at a compromise with the Indians. I don't think they will turn him over to the Indians. It seems they will administer the punishment."

Pierre asked one of the men who was moving beside him, "What's happening? Where are we going?"

The man grinned. "The hanging tree."

"Do you mean they're going to hang the poor fellow?"

"Yes, it's him or us. Hanging him will satisfy the savages. So he must go."

"But he hasn't had a trial. I understand he killed the Indian accidentally. Wasn't he attacked first? He was defending himself. He didn't mean to kill the Indian."

"That may be true, but the Indians don't see it that way. They've lost a valued warrior. A slave killed him. So the slave must die. There's no other way."

Pierre was appalled.

Quickly, the milling group arrived at a tall red maple that dominated a small clump of trees. It was the tallest tree in the grove that was a mixture of spruce and pine.

Belleisle's two soldier-retainers threw the black man to the ground.

The terrified man struggled and squirmed to free himself. One man pressed the black man's head between his knees and forced his arms behind his back; the other tied his wrists tightly together with a rawhide thong.

A sturdy hemp rope was procured; Pierre did not know where it came from. One end was flung over a hefty limb of the red-barked tree; eager hands grabbed the standing part of the rope.

Pierre stepped into the open space left by the now subdued crowd. He faced Belleisle. “Sir, this isn't just. This poor man hasn't had a fair trial. He's been sentenced without anyone hearing his side of the incident.”

Belleisle shook his head wearily. “Monsieur Marin, we have no choice. If we don't mete out the punishment, the Indians will. And his fate won't be a pleasant one. At least here, our punishment will be quick, and he will have the benefit of a priest to help him on his eternal journey. My dear Monsieur Marin, if we don't do this, the whole colony will suffer. These Micmacs are not an easy people; they have long memories when they think they've been wronged. It's better to sacrifice one black slave than to have everyone live in fear. What must be done, must be done.” It sounded final.

Pierre continued, “But we've done nothing to save this poor creature. We're many here. We could easily protect him from these Indians.”

“You don't understand. True, they're few now, but they are many in the neighboring countryside. These would let their brethren know of this incident, and we would be their enemies. We'd never be safe. Now we have their friendship, and the only way to keep it, is to hang this man.”

The priest enjoined, “Pierre, it's for the best. It's God's will. This slave will be helping to bring God's word to these poor ignorant savages. This man will get his reward this day in heaven. I will hear his confession and absolve him of his sins. He will be saved, and his eternity will be assured.”

Pierre could see that nothing he could say would save the black man's life. So he stepped back into the crowd. Jacques patted his shoulder.

“Well done, Pierre. At least you tried.”

They raised the trembling black man to his feet and tied a piece of linen cloth over his eyes. Silently the men drew him erect. The priest stepped to his side and spoke to him quietly in a voice so low that the bystanders only a few feet away could not hear. They saw the man's lips quiver as the priest blessed him.

A hush descended over the crowd as a slip-knotted noose was placed over his head and tightened about his neck. Four men and two youths holding the standing part of the rope prepared to pull the doomed man off his feet. One of the Indians joined them, and they stared toward the Indian leader who held his right hand in the air, and solemnly and dramatically became statuesque. The silence was pregnant.

He dropped his arm. The men at the end of the rope ran away from the tree, quickly taking up the slack. The moving rope jerked the man's body sharply. His head snapped back. His feet lifted from the ground. His legs jerked convulsively. His body struggled momentarily. No sound escaped his lips. The suddenness of the action cut his breath, and no sound came from his strangled lungs. His face turned blue. His mouth popped open exposing his gleaming teeth and protruding tongue. His movements slackened. His rigid body relaxed. His head dropped forward. Slowly his body went limp. It hung swaying slowly in the slight breeze of the autumn day.

Many signed themselves with the Sign of the Cross, bowed their heads, and turned away.

Later that evening, Pierre described the events of the afternoon. Françoise cried softly as he told her of the fate of the black man.

"Pierre, was there no way to save the poor fellow?"

"I tried to persuade Belleisle and Father Molin to give him a trial, but they seemed to think the Indians wouldn't understand that. To them, he was guilty of killing one of their warriors even though he started the quarrel."

As Françoise wiped the tears from her eyes, she said, "That could happen to anyone. What would happen if a Frenchman killed a brave? Would he be so easily sacrificed?"

"I don't know, Françoise. But you're right. I think a better defense would have been made. That poor slave was expendable; his death was a simple solution to the problem. I think Belleisle and Father Molin could have done more. To me, it seems that Belleisle wanted to keep the Indians' favor at all cost, and Father Molin was more interested in the poor man's immortal soul."

"Oh, Pierre, this country's mean! I don't think I can stand it. Each day I miss Le Havre and city life. The wildness and savagery frighten me. I'm nervous. We're too far from the fort and the other colonists—they're closer together and can help each other in a crisis. Pierre, we should move closer to the fort."

"Françoise, we're safer here. The Indians, the pirates, the privateers will attack the fort before our simple abode. The Indians are our friends; the settlers are near enough to call for help, and our home is strong enough to defend, if need be. No, Françoise, we're safer here."

Françoise's shoulders sagged. She saw that no matter how much she argued Pierre's mind was made up; he intended to stay at this location. It was far enough from the fort that Belleisle could not keep an eye on his activities—particularly his trading activities.

In the following week, the settlement returned to routine. The incident of the Indian and the black man was forgotten by most of the settlers. The mild weather continued. October turned to November, and still the snow did not come.

Pierre accumulated goods from the farmers—their surplus grain, vegetables, dried meat and fish, and salted fish as well. He made no overtures to the Indians for furs, as he felt they would be of poor quality. The Indians had not yet departed for their winter camps in the forests due to the mild weather. Bands came and went, but most were still camped around the fort and Belleisle's house.

On Wednesday, the second week in November, Pierre was surprised to see a canoe with an Indian man and woman approaching his small landing. As they came toward the shore, he walked slowly down the path to the stream to meet them. The dark-skinned man skillfully beached his light craft. The young woman in the bow leaped nimbly to the shore and drew the craft on land. The man in the stern stepped gracefully from the canoe and raised his hand in greeting.

Pierre's brow lifted in surprise. It was the same Indian who insisted on the punishment of the black man. Pierre was puzzled. What did this man want with him?

The Indian raised his right hand and said in fractured French, "Friend."

Slowly Pierre raised his hand in similar fashion and repeated, "Friend."

"Me, Miskoo, great warrior."

Pierre reciprocated, "Me, Pierre. Friend of Miskoo."

At this, the Indian grinned widely, showing a mouth with many missing teeth. "Me come to trade."

For a moment Pierre was speechless. How did the Indian find out he was a trader? Pierre was careful to keep his activities unobtrusive. He hoped to avoid trouble with Belleisle whom he was sure would not approve of his activities. All that he accumulated was under the pretext of using it for himself. Only Jacques and Marguerite were aware of his plans. He recovered quickly. "You have furs?"

"Me have furs. You have firewater?"

It was only when the Indian mentioned his desire for spirits that Pierre noticed that both were drinking. The sweet-sour smell assailed his nostrils. That smell, mixed with the smoke smell of their skin clothes and the stale smell of perspiration and other unrecognizable odors, hid the alcohol scent from him. They were not inebriated, but they were influenced by the quantity they consumed.

"No firewater, Miskoo. Much meat, fish, kettles, knives, axes, and other things."

"Miskoo and Neremoosin," he pointed to the woman, "want firewater."

Pierre looked at the woman. She was young, he could tell. But he was not sure how old she would be. Her hair was neatly plaited into two long braids that hung down her back. She wore a simple, undecorated light doeskin gown that came below her knees. Around her waist, it was held by a thin rawhide thong, which emphasized her slim figure and accentuated her breasts. The hem of the skirt was fringed, and she wore high-vamped moccasins of golden moosehide. She was shorter than Françoise and slighter in build. Pierre thought her dark almond-shaped eyes gave her an intriguing appearance.

Pierre looked to the tall, well-built brave and repeated, “I don't have firewater. You don't need firewater.

Françoise heard voices and appeared at the door of the dwelling. She stood framed in the opening as the bright November sunlight shone upon her. The cascades of her dark brown hair glimmered as it fell around her shoulders. Even from that distance Pierre thought she looked pretty. He could see an anxious look on her face, almost fear.

The Indian stared unabashed at her. He turned to Pierre. “Nice woman. Strong. Good for much work.”

“Yes, good woman. My wife. Françoise.”

The brave repeated the name with difficulty. Several moments passed as the two men studied each other. Then the Indian pointed to a small bundle in the canoe. “Good furs. Three beavers. Many squirrels.”

“No firewater. No trade.”

A scowl crossed the man's brow. Then, as quickly, it left. “Woman want firewater. Miskoo no want.”

Pierre did not answer. He pondered the situation. He did not want to antagonize the Indian. Since he owned no rum or brandy, he hoped he could persuade the Indian to trade for other items. This opportunity to establish a trading relationship with the Micmacs through this chief—for that's what he seemed to be—interested Pierre. He showed great influence when the incident with the black man occurred. If Pierre could win his respect and friendship, it might help him to establish himself as a trader. Already, he knew that Pierre maintained items to trade. “Show me your furs, Miskoo. Maybe we can trade.”

The Indian drew himself up rigidly and exclaimed firmly, “No firewater, no trade!”

“No firewater, Miskoo, but many other things. No trade, Miskoo.” Pierre turned away and started up the path toward Françoise. He hoped the man would not be offended, but he could see no reason to harangue further. The man and woman wanted liquor that he did not have.

“Stop!” The authority in the brave's voice stopped Pierre. He turned back to face the Indian. “We trade.”

“I've no firewater, and you want nothing I have.”

The dark eyes turned toward Françoise, and a gleam appeared in them. He waved his right hand toward her. “You have woman; me have woman. We trade.”

Pierre heard of the easy manner in which Indians traded their women. He heard it was not unusual for an important brave to have several wives that he traded regularly with other braves or used as chattels to obtain whatever he needed from other men, white or red. But he never heard of a trade of women between a white man and an Indian. The idea surprised him. He knew the situation was becoming critical. He could not trade for firewater as he did not have any, but he did have a woman, and, he supposed, to the Indian, she was a proper item of trade. He did not want to offend his visitor, but he certainly did not want to trade Françoise for the Indian woman. "My woman is not for trade, Miskoo. I need her. She's strong and works hard. She keeps me warm at night." He added the last in hope he could convince Miskoo of her value to him, but he soon grasped that he made a mistake. Instead of extolling her, he should be depreciating her. He was making her more desirable.

"My woman do that too. She hunt. She fish. She cook. She better woman."

"If she's so good, why do you want to trade her?"

"Miskoo never have woman with white skin. Miskoo like try woman with white skin."

Pierre needed to convince this man that his wife was not for trade; he must persuade Miskoo that his woman was too good to trade for Françoise.

At that moment, Françoise shouted, "Pierre, what do those Indians want?"

"They've come to trade. They're looking for liquor. They think I've rum and brandy, and they want some."

"Tell them to leave." The hysteria in her voice was noticeable, and he was sure the Indians noted it too. The brave moved up the path toward Françoise. She became rigid; her eyes opened wide.

Although the Indian's command of the French language was limited, he seemed to understand all that was said. Pierre could see that fear and apprehension possessed Françoise; perhaps she would act rashly. He wanted to soothe and calm her, but he did not want his visitors to see her panic. "They will be leaving soon, Françoise. Stay. I will handle this." She relaxed, and it pleased him. He turned to the Indian. "Miskoo, my woman isn't for trade. I've other things to trade—pots, kettles, knives, axes… many things. If you want to trade with Pierre, then I will trade. But I won't trade my woman."

Disappointment showed in the Indian's face. He called to the Indian woman who came meekly to his side. He turned her to face Pierre. He took left arm and squeezed it firmly. "See, strong. Good for much work." Then he lifted her doeskin skirt to her loins exposing her pubes. "Good for man." Then he dropped it.

Again Françoise shouted, "What does that savage want, Pierre? Why is he showing you his woman?"

"He wants to trade his woman for you."

Françoise's hazel eyes opened wide; her mouth opened slightly; her body became rigid again. Her voice trembled. "Pierre, send them away!"

Pierre forced himself to remain calm. "Miskoo, I don't want your woman. I need mine. You need yours. My woman wouldn't be good in your camp. Yours wouldn't be good in my house. You keep your woman, and I will keep mine." Pierre hoped his firmness would dissuade the persistent chief.

Miskoo pushed the woman roughly toward the beached canoe and growled a command in his language. She stumbled, caught her balance, and deftly stepped into the canoe. She retrieved the small bundle that lay amidships. The Indian scowled, but said, “We trade for other things. What do you have to trade?”

“Come, I will show you.” Pierre waved his hand toward the house.

Françoise muffled a scream and turned to the dark interior of the building.

“Your woman makes much noise. Needs training, like a dog.”

Pierre smiled. He could not understand the Indian mind. They were so different from the French or English. He murmured to himself, “I must try to understand them if I'm to deal with them.”

Chapter Twelve — Terror

The sun was still high in the sky when Miskoo and his woman left Pierre's place. Pierre felt good about the visit: he established a friendly trading contact with the Micmacs; he and Miskoo developed a positive relationship between them. Pierre liked the young brave. He probably was a few years older than Pierre's twenty years, but he seemed much older. Already he was an honored and respected warrior of his band with several victories to his credit, both personal and tribal, for several enemy scalps adorned his vestments, particularly his medicine bag. These he showed Pierre with pride, as a badge of honor.

His young wife, he treated with indifference and disrespect, almost as a slave. She did all his errands and attended to his every need solicitously. On a number of occasions when she was slow to respond, he did not hesitate to cuff her soundly across the head or back, and she scurried to obey.

Françoise remained inside the house, but she observed the proceedings through one of the many chinks in the log wall. Later, she accosted Pierre, "That Indian's a savage. He treats that poor girl like a slave, a piece of property."

"Françoise, to him, that's what she is. To obtain her, he gave much to her family. Since he paid for her, he can do as he pleases with her. She belongs to him, body and soul. As well, he told me he has another woman that belongs to him. He was willing to exchange her for you." Pierre laughed at his own joke.

Her fury surprised him. "You think that savage's all right. Maybe you like one of those Indian woman," she shouted.

Pierre stared at her in disbelief. He had not noticed how upset she was. He tried to repair the damage he did. "My darling, I was only joking. You must learn to understand these people. They're all about us, and they outnumber us. We must, if we're to establish ourselves here, be on good terms with them."

Françoise would not listen; she heard not a word that he said. She shouted louder, her voice rising to a shriek, "Those savages will kill us. They will destroy us. They will attack us at night. I saw those horrible scalps he showed you. He will do the same to us."

He tried to reason with her. "Those are enemy scalps. We're friends. As long as they remain friendly with us, they won't do that to us."

"How do you know that?" she stormed. "Today we're their friends, but, who knows, tomorrow we may be their enemies. If they get drunk, they may change their minds. Remember the black man. He did nothing to that Indian who attacked him, yet they hung him. Maybe they will do the same to us."

As she spoke, she waved her arms and paced back and forth in the small room. Pierre rose from his seat by the small table and approached her, speaking calmly and soothingly. "Françoise, something like that could happen, but there's no reason to think it will. You're creating a situation that may never happen. Yes, their customs are different from ours, but they're still men and women—with the same feelings: love, hate, anger, and greed. If we treat them honestly, they will treat us the same way." He paused. "You must think of them as fellow human beings, not savage animals."

She almost growled. "How can I do that? They behave like animals! Did you see how he treated that poor woman? Like a slave; he beats her for no reason. That's animal-like and savage."

"Françoise, that's their way. Some Frenchmen treat their women in the same way. We must show them that's not the Christian way. We must teach them to love and respect God."

She looked at him with hard eyes. "That's the priests' and missionaries' job. Until they're civilized, I don't want anything to do with them." Her voice was high-pitched and rasping.

Pierre shook his head. "But, Françoise, that's impossible. If I trade with them, they will be around." He spoke slowly, like a parent to a small child. "I know it's the first time you've been close to them; you will find out they're not to be feared."

Pierre saw that she was on the verge of hysteria—tears were not far away.

Her voice cracked, and she broke into wild laughter. "I didn't come to this country to make friends with the Indians. They can stay in the woods where they belong. I don't want them around me." She sobbed and wrung her hands. "They're not my friends, and they will never be. That Indian's a dirty man. He lifted his wife's dress to show you her body. He's a beast!" she shouted.

He never before saw her so distraught and irrational. For several moments he stared at her, nonplused. He tried to approach her, but she retreated. She looked wildly about, sobbing and laughing at the same time. She moved to the open door and appeared about to scurry away. Pierre was worried. What was he to do? Had she lost her mind? She seemed to have lost control. He called softly, "Françoise, please sit down. Listen to me."

She darted toward the door; she sidled through it and scurried to the outer door of the storeroom. Pierre rushed after her; he caught her as she opened the exterior door. She whirled on him, her eyes wide— her hands opened into claws— and she flailed at his face. The suddenness and fury of her attack caught him unprepared. Her fingernails raked his left cheek. He felt a burning sensation as the skin was stripped in furrows. Instinctively he grabbed her wrists. She struggled and writhed vigorously; then she started kicking. He shook her like a dog with a small animal in its mouth, but she continued to wrestle, her lips curled back in a snarl. Her ferocity frightened him.

She freed her right hand and stabbed at his eyes with her fingers; he ducked and whirled her around, wrapping his arms around her torso. He caught her free hand and twisted her to face him. Then he brought his right hand up sharply. His open palm struck her left cheek with a resounding smack. The imprint of his fingers left four white bars on her cheek as the blood was driven from the rosy surface. Her eyes filled with shock and bewilderment; she crumpled against his chest, sobbing noisily.

The next two days were difficult for Pierre. Françoise moved about, doing her work, silently, morosely. After Pierre struck, he was mortified; his guilt made him solicitous and sycophant; he anticipated her every whim and showered her with love and affection—but nothing lifted her depression. Her withdrawal made him distraught and worried.

Finally, he hoped the situation would return to normal if he ignored it. He went about his work with a vigor that belied his feelings for them. The activity did keep his mind off his problem with Françoise. Several times he thought he would discuss his problem with Jacques and Marguerite; he even considered talking to Father Molin, but he decided the problem was not that serious; Françoise would return to her usual cheerful self, and later they would laugh at the incident.

That evening, as they lay abed, he put his arms around her and whispered in her ear, "My darling, I love you."

Françoise did not respond, but lay silent and rigid.

"My dear, I'm sorry I struck you, but it seemed the only way to bring you back to reality. You were losing control. And I knew of no other way. I must confess I was a bit annoyed as well; I lost my temper. I promise it won't happen again, but you must promise that you will try to be more patient with me."

She turned away; she still said nothing.

"Françoise, we can't go on this way. It isn't right. And the longer you remain angry, the more difficult it will be to reconcile."

She stirred and twisted to face him. "I want to go home." A wistful sadness filled her voice.

"But, Françoise, this is our home. We made that decision months ago…you agreed to it. We can't go back to France. We have no future there. All our opportunities are here." He was happy she broken her silence; at least they would be able to talk about their situation.

She was dry and emotionless. "Pierre, I can't stay in this country. I'm not suited for the life of a pioneer. I'm not strong enough to live this kind of life. The work's too hard, the conditions too rigorous, the country too wild. I won't survive."

"My darling, you've been superb. You've been everything a man could want in a wife. You're strong and healthy; you're smart and willing; you're loving and satisfying. My darling, you're too hard on yourself."

As she continued, Pierre noted that feeling was returning to her voice. "But Marguerite seems to enjoy life here. She's so capable and comfortable with what she's doing while I'm miserable. Everything is difficult and cumbersome. Even the most simple task."

Again, Pierre was annoyed that she compared herself to Jacques's wife. It was true that Marguerite was radiant and effervescent. Each day, as her stomach expanded with the growing child within her, she became more buoyant and happy. Her joy seemed to sadden Françoise more. He hoped that Françoise would share Marguerite's happiness, but it seemed she was jealous of her friend's joy. "Dear Françoise, you mustn't compare yourself to Marguerite. You're another person. You've your own qualities, and they're different from hers. For one thing, I love you the way you are. You mustn't change into someone else. You must remain you."

She whispered, "Pierre." She had not used his name for the past two days. "That's why we must move from here. I can't live in isolation; I must have people around me. If I'm to here, we must move nearer to the fort. I need people nearby. Here, our nearest neighbor is more than a league away. I'm too lonely without people around."

Annoyance flitted through his mind. Here it was again: her desire to move nearer the fort. Could she not understand it was impossible? For one thing, he no longer possessed the resources to build another house, and it was too late in the season for that; second, he would be too close to the watchful eye of Alexandre Le Borgne de Belleisle? He would not be able to carry on his business as easily as he could here. So he argued, "But, my darling, you know that's impossible this year. I've spent all my money on this place, and it's too late in the season to build anyway. No, for now, we will stay here. Perhaps next spring, I will be able to make other arrangements. So, my darling, you must be patient. During the winter, I will be here. I won't leave you alone, and in the spring we will see what can be done to make things more pleasant for you."

"No, Pierre, I can't spend the winter here. I will be crazy before the winter ends. If you won't move to the fort, I will return to France on the next ship that leaves."

Although the season was late, he knew that a ship in the basin was about to leave for France shortly. Her stubbornness worried him. "Darling, be reasonable. I've promised to consider moving to the fort in the spring. We must stay here for the winter."

Françoise raised herself to her elbow. Her eyes glinted steelily. "Pierre, I'm going to the fort tomorrow. If we don't move, then I will be boarding the ship in the basin and return to France. I can't stay here."

Her ultimatum disturbed him, but his decision became more resolute. He could not let his wife dictate their destiny. She was being stubborn and unreasonable. If he let her have her way in this important undertaking, she would forever be testing his will. No, he could not let her have her way now.

"My darling, I'm sorry to hear you make such a decision, but my life is here, on this piece of land. It's not at the fort. I asked you to share this life with me, and if you choose to do otherwise, that will be your decision. If you can't stay, then I can't hold you against your will."

He hoped she would capitulate, but she did not.

"Tomorrow I will get my things together and move to the fort."

Her determination stunned him, and a deep sadness overwhelmed him. He pondered the situation. The deepness of the rift did not strike him immediately, but when she turned away from him, the enormity of her decision seized him: his wife of a few months was about to leave him.

The next morning, early, Françoise rose and packed her few belongings. Pierre feigned sleep, and through slitted eyes he watched as she moved about their tiny home gathering her possessions and packing them into bundles. Silently, she prepared to leave him. A single candle sputtered and wavered as vagrant currents of air moved through the small abode. Wisps of smoke wandered toward the ceiling. The subdued darkness of the area away from the candle seemed as heavy as his spirit.

He was tempted to try once more to change her mind, but he found the idea revolting; a wife was subject to her husband: she promised to love, honor, and obey. He had every right to expect her to remain with him. He turned noisily away from her to face the wall. He hoped she would make an effort to talk to him, but she did not. The atmosphere between them remained charged and oppressive. He could feel her stubbornness; her position hardened rather than softened. Well, if that's the way she feels about our marriage, then she can go, he thought. He could not and would not move near the fort and Belleisle's house. He made his decision, and he would not let a stubborn wife change it; he was the master in his home.

Daylight came slowly this late in the fall. The late October weather was exceptionally mild; at least, that was what the older inhabitants claimed. Winter, this year, was late in coming. Although temperatures diminished, no snow fell. Although a chill was in the air, a fire was not needed to keep the house comfortable. Pierre rose silently, sat at the table, and munched on a piece of stale bread and smoked fish while Françoise sat in a corner, blank.

Finally he said, "When are you leaving?"

"As soon as it's light enough."

"I will take you."

"There's no need. I can handle the canoe myself." It was true. She was now a proficient canoeist— even against the tidal bore that inundated the basin twice daily.

"But I will take you. I will be needing the canoe later." He did not explain that he and Jacques planned to go hunting, for a moose, they hoped, as it was the end of the rutting season, and bull moose could still be drawn to their muskets.

Pierre and Françoise were leaving when they heard a shout from the landing by the stream. Pierre recognized Jacques's mellow voice, and he saw that Marguerite was with him. He waved as they made their way slowly up the path toward the house. Marguerite was the first to notice the tightly bound bundles on the ground before Françoise.

"Well, where are you off to?" she asked.

Neither answered, and the silence became embarrassing.

Jacques looked at Pierre inquisitively. "My friend, what's going on?"

Pierre mumbled, "Françoise is going to live at the fort."

"I don't understand!" Marguerite interjected, a shocked look on her face.

"I'm leaving," Françoise said simply.

Shock registered on Jacques's face. He recovered first. "Maybe we should have a cup of tea and find out what's happening."

Marguerite affirmed, "Yes, I think Jacques has a good idea. I will make us a cup of tea, then we will talk about what's happening."

Pierre nodded silently, and Françoise made no reply; none gave a sign of opposition.

They returned inside. As Marguerite quickly and efficiently prepared the kettle and teapot, Jacques laid wood on the hearth and soon a fire roared. In the meantime, Pierre and Françoise sat staring at the floor. No one spoke. Steam from the hot liquid rose slowly from the heavy pottery bowl as the visitors joined the silent, sullen couple. Jacques twirled his bowl nervously; Marguerite sipped tentatively.

Jacques sighed and said, "Pierre, would you please tell us what this is all about?"

Pierre shrugged his shoulders. Even though Jacques was a good friend, he was embarrassed that Françoise decided to leave him. He turned to Françoise and said in a low voice, "Would you tell them why you decided to leave me?"

She stared at the floor for several moments, then lifted her head quickly and in a quivering voice, said, "Yes, I will. You're being stubborn and won't listen to me. I'm afraid to stay here. The Indians horrify me. Two days ago an Indian chief and his woman visited us. They came for liquor, but the brave wanted me." Her voice rose shrilly, and she wrung her hands nervously. "He wanted to trade his woman for me." Her eyes glistened. "The way he looked at me frightened me. I can't forget the look on his face…and the way he treated his wife. I'm afraid he will come back when I'm alone, and he will carry me to his camp, God knows where." She paused as if to catch her breath. "Pierre won't listen to me. He seems to think I'm imagining these things, and they're of no consequence. I want to live by the fort so we will have protection from those savages." She sighed deeply.

Pierre pleaded, "But, Françoise, these savages are Christians. Father Molin says that most of them are better than the colonists here in the basin. They are not dangerous. The soldiers and sailors are probably more menacing to you women than the Indians. That's why I see no reason to move to the fort. Marguerite, are you afraid of the natives?"

She answered slowly, "Yes, I am. And like you, Jacques assures me that I've nothing to fear. But several incidents have bothered me. Of course, the worst was the hanging of that unfortunate black man."

Jacques joined in, "But that was an isolated incident. Most of the time the Indians are our friends, only when they get liquor are they unmanageable. I've no trouble with them, but I'm sure we won't see them as much as you do. I'm not involved in trade with them."

"Jacques, that's the only occasion I've dealings with the Micmac. True, I hope to have more. And after Miskoo and I got to know each other, it was different. He's an important man in his band, a mighty warrior and brave. His people listen to him, especially in time of war."

"That's what frightens me, Pierre. He's a warrior, not a chief. I'm afraid his people only listen to him when they're at war," Françoise, on the verge of tears, remonstrated.

Jacques looked at the two. "Surely there's a better way to resolve this problem. Maybe it would help if you were to move in with us for the winter?"

"Jacques, that's very generous of you, but winter is the best time for us to stay here; the Indians will soon be gone to their winter camps, and we won't see them until spring. Now's the time for Françoise to become accustomed to this place."

"That's true, Pierre," Marguerite added, "but Françoise had an unsettling experience. Perhaps if she came to live with us for a short while, she will be able to conquer her fears, and she can rejoin you here."

During this exchange, Françoise remained silent, but she followed the conversation attentively. Pierre noticed that she seemed interested in Marguerite's suggestion. He looked at her hopefully. "What so you think of that idea, Françoise? Maybe we could stay with them for a week. Perhaps by that time, you'd be ready to move back here."

She remained silent.

"You know I love you, Françoise. Please don't leave. I don't want you to leave me, not even to stay at the fort. I'm more worried about you if you stay at the fort."

She raised her head slowly. "I don't want to leave you, Pierre, and I don't want to live with Marguerite and Jacques. All I want is to move nearer the fort for a while, until I feel more comfortable in this land. We're too far from everybody. Jacques and Marguerite are upriver on the opposite shore; the fort's several leagues away…Pierre, it's just too isolated here. I'm too afraid."

A thought struck Pierre. "Darling, let's go to Father Molin. Maybe he can settle this dilemma for us. Would you listen to him?"

Françoise brightened. "Yes, I'd listen to Father Molin. He's wise, and Holy Mother Church is comforting. I'd do what he recommends."

"Good, Françoise, we will go see him right away."

Father Molin just finished his early morning Mass as Pierre and Françoise landed before the newly completed chapel four leagues upstream from the fort. The priest's sturdy cabin was located to the north of the chapel. He waited at the door as they threaded their way through the small group of colonists and a few Indians who attended the early morning service. They nodded and spoke a soft greeting to the worshippers they knew, which was most of them.

"Good morning, Pierre, Françoise. What brings you to see me?"

"Father, Françoise and I have a problem that we hope you can help us with. It's very serious."

The priest, whose hair was graying along the sides, waved his hand to invite them into his abode. He waited until they entered; then he motioned them to two ornate wooden chairs that were brought from France.

After they sat down, he turned to them and asked solicitously, "What's this very serious problem that you've been worrying about?"

"Father, I will let Françoise tell you about it."

Françoise raised her eyes to the priest's face. "Father, I want to go back to France. I'm not happy here."

"My dear, that's a serious decision. I assume that Pierre doesn't agree with you; that's why you're here."

She paused, licked her lips, and answered slowly, "Yes, Father, that's it."

"How does Pierre feel about this?"

"He doesn't want to go back. He believes that his destiny is here. He thinks he can make a fortune farming and trading with the Indians."

"H'm…what's wrong with that? Surely that's not what persuaded you to return to France?"

"No, Father, it's the loneliness and the fear."

"What are you afraid of, my dear?"

"I'm afraid of many things…the wilderness…and its wild animals. But especially the Indians. Their way of living…their way of acting…makes me afraid of them. Their cruelty and savagery worry me."

"My dear, these Indians, the Micmacs, are our friends; many of them are Christians and good members of Holy Mother Church. They will never hurt you. They're allies of the French. They don't like the English. The stories that you hear about their savagery and cruelty are nothing but that—stories. They're good people. Most of them are seeking salvation. My dear, what you must do is pray for them and for you. You must go home with your good husband and work with him to make a fine home here, in Acadia."

Françoise started to cry quietly. Pierre moved to her and placed his arm around her shoulders. He drew her close and patted her shoulder awkwardly.

"You mustn't cry, my dear child. Remember your marriage vows. You're subject to your husband. If you pray to Christ, he will help you; you will find strength to endure the little daily sufferings that come your way, and life will become satisfying."

"You're right, Father," she mumbled through her tears. "I've been selfish and sinful. I will pray for God's forgiveness and ask for his help."

She lifted her face to Pierre. "I'm sorry, my love. I was angry with you for no reason. You were right. We must work together."

Pierre was astounded that the priest's few words could effect such a change. But he recognized that Françoise drew strength from the Church and from this man who represented the risen Christ. Pierre always felt the power of God in the Church, but he never comprehended its deep influence on his wife. He took her hands in his and smiled. "My darling, I'm so pleased that you've changed your mind. Does that mean you won't be moving to the fort? That you will be staying at our home?"

She raised her bowed head, and, through her tears, she smiled. "Yes, I will be going home with you. To stay."

The next three days were joyful ones for Pierre and Françoise. It was like a new discovery. Pierre was solicitous and considerate. He did everything he could to make her comfortable and at ease. He worked around the homestead doing all the minor chores that he neglected before. He built a small barn and purchased a nanny goat and her kid. Françoise found them a source of delight. She even learned how to milk it. As well, by some judicious trading, Pierre was able to obtain three mature sheep which he hoped would provide them with wool, and if need be, some meat. He attempted to obtain a milk cow, but the deal fell through at the last minute, and, in a way, he was glad, as he did not have sufficient hay for the winter.

The weather remained mild and pleasant. Most of the old-timers said it was the mildest winter they could remember. Jacques and he worked together building dikes on their respective properties. The work was arduous, and each night they were happy to retire early.

October turned to November, and still the snows did not come. Only an occasional wet and cloudy day marred the weather. Surprisingly, most days were sunny and warm with a pleasant southwest wind.

Pierre noticed that Françoise became her happy, buoyant self. Only once in a while did he see wistfulness in her eyes. To help matters, most of the Indian bands left the vicinity and disappeared into the vastness of the wilds. Grandfontaine made an appearance from Fort Pentagouet; all seemed quiet in the colony. The deputy-governor still tried to collect his rents and dues, and occasionally threatened to banish some of his landholders. Father Molin exhorted the parishioners to pay their tithes, and grudgingly most of them complied. The usual disputes between members of the colony occurred: dogs that chased and bothered the neighbors' animals, boundary disagreements, dowry rows, family quarrels, and even a few scandals—husbands who were being too attentive to females other than their wives, and a few young rakes too ardent in their pursuit of the young ladies they were courting.

Generally, though, the colony was contented and peaceful. The old-timers seemed pleased that once more they were being ruled by their mother country although most complained that they were not receiving the attention from the king and his minister that they deserved.

Françoise was still a bit jealous of her friend, Marguerite, whose pregnancy was well established. As the months went by, Marguerite became more excited and happy about the upcoming event; she was expecting her baby in early spring, about the middle of March. Jacques was as expectant as the mother was, and his happiness showed as much as Marguerite's.

Pierre knew that Françoise was disappointed that she was not pregnant, but they made love regularly in the hope that she soon would be. Each month, as Françoise's periods came, he could see her become depressed, and for several days he worked hard to restore her confidence and spirit.

Pierre was happy that winter was so late, for it gave him the opportunity to improve his homestead and to plan the crops and animals he would need in the coming year.

Only one incident marred the tranquility. Early one morning late in November, he went out to feed the few animals he owned; he was angry when he discovered that marauding wolves killed his three sheep. He found the torn carcasses in the low shrubs that bordered the flats at the base of the uplands along the north edge of his lands. What angered him most was that all three were killed, but only a small amount of meat was torn from each body. The slaughter was wanton.

He heard from some of the other settlers that a small band of wolves was active in the neighborhood, taking a sheep here and a lamb there; this was not unusual. In years past, this happened, and the farmers considered it as one of the hazards to contend with.

When he returned to the house and told Françoise about the incident, her reaction surprised him although he recognized it should not have.

She broke into tears and sobbed, "There, you see. Those animals will be the death of us. They come to our door and steal our stock. The next thing you know, they will be attacking us."

Pierre tried to console her. "Françoise, this happens every year. The others told me about those wolves. I was careless. I should have enclosed the animals last night."

She continued sobbing. "Every day I pray to God to help me understand this country. I listened to Father Molin, but I'm still afraid. Each night I dream about all the horrors that could happen to us. I see us attacked by Indians, and now it will be wild animals."

"But, Françoise, it's getting better. I see it each day. You're more relaxed. You seem more happy."

"Pierre, each time something like this happens, for many days and nights, I'm so nervous I feel ill."

"I know that, darling, but you're improving. I see it more and more. I know that soon you will accept conditions here, and you will learn to cope with them."

"Pierre, I still think about returning to France. I don't know if I will ever be able to call this country home."

"You will, my darling, you will."

She looked up through her tears, a small smile tugging at the corners of her mouth. "I try, Pierre. I try, my love. For you."

"I know, my darling, and I understand and appreciate your suffering."

He drew her close and kissed her tenderly. He wondered if her fears would ever leave her. They had not surfaced for many days, but he perceived that they were only suppressed, not eliminated.

Chapter Thirteen — The First Winter

January 12, 1671 was a memorable day for Pierre and Françoise; it was their first Acadian snowstorm. The icy winds came howling from the northwest, rolling the clouds like waves. This advent of cold air was sudden and dramatic; one moment the sun was shining; a moment later a deep darkness descended, covering the entire land. The strident winds whipped along the ground hurling anything that was not tied down until it was obstructed by a rail fence, a dike, or a row of bushes or trees. The icy rain came slanting down in moving sheets, and then it turned to white smoke, as the droplets of water became ice crystals. The afternoon haze turned into a blanket of darkness as night came early, the snow and wind tearing around their small, snug home.

By morning, the sudden storm blew itself out, but a soft blanket of snow covered the countryside. The bleating of the nanny goat in the lean-to barn attached to their home awakened Pierre who looked at Françoise. In the morning darkness he could see nothing so he reached across to brush her face. She stirred slightly, murmuring peacefully as she snuggled closer to him. The rush mattress whispered and groaned under its canvas cover as she stirred. The heavy coarse woolen blanket and the down-filled counterpane felt warm and inviting as Pierre contemplated rising to do the chores.

He and Jacques planned to work on a ditch on Jacques's property that would drain an area he hoped to seed to wheat in the spring. It was a back area that seldom received salt water from the tidal bore; therefore he hoped the soil would not be too saline allowing him to harvest a crop from it in the coming year. But, now, Pierre knew they would not be working in it.

He lay quietly pondering his plans for the day.

A pounding on the exterior door awakened him instantly from a half-sleep, and he bounded out of bed. In the darkness he searched for his clothing that he deposited on the floor the evening before. Jacques's voice had urgency about it as he shouted through the barred door. "Françoise! Pierre! Open up! I need your help!"

Françoise, also awakened at the first pounding, called to Pierre, "That's Jacques. Something has happened. It sounds urgent."

"Yes, it does." Then he called to Jacques who was still pounding on the door. "I'm coming. I will be right there."

He hurried into his short trousers and slipped his coarse-spun shirt over his head as he rushed from the bed across the kitchen area, through the door into the anteroom storeroom. He removed the three wooden bars from the door and pushed it outward. "What's the matter, Jacques?"

"Marguerite's had an accident." He paused to catch his breath. "She fell last night as she was helping me drive the animals into the barn." He entered the low room, stamping his moccasined feet. "She seemed all right last night, but this morning she's in pain, and she has a fever. She asked me to get you, Françoise."

Françoise rose quickly; she met the men as they entered the house area. She lighted a candle from the small fire that burned in the hearth.

"Come in, Jacques. I heard you tell Pierre that Marguerite had an accident. Is she bleeding?"

"No, I don't think so, but she's in pain and has a fever."

"I will come."

They made the canoe trip to Jacques's home quickly as the incoming tide helped the upstream journey.

Françoise found Marguerite in bed, writhing and moaning in pain. She shooed the two men from the bedroom and told them to prepare plenty of hot water. She was not sure of the situation, but the baby might come early. Since it was the sixth month of Marguerite's pregnancy, she knew it would be impossible to save the baby; she hoped she could save the mother.

As Jacques walked back and forth wringing his hands and muttering to himself, Pierre stoked the fire, and soon a large cauldron of water bubbled on the hearth. He busied himself at the fireplace, keeping the fire roaring, and heating water in several pots that stood or hung from the iron crane.

He turned from the hearth and looked at his friend. "How did it happen?" He asked the question more to divert Jacques's attention than to know the details of the accident. He knew it was an easy matter to slip and fall while driving animals, especially in the wet, snowy weather of the evening before.

Jacques stopped pacing, and more to himself than to Pierre, said, "I told her not to come out in that storm, but she wouldn't listen. We were driving the cattle into the barn, and, you know that old red and white horned one, she suddenly bolted. Marguerite turned to head her off, and she slipped. I saw her fall. She fell backwards and landed…not too hard…on her behind. I asked her if she was all right… she said she was fine. It wasn't until the middle of the night that she began to have pains…and the fever started."

"It isn't too serious, Jacques. I'm sure she and the baby will be all right."

"I hope so. Marguerite has been feeling so well up to now. I hope this won't set her back."

"Ah, Jacques, a few days rest and she will be back to her old self."

Françoise came from the bedroom. "She's resting now. I don't think she will have the baby, but she will have to be careful for the next few days. She's strained something so we will have to keep her quiet until the injury's healed. For the moment she's fine. Perhaps some of her problem was fear and anxiety. Pierre, I will stay with her for the next few days to make sure she behaves herself and stays in bed."

Pierre nodded his assent.

For the next two days, Françoise maintained her own home and looked after Marguerite. The fever subsided, but Marguerite still complained of pains in her lower abdomen. Françoise recalled one of her mother's pregnancies; she remained in bed from the fifth month on in order to avoid a miscarriage. Now she wondered if Marguerite would have to do the same.

Her friend seemed to be improving, but as soon as she tried to leave her sick bed, her pains became intense, and she broke into a cold sweat. She grimaced and fell back onto the bed, exhausted. Jacques was so concerned that he hovered over her like a hen over her brood of chicks. Pierre understood and insisted Françoise stay with Marguerite as long as necessary.

During the afternoon of the second day, as Marguerite lay propped up in bed, Françoise brought her a cup of warm goat's milk. As Françoise handed her the steaming bowl, Marguerite wrinkled her nose and sighed, “I liked goat's milk before, but now the smell nauseates me. I'm not sure I can drink it.”

Françoise smiled and urged, “You must, Marguerite. If not for yourself, at least for the little one. That one must continue to grow and develop. The baby still has four months to grow, you know.”

“I suppose you're right. But before, I could eat anything. Now almost all food makes me sick.”

Françoise smiled again and encouraged her. “Marguerite, that will pass. As soon as your injury heals, you will be back to your old self.”

“I hope that's soon. You've been kind to stay with me. Jacques and I are grateful to you and Pierre for all your kindness.”

“Don't worry about that. I'm very happy to help. And you know that Pierre would insist that I stay with you until you're well again. No matter how long it takes.”

“I know that, Françoise. But you have your own work to do. And I'm sure Pierre misses you in his bed.” A mischievous grin curled her lips.

Françoise grinned back. “Yes, you're right. Pierre's eager for a son to help him on the land. He's looking forward to the time when I will be pregnant. But he's patient.”

“Oh, yes. I know how patient men are. Jacques couldn't wait until I was pregnant. He was in a hurry to have a child. I dearly hope that nothing happens to this child. Jacques will be extremely disappointed; he was overjoyed when he found out I was expecting.”

A twinge of guilt made Françoise shudder. She recalled the times she rebuffed Pierre when he tried to make love to her. He, too, was eager for a son. Somehow he could not see that their first child would be other than a son. Several times, when Pierre spoke of his son as if the baby was already born, she suggested their firstborn might be a daughter, but Pierre simply ignored it.

“Well, Marguerite, we mustn't disappoint Jacques. We must do everything to be sure the child arrives safe and sound.”

Two days later, Françoise was still at the Breton homestead. Marguerite appeared well, but when she tried to rise from the bed, she could not. The same abdominal pains returned, and a look of fear and anxiety masked her face. Françoise did not encourage her to overexert herself. As long as she remained prone and quiet, the pains subsided and she was comfortable.

That evening, Pierre came from his work and entered the bedroom. He smiled reassuringly at Marguerite. "You're looking much better, Marguerite."

She smiled wanly and lifted her hand in greeting. "I'm fine…until I try to leave the bed…then I feel as if I'm about to die."

"I know. Françoise told me. Don't worry, Marguerite. Françoise will stay with you as long as you need her…even if it means until the baby is born."

Marguerite looked shocked, and Pierre noticed he should not have said that. He continued, "You must understand, Marguerite, that it's possible to spend the rest of your term in bed. I've heard of many women who've had to do that. I think that Françoise's mother had to do that for one of her children. It's not the end of the world."

Françoise entered the room with a large bowl of steaming stew. The savory odor made Pierre's mouth water even though he had eaten his evening meal. "What've you been telling this woman?" Françoise teased.

Neither responded, so Françoise continued, "I hope I haven't interrupted a secret conversation."

"Don't be silly. Pierre scared me half to death. He told me I might have to spend the rest of my term in bed. That's horrible!"

Françoise smiled. "He may be right, Marguerite. You've taken a nasty fall. You've injured yourself inside. You can't leave your bed until you're healed. If you do, you may injure the child. Pierre's right. If it's necessary, you will stay in bed until you're due…I will look after you…and you will not worry about it."

Pierre nodded his head vigorously.

Jacques came in. He heard the last of the conversation. "What's going on here?"

Pierre looked at his friend. "Jacques, we're just telling Marguerite that she must stay in bed until she's completely healed…no matter how long it takes. Even if it means until the baby comes."

Françoise interjected, "I will look after her." She added, "And you. And Pierre."

"Do you think she will have to be in bed that long, Françoise?"

"I don't know. But it's possible. My mother stayed in bed four months when my young brother, Antoine, was born. She had pains like Marguerite, and they didn't leave until my brother was born. So you must be prepared for that possibility, Marguerite. If it happens, at least she's lucky it's during the winter. Some people have all the luck. If it were to happen to me, I'm sure it'd be during the hottest time of the year." Françoise laughed and the others joined her.

The weather remained mild and balmy, and Marguerite remained in bed. Françoise continued to nurse her. Each time she thought she was well enough to leave her bed and she tried to rise, the pains returned. So finally she sensed she must remain in bed until the baby arrived.

Françoise developed a routine. Each day, after she finished the chores in her home, she took the canoe and paddled to Marguerite, or Pierre came with her if he and Jacques had something planned.

The snow from the mid-January storm all but melted; no further storms occurred. Occasionally, a squall would pass through, depositing some rain and even a bit of snow, but it did not last. In the sheltered spots, small piles of snow remained, but it was not necessary to keep the animals in the barns. They were pastured or allowed to roam over the marshlands, foraging for themselves.

Pierre was concerned that the mild winter would have a deleterious effect on the furs that he expected to obtain from the Indians, especially his friend, Miskoo. Throughout the winter, he and Jacques were able to continue their work on the dikes and fences because they did not spend so much time obtaining firewood for the voracious fireplaces.

When some of the older settlers joined them in their work, it became a celebration. Someone would bring a small cask of wine that was passed from one to another. By evening, one or two imbibed too much. On such occasions, they went to a neighbor's home and feasted. After a good meal, the fiddles, the fifes, and the drums would magically appear, and everyone joined in a round of dances while another cask of wine would add to the merriment.

Twice such impromptu celebrations were held at Jacques's. Marguerite watched from her bed; the change distracted her: she loved the jokes, the laughter, the music, and the dancing. The neighbors were kind, and a steady stream of women, and sometimes men, came into the room to cheer her up. Jacques was always nearby, and Françoise made sure that she was well cared for. Other than the exasperation of her inactivity, the winter passed pleasantly.

Father Molin came to see her regularly, hearing her confession, and giving her the Eucharist. Although she was unable to attend Mass, she found comfort in the recitation of the Rosary. When she was alone and time hung heavy on her, she reached for the beads that hung over her bed and repeated the prayer to the Blessed Mary with great reverence, asking for the safety of her unborn child and her home.

On March 14, 1671, in mid-morning, she awoke from a nap that she fell into as she recited her prayer when a sharp cramp seized her. Its sharpness and severity startled her awake; she gasped instinctively. She was alone in the house as Jacques and Pierre left early on a hunting expedition; they hoped to bag a deer for the larder. Françoise had not yet made her daily appearance although Marguerite expected her any moment.

Another sharp pain tore at her inwards, and she moaned softly. Then she felt the flow of liquid dampen the mattress between her legs. She knew her time had come; she was about to give birth. The suddenness of the pains and the quickness of the rupture of the placenta unnerved and frightened her. She prayed Françoise would soon arrive. She tried to relax and lay back on her pillow. She was not due for another month. How would this affect the child? Would it survive? Would the birth be normal? Would complications occur? Would she hemorrhage? Would the baby arrive before someone came to help her?

Another spasm wrenched her, and she felt the muscles of her abdomen stiffen and tremble. The pain and tightness lasted for several moments and then subsided; beads of perspiration dampened her brow, and her mouth felt dry and parched. She relaxed as her body sagged and her muscles loosened. She drifted into a mild stupor; she was not sure whether she dozed or became semi-comatose. At any rate it felt pleasant.

She did not know how long she reposed when the next seizure came, but she felt it more intensely than the one before; the pain rolled along her abdomen, through her back, and up to her breasts, strangling the air from her. Her breath whooshed out in a great heave; she fought for air, but the tension in her body refused to allow her to inhale. She felt asphyxiated, and darkness enveloped her. At the moment she felt she would lose consciousness, the muscles loosened, and the pain subsided. She gasped in great gulps of air, she moaned as sweat poured from every pore, her body gradually relaxed, the pain lifted, and a lassitude possessed her. She gripped her rosary tightly as she waited fearfully for the next contraction.

The time between each contraction was dreamlike and agreeable. She dreamed of a little boy, blond-haired and blue-eyed, romping about her knees. She looked at him with loving eyes, and she caressed him gently. Her heart welled up with love when she saw the pride in Jacques's eyes as he admired the child.

Her reveries relaxed her so much that the next spasm surprised her. The pain in her groin was more intense than before; instinctively she raised her legs and spread them apart to make room for the tiny life that struggled to enter the world.

She did not hear Françoise enter the room so, when she heard her voice, she was startled.

"You're doing fine, Marguerite. The child will be here next time."

An immense feeling of relief came over her; the pain and fear of moments before seemed nothing. Through a haze she gazed up at Françoise and whispered hoarsely, "Thank God, you're here."

Another burst of pain interrupted her, and she could feel herself pushing trying to hurry the event along. Through the mist, she heard Françoise encouraging and urging her. Her pelvis seemed to burst, and then a great weight lifted from her; for a few moments darkness closed about her. A feeling of well-being overcame her, and she lay back, relaxed and satiated. Her job was done—the silence was gratifying and luxurious. She knew that Françoise was attending to her and the life expelled from her body. But the pleasure of the moment was boundless, and for the time being, she was not interested in the child. The birth tired Marguerite; she fell into a deep sleep.

Sometime later—she did not know how long—she awoke to subdued conversation. As consciousness returned, she recognized the voices of Françoise and Jacques.

"The child's very small and weak."

"Do you think it will live, Françoise?"

"That's in the hands of God, Jacques. He will decide that. Fortunately, Marguerite's fine. In a matter of days she will be up and about, as good as ever."

"Thank God for that. And thank you and Pierre for standing up for the child. I'm happy that Father Molin came and baptized the child immediately. It was unfortunate that Marguerite wasn't awake when the child was christened. I hope she won't be too unhappy about that."

Marguerite struggled to a sitting position. "Where's the baby? Jacques, Françoise, where's the baby?"

They hurried into the bedroom, Françoise carrying the small blanket-shrouded bundle. "You've had a long sleep, Marguerite. That's good. Now you're stronger."

Marguerite smiled. She felt sore, but better than the past three months. "I'm feeling better. How's the baby? What is it?"

Jacques laughed. "We've a beautiful daughter, who's already baptized."

A knot of fear tightened her breathing. "Why has she been baptized so soon? What's the matter?"

Françoise looked quickly at Jacques and then answered, "She's very small and weak, Marguerite. It's just a precaution. But she will be fine. You're strong and have plenty of milk. She will soon grow strong and robust too."

A slight squirming and mewing issued from the blanketed infant; Marguerite raised her hands to accept the child. Françoise handed her the bundle gently, and then Marguerite pulled back the coverlet to look for the first time on the product of her body. The smallness and redness of the tiny being startled her. She saw many babies, but none seemed as small and as vulnerable as this one. The child lay still and silent; she was not sure it was alive.

Françoise said, "While you slept, the child fed twice. At least she knows how to take the breast."

"Will she feed again?"

"You can feed her as often as possible so she will grow and develop quickly. The next few days are important for her. She must make up for the time she lacks."

"Will she live, Françoise?"

"That's in God's hands, but I think so. She seems to be a fighter, your little Geneviève."

"I like that name. You remembered, Jacques."

"Yes, Marguerite. She's Geneviève Marie…just as we decided. If something should happen to her, she will be our little saint."

Marguerite drew her close, opened the front of her chemise, and proffered her ample right breast to the child. She forced the gorged and swollen nipple into the tiny mouth, and she felt the gentle drawing of the sucking child.

For the next two weeks, the child alternated between periods of vigor and weakness. At times she seemed normal and lively, but during other periods her body functions seemed to disappear—her breathing became shallow and almost nonexistent. Several times, Marguerite thought she died, but each time, her breath returned with a noisy shudder. Marguerite held the struggling child in her arms most of the time, afraid to leave her. Françoise stayed with the apprehensive family, providing sustenance and support.

Each day the child survived improved its chances, but she still remained weak and sickly. By the end of the second week, Françoise was sure the child was out of danger, although she was not pleased with its progress. She strengthened, but she became fretful and demanding.

Early on the morning of the fifteenth day, Marguerite, sitting in a chair before the fireplace, studied the sucking child. "Françoise, I'm well enough to assume my duties here. You must return home to Pierre. I will be able to manage now. My strength has returned, and Jacques and I can handle things. I thank you and Pierre so much for the help you've given us."

"Marguerite, I'm happy that I could help. I know if I'd been in the same position you'd have done the same. You're right. I must return home. I will visit often to be sure that all is fine."

Due to the mild winter, spring came suddenly, surprising the community. By early April the snow disappeared, and the early morning warm sun burned mists and fogs away. The animals awakened early from their winter doldrums, enlivening the countryside with their mating. Calves and lambs appeared magically. Because of the mild spring, the new-borns survived with surprising ease. Even the farmers started their spring work, tilling and seeding, with a verve and eagerness that astonished all.

When Françoise returned home at the beginning of April, it seemed like a new beginning for them. Their passion was insatiable; they made love often—sometimes several times a day. Pierre said it was 'spring fever', but Françoise insisted it was 'absence that increased desire'.

Early one morning, after they made love, Françoise kissed Pierre gently, and then turned his face toward her. "Pierre, I think I'm pregnant. I'm a week overdue, and I feel different."

Pierre laughed. "It's only spring fever. We all feel different at this time of year. Don't get your hopes up. It may be a false alarm."

"No, I don't think so. You know I'm very regular. I will be absolutely sure by next week."

He drew her into his arms and kissed her forehead, her eyelids, and her nose; then his lips sought hers. She opened her mouth and flicked her tongue into his. He felt stirrings, and caressed her breast gently, first one then the other. He kissed her neck and shoulders, following down to her budlike nipple that he licked and nibbled delicately. She responded, and they made love again.

April turned to May; it was mild and balmy. The migratory birds returned and filled the estuary and the creeks with their cacophony as they nested in the reeds and rushes along the shores. Pierre watched their mating and nesting activities with a new understanding of their paternal and maternal instincts. Their industry matched his own as he dreamed of the day that his child would be born, for it was now certain that Françoise was with child.

He was overjoyed at the change that took place in Françoise: each day she awakened with anticipation of life to be lived; her joy at the prospect of becoming a mother filled her with happiness; her cheeks sparkled; her eyes twinkle; and she bubbled with laughter. Her happiness overflowed into Pierre. Brightness and joy filled their home; the world belonged to them—no matter what happened, it could not dampen their enthusiasm and optimism. Pierre looked on each day as a foreshadowing of Paradise.

On a sunny morning in mid-May, a surprise visitor beached his canoe at Pierre's landing. The noisy birds that filled the creek and the nearby river heralded his arrival. Pierre leaned against the handle of the mattock that he was using to cultivate a small area of land north of the house that Françoise wanted to plant to corn and turnips. He watched, interested, as the canoe approached his landing, and three men beached it and drew it on the shore.

As they approached, following the path, Pierre recognized the leading figure as Sieur de Belleisle. His homespun clothes did not distinguish him from the other inhabitants of Port Royal. He was dressed in the typical costume of the colonists—homespun knee breeches, a heavy cotton shirt, and a low-crowned wide-brimmed beaver hat decorated with a simple ribbon around the lower crown, fine woven stockings, and on his feet, a pair of plain moose hide moccasins. His stocky frame carried this costume with an air of authority.

Pierre left the cultivated plot, placed the mattock against the corner of the house, and went forward to meet his seigneur. He waved his hand and called, "Good morning, Sieur de Belleisle. It's a pleasure to welcome you to my humble home."

"Good morning, my friend Pierre. I'm happy to visit you. I'm making the rounds of my concessionaires to see how they're doing, and to see if I can be of any help."

"Ah, my seigneur, that's considerate of you. I'm doing well, and soon I will have some land ready for planting." Pierre nodded to the other men who accompanied Belleisle. He knew them as Belleisle's hired men, tradesmen.

"You've a nice place here, my friend. I'm happy to see you're improving your land."

Françoise appeared at the door and curtsied to the man who stood talking to Pierre. He nodded in acknowledgment, and then turned back to Pierre.

Pierre wondered at the true motive for the seigneur's visit. Was he truly here to see if he could be of help, or was he trying to find out about Pierre's trading activities? He knew that Belleisle's reputation was more self-centered than that.

Belleisle was only a few years older than Pierre although he was in Acadia for many years. Belleisle's father, Emmanuelle Le Borgne, was one of the major creditors of old Charles de La Tour who died only a few years before in 1666. Through this relationship, and the fact that Belleisle married La Tour's daughter, Marie, be became the seigneur of most of the lands around Port Royal. Pierre could not bring himself to like this man, yet he could not understand why. He was pleasant enough, and he treated Pierre with honesty and fairness, yet something about his personality irritated Pierre.

Belleisle smile widely. "I've some dyking to do on my land, and I'm arranging to have it done soon. Which days do you think you'd be available? Others are saying that two days next week would be the best time. Do you think you could be available next Monday and Tuesday?"

Pierre considered. Work for the seigneur was one of the conditions of his grant, and the sooner he got it done, he would not have to consider it again for some time. "If that's what the others have agreed to, then it's fine with me."

Without acknowledging Pierre's reply, he immediately took another tack. "Rumors abound that you're trading here. You know that I've the right to trade with the colonists and Indians, and I only can give permission to others to conduct such trade."

His directness left Pierre speechless as he considered how he would answer the accusation. Finally, he replied, "My lord, I've only bartered with the other colonists for my own needs. I've not traded with others as a business." It was true that he planned to become involved in the trade, but so far he only accumulated produce and surplus goods that some of the concessionaires possessed. He was not yet seriously involved in trade.

"That's good, Pierre. I wouldn't like to banish you from this land because you've broken the rules. As you know, I forced some from the land; they refused to acknowledge my inheritance."

"Do you have time for refreshments, Sieur de Belleisle?"

"No, I'm afraid not. We've many to visit this day, so we will take our leave. We meet at my house on Monday of next week. Bring your tools."

He turned and walked slowly toward the beached canoe. His retainers followed. At the canoe, he turned and waved to Pierre who trailed behind the group.

Pierre watched as the canoe drifted down the small stream to the main river. *Why do I dislike that man? Is it his position? Is it his manner?*

Does he intimidate me? He's done nothing to me, yet I can't feel comfortable with him.

The following Monday, after Pierre spent a long, hard day working on the dikes on a piece of land known as Belleisle Marsh on the north side of the Dauphin River, he drifted his canoe down the smooth flowing river toward his land. Dusk descended slowly making the area peaceful. Female ducks with their newly hatched clutches played hide and seek among the rushes that lined the shores. He watched as a hen shepherded her brood in search of food. If he drew too near, she clucked and the young disappeared into the shore grasses while she tried to lead him away from her family. The sun almost disappeared behind the South Mountains as the shadows lengthened over the quiet flowing river.

He made his approach to his landing slowly and languidly. The deepening dusk gave his homestead a feeling of peace and contentment. Once he beached the canoe, he trudged silently up the incline toward the two-room structure that was home. Suddenly, he perceived it was unusually quiet. He could hear no sounds emanating from the building; he looked about to see if Françoise was busy outdoors. He could not see her. A sheep bleated from a nearby pasture; a dog howled dismally from one of the farmsteads, but only an ominous silence greeted him. He called, "Françoise, I'm home. Where are you?"

He stopped, waiting expectantly for an answer, but none came. The deepening shadows now seemed threatening. His heartbeat quickened. Had something happened to Françoise? Why did she not answer his call? He hurried up the last few yards of the path and rushed through the open door of the storeroom. His eyes took several seconds to adjust to the darkness inside. The inner door, the entrance to their living quarters, was closed, but he heard a muffled, sobbing sound. He stopped and then approached the door cautiously. A multitude of worried thoughts flashed through his mind. Was it Françoise who was making the sound? Or had some stranger, Indian or Frenchman, invaded his home?

He listened at the closed door, hearing only the same muffled sobbing sound. It must to be Françoise; why was she crying? Carefully he opened the door and peeked into the gloom. Before the fireplace, her head in her hands was the shuddering figure of Françoise. She did not look up when he stepped through the doorway. Pierre rushed to her, stooped to one knee, and put his right arm around her heaving shoulders. "What's the matter, my darling? Why are you crying?"

She leaned into his arms and flung her arms around his neck. Through blubbering sobs she tried to tell him something, but he could not understand her. He took her arms and unwound them from his neck and said gently, "My darling, stop crying, get hold of yourself, and tell me again, slowly, so I can understand."

She looked up into his face, and with a great effort she stopped sobbing; her lips quivered, and her large eyes stared at him, but no words came.

He stroked her hair gently, and held her close, kissing the top of her head. "Take your time. When you're ready, you can tell me what it's all about." He felt her body shudder as she worked to gain control. After what seemed a long time, she quieted and snuggled against his chest.

In a monotone, she murmured, "Pierre, the baby's gone."

He stared at her, uncomprehending.

She repeated, on the edge of more tears. "The baby's gone. I lost the baby."

Understanding came like a bolt of lightning. He seized her by the shoulders and swung her to face him. "What happened? Did you have an accident?" Disbelief sounded in each word he uttered.

Wearily she answered, "No, I lost the baby."

She started to weep again. Pierre drew her close and awkwardly tried to comfort her. He felt useless.

Chapter Fourteen — The Route

Wednesday, June 4, 1671 was a dull, overcast day with the threat of rain. The guard at the entrance to the basin notified the settlement of Port Royal the evening before that the brigantine "L'Oranger" would be anchoring the next day. Since the arrival of a vessel from France was such an important event, most of the inhabitants put on their best clothes, packed a picnic lunch, and planned to spend the better part of the day at the fort welcoming the newcomers. Rumors abounded that this ship carried a large contingent of new settlers, especially marriageable young women.

The young men of the colony were particularly excited, as a shortage of females was a serious problem in the small community. Grandfontaine commissioned the priests to take a census: 363 souls at Port Royal consisted of 68 families of whom 200 were under the age of 20: 125 boys and only 91 girls.

Pierre and Françoise, Jacques and Marguerite with little Geneviève traveled together to the anchoring basin. They arrived near noon and joined the others as they milled about the tumbled down fort that was slowly being repaired to make it serviceable. They greeted most of the people by name as all attended the small chapel upstream where Father Molin was the pastor. The occasion was gala: All were dressed in their best; many children ran about renewing acquaintances; young men and women eyed each other critically, the young men vying for the eye of the lesser number of young women. Mothers kept a stern eye on their nubile daughters, not allowing them out of their sight.

A few Indians, who returned from their winter camps and hunting grounds, surveyed the confusion with quiet dignity and aloof bearing, although a few Indian children joined the French ones in romps and noisy games.

Pierre and the others found a vantage point on a knoll along the small Allain River, which flowed from the south into the Dauphin River, a few hundred yards south of the fort. They spread out reed mats that Marguerite wove, and they prepared to wait the arrival of the ship. The overcast started to break up, the sun occasionally breaking through the disintegrating clouds. As they waited, sunshine replaced shadow. The group was about to start their lunch of cheese, loaves of wheat and barley bread, ample quantities of goats' milk, and a flagon of wine that Jacques brought, when someone signaled that the L'Oranger was coming into sight.

Everyone rushed to the bank, but Pierre said quietly, "It will be at least an hour before she's about to anchor. Let's finish our meal, then we can enjoy the disembarkation."

They agreed, so they enjoyed their meal as most of the crowd jostled for a better view.

Within the hour, the hundred-ton vessel anchored to the cheers of the crowd along the bank. The spot Pierre chose allowed a good view of the activity taking place, and he and the others reminisced about their own landfall a year ago.

Longboat after longboat of passengers and cargo was unloaded and deposited on the quay and along the shore. Pierre counted approximately sixty passengers and settlers, but he was sure of the number of females: five. As each landed a cheer went up from the waiting crowd, especially the men. Eager hands were available to help each ashore, and as many hands tended to their luggage.

Belleisle attended, dressed in his best, though outdated, costume. Nevertheless, he looked resplendent in a dark felt hat decorated with a white ostrich plume and brilliant loops of blue ribbon. He wore a short cloth jacket of royal blue with short sleeves that ended in a fringe of looped ribbons; beneath the jacket he wore a fine lingerie shirt with full sleeves; at his neck was a lace falling band, while lace ruffles encircled his wrists. A dark blue fringed and embroidered baldric crossed his chest from his right shoulder to his waist at the left, and from it hung a shining sword that fell behind his cloth rhinegrave breeches that ballooned and came to a band at the knee. Brilliant blue loops of ribbon formed cannons that emphasized his blue silk stockings. In contrast to his blue costume, he wore dark brown leather square-toed shoes with bright red heels. Of the motley collection of uniforms and clothing, his was the most striking.

"The governor made a special effort today," Jacques remarked wryly, smiling. "I guess he's trying to impress the new arrivals. Maybe he's trying to recruit more settlers for his lands. What do you think, Pierre?"

"You may be right, Jacques. But it seems to me that most of the seigneurs are more interested in the fur trade than in establishing farms."

"That's true. I've heard Belleisle is about to banish Fauchard, Dumets, and Fortier from their lands. If he's really interested in farming, he'd be more lenient with his people."

"That's true, Jacques. And it's too bad Father Molin seems to side with Belleisle. His last sermon, I think, was aimed at them. 'Give unto Caesar what's Caesar's and give unto God what's God's' seems to say that Belleisle is like Caesar, and, of course, the Church always needs more money." Bitterness rasped his voice.

"Do you think he will actually throw those men off their lands?"

"Well, I wouldn't be surprised. He certainly seems prepared to show his authority. He came to see me the other day and hinted very pointedly that I was not to trade, either with the settlers or the Indians. He told me he was the only one with that authority. But I don't intend to change my plans."

Françoise entered the conversation. "You must be careful, Pierre. You could get into trouble." She spoke slowly in a small voice. The loss of her child did not help her attitude; Pierre could see she was reverting to her unhappy state of earlier. Although she did not mentioned returning to France, he knew the idea was never far from the surface of her mind. She still looked wan and pale, and she seldom smiled. The contrast between her and Marguerite was remarkable.

Although little Geneviève took most of Marguerite's time since she was puny and sickly, Marguerite bubbled with happiness. Her old vigor returned, and she worked from morning until dark as if the whole day was play. Her cheeks glowed with health, her whole body alive and quivering with joy.

Jacques, also, was euphoric, especially when he talked about his tiny, brown-haired daughter, who, in appearance, was a good combination of him and his wife. In two weeks time she would be four months old, yet she was still small and underdeveloped for her age. Although she grew, she was restless and colicky, and many nights she kept them awake as she fretted and cried. Both, then, took turns holding her and rocking her in their arms before the fireplace. Neither complained as the bond between them and their daughter strengthened. Often, if another person took the child in arms, she seemed to sense it was a stranger and she started to fuss. At present, she lay wrapped in a layer of soft blanket, quiet and contented.

Pierre looked tenderly at Françoise, feeling sorry that she was deprived of the child she so desired. "Françoise, you know I will be careful. I must, for we will have children like Jacques and Marguerite. Geneviève is being an angel today. Is she always like this?" Pierre knew she was not, but he felt he might make Marguerite feel better.

"Pierre, she's always an angel. Even when she keeps us awake at night. Isn't that right, Jacques?"

They spent the afternoon meeting and talking to the newcomers, who were thankful that their long journey ended successfully. Some of the new arrivals planned to continue their journey to Fort Pentagouet to establish their homes, but many decided Port Royal was a better place to settle because it was already a well-established community.

The five women aboard disappointed the bachelors: three were already married, one was a nun, and the last was a widow of some fifty years. Some of the older bachelors showed an interest; it was obvious she would have little trouble finding a husband.

As the evening sun dipped into the west, Pierre and the others decided it was time to return home and the evening chores—feed the animals and milk the goat and cow. Jacques acquired a milk cow as a precaution, in case Marguerite could no longer nurse little Geneviève.

Two weeks later, early one morning, Pierre heard a shout from his landing. He hurried down to greet his Micmac friend, Miskoo, who, with the help of two young Indian women, pulled a large birch bark canoe onto the beach. The canoe was heavily laden, the cargo covered with a skin blanket.

Miskoo raised his hand in greeting and smiled broadly. Pierre tried to speak a greeting to Miskoo in the Micmac language, but Miskoo broke into gales of uproarious laughter at the attempt. Even the women grinned. Pierre realized he must learn their language if he was to deal with them. After Miskoo laughed himself out, he said in his fractured French, "It nice see my friend again. My band come trade…live by sea for summer."

It was the Micmac custom to spend the winter in the deep woods hunting the deer and moose and any other animals that were available. In spring and summer, they moved to the seacoast where clams, oysters, and fish became the staple of their diet. As a result, during the summer many Indians camped in the vicinity of Port Royal.

"Welcome, my friend. Where is your camp, Miskoo?"

"Me camp at mouth Orignal River. Fishing good, it is peaceful." The Orignal River was located several leagues to the west on the south shore of the basin.

The two Indian women, each with a papoose strapped to her back, unloaded bundles from the canoe. Pierre saw that each bundle contained prime furs — beaver, muskrat, wolf and other animals. Although Pierre heard the fur catch of the winter was poor, it seemed that this band enjoyed a successful season.

Pierre raised his hand to stop the women from further unloading. "Miskoo, I've very little to trade. A few pots and kettles, some axes, and a few other tools, plus one musket and balls…a bit of powder. You've many furs."

"Miskoo not trade with Belleisle. He cheat. He steal. He not give Indian enough for furs."

Pierre laughed. "But, Miskoo, I can't give you enough for your furs. I have little."

It was Miskoo's turn to laugh. "I take your woman. She worth one bundle beaver."

Pierre knew the young brave was joking, for never would a brave of his stature offer that much for a woman. Pierre gestured toward the two women who stood waiting an order from Miskoo. "You've more women than you can handle now, Miskoo."

"No, Pierre, Miskoo handle many women. Miskoo great brave. Need many women."

"You know, Miskoo, my woman's not for trade. I need her myself."

"You my friend, Pierre. I not want your woman. I want gun, balls, powder. You have, so we trade."

Pierre saw that Miskoo made up his mind; he would trade with Pierre whether Pierre wanted it or not. He nodded in assent. Miskoo spoke softly to the young women; each picked up a bundle and followed Miskoo as he and Pierre walked toward the combined trading post dwelling. As they approached, the sharp aroma of baking biscuits assailed their nostrils from the open door of the log structure.

Pierre called, "Françoise, we have visitors." He did not want to frighten her, as he knew she was uneasy about Indians. She came to the door. A look of amazement and fear transformed her flour-smudged face. For a moment she stood thunderstruck, then she smiled tentatively.

"Françoise, you remember Miskoo. He came to visit last fall. I did some trade with him, and now he's back for more. He has many furs from his winter trapping."

Françoise looked inquisitively at the two women who stopped discreetly behind Miskoo.

"These are Miskoo's wives. An Indian can have as many wives as he's able to maintain. Many wives are a sign of importance. So you see, Miskoo is an important man in his band. He now has two women, and each have a child."

"They're not Christians!" She turned and re-entered the building.

The two young women sat on the bundles they had been carrying. For the first time, Pierre looked them over carefully; they were young, not more than fifteen or sixteen. They were so alike that he thought they might be sisters, even twins. He tried to decide which was Neremoosin, the one that accompanied Miskoo last autumn, but he could not be sure. They were the same height, and each wore her hair in two long plaits that hung down her back. Each wore a narrow leather headband, and each was attired in a simple undecorated doeskin gown belted with a rawhide thong. On their feet, they sported high vamped decorated moose hide moccasins. Dangling from a strap over each forehead was a cradleboard with a slumbering infant laced in. Even the children looked like twins.

One of the babies started to mew; the woman deftly swung the cradleboard to her breast, opened the front of her gown, and inserted the dusky nipple into the child's quivering mouth. It immediately started to suck noisily and contentedly. The naturalness of the action filled Pierre with a longing for a child of his own. He hoped that Françoise would soon be pregnant again.

Pierre motioned Miskoo forward. The two men entered the dim storeroom.

Two days later, on June 25, Governor Grandfontaine arrived at Port Royal. Although he was expected, he arrived with little fanfare. He had much work to do and many problems to solve. Belleisle banished three of his concessionaires for non-payment of rent and dues; the community was agitated. The census that he ordered was still being carried out, and he was trying to get the defenses in some semblance of order. He established his headquarters at Fort Pentagouet on the Penobscot with his garrison since he was trying to define the boundary between the English colonies and Acadia. Many of the English, especially the traders that were active in the fur trade, were unhappy with the present state of affairs and did all they could to harass and disrupt the establishment of French authority.

Grandfontaine also received another task from Courcelles, the Governor of New France at Quebec: He was ordered to find the best route overland from the Acadian colony to Quebec, the capital of New France. Several routes were in use by the Indians: up the Penobscot River over the height of land and down the Chaudière River to Quebec; up the St. Croix

River across to the St. John River to Rivière du Loup to the St. Lawrence and up it to Quebec; or up the St. John to its source, across the height of land into one of the many streams that flowed into the St. Lawrence.

A soldier arrived in the late afternoon to inform Pierre that the governor would like to see him the following day at his earliest convenience. Pierre was surprised and flattered by the summons, especially the courtesy with which it was delivered.

The following morning he left early for his rendezvous with Captain Hector. The meeting took place aboard the governor's ship, "Le Cygne", the same ship that brought them to Acadia. He ducked his head instinctively as he entered through the low door to the governor's cabin. The soldier who accompanied him from the main deck, saluted, and left.

From the gloomy interior, Pierre heard the captain's bass voice before he could see him. "Come in, Pierre. It's been a long time since I've seen you. You're looking well."

"Thank you, sir. Yes, I'm well. Life's favored me."

"Ah, that's good. Come. Sit down. I've much to discuss with you."

Pierre's eyes adjusted, and he saw the governor was attired casually, but still more in the dress of a Frenchman from the court than in the manner of a frontiersman of the New World. He was wearing a full, frilly silk shirt with lace cuffs; he wore on a pair of velvet breeches with long narrow legs stuffed into a pair of knee length boots with folded tops. He sat in a sturdy captain's chair behind a small, but heavy table used as a desk. He leaned forward with his Vandyke chin resting in the palm of his left hand. He motioned with his right hand to a heavy chair to his right.

Pierre took the proffered chair. "Sir, it's nice to see you again. Much has happened since I last saw you."

"So I understand. It seems there's been some trouble. I've many complaints from the old-timers about Monsieur Belleisle. You're one of his concessionaires. How do you see it?"

"Well, sir, there's been much commotion. Some of it's no doubt Monsieur Belleisle's doing, but much of it's not his fault. He's trying to get what's due him."

"First, about the killing and hanging. Was it justified?"

"No, I don't think so. But, in all fairness to Monsieur Belleisle and Father Molin, they could do little about it. The Indians were very angry at the death of one of their warriors even though he brought it on himself. It seems he attacked the black man without provocation. The Negro defended himself, and in the ensuing struggle the black man killed the Indian. The Indians insisted on retribution; Monsieur Belleisle felt it better to sacrifice one slave than to jeopardize the whole community. So the slave was hanged."

"What about the three men banished from their lands?"

"Here, I believe Belleisle is wrong. I'm sure, had he been more diplomatic, such action would be unnecessary. But Belleisle issued ultimatums, and these old-timers have been too long without authority, so they refuse to be dictated to. If he used persuasion rather than dictation, he'd be able to achieve more."

"Do you think I should replace him?"

"That's a tough question. The people here need someone to rule them. Without authority, they're a quarrelsome group. The older settlers have done what they think is right for too long. They're very independent."

"The problem is I have no officers to spare at the moment. Lieutenant Richard's commission is up; he's more interested in his seigneury than soldiering. St. Castin, my man at Pentagouet, is more interested in the Indians and women than the rule of the colony. Lieutenant Soulanges, the last of my officers, is under detention for insubordination. I'm asking for his return to France as he refuses to obey my orders. So you see, Pierre, I've no one I can trust here at Port Royal. As well, I've been ordered by Governor Courcelles to find the best overland route from here to New France. I must also re-establish Fort Latour at the mouth of the St. John River. Pierre, I'm short of capable men. That's why I summoned you."

"Sir, I will help if I can."

"I hear that you're friendly with one of the Micmac leaders…a young brave called Miskoo."

Pierre replied cautiously. "Yes, I know him. I consider him a friend."

"How well do you know him? Do you think you could persuade him to join you in an expedition to find the best route from here to Quebec?"

He presumes too much, mused Pierre. He's not asked me to undertake such a task. He assumes I will do it.

"Sir, I'm not sure I'm the person to undertake such a trip. I'm not familiar with the wilderness. I don't think such an expedition through unknown country is for me. I don't think I'm ready to lead such an expedition."

After more discussion, Pierre agreed to undertake the exploration expedition to find the route, but it was conditional that he could persuade his friend, Miskoo, to accompany him.

At first Françoise was vehemently oppose to Pierre's absence for most of the summer, but, after much persuasion, she agreed the expedition might be beneficial to them as well as the colony. Now, they were isolated from the main centers of New France, and, particularly, from the seat of government in Quebec. If a safe, easy route overland could be found and established, it would, no doubt, be of benefit to the colony. For one thing, trade might be established between Port Royal and Quebec rather than with Boston. They might be able to get better deals from their own countrymen than with the English. Some of the attention that Versailles paid to the St. Lawrence might be directed toward them; more money and royal help might be forthcoming. Pierre also saw it as a chance to extend his influence with the Indians, especially in the fur trade.

Françoise agreed when he promised to hire the young Doucet to be with her while he was away. Young Albert developed into a sturdy and independent eleven-year old who was capable on the farm. The family would appreciate the extra sous that his employment would bring.

Miskoo proved more difficult to persuade than Françoise. He was in no hurry to abandon his easy summer life for the difficulties of travel in the hinterland. He knew a great deal about the country into which they would be traveling. His greatest fear was the Iroquois they might meet once they crossed the height of land into the streams that flowed to the St. Lawrence. According to Miskoo, the Iroquois vowed to destroy the French settlements along that river and were presently preparing for a major war against the French. That was the reason why he was not in a hurry to journey anywhere near their territory.

Pierre went to see Miskoo at his camp on the Orignal River. Miskoo and several of his followers set up a summer camp of five lodges consisting of a pyramid framework covered with several layers of bark, mostly birch bark. When Pierre visited the camp, the women were busy catching and smoking fish. A weir was built at the mouth of the river, and at low tide, the fish that were trapped behind it were netted or harpooned; then they were split and hung over a smoky fire to cure.

Miskoo sat before his lodge staring into a small fire that smoldered before it. Pierre sat across from him and waited patiently for Miskoo to speak. He learned never to rush the Indian chief's decisions. For several minutes Miskoo gazed into the wisps of smoke that rose on the still morning air as if he was seeking wisdom from the gray-blue mist that rose from the firepit. Finally he spoke, "Pierre, my friend, I go with you, but I bring my camp with me." The Indians could not understand how the French could leave their women and children behind whenever they traveled.

"But they will slow us down."

"No hurry. Summer come. Summer go anyway. We live anyway."

Pierre remonstrated. "But we must hurry, Miskoo. The captain wants to know the best route as soon as possible.

"Trail not move. Trail still be there. We move. Wife and children no go, me no go. My people no go. We need my people. They help much. We need."

Pierre wondered if Grandfontaine would be willing to give Miskoo and his band the presents they would expect. His orders were to find the best route to Quebec. Grandfontaine promised him he would be well rewarded—maybe further grants of land, certainly some gold pieces, and possibly a license to trade with the Indians and the Bostonians.

Pierre resigned. "Agreed, Miskoo. We will travel with your camp."

Miskoo's stoic face brightened, and he spoke sharply to one of the young women who accompanied him to Pierre's place earlier.

"When can we leave, Miskoo?"

"Tomorrow."

"No, Miskoo, too soon. I've much to do. Three days." He held up three fingers. Miskoo grunted as if he was annoyed at the delay; then he barked another order to the women.

Pierre continued, "I will be ready in three days. We will leave then."

Early, three days later, five canoes filled with gear, supplies, women, and children left Pierre's landing. Pierre looked back as the canoes floated down the stream away from Françoise who stood with young Albert Doucet by her side. They waved until the flotilla was out of sight; her sad, wistful figure made Pierre wish that he had not agreed to this trip. He knew he would be away most of the summer, and the responsibility for the animals and crops would be on her shoulders. He hoped no major emergencies would arise while he was away, although he knew Jacques and Marguerite, as well as the other neighbors, would help her.

Everyone with whom he discussed his commission was favorably disposed to the idea of a better and shorter route to Quebec. The present sea route was long and unpredictable, depending on the vagaries of weather, pirates, privateers, and other hazards. If he could find a dependable, safe and shorter route to Quebec the entire colony would benefit, so all his neighbors indicated they would be available if Françoise needed them.

The plan was to cross François Bay to the mouth of the St. John River, to ascend to its origins, to portage across the height of land, and to find the best stream or river to the St. Lawrence River, and then to Quebec.

Pierre never made an extended canoe trip before, so the prospect excited him. Five canoes made up flotilla: Miskoo and his wives manned the two lead canoes. Pierre was given the bow position with Miskoo in the stern; the other, heavily laden, was assigned to Miskoo's two young wives and his children. The three others were loaded with, what seemed to Pierre, three families: one canoe with three occupants, two young braves and an older woman; the next with an older couple; and two young braves occupied the last. Each of these was heavily laden, the water coming within inches of the gunwales.

The stamina of the Indians amazed Pierre; they paddled for hours without stop while Pierre's muscles screamed in agony. This went on day after day with but brief stops for rest and food. Miskoo and Pierre led the way, down the Port Royal Basin to its outlet, then the long trip across the salt water François Bay to the mouth of the St. John River. They made their first portage: first across the peninsula directly east of the abandoned, dilapidated old Fort Latour that was not used for several year; the second, across another peninsula that jutted southward, circumventing the reversing falls which Pierre found fascinating. This second portage brought them to the St. John River proper, north and west of the falls. Since summer was well advanced, the river was slow moving and languid; the spring run-off long since made its way to François Bay.

During the days that followed, as they made their way up the St. John River, Pierre worked at learning the Micmac language. To his surprise, he had a facility for learning the language, and since conversation was only in that language; he learned it quickly. He found his Indian companions to be a fun-loving group with a well-developed sense of humor. They laughed at his mistakes with the language, and they often taught him to say things wrong so they could make fun of him.

Their easy morality and lack of inhibition unnerved him. In camp, he noticed both men and women made little effort to cover their nakedness, and it did not seem to bother them if their genitals and other parts were exposed. The men, for the most part, wore a loincloth, while the women wore a simple skin gown that hung loosely about their bodies. As they went about their activities, they often hiked up their gowns about their loins exposing themselves to whoever happened to be looking. If they felt like removing their garments before the men, they did so.

One evening as Pierre and Miskoo sat about the campfire after they ate, Miskoo looked at Pierre and remarked, "I see you have been looking at my wives with interest, my friend. Would you like one as a sleeping companion?"

Pierre was astonished and speechless. He did not realize that his feelings were so exposed. For several moments he was so embarrassed that words would not come. Finally, he mumbled, "No, my friend, I'm not used to seeing such beauty exposed."

Miskoo laughed. "Indian women have nothing to hide. Nor have Indian men. Making love is a natural thing. Even if your priests tell us it is forbidden until your god makes it available, we know our god finds it a thing of beauty."

Now it was Pierre's turn to laugh. "You're right, Miskoo. My god makes it a sin. A man and a woman must be joined by the Church before we can make love, and then it's only to create children."

"Your god is good in many ways, but he who created man does not understand his needs. I will share one of my women with you while we are on this journey. That's the way of the Micmac. Which one of my wives do you want?"

Pierre was not sure how to answer his friend. He did not want to insult him or displease him by refusing his offer. He pledged fidelity to Françoise, and he took his oath seriously, even though he found these two young women attractive. Their dusky color, their black hair, their dark brown eyes, as well as their sensuous bodies attracted him. More, though, was the excitement that stirred his groin. As he watched them move lithely and provocatively about the campfire, their swinging hips and jouncing breasts drew his eyes repeatedly.

Miskoo watched with an amused grin and a twinkle in his eyes. He called one of the women to the fire. "This is Debit Iskisy. She is named for the light that shines at night. If you want her, she is yours while we are on this journey."

"My Françoise would not approve. She would be very angry with me if I were to make love to another woman. I thank you, Miskoo, but I can't accept your generous offer."

"Oh, my friend, it isn't that generous. I would expect you to do the same for me one day. I would like to make love to a white woman, although I'm sure she would not be as good as an Indian women."

Concern showed on Pierre's face. So, Miskoo was not joking when he wanted to trade for Françoise. He wanted to keep the Indian's friendship, but with no intention of doing so by offering Françoise as a piece of trade goods.

After a slow trip up the St. John River, they arrived at the English-built Fort Jemseg located at the juncture of the Jemseg and St. John rivers. Now, it was vacant as the English abandoned it, and Grandfontaine, due to a paucity of soldiers and officers, was unable to garrison it. So it lay abandoned and unoccupied; not even an Indian encampment was at the site.

Pierre examined the small fort located on a low-lying spit of land on the south shore of the Jemseg River a short distance from where it flowed into the mighty St. John. He could see that it would be easy to resurrect and use as a defense point far inland, even though it was poorly built.

The St. John River turned westward, and in two days they came upon a large Indian encampment, the Malecite village of Nashwaak where several bands congregated for the summer. They proved friendly, and Miskoo and his entourage were welcomed with feasting and festivity. Their language, although similar to Micmac, was different in many ways. As a result, Pierre understood them with great difficulty although Miskoo and his people seemed to have no trouble, but their peculiar way of speaking was the butt of many jokes when Miskoo's people returned to their own camp.

They spent two days with the Malecite before proceeding up the river. A short distance to the west, the river narrowed perceptibly, becoming more difficult to navigate, as the current became swift, with many rapids. Often they portaged around particularly difficult sections of the river, and Pierre despaired that the route would be an easy one for transportation and communication. As they traveled further westward, Miskoo talked more and more of the feared Iroquois who lived in that direction.

Two days later, they reached the height of land and made a long portage until they reached a stream that flowed north. This was Iroquois country, and now Miskoo traveled slowly and cautiously. At any moment they might run into an ambush and be annihilated. The Mohawk tribe was the master of the area; Miskoo was involved in several battles with them, thus he knew they were redoubtable warriors—fierce, tenacious, and cruel. He knew of their conquest of the Hurons; their expansionist policies were talked about at all the tribal councils of the east.

Pierre tried to assure Miskoo that the Iroquois would be no problem because Governor Courcelles concluded a peace with them; they were no longer at war with the French. None of his arguments satisfied Miskoo, and he and the rest of the party were uneasy. Several times, he tried to convince Pierre not to continue, as the river they were on grew broader and easier to navigate the further they proceeded downstream. Pierre insisted he must see for himself. He could see that the river flowed strong, and its bed was very rocky so he did not feel satisfied with Miskoo's assessment. As they paddled downstream, the river became more turbulent, rapids more common. In fact, they spent a great deal of time making portages around rapids that were difficult due to the heavy growth that lined the shores. Fortunately, at each portage many previous voyagers established a well-defined path.

Early one morning, as they were paddling down a quiet stretch of the river, Miskoo called softly to Pierre, "Turn toward shore. All is not right."

From the urgency in his voice, Pierre knew he must obey, and without a reply he headed the canoe toward the east bank. Miskoo paddled silently. The other canoes followed Miskoo's example. Once ashore, they quickly hauled the canoes into the thick underbrush that lined the shore.

Pierre whispered, "What is it, Miskoo. Why are we stopping and hiding?"

"All is not right, my friend. Did you not notice how quiet the birds were? We are not the only ones on the river."

Pierre paid not much attention to the animals and birds, but he knew that Miskoo and the other Indians were more attuned to nature than he was. "Who do you think is on the river?"

"I don't know, but I intend to find out before we go further."

They huddled in the deep underbrush, silent and unmoving. Soon the forest noises returned to normal—birds twittered, squirrels and chipmunks chattered, other small animals scurried about, and the insects buzzed. Pierre and the Indians gazed intently over the waters of the swift flowing stream; all seemed peaceful and in harmony.

Then Miskoo pointed to the far bank. Pierre followed his finger and saw a slight movement in the bushes on the far shore. He stared at the area where the bushes moved, expecting to see some large animal, perhaps a moose or a deer. But as he watched, two human figures slipped from the cover and looked at something on Pierre's side of the river. They were two Indians, dressed and painted for the warpath. "Who are they?" whispered Pierre.

"Mohawks!"

"Why are they looking this way?"

"I think they've been following us. They know we're here. I think they will try to capture us."

"Why? We're not at war with them."

"But we're in their territory, and anyone who comes into their country is an enemy."

"Maybe we should make our presence know and show them that we come in peace."

"No! You don't know the Iroquois. They kill first and ask questions after. Then it's too late. Pierre, we must leave this country. Now. We're not safe here. I won't take my people any further."

Pierre realized that this was not the time to argue. He was at Miskoo's mercy. He needed him to accomplish his mission. So he fell silent and watched the figures on the far shore.

Chapter Fifteen — A Child is Born

The late sunrise and the cold weather kept Pierre and Françoise abed. As they lay in each other's arms comfortable beneath the thick goose-down coverlet, they praised the Lord for their good fortune. The Christmas season was past, and the New Year festivities were over. 1671 was a fruitful year: the harvest bountiful, the trade with the colonists and Indians successful because Grandfontaine issued him a license, his pay for the report on his explorations.

He twisted onto his elbow toward Françoise and smiled at her. He kissed her gently on the nose and whispered, "Darling, how I love you. You get more beautiful each day. This country agrees with you."

She wrinkled her nose, and he knew he should not have made the last statement. Although she seldom complained anymore, he knew she did not accept Acadia as her home; she still longed to return to France, and, particularly, to Le Havre and her family.

He changed the subject. "My darling, I hope this year will be as successful as the last."

"I hope so too. Then maybe we will be able to make a trip to France and visit our families."

"That's always possible, my dear. If we're as prosperous this year as last, I will think of sending you to visit your family."

Her voice brightened. "Oh, would you? That would make me very happy."

"But that means I'd have to work for the governor again. I'm not too sure he was happy with my report on the route to Quebec. He was disappointed. He wasn't happy because I didn't make it to Quebec. Miskoo insisted we turn back once we met those Mohawks. He insisted we were in danger, but I still have my doubts. Anyway, I did find out that the best route was the one we took. The route back was more difficult and dangerous."

She snuggled against him. "I'm glad Miskoo was sensible and didn't take chances. You're home safe and sound."

He kissed her again, and she responded passionately. Their lovemaking was satisfying; they lay satiated and languorous, enjoying the post effects of their passion. Pierre dozed in a semi-stupor of contentment. Françoise cuddled against him, her head on his chest listening to the strong rhythm of his heartbeat, caressing and twisting the growth of masculine hair on his strongly muscled chest. The acuteness of the pain jerked him upright and awake. His gasp and cry caused Françoise to break into loud laughter as she sprang away from him. He made a wild grab for her and caught her by the upper right arm, pulling her roughly to him. He started to tickle her, and she struggled to avoid his moving fingers. After a few moments, she became helpless; he made her beg for forgiveness. She conceded defeat and searched again for his mouth with hers. "My darling, I love you so much," she whispered. "I've a secret for you."

He looked at her quizzically.

"Can you guess what it is?" she teased.

For a moment he thought she meant to tell him she was pregnant. Then he dismissed that as impossible. If she were pregnant, she would have told him sooner. After all, she had many chances during the past festive days. What could it be?

"If you tell me, it will no longer be a secret. I will tell everyone. I know," he teased, "you've a new lover."

She flailed at him with her clenched right fist. He grabbed it with his left hand and twisted her onto her back. Then he kissed her fiercely. "I will torture you until you tell me."

She struggled as he kissed her so long that she was breathless. She flung herself to one side, gasping for breath and she muttered, "You're cruel." Then she laughed. "Now I will never tell you my secret."

He grabbed her again. "I will kiss you until you're unconscious."

She squealed, "No, please, sir. I surrender. I will tell you my secret."

"What is it, my darling?"

"Remember, now, you must keep it a secret. You mustn't tell anyone."

"I promise," but she knew by the twinkle in his eye that she could not believe him.

"Marguerite is pregnant again. They're going to be parents again. She tells me she's due the last part of August. Isn't it a shame; she will be carrying during the worst part of the year during the hot summer month—but she's happy."

Pierre's disappointment showed in his face; for several moments he said nothing. Then he muttered slowly, "I'm happy for them. Maybe another child will be good for little Geneviève."

"I do hope so," said Françoise wistfully.

"It's not easy for them," Pierre mused sympathetically. "She's not a healthy baby. I hope this one will be strong and healthy…as I'm sure it will be."

"She's already nine months old and she's not sitting yet. Marguerite is very concerned about her. I try to reassure her by reminding her that the poor darling arrived early. Yet Marguerite knows she should be stronger than she is. It's a pity…since she's weak, she gets every cold or flu or disease that comes along. Twice I thought she'd die…once when she got a fever, and the next time when she had such a severe cough. But she's a fighter; she's got a heart."

Pierre nodded his head in assent, and then his face broke into a smile. "I tell you, Françoise, I will make love to you until you're pregnant again. It's our turn to have a child. You're strong. I'm strong. We will make a baby even if we spend the rest of our lives in bed."

She laughed. "We've spent too much time in bed already. Much work must be done, and we're not doing it."

"Come, we must work on making ourselves a child."

"No need, Pierre. We've already done that."

He stared at her for a moment, incredulous. "What are you trying to tell me?"

She looked at him coyly. "I'm trying to tell you another secret."

He stared at her. Then he became solemn. "Are you serious, my darling? Are you telling my you're with child?"

"Yes, darling. I'm expecting about the same time as Marguerite."

Pierre's whoop of joy startled her. Her eyes opened wide with shock; then she started to laugh. He grabbed her into his arms, and howling and laughing, he caressed her to demonstrate his happiness.

The next eight months passed slowly, or so it seemed to Pierre. He was solicitous and attentive to Françoise; he monitored the subtle changes in her body as the child developed within.

August 24, 1672 was a warm, pleasant day—tufts of clouds dotted the azure sky, and a light wind blew in from the Port Royal Basin rippling the surface of the bay and river. Pierre and Françoise were busy with the harvest, particularly the wild fruits that grew profusely along the banks of the Dauphin River and the streams that fed it. For the past days she picked berries along the creek that flowed through the west side of their property. When he could, Pierre joined her as she was heavy with child, and Pierre was concerned for her welfare. Her swollen stomach made her clumsy, and he feared she might fall and endanger the life of the child she carried. Although she insisted she was capable of looking after herself and the child, he tried, whenever he could, to accompany her on these berry-picking expeditions.

This Wednesday morning she planned to pick some serviceberries that grew abundantly along the high banks back from the water's edge. She watched these berries mature throughout the summer; she hoped to preserve some of them for the cold winter months, but she was especially eager to make some pies with the lush, juicy berries.

Immediately after breakfast, she turned to Pierre and announced, "Today I will have a surprise for supper."

Pierre glanced at her and smiled appreciatively. Ever since she became pregnant, her attitude changed. Not once did she complain about the country, not even in mid-summer when the humidity and heat were greatest, and the myriads of insects, particularly the mosquitoes, were the most bothersome.

"I know. You're going to pick more berries, and we will have a new dessert for supper."

She wrinkled her nose and grimaced good-naturedly. She filliped a stream of water toward him from the wooden bucket, which she was using to wash the heavy clay dishes that they used for breakfast. "You always know when I've a surprise," she grumbled jovially.

"Where are you going today?" Concern permeated his voice.

"Oh, not far. Just back along the ridge next to the creek. The blueberries are ready. And they're plentiful."

"Just as soon as I've finished the chores, I will join you. In the meantime, be careful. The land's rough with many snags and windfalls. Be careful not to trip. Your time's near. I wouldn't want anything to happen to my son." Although he smiled, his voice betrayed his real feelings.

He patted her rump as he passed by on his way to the daily chores of an Acadian farmer although the cows and goats were pastured on the thick grasses that grew in the tidewater meadows, he must feed the chickens and the two hogs he acquired. As well, he needed to milk the single cow that he kept separate from the others to provide them with milk, cream, and cheese. These chores occupied him for over a half-hour morning and evening.

As he milked the brown and white cow tied to a corner of the split-rail fence that kept the calves from their mothers when he weaned them, he watched Françoise waddle toward the uplands to the north. She carried a birch bark basket on her arm; he smiled as he watched her clumsy swaying gait. She wore a cloth sunbonnet to protect her from the strong rays of the sun.

Milk spurted into his wooden bucket with a satisfying swirl as each pulse of the stream, which he forced from the cow's udder, frothed into the pail. Pierre enjoyed these quiet moments in the early morning when he allowed his mind to wander over various aspects of his life.

This new country was good to Françoise and him. It was little over two years since they arrived; already they were well established. They owned a dozen chickens, two swine, and four heads of cattle—two cows and two calves, and one of the calves was a heifer that would help to increase his small herd, while the little bull would be castrated and allowed to grow to provide them with beef when he matured enough to be butchered. His building was comfortable; although Françoise insisted once the baby arrived, they would need more room. He would add a lean-to, or, preferably, he would build a new house. He was more concerned about the new barns and sheds for the animals. The winters could be severe, and the animals required more shelter than they now had.

A shout from the river startled him from his musings. It was his friend Jacques.

"Hello. I'm over here."

Jacques came up the path quickly.

"Is Françoise about, Pierre? Marguerite's time has come. She'd like Françoise to assist her." Jacques looked agitated.

Pierre understood the concern in Jacques's voice. Their first child, Geneviève, was a tiny, sickly child who required much care, who, on several occasions, nearly died from the various diseases that she seemed prone to. "She's back on the ridge picking blueberries…you know, the tall ones. If you will go for her, I will finish the chores and go with you."

Without a word, Jacques turned in the direction Françoise took just minutes before, and, almost running, he shouted as he went. His bass voice reverberated over the landscape as he called her name.

Pierre frowned; would he be as nervous when it came time for his child to be born. The prospect of an heir and more hands to help on the farm, his trading activities, and other ventures pleased him. He wanted a son, but he knew Françoise was hoping for a daughter as a companion and helper. In this land, many hands meant light work, and everyone contributed a share to the family welfare. Since the government, the companies, and the seigneurs did not encourage immigration, it was up to the settlers themselves to provide for the growth and expansion of the colony. Many children were desirable, even necessary. Well, Jacques and Marguerite were doing their share; this was their second child.

Pierre could still hear Jacques's deep voice shouting for Françoise. Even at this distance, he could hear the urgency in Jacques's voice.

Within the hour they were at Jacques's house. This time the birth was uneventful and quick. The only thing to mar the event was Jacques's disappointment that it was another daughter. Unlike the first child, who was brown-haired and delicate, the new child, Angelique Louise, was blonde and robust. Her first cries were shrill and lusty. Jacques and Pierre, who awaited the arrival in the cozy kitchen, looked at each other and smiled.

"That one has a pair of strong lungs," Pierre chortled.

Françoise called from the bedroom. "Come, Jacques, come and see your new daughter."

Pierre saw the disappointed look that crossed Jacques's face, but it was only momentary; then it broke into a relieved and satisfied smile.

"I'm coming," he roared, and quickly crossed the room to the parturient chamber. Françoise stepped back from the bed as Jacques knelt beside it and drew Marguerite's hand into his own. "My darling, how are you? You look so much better than you did for Geneviève."

She smiled wanly as she lifted the cotton blanket that swaddled the small bundle making luscious sounds at her breast.

Jacques grinned. "My, she surely a hungry one. Look how strong she is."

Already her tiny hand was grasping at Marguerite's firm and swollen breast. The tiny head was still dark from the moisture of birth, but even so, it was apparent the slight fuzz was light in color.

"I think she will be blonde…just like my mother. She has light hair."

"Well, no matter, Jacques. She's strong and healthy." Marguerite glanced toward the tiny bed that stood in the far corner of the room where Geneviève slept peacefully. She could walk, but she was a quiet child who still slept much of the day. At that moment, she awakened and began to fuss and whimper.

"Jacques, please see what's the matter with Geneviève." Her voice was tender.

"Never mind, Jacques," Françoise interposed, "I will tend to her." She moved to the child and took her in her arms. The child stopped mewling immediately and clung to Françoise. Françoise patted her dark head and soothed her, crooning softly. "See, Geneviève, you've a new little sister. You will have someone to play with and to keep you company. She's a sweet little girl. Do you want to see her?"

The child understood, shook her head affirmatively, but did not smile. Françoise drew her close. What a contrast in the two children! The newborn was almost as big as the tiny creature she held in her arms, and already the newborn was assertive and demanding. Did that give an indication of their future characters? Françoise wondered.

She drew near the maternity bed, and Marguerite pushed back the coverlet to let the older child see her new sister. "See, Geneviève, you've a new baby sister. See how tiny she is. We will have to take care of her until she's big enough to play with you." She smiled up at her firstborn, and a glow of love glistened from her eyes.

Françoise noticed it and whispered to herself, "There's nothing like one's first child."

The sun was low in the west when Pierre and Françoise paddled their way slowly down the river toward their home. Françoise paddled languidly as Pierre's powerful strokes propelled the birch bark canoe swiftly over the quiet waters of the static river—the swift current and the tidal bore negated their opposing forces; the river was currentless like a lake.

Françoise thought of the surprise dessert she promised Pierre that morning. Her plans were disrupted; she did not picked a single berry. Her promise would have to wait till the morrow. The sun, low in the cloudless sky, promised a pleasant day. She half twisted as she knelt in the bow, and she said to Pierre, "I'm sorry I couldn't keep my promise."

Pierre was perplexed. "What promise?"

As Françoise turned to resume paddling, a sharp pain seized her; she grimaced and winced. She stopped the paddle in mid-air and remained frozen and still.

"What's the matter?" His voice was urgent and concerned.

The pain caught Françoise's breath; she struggled to reply. "I think it's my turn."

"Oh, my!"

As he thrust the paddle into the turgid waters with increased vigor, he thought, Whom will I get to help Françoise? I need someone to aid her in her accouchement. But first, he must get her home.

"Put the paddle aside, Françoise. Don't strain yourself. We're nearly home."

The pain subsided, and she felt relieved and comfortable, but she decided Pierre was right. She would not be careless; Pierre was capable of bringing the canoe swiftly to the landing. She placed the dripping paddle behind her in the bottom of the canoe and leaned back on her legs. The kneeling position seemed acceptable if not comfortable. She doubled over as the cramp stiffened every muscle of her lower body, even those of her legs. She grimaced from the intensity of the pain, and she could feel tiny beads of perspiration ooze along her upper lip and forehead. Her hands gripped the gunwales; her head slumped forward; the cords of tendons along her neck were taut and prominent.

Pierre watched her stiffen; deep furrows of worry lined his forehead. "Are you all right?" The anxiety in his voice unhidden.

She struggled with the pain, trying to relax. "Yes," she mumbled, but the tension and tremor in her voice belied her words.

Pierre's powerful strokes brought the canoe to the entrance of the stream leading to his landing. Silently he pulled the paddle as he hurried to bring them home. As he maneuvered the canoe to shore, he saw Miskoo's canoe drawn up on the beach.

What a time to come trading! He would have to convince Miskoo to come back at a more appropriate time. He was too busy now. First, he must get Françoise to bed and then to get the fire going to heat water; then he would have to locate one of the midwives of the colony. Several were competent and efficient. He knew Françoise hoped Marguerite would aid her as she helped Marguerite, but neither planned their times together. Who would he get? He would discuss that with Françoise.

Carefully he brought the canoe to shore; he nosed the prow gently to the small beach that he developed especially for the ubiquitous canoes that provided the main transport on the river and its streams.

Again he studied the canoe on the beach; the symbol on the bow identified it as Miskoo's. The late afternoon quiet was broken by the gentle lapping of the now rising tide. As he steadied the canoe with his paddle, he called to Françoise, "Are you able to get out?"

"I'm fine now. The pain has subsided; I'm fine." She clung to the gunwales as she gingerly lifted herself to an almost upright position. She steadied herself and tested her strength. The pain disappeared, and only a slight stiffness and a lightness of her head remained.

She paused to clear her head, and then slowly lifted her left leg over the side of the canoe. Nausea and dizziness swept over her, the world whirled in a maelstrom, and darkness engulfed her. She could feel herself falling; then the world disappeared in blackness.

A whirling fog whisked her to consciousness. She seemed to be twirling like the vanes of a windmill, and her mind drifted in and out of the gray mist that absorbed her. Consciously, she strove to bring her body and mind into the reality of the world; slowly her efforts were successful. She could hear the muted sounds about her: the hiss of a sputtering candle, the crackle of wood burning, the gurgle of water being poured, and the rustle of garment as someone moved about.

An involuntary contraction of the muscles within her body made her cry out sharply. She squeezed her eyes tightly to alleviate the agony and to stop the hot tears that tried to course down her cheeks. She noticed her cheeks were wet, other tears already found their way down. She licked her hot, feverish lips and the saltiness of stale tears tainted her tongue. She arched her back trying to hold back the pain that roiled through her lower abdomen along her sides to her waist and then around to her lower back. She held herself stiffly, and slowly, very slowly, her taut muscles relaxed.

She tried to open her eyes, but the effort was too much, and she crumpled into a quivering heap. The pain passed; her body seemed weak and jelly-like; the muscles quivered without strength. She shivered, and the tears streamed uninterrupted down her flushed cheeks.

She felt coolness on her forehead and cheeks. The roughness of the damp cloth felt soothing. The crooning of the soft, sibilant voice quieted her jangled nerves, and the quivering subsided as a gentle hand smoothed the damp wisps of dark brown hair that clung limply to her smooth, broad forehead. She moaned in unison to the low chanting song.

The strange sounds startled her; her eyes popped open. The black hair and brown skin of the face smiling into hers surprised her, opening her eyes wide with fear. Where was she? Who was this Indian woman? Why was she here? A thousand questions burst into her mind, but she could not answer a single one.

Slowly her eyes focused, and she looked about her. The familiarity of her own home reassured her, but the stranger frightened her. Before she could move or say a word, another jolt of pain rocked her body, and again she could feel herself spinning into the black abyss that robbed her of time and space. She fought frantically to maintain her lucidity, thrashing and tossing about. She felt strong hands restrain her, and a soft voice soothe her. She quieted and felt waves of hot and cold sweep over her body; perspiration soaked her, and she realized she was naked. The discovery shocked her, and she tried to curl into a tight ball to hide her nudity. The largeness of her stomach prevented her from curling into the fetal position; she writhed and groaned in agony—mental and physical.

Gentle hands stroked her body and turned her onto her back; then her legs were drawn up and spread apart; her lower body felt bloated, distended; she lay back exhausted and weary.

A knife-like pain, excruciating and piercing, stabbed at her genitals, forcing her to cry out, and a swishing sound like the gurgling of a noisy stream emanated from her lower body. Her body spewed forth.

Her abdomen collapsed, and she lapsed into a void. The darkness lasted she knew not how long; although it seemed hours, it was only minutes. She felt a damp, slippery, glutinous object on her belly, warm and vibrant, and a feeling of joy invigorated and enlivened her, and her senses responded. She produced a child. She wanted to grab it and clasp it to her breast— to possess it and cling to it as part of her body. It came from within her; it would always be part of her, close and linked as it was now by a moving and pulsing umbilical cord. She tried to rise, to take the child in her arms, but as she did so, the strange woman who was tending to her and the child, forced her back onto the mattress.

The child, lying across her, face down, wriggled and squirmed, and a strong, vigorous cry erupted from its lips. The sound entered her mind, and the urgency of its appeal made her breasts overflow: milk seeped slowly from her engorged nipples. She stared at the busy dark-skinned woman and whispered, "Please give me my baby."

The woman glanced at her, smiled, and turned back to the job at hand. Françoise saw the flash of a knife-blade; a cry of fear escaped her lips. The woman was cutting the cord that connected her to the life on her stomach. The separation struck her, and she mouthed a pray. "Dear Lord, keep this child safe. Make him your worthy servant and a joy to Pierre and me."

But was it a boy! She did not know. Finally the child was wiped dry, its cries continuing as the Indian midwife prepared it for the mother's breast. She handed the child to Françoise who lifted it to determine its sex. She gave a cry of joy. "Pierre will be happy!" She drew the boy to her waiting breast where it snuggled comfortably and pulled vigorously. The stimulation elated her; she moaned softly and ecstatically.

The young Indian woman cleaned the small room, replacing the soiled bedding with other coverlets and blankets that Françoise prepared for the occasion. Once Françoise and the child were comfortable, she slipped out. Pierre's joyful whoop roused her from her lethargy; she smiled weakly, but animatedly as he entered the room. It was apparent that he already knew he was the father of a robust, healthy son. His eyes shone, and his face beamed as he approached the bed. He threw his arms around both and kissed her tenderly; then he looked at his new son.

Françoise murmured, "Be careful, Pierre, he's still small and delicate, but he will grow into a strong man."

Pierre lifted the cover and looked with sparkling eyes at the firm, strong body of his child. To him, it was the most beautiful baby he ever saw. The child's body glowed pinkly, his head covered with a thin mat of dark brown hair. Even now his limbs were sturdy. Pierre's chest puffed with pride and love. "May I hold him?" he pleaded.

"You must wait. He hasn't finished feeding. Be patient."

"I'm sorry, my darling, but I'm excited. It's not every day that a man becomes a father for the first time. And has a son!" He could not contain his joy.

In the hours that followed, Françoise marveled at her son. Her strength returned, and the child suckled and slept; seldom did he fuss or cry. Françoise remained abed, and time became unimportant as Pierre ministered to her needs.

The following morning, Pierre threw open the shutters, allowing the sunshine to filter into the room. Although the brightness cheered her, she felt a lassitude she could not explain. As well, her mouth was dry and thick, and she did not feel hungry as she thought she should. Pierre prepared her favorite morning meal—boiled oats with lumps of maple sugar scattered atop, and the whole smothered in rich, golden cream; small hot rolls dripping with saffron butter; and a bowl of warm goat's milk. The smell of the food nauseated her, and she retched. Her empty stomach had nothing to expel so only a spasm of pain went from her midriff to her lower body; she coughed, and it pained her more than the strain of vomiting.

Pierre smiled at her apprehensively and quickly removed the offending food. "I hope it's not my cooking, darling."

She tried to smile, but the effort was too much, and she fell back onto the pillow as waves of dizziness and nausea pulsed through her body. Pierre set the tray on the crude table, and then came slowly to the bed. He sat on the edge and took her left hand in his; it was hot and dry. He touched her forehead with his right hand; it was also hot and dry; it felt rough, almost scaly. Weakly, Françoise opened her eyes; they were dull and listless. Concern furrowed his brow. "Are you all right, my love?"

Françoise did not move, but her eyes closed slowly, and she seemed asleep.

Pierre's hand went to her cheek, which was ruddy and fiery. Slowly he slid his hand to her neck and then to her breasts; her whole body was burning with fever.

In fear, he reached across to the child that lay beside her. Slowly he pulled aside the coverlet and gazed at the sleeping child, its breathing regular and strong. His rough, work-callused hand gently touched the smooth forehead and tender cheeks. The child's skin was cool and velvet to his touch. He gazed at the sleeping infant; a rush of emotion filled him. Oh, what a beautiful child! he thought.

Françoise moaned, and her lips moved, but no sound came from them.

Pierre covered the child and bent over the feverish woman. "What did you say, darling?"

Her lips moved again; he bent low to catch the words. "Water, water," she whispered.

Pierre moved quickly to bring a bowl of water from the table. He raised her head carefully and touched the edge of the bowl to her cracked lips. He tipped the bowl slightly, trickling water into her mouth. Some of the water dribbled past her lips while some dripped along the side of the bowl, along her chin, onto her bosom. He gazed at his wife, frightened, wondering what to do.

Neremoosin, Miskoo's young wife, helped with the birth, but now they returned to their camp. Maybe she would know how to deal with the sickness that now plagued Françoise. Pierre knew that such fever was common at the birth of a child, and if not treated, the mother and, often, the child succumbed to it. If a wet nurse could not be found then the child would have to be fed cow or goat's milk. Some babies adapted to the new diet while others did not and wasted away.

What should he do? He knew he must to take the child away before it got the fever that was ravaging Françoise. Where would he take the child?

A thought struck him. Marguerite had a new child; maybe she would be able to suckle both. He knew she was a robust woman with ample breasts. Now, if only those breasts could produce enough milk for two, then maybe he his problem was solved.

Maybe he could persuade Neremoosin to return and take care of Françoise. First, he would take the child to Marguerite, and then he would go to the Indian camp on the Orignal River. He would leave Françoise alone; nothing else could he do. He would place water within her reach; he would try to make her as comfortable as possible. He hoped she would be all right while he was gone.

Chapter Sixteen — Adoption

With the child well wrapped in heavy woolen blankets, Pierre left the house and trudged down the path to his beached canoe. As he approached the landing place, he was surprised to see Miskoo and his two young wives drawing to shore in their canoe. Miskoo waved a greeting, and as his wives beached the canoe, he hurried to meet Pierre. Pierre lifted his hand in greeting and waited to hear what errand brought Miskoo to his home. As usual Miskoo spoke in a mixture of French and Micmac, although Pierre was quite proficient in the Micmac tongue. "The child is well?" he inquired.

Pierre answered in Micmac. "Yes, Miskoo, the child is well, but my wife is very ill. I was about to go to your camp to ask Neremoosin to care for Françoise. She has the fever."

Neremoosin and Debitkat Iskisy beached the canoe and retrieved the cradleboards that contained their infant sons of the early spring. The wives delivered within days of each other—Neremoosin's child was born on April 10 while Debitkat Iskisy's was born on April 14. Both children were strong and healthy; Miskoo was proud of them. The older was called Wazoo, meaning yellow, as he turned yellow from jaundice shortly after birth, while the other was called Miskuy, meaning red, because he was a bright red color at birth.

Both women slung the cradleboards to their backs and adjusted, almost simultaneously, the decorated headbands on their foreheads. They smiled a greeting to Pierre; he returned it with a smile and grunt. Then in a few words, he explained the situation.

Furrows of concern creased their brows. Miskoo raised his hand. "We will help, my friend. My wives know of medicine that will cure the fever. My wives will be able to feed the child; they have plenty of milk."

Pierre tried to remonstrate, but Miskoo stopped him before he could say a word. He stepped past Pierre and beckoned his wives forward. Pierre shrugged and followed the three Indians as they hurried toward the house.

Maybe their plan was better. He was not sure he liked the idea of his son being nourished by a native woman, but he decided her milk would be as good as any other woman's milk. After all, the color of the cow did not have much to do with the quality of the milk. He was pleased that his Indian friend was so generous, but he wondered what Miskoo would expect in return. Although, by nature, the Indian was a generous person, his prestige was related to that generosity. He hoped that Miskoo considered the present situation one of need, and not one that required a favor for a favor.

Once inside the small back room, which served as their home, Neremoosin propped the cradleboard against the north wall, and then she moved to the bed along the south wall where Françoise lay pale and still. She examined the shallow breathing woman, and then she signaled to Pierre that she wanted a basin of water and a cloth.

The child in his arms started to cry loudly. The other woman,

Debitkat Iskisy, set her cradleboard beside that of her twin sister and moved toward Pierre. She took the bundle from his arms, moved back beside the propped cradleboards, squatted on the floor, drew her right breast through the opening of her doeskin gown, opened the blanket that covered the child, and with her left hand, steered the dark brown nipple toward the mewling child's mouth. The child wriggled his head, searching, found the warm protuberance, and started sucking contentedly.

Miskoo looked at Pierre and laughed quietly. "The child was hungry," he stated. "He likes Micmac milk."

Pierre noticed the breast was large and full. The woman seemed to have an ample supply of milk. The child's hunger would be assuaged for the moment, but how would he feed the child in the future?

Miskoo watched the white child. The child's whiteness was stark against the woman's tawny skin. His tow hair glinted in the sunlight that entered through the unshuttered window as a sunbeam played on the squatted woman and her sucking charge. The tiny lips worked furiously as they drew milk from the tawny breast; slurping sounds and a slight dribble of liquid escaped from the tiny mouth sending a moist rivulet over the curving pap. Miskoo looked at Pierre. "He's a beautiful child…strong. His hair is like the morning sunrise…golden and silky. His cheeks are like the evening sunset…pink and white. He is beautiful."

Pierre's chest rose. He was so busy he was unable to admire his son. But as he listened to Miskoo extol his beauty, he looked at him with new appreciation. It was seldom that the Indians indicated the white man was their equal, let alone attractive. They usually found the white man inferior to them, not only in looks and physique, but also in intelligence and knowledge. That made Miskoo's remarks more satisfying.

Neremoosin spoke sharply. She was still waiting for the water and cloth. Pierre hastened to do her bidding. Once she had the water, she whipped back the covering and started to bathe the feverish woman from head to foot. Pierre was shocked that his wife was stripped naked before the group; he knew Françoise, if she could, would do her best to hide her nakedness; in her present state she moaned and groaned but did not resist the ministrations of the Indian woman.

Pierre watched fascinated as the Indian woman bathed her face and forehead with the cool water. Then she bathed her bosom and her soft stomach. Slowly she allowed the cooling water to moisten the sick woman's loins and legs. As she worked, Françoise quieted and became calm. Her moans changed to whispered whimpers, and she fell into a restless sleep.

Neremoosin covered Françoise with a light cotton sheet, and then she sat beside the bed crooning softly. By this time, the child in Debitkat Iskisy's arms was replete and sleeping peacefully.

Miskoo took Pierre by the arm and led him through the outer room outside. The sun shone brightly, and the world seemed pleased that it was high summer. Birds were flocking, practicing their flights, preparing for the long migration ahead. Already, an occasional leaf turned its fall color and fell to the ground, and the grasses, although still green, slowed their luxurious growth of early summer. Water and sea birds squawked and cackled from their chosen areas on the streams and river. Pierre and Miskoo listened to the stirrings of nature; then Miskoo put his hand on Pierre's shoulder. "My friend, I will leave Neremoosin to care for your wife, and I will take your son with me. Debitkat Iskisy will care for him. She has ample for both our sons."

The idea startled Pierre. He did not want his son to leave him. He appreciated the generosity of the Indian chief, and he was grateful for his offer, but he did not like the idea of his son going to Miskoo's camp. He wanted to keep his son at home. "I thank you for your help, but, Miskoo, I can't let my son leave home. He must stay with his mother. I'm sure his presence will help Françoise to regain her health quicker. I will get my friend, Marguerite, to feed him."

"He will be safe with me, Pierre. I will treat him like my own son."

Pierre was apprehensive. He knew adoption was a common practice with the Indians—of children and even adults. If he allowed his son to go to Miskoo's camp, he might have difficulty getting him back. Miskoo might claim him as his own. If he took a fancy to the child, it was not unlikely he would want to adopt him. Already he indicated he thought the child was beautiful. He stared at Miskoo, trying to fathom his mind. "I know you will treat him well, Miskoo, but I can't let him go. He's too precious to me and Françoise. We'd be too lonely and sad if he was missing from our lodge."

"But, Pierre, your wife can't care for him or feed him. She's too ill." Miskoo's voice hardened and his brow knitted. His eyes sparkled brightly.

Pierre perceived that Miskoo was becoming angry. As a chief, his wishes were usually fulfilled. Miskoo's anger intensified Pierre's resolve. He must keep his son with him; he could not allow Miskoo to take him. "My son must stay with me." Pierre's voice was hard and brittle. He tried to contain his anger, but he would not let Miskoo persuade him to do something he did not want to do.

Miskoo's face scowled. "I see you do not trust me, your friend. I want to help you, and you will not let…"

Pierre interrupted him. "You can help me, Miskoo, as you've already done. Let Neremoosin stay at my lodge, and care for my wife and son."

"No, that can't be, Pierre. She does not have enough milk for her son and your son. Only Debitkat Iskisy has enough, and only Neremoosin has the knowledge to cure your wife. So you see, it's necessary to take your son with me. I can't leave both my wives with you. I need one in my lodge."

Pierre was not sure he believed Miskoo. Neremoosin appeared as strong and bosomy as Debitkat Iskisy; she could probably provide milk for her son and his, but was no way could he be sure. He felt Miskoo was trying to deceive him. "My son must stay with me, Miskoo."

"I like your son. He is like the morning sun, bright and pleasing. I would like him for my own. I will give you one of my sons for yours. And many furs as well."

Now it was out in the open. Now Pierre knew why Miskoo was so eager to have his son accompany him to the Indian camp. Pierre had a dilemma; he did not want to lose the chief's friendship, but neither did he want to lose his son. He knew Miskoo could be adamant. What was he to do?

"You're my friend, Miskoo, and we can share many things, but I can't let you have my son. He's my most treasured possession, along with my wife."

"But I will give you one of my sons. Do you not think that an Indian son is not worth a white son? I tell you, Pierre, an Indian child is worth two white sons."

"That may be true, my friend. But your son is not the product of my loin. My son is."

"That's of little consequence, Pierre. The product of one's loins can be many. Many women are willing and capable, both white and Indian, and a man can produce many children. I will give you any one of my women as well. Then you can produce more from your loin."

Pierre detected that any argument he put forth would be specious. The Indian mind did not work the same as the French mind. They did not believe in the same doctrine or religion as the white man even though they might be Christian.

"No, Miskoo, you can't have my son, and I don't want your son, or your woman. I've a son and a woman; I will keep them."

Miskoo's eyes glittered, but nothing else about his face changed. "Then I will leave. I will leave Neremoosin to care for Françoise, but Debitkat Iskisy must come with me. I will return tomorrow to see how your wife is. Maybe you will change your mind."

Pierre was astonished that he would leave Neremoosin, but he was grateful. Perhaps he was not as angry as his eyes indicated. Yet Pierre was worried. He was sure Miskoo would not give in that easily.

Without another word to Pierre, he called to his wives with instructions and turned down the path to the beach. Pierre stood looking after him apprehensively. Had he insulted the Indian to the extent that he lost his friendship? He hoped not. The Micmac was important to Pierre. His influence with the other Indians made it possible for Pierre to carry on a lively trade. Pierre supplied them with goods that he obtained from Boston, and they supplied him with furs, canoes, and snowshoes. This spring his storehouse was full; he made a tidy profit once he disposed of it to his man in Boston. He hoped he could somehow appease Miskoo.

As these thoughts flitted through his mind, Debitkat Iskisy, with her cradleboard on her back, hurried through the door, and without a backward glance, she followed after the striding Miskoo.

Neremoosin and her son remained behind. Pierre, after he realized he could do little, decided he would inform Jacques and Marguerite of the birth of his son.

As he drew his canoe onto the bank before Jacques's log house, he heard Jacques shout, “Welcome, Pierre. What brings you here?”

Pierre smiled. His friend was in a cheery mood. All must be well with Marguerite and the new child. “Good news…and bad,” he returned.

As Jacques joined him and said, “Give me the good news first.”

“I'm the father of a wonderful son!”

Jacques grasped his hand firmly, shook it vigorously, and threw his arm across Pierre's shoulders as he steered him up the path to the house. “Congratulations, my friend. I'm happy for you.”

Pierre noticed a wistful sound in his voice. He knew how badly Jacques wanted a son. “Jacques, that's the good news. The bad news is Françoise is very sick with the fever. She's so ill she can't feed the child.”

A sad look came over Jacques face. “That's too bad. Can Marguerite and I help? Maybe Marguerite can look after the little one until Françoise's strong again. This time, the child and she are very well, and she has enough milk for two children.”

Pierre stopped and gazed into his friend's face. Jacques's concerned expression touched him, and he drew the other into his arms. “My friend, I thank you. Your generosity touches me.”

Jacques shrugged his shoulders. “That's what friends are for—to help each other.”

“Let's tell Marguerite. Let's see what she has to say about that.” Pierre grinned at his friend.

Marguerite was as enthusiastic about the news as Jacques was. Although it was only the third day since the birth of their second daughter, whom they named Angelique Louise—because Jacques said she looked like a little angel—Marguerite was already up and about. She said she felt a little weak, but she was strong enough to do her household chores since the children were so pacific.

As she went about her chores, Pierre elaborated on the situation at home. “Françoise is very ill. Her fever's high, and she sleeps most of the time. It's the birth fever, I think. At least, that's what Miskoo's wife, Neremoosin, says. I was about to bring Louis Joseph here when Miskoo arrived with his two wives. Do you know them?

Both nodded negatively. Pierre was certain they did not know the Indian women although he was sure Jacques met the chief on several occasions when he came to visit or trade with Pierre. “He has two young wives, twin sisters. Both gave birth to sons in April, within days of each other. Miskoo insisted he and his wives would care for Françoise and little Louis. I was unsure, but I gave in, and now Neremoosin is with Françoise and the child. Miskoo wanted to take Louis to his camp; I couldn't agree to that. I fear Miskoo wants to adopt my son. His light hair and complexion captivate him. I'm worried because he seemed angry when I refused to let the baby go with him. But, he did leave, and he allowed Neremoosin to stay behind."

Jacques and Marguerite were silent. Pierre knew they did not approve of his relationship with the Indians. Pierre was friendly with them, but his friends avoided them. They were afraid of them and considered their ways savage and barbaric. Pierre tried to explain that the nature of their culture and lifestyle made them behave the way they did. No matter how Pierre argued, they would not accept the Indians.

"I can't stay long. I wanted to let you know of my good fortune, and I wanted to let you know Françoise isn't well."

Upon his return home, he found the situation little changed. Françoise slept restlessly, her fever still high. After he felt her forehead, he turned to the child. Neremoosin placed him at the foot of the bed where he slept peacefully wrapped in his knitted coverlet. Neremoosin squatted on the floor next to the cradleboard holding her son. Her child also slept peacefully. Pierre studied the ruddy complexion and the mass of straight black hair that covered his head; the child looked sturdy and healthy. Pierre knew the child was born in the spring, and he marveled at the growth that took place in the elapsed four or five months. He hoped his son would be as big when he was the same age. Neremoosin's milk supply must be abundant to produce such a sturdy child.

Because the events of the day took their toll, Pierre retired early. He, like Neremoosin, sprawled on the floor, a light blanket covering him, and within minutes he slept deeply.

The crowing of the cock from his small flock of chickens awakened him; he lifted himself to one elbow, disoriented for a moment, then he discerned where he was. The room was very quiet. In the gloom, he made out the supine form of Neremoosin as she slept along the north wall. Only subdued sounds of breathing broke the stillness.

The quiet startled him. Was Françoise still breathing? Fear gripped him. Was she all right? The thought awakened him completely, and he leaped to his feet. His sudden movement awakened Neremoosin; she whispered, "What is it?"

Without replying, he hurried to the bed. In the grayness of the dawn light, he searched for his wife. His hand grasped hers; the fiery heat made him gasp. At least she was still alive. The fever was still with her. He bent forward, listening to her breathing. It was shallow, but strong. He sighed with relief. Although she did not seem improved, her condition had not deteriorated. He touched her forehead. It was hot and dry. She moved her head and groaned audibly.

He whispered, "My darling, how are you?"

She whispered hoarsely, "Please bring me some water. I'm thirsty."

He patted her cheek; she squeezed his hand. "Where's my baby?"

He looked to the foot of the bed where the baby was placed; he saw no bundle. Fear rose like a tidal wave. His heartbeat quickened, and a band like a vise squeezed at his chest. What happened to the child? He felt with both hands, but nothing. The child was gone. He turned to Neremoosin who rose and stood cowering against the wall. "Where's the child?" he shouted.

The woman raised her hands to protect herself and mumbled almost incoherently, "Miskoo has taken him."

The sun was rising over the eastern horizon as Pierre strode into the center of Miskoo's camp. His fury abated somewhat, but his breathing was still quick and deep—some from the exertions of paddling the several leagues from his home to the Indian camp. He was still affronted by the actions of his friend. During the dead of night, Miskoo stole into his house, and, with Neremoosin's help—she unbarred the door—he took Louis Joseph and left his second son, Debitkat Iskisy's child, in his place. The more he thought of it, the angrier he became.

Although Miskoo's camp was a small one, he knew if he used force, he would be at a disadvantage. His single musket against the combined weapons of the camp would be futile. He doubted that no more than two muskets were in the camp, but he knew several bows and arrows, and, worse, many tomahawks—metal, as well as stone—were the favorite weapons and at close quarters, they were devastating. The more he thought of the situation, the more he knew he must be calm and reasonable. He could not let his emotions take control, or he would worsen the situation.

He stopped before Miskoo's hide-covered wigwam, and for several seconds he sucked in his breath in great gulps. He cradled the musket in his left arm, then cried out, "Miskoo, my friend, I want to speak to you."

He heard stirrings from several other hide and bark covered abodes. No sound emitted from the lodge before him. Was Miskoo ignoring him? He was sure Miskoo was inside. He waited several seconds, and then he shouted again, "Miskoo, it's me, Pierre. I've come for my son. I know you have him. I want him!"

He heard a baby cry from within. It must be his son. "I know you're inside, Miskoo. You're my friend, but you've not treated me as a friend. You've stolen my property. I want it back."

Pierre waited impatiently. What would he do if Miskoo refused to talk to him? Would he enter the lodge and take the child? Should he dare the enmity of this Micmac chief to get his child back? What should he do?

He was angry, and his frustration made him grit his teeth and curse under his breath. How could his friend invade his home and steal his son?

He hefted the musket and transferred it to his right hand. It was loaded and ready to fire. At least he would kill Miskoo before the remainder of the camp got him. His rage subsided, and he stepped to the entrance of the wigwam.

Several curious braves came from their lodges and encircled Pierre.

He glanced around. Although the faces were not hostile, neither were they welcoming. He saw that most were armed with weapons in their hands or on their person. The situation did not favor him. He turned back to the closed doorway to Miskoo's lodge.

Again he shouted, "Miskoo, it's me, your friend, Pierre. I know you've something that belongs to me. I want it back. Come out. I want to talk to you."

All was quiet. No movement, not even among the gathered Indians who now included several women and a large number of children, transpired. They waited silently and stoically, assessing carefully the attitude of this white man who trespassed into their camp.

Someone stirred in the lodge, and the rawhide door was pushed aside. Debitkat Iskisy stepped through the opening and came forward. "You have my son, white man. That's a fair trade. My son is strong. He's no longer a baby; he's a little man. Your son is weak and young; it's not certain he will live."

Apprehension flashed across Pierre's face. It did not go unnoticed. The young woman smiled and hurried on, "He's well. He's not sick. For so young a child, he's strong and handsome. My son is older, bigger. The white child is young and untried."

Pierre heaved a sigh of relief. At least the child was well; he was without his mother's fever. "I don't want to talk to a woman. This is a man's problem. I will speak only to Miskoo."

"Miskoo is not to be disturbed; he still sleeps. He will not talk to you now. You must wait until he awakes."

Pierre could feel the heat rising to his face. He clenched his fists, and the muscles along his jaws and cheeks quivered with tension. He breathed deeply, trying to control his emotions. Foolish anger would not solve his problem; he must keep his wits about him. "No, I must see Miskoo now. If you don't awaken him, I will."

He took a step forward. Debitkat Iskisy raised her hands and placed them on his chest to restrain him. She did not push; she barred his way. He saw the determination in her dark brown eyes raised to his.

"I will speak to Miskoo." She turned and entered the lodge, letting the skin door fall into place over the opening.

Several sounds came from the dwelling: the soft, mewing cries of a child, the muted whispers of a female voice, and the guttural grunts of a disturbed male. Pierre stood helpless before the flimsy shelter assessing the situation. How would he persuade the warrior to return his son? The situation seemed hopeless.

After several minutes, the covering was flung open, and Miskoo stepped through the opening. He was dressed in an undecorated doeskin loincloth and low moccasins. His bronze body gleamed, as if oiled, which Pierre surmised was the case. His shining black hair was parted in the middle, and two braids, unadorned, hung down onto his chest. He stepped in front of Pierre, raised his right hand in greeting, and said stentorously, "Welcome, my friend Pierre, to my camp. I am sorry that I was not prepared to greet you in a more hospitable manner, but I did not know that you would be coming to visit." He smiled sardonically. "Sit. We will talk."

He sat down cross-legged before Pierre. Pierre squatted, facing him. A shuffle whispered as the other inhabitants of the camp moved to form a circle around them. Pierre stared into the black eyes of the Indian whom he thought was his friend. His vulnerability struck him once more—the vulnerability of all the white men in this country. They were here at the pleasure of the natives. If, for some reason, the Indians decided they no longer wanted the white men as neighbors and visitors, they could easily force the white men to leave. His situation was typical of the colony—surrounded and overwhelmed by numbers.

Miskoo did not invite Pierre into his lodge; he did not bring out the calumet, the traditional pipe that was smoked whenever the Indian negotiated important issues. Miskoo did not feel that the kidnapping of a child was important enough to warrant this nicety. It was not as important as trade in furs, fish, or meat.

They stared into each other's eyes as if trying to fathom their intent and resolve. Finally, Pierre could restrain himself no longer. "Miskoo, you've stolen my son. I want him back."

"Pierre, Miskoo does not steal. He takes what he needs for his fulfillment. He is fair; he replaces what he takes with equal value."

Pierre found it difficult to understand the nature of the Indian mind. Somehow he must make this chief recognize that the Indian value system was counter to his own, and that the son he loved so dearly must be returned. "That's true, my friend, but I don't want your son; I want my own son. He belongs to me; he's the fruit of my loins; he's part of his mother's body. She loves the child and needs him."

"A woman can produce other children. She can learn to love any child. Your woman will learn to love Miskuy, Debitkat Iskisy's child."

Pierre saw the arguments he was using were hopeless. He was forced to try another tack. He remained silent for several moments as he considered Miskoo's statements. He spoke gravely, "Miskoo, perhaps we can share the children. I will take your son into my lodge for part of the year, and you can have my son in your lodge for the other part."

The Indian blinked his eyes. He stared stonily at Pierre, his face unmoving. Pierre could tell his idea was appealing. "How do you mean?"

"For part of the year, Françoise will care for your son while your woman will care for mine. When Miskuy is with me, I will raise him as my son, like a white man; when Louis, my son, is with you, you will consider him as your son and teach him the ways of the Indian. Thus, our children will understand each other better."

Pierre could see how that arrangement would help him in his dealings with the Indians as he was sure Miskoo could appreciate the benefits he might derive from having a member of his family closely allied to a white family.

A smile came over Miskoo's swarthy face, and his eyes crinkled at the corners. "That's a good idea. Our families will be united as one."

The enormity of what he proposed struck Pierre. What would be the consequences of such an arrangement? Who would benefit? Would Françoise understand that he was backed into a corner? Would she understand that it was the only way he could retrieve their son? How would she react to the idea of having an Indian child for part of the year, perhaps half of the year? How could he be sure Miskoo would keep his end of the bargain?

Pierre's silence seemed to communicate his last thoughts to Miskoo who seemed to have similar ones, for he said, "This agreement must be sealed properly."

"Yes, my friend, your people have heard our talk. They must remember it and know that we are now one family."

"That's not enough, my friend. We must become blood brothers."

Pierre heard of the manner in which Indians could be united by a solemn ceremony whereby two men pledged themselves to each other for life by mixing their blood, but he did not know how it was done. His startled look showed his ignorance and apprehension.

Miskoo peered at him. "Are you willing to become my brother?'

Of the Indians he knew, Miskoo was the one he most admired for his sagacity, intelligence, and courage, but he was not sure he wanted to become so closely tied to the Micmac warrior. Although he accepted Christianity and was baptized, he retained most of his Indian customs and habits. Miskoo chose what suited him from the rituals of the Church, as well as those that suited him from his own culture. The blood brother ceremony was one he retained for his own purposes.

Pierre knew that Françoise would be horrified at the step he took to retrieve their son, but Pierre could argue that the child would be damned forever since he was not yet baptized. Françoise's piety would work to his advantage. He was without choice. But this blood brother business would be another thing.

Françoise feared the Indians. Stories of their savagery and barbarity were numerous. Each one she heard made her more fearful. Pierre reasoned: If she gets to know them well, she will see they're like all other people. They're kind, considerate, and sympathetic. They exhibit the same emotions as the white man: they love, they hate, they rejoice, they anguish, they beguile, they disappoint, they soothe, they aggravate—they're human.

Slowly he nodded his head. "Yes."

"Then it will be done."

A hubbub of excitement gripped the assembled camp as it grasped what their leader proposed. The ceremony was unusual and solemn. When it happened with a chief and warrior of Miskoo's stature, it was an important event, and more momentous when it occurred between an Indian and a white man.

Within minutes, a fire was lit in the fire pit behind Pierre; then the two men sat side by side facing east to the risen sun. Debitkat Iskisy was dispatched to fetch the calumet and the pouch of ceremonial tobacco. She returned with it, handed it to Miskoo who took it reverently from her hands, and carefully opened it.

The calumet consisted of two parts: a stone-carved bowl with intricate designs, geometric in shape encircling the base, and a long wooden tube that was inserted into the base of the bowl. From the pouch, Miskoo removed some powdery material mixed with greenish-brown leaves and particles of fine twigs. This, he tamped carefully into the bowl; afterwards he took a small brand from the fire and lit the mixture with short inhalations. The material glowed brightly as he sucked; a small wisp of smoke ascended skyward in the still air. He tossed the burning twig into the fire.

Grasping the pipe in both hands, he lifted it toward the sun and raised his head skyward. His lips moved as in prayer, but Pierre could not make out what he was saying. He then placed the end of the pipe into his mouth and drew strongly on it, causing the fire within the bowl to glow brightly; then it turned to gray ash as he inhaled the smoke into his lungs. He held the smoke in for several seconds and then blew it toward the sun. Without speaking, he handed the pipe to Pierre. Pierre followed Miskoo's example and raised it solemnly toward the sun. He placed the end of the stem into his mouth and sucked.

The acrid smoke entered his mouth and throat. It gagged him as he inhaled. His mouth, his throat, his lungs rebelled at the unfamiliar substance that irritated and burned; he fought to keep from coughing. The fiery sensation spread through his chest, choking him. He felt his muscles reacting involuntarily. He thought his lungs would explode, but he knew it would be improper to cough or sneeze. His host might be affronted.

He took the pipe from his mouth; his muscles quivered as he tried to control them. Then he blew the smoke skyward. Slowly his irritated membranes recovered, and the tears in his eyes dissipated. With blurred vision, he handed the calumet back to Miskoo.

Miskoo smiled as he accepted it. It was apparent that he understood Pierre's discomfort, yet he admired Pierre's self-control.

Debitkat Iskisy handed Miskoo a shiny trade knife. He accepted it as he had the calumet; he held it in both hands raising it toward the sun. He took it in his left hand and quickly drew the sharp blade across his right wrist cutting a fine line across the base of his hand. Bright red blood seeped from the superficial wound. With both hands he passed the knife to Pierre. Again Pierre followed Miskoo's example. Bright red blood oozed from the slight wound. Pierre's heart beat rapidly; he felt the intensity of the situation. Miskoo took the knife from Pierre and handed it to Debitkat Iskisy.

He reached for Pierre's right hand; Pierre did the same. Miskoo's hand grasped Pierre's arm above the wrist. Pierre did likewise. The blood from the cuts oozed and mingled together. Both men held firmly for several minutes, peering into each other's eyes.

Miskoo spoke solemnly. “Now we are brothers. Your blood is mine; mine is yours.”

Chapter Seventeen — Illness

In the months that followed, Françoise remained in bed, ill and depressed. For several weeks, at the outset of her illness, she was semi-conscious and did not respond to the ministrations of Monsieur Bourgeois, the colony physician, or Neremoosin's herbs and incantations. Marguerite and Jacques helped in many ways, spending days at Pierre's home doing the household chores. Other women of the colony also helped.

Late in October, when the leaves fell from the trees and most of the birds left for the south and the chill of winter was in the air, Miskoo arrived one morning with Debitkat Iskisy and the child, Louis Joseph. He informed Pierre, "I am going with my people to the winter hunting ground, but I will leave Debitkat Iskisy and our son with you for the winter. She will stay to take care of our son. Your woman is not fit to do that. She is still too ill."

Pierre stared at him. It was true. Françoise was not yet recovered; she was ill and weak, spending most of her time in bed. She lost much weight and looked frail and emaciated. Dark circles rimmed her eyes, which were sunk deeply into her head. Sometimes they glittered brightly, but most of the time they were dull and lifeless.

Why was Miskoo leaving Debitkat Iskisy and taking Neremoosin? Since they became blood brothers, Neremoosin stayed with Pierre and Françoise ministering to her and tending the household, as well as Miskoo's two sons that she cared for diligently as if they both belonged to her. Both thrived on the nourishment from her body, outgrowing their cradleboards. They spent a great deal of time outside on the ground and inside on the crude floor, frolicking.

"Why are you taking Neremoosin and leaving Debitkat Iskisy, my friend?"

"Several reasons, my brother. Our son, Louis Joseph, needs her, and it is time for me to live with our Indian sons. Soon they will not know Indian ways." He smiled.

Pierre smiled back at him.

Miskoo continued, "It is time for my wife, Debitkat Iskisy, to learn the ways of my white family. She asked to come and be with you. And I am lonesome for my wife, Neremoosin."

Pierre bowed his head in acquiescence. Miskoo's reasons were logical. He knew that Miskoo grasped that he could use the help of one of the women, but he resented Miskoo's lack of consultation on these decisions.

The change was made. Françoise, in her weakness, made no comment.

During her illness, Pierre fashioned a bed on the floor for himself. Neremoosin simply wrapped herself in a blanket and stretched out near the cradleboards in which the children slept.

Pierre missed the comfort of his bed, but most he missed the soft warmth of Françoise's body next to his. Often he would awaken, dreaming he was making love to Françoise, and then noticed that he was not sleeping in the same bed. Several times he approached her to take her in his arms, but she pushed him aside even though he intended only to hold and cuddle her.

Her lack of progress worried him. Some days she seemed to be improving, and then she would relapse and the fever would return although it never got as bad as it was at the outset. Just when she seemed to be recovering and her strength seemed to be returning, she would be sick again, and she lingered in bed, weak and unresponsive. During those days she would not talk to Pierre, but she needed constant attention. Debitkat Iskisy was more solicitous than Neremoosin was. She cared for Pierre, Françoise, and little Louis attentively and lovingly.

Winter came slowly but inexorably. No sudden storm ushered in the season; the temperature lowered daily and it snow regularly, so that by mid-January a thick layer of snow blanketed the countryside, and the streams were covered with a dense sheet of ice. Pierre was well prepared for winter: his animals were housed in the barn he built; he had sufficient quantities of feed and hay to last longer than was necessary. During the short winter days, he spent his time cutting firewood, although he had a stockpile from the last year. He liked the activity.

One January afternoon, as he tramped down from the uplands to the north of his homestead, he stopped and surveyed his home. The combined home-storeroom-trading post looked warm and comfortable as a thin wisp of smoke curled from the thick clay chimney of the stone fireplace. The log barn to the east of the house looked sturdy and utilitarian. His few animals were healthy and comfortable. The haystacks that he accumulated were fragrant, nourishing, and plentiful. He owned a home in this raw land. He possessed property, and he acquired plenty of food—domestic and wild. He would never have been able to do that in France. He was pleased he that he had decided to make his home in the New World. But two things marred his pleasure: Françoise's illness and her unwillingness to accept this land.

He was sure she would overcome her illness, but he was not sure she would ever accept the land. Often she complained about the loneliness and isolation. She still wanted to return to France, to her homeland, and her family. Pierre was sympathetic; after all, she was born and raised in the city; she was accustomed to the hustle and bustle of city life; now she found herself in a rural, almost wilderness environment. If they continued to prosper and he acquired enough money, he would send her to France on a visit. But, if he did, she might not return. The thought jolted him; he could not see himself without Françoise.

He shrugged his shoulders and resumed his trek to the barnyard. It was time to do the evening chores. Debitkat Iskisy came out of the house carrying a wooden bucket. She headed toward the well that he dug. In fascination he watched her. She threw a blanket over her head and around her body. Only her feet, encased in moose hide moccasins, showed below the blanket. He admired her; she kept his house without murmur, doing the many chores efficiently: caring for the baby, nursing his wife, tending to his needs, and not once complaining or remonstrating. For the first time, he looked at her as a woman.

Two days later, on Wednesday, as Pierre was feeding the cows in the log barn, a form filled the small doorway, shutting out the sunlight. Pierre looked up from where he was spreading hay in the log manger. For a moment he thought it was Jacques coming to propose an activity for the day: a hunting expedition, a trek to the fort, a visit to one of the other colonists, or even to one of the seigneurs of the area. Instead he was delighted by the sound of Miskoo's low, guttural voice. "My brother, it is time to see if my family is well and everything is in order."

Pierre laughed in invitation. "I'm happy to see my Indian brother. How's my Indian family? Are the little braves well and growing?"

"You would be surprised to see them. They are growing stronger each day, and they will soon be walking."

"All is well with Neremoosin?"

"She is well, my brother. I think that she is with child, but she did not tell me yet. In our culture, the father is the last to know." He laughed as if he made a joke. Then he looked at Pierre pointedly. "Is my other wife pregnant yet?"

Pierre looked at him solemnly as his implication sunk in. "She's not my woman, Miskoo."

"But, of course, she is. Brother, what is mine is yours. I left her here for your use, to care for all your needs."

Pierre never thought of Debitkat Iskisy as a lover; to him she was a woman to do the chores. He thought of her as a servant. "Miskoo, she's your woman. I have my own woman. In my culture, when a man chooses a woman, he's faithful to that woman…and to her alone. When he marries her, he promises to love her, and her only, for the rest of his life. So you see, I can't take your woman; it would be breaking my vow to my wife."

Miskoo shook his head in disbelief. Many things about these Christians he did not understand, and that he did not wish to understand. Their priests and shamans made life complicated for a man. If a woman was available for a man's pleasure, it was only right he take advantage of that opportunity. The Christians preached brotherhood, but, to Miskoo, they did not practice it. What did it matter who sired a child? If we were all brothers, then that child was the responsibility of all, not just the mother and father. He could not understand how the white man thought about his children. It seemed to him they were treated as a piece of property to be used and exploited. The white man used his children as slaves and workers; that was why he treasured them. The Indian used them as a gift and beneficence; that was why they belonged to the tribe.

"Is your wife with child?" Miskoo demanded.

The question irritated Pierre. That was not the Indian's business. Yet he felt compelled to answer. "No, my wife is still too sick. I don't sleep with her."

"That is the more reason you should be sleeping with Debitkat Iskisy."

Pierre did not like the direction the conversation was taking. Although he had not made love to Françoise for many months, and he often dreamed of the day she would be well enough to accept him back into her bed, he was annoyed by Miskoo's suggestion. That would be adultery and a sin, which he would have to confess to the priest. He could never be unfaithful.

Miskoo looked at Pierre wryly. "I have spoken to Debitkat Iskisy. She will make love with you when you are ready."

Pierre breathed deeply, and he felt his face heat up. The indifferent manner in which the Indian treated sex unnerved him. It was not love, or even lust; it was simply one of the needs of men and women that required fulfillment. It was another body function that must be attended to.

Miskoo continued, "You do not like my Debitkat Iskisy? You do not think she is beautiful?"

Pierre hesitated. He never considered her as a desirable woman. He never thought of her as a mate. He did not want to insult Miskoo, so he considered his answer carefully. He thought of Debitkat Iskisy's face. It was oval with a pleasant tawny color. Her black hair was parted in the center and neatly braided into two long plaits that hung down her back. Her forehead was broad and smooth; her dark eyes, large and deep-set. Her ruddy cheeks dimpled when she smiled, which was often. Her mouth was small and tidy with well-defined lips, neither thin, nor full. Pierre admitted that she was pretty.

Her body, he could not judge, for most of the time she wrapped herself in a coarse trade blanket over a nondescript doeskin dress that hung below her knees. The only thing he noticed was her breasts that were ample and full, topped with deep brown nipples. These he noticed as she fed his child, Louis Joseph. "Yes, your wife is a beautiful woman. I'm sure she'd make any man happy." He finished spreading the feed before the animals and then leaned against the doorframe.

"Since your woman is sick and cannot make you happy or give you pleasure, you may use mine."

"That won't be necessary. I will wait for mine. Soon she will be well, and we will make love, and I will sire another child. Thank you."

In the days that followed, Miskoo's words echoed through his mind, and he looked at Debitkat Iskisy differently.

In the evening, by the dim light of a candle and the flickering illumination from the glowing logs of the fireplace, he watched her as she moved silently and wraithlike about the small room of the living quarters. Françoise lay quiet and sleeping, or seeming so, in the far corner of the room. Pierre sat in a chair he constructed from saplings and strips of rawhide woven as a seat and back. He relaxed and stared into the flames, sometimes contemplating his future, and at other times, enjoying the warmth and glow of his home. It was then that his mind turned to love; he recalled the pleasure of Françoise's body, and his blood heated. His desire flamed; he contemplated the women who inhabited his world.

Françoise was sick and unavailable, weak and unable to satisfy, debilitated and not responding; feelings of guilt nagged at his conscience that he should think of her in that way. Then his thoughts turned to Debitkat Iskisy. She was healthy and available, strong and able to satisfy, vibrant and responding. He recalled, when their hands touched as she passed him a plate of food or placed the child, into his arms the warmth and pulsing feel of her flesh, the longer than necessary contact, and the glow of her eyes as they met his.

He noticed the swing of her hips beneath the shapeless gown. He admired the curved and globular breast as she fed the growing Louis Joseph. Each time the sepia nipples hardened as the child sucked, he could feel his fingers fondling and caressing them, and his lust stirred within him.

Each time he found his mind so occupied, he growled and struggled with his thoughts and body, and he said a silent prayer to banish his temptation. He tried to avoid contact with the young woman. During the day that was easy. He kept busy with the many chores that needed doing, or he visited neighbors and helped them with their many jobs. Often he visited Jacques and Marguerite, and one day toward the end of January, Marguerite who noticed his frequent visits, remarked, "Françoise must be improving. You spend a great deal of time away from home." She laughed as if it was a joke, but he sensed she was serious.

He laughed softly. "It's hard to keep two women satisfied."

Marguerite looked at him sharply. "Do you consider that Indian girl…a woman?"

The acuity in her voice annoyed Pierre, and he peered at her. Guilt flooded through him; he wondered if Marguerite read his thoughts and if his lust for Debitkat Iskisy was apparent. "Miskoo certainly considers her a woman. She's the mother of one of his sons. He considers her more beautiful than any white woman. You know, Marguerite, it's surprising how the Indians view white women. Actually, they think we're ugly, and their people are comely and attractive."

Jacques, who was silent to now, interjected, "If a man had no other woman, I'm sure he'd find an Indian girl attractive. I've heard they're uninhibited in their love-making and could teach a white woman a thing or two." He studied Marguerite with a twinkle in his eye.

She picked up a nearby wooden ladle and waved it at him. "Don't you ever try to find out, or I will ruin you for life. You will never be good for any woman, white, red, or yellow."

Jacques reached down to protect himself; Pierre laughed loudly.

Marguerite watched Pierre closely. "If those Indian women are so uninhibited, I'm worried for Françoise. Is she any better these days?"

Pierre shook his head sadly. "She's the same. If she's improving, it's very slowly. The doctor doesn't seem to be able to effect a cure, and the herbs Debitkat Iskisy gives don't seem to have any effect either. One day she seems to be improving, and the next, she has a relapse. She tries to rise from her bed, but the effort seems too much for her. I worry a great deal about her. I hope she recovers by springtime when everything else comes to life.

The months dragged on, as did Françoise's illness. Her condition changed little. Pierre was solicitous and tried to encourage her and enliven her spirits, but he could not please her. She grumbled and berated everything about the house, the farm, the neighborhood, and the country. He listened patiently and sympathized with her. She reiterated often that when she was well she would return to France and leave this God-forsaken country. He did not try to convince her otherwise; he even promised that she could return to France, but he meant for a visit, while he believed she wanted to go back permanently.

The last days of March saw the return of warm weather; the sun shone brilliantly, burning the snow from the fields and woods. Soon bare patches of earth appeared, and the dormant grasses turned green. The early birds returned, the rabbits and other varmints became apparent, and life was renewed. Pierre noticed a change in Françoise; she was improving, slowly, but noticeably. She often sat at the door and watched the plants and animals enjoying the springtime. But she was still too weak to leave the house and spent a great deal of time in bed. She depended on Debitkat Iskisy to do the work.

Pierre, too, depended on the Indian woman to tend to Françoise and little Louis. The child grew: he could sit by himself, and he crawled about the crude floor of the house. He was strong and loved to be on his feet. Whenever Pierre played with him in the evening, he held onto Pierre's fingers and bounced up and down vigorously. His hair grew; it ringed his head with golden curls. Pierre was proud of him.

Debitkat Iskisy seemed just as proud as Pierre. She treated the child as her own; sometimes Pierre felt Françoise was jealous of the surrogate mother. As she lay in bed, her eyes followed the Indian woman when she moved about the room, and, to Pierre, they glittered unnaturally. Debitkat Iskisy did not seem to notice as she cared for Françoise tenderly. The more Pierre watched the Indian woman, the more he appreciated her. Her tenderness, her concern, her desire to please, her willingness to help, her quiet ways, her calm efficiency made him feel he could never manage without her.

Although he never attempted to make love to her, he knew that if the right circumstances came about, he would have difficulty controlling himself. Many times he visualized the possibility. Her wholesome figure beneath the sack-like dress intrigued him, and in his mind he could see her smooth limbs, the curve of her hips, the softness of her stomach plunging to the darkness between her legs. Her tawny breast beguiled him, and he admired them each time she fed the child. They rose from her chest, high and full. Although they were unrestrained beneath the bodice of her dress, they were firm and up thrusting, the breasts of a young woman. The small berrylike nipples centered the smooth brown areola that extended in a wide band on them. He found them beautiful, more beautiful than Françoise's small, almost flat, breasts.

He tried to dismiss his lustful thoughts, but no matter how he tried, they returned to haunt and stir him. He knew that she was attracted to him also. On many occasions, she smiled at him in an inviting manner, and her eyes caught his and held them, asking him to possess her. Often she accidentally touched his body with her thigh or hip, and it lingered longer than it should. Then he felt his blood rushing, and it took all his self-control not to touch her. His hands seemed to have a mind of their own, wanting to grope and caress, but he held them back, feeling miserable because his passion was so strong.

Each Sunday, he rose early, did his chores, and then headed for the small church upriver to attend Mass. The entire community, except for the ill and infirmed, went to the chapel to fulfill their Sunday obligation. As well, it was a time to meet neighbors, to find out the latest news and gossip, and to learn about what was happening in the community.

The last Sunday of March was a perfect spring day. Most of the snow melted, the grass was greening, the bushes and trees, budding, and the birds were singing. The entire world was alive; Pierre felt especially alive.

On his return from church, the sun was high in the sky. It was midday as he sauntered up from the landing where he beached his canoe. He enjoyed the brilliant sunshine and the warmth it imparted to the world. He thought of the many things he must do in the coming season: the trade with the Indians, the land to prepare for seeding, the dikes that needed repair, and those to be constructed.

Because of his preoccupation, he did not notice Debitkat Iskisy waiting for him at the door. He started when her hand touched his arm. She placed her right hand over his lips and whispered, “Françoise and Louis are asleep. Let's take a walk and enjoy the beauty of the day.”

Her nearness flustered him. Before he could answer, she directed him north of the house toward the bank of the stream that flowed from the uplands. As she drew him along, he noticed that she prepared herself. She washed and redone her hair; the long plaits hung down over her breasts, from each plait a piece of colored cloth entwined and was tied in a neat bow at the end. Her ruddy face shone and glowed, and her cheeks gleamed as if she rubbed them vigorously. She led him along the path that bordered the stream, northward. As they moved slowly along it, the small animals and the chattering birds became silent; stillness followed them.

“It's such a beautiful day that I had to come to the woods to feel life stirring.” She spoke in Micmac, although she learned some French over the winter. Pierre improved his Micmac, yet it was not as fluent as his French was.

He answered in Micmac. “Yes, it is. But I must get back to my wife.”

“They're sleeping. They will not miss us for a short time. I want you to enjoy this day with me.”

He looked at her suspiciously. He was not sure what she was contemplating. If they went to a secluded spot along the stream, he was not sure he could control himself. She looked enticing to him; it was a long time since he enjoyed a woman.

She seemed to understand what was going on in his mind because she looked at him coyly, took his hand in hers, and smiled, showing even, white teeth. Her lips were moist and open, inviting, but he restrained his desire to take her in his arms and kiss her.

She skipped forward gaily, pulling him along. Her vivacity and vitality stirred him; he smiled down on her. Her fingers twined more intricately with his, and he could feel the warmth of her palm against his. The feeling pleased him; he knew he was heading for pleasures that should not be. He tried to stop, but he could not. The idea of returning to the gloom of his home skipped through his mind, but he dismissed it and followed the lively, pulsing body of the woman beside him.

His heartbeat quickened as he anticipated the possibilities within his grasp.

She found a small open area with new grass intermingled with that of the previous year forming a soft, springy mat. She threw herself to the ground and, still holding his hand, drew him down beside her. He sat down and gazed into her dark eyes. They glistened and glowed, inviting. For several moments he sat looking into their dark depths; they were large and almond-shaped, dark brown flecked with gold. She raised his hand to her lips and kissed the center of his palm.

The movement of her lips tickled, and the energy of it traveled up his arm through his body to his genitals. He placed his left hand on her stomach and caressed it through the thin leather of her dress. She sighed and placed her hand behind his head, entwining her fingers into his long dusky blond hair and drew his head down to hers. Her lips found his, moist, warm, and moving. Her tongue slipped into his mouth, electric and tingling. Pleasure shook his body, and he sighed noisily; it was so long since he experienced the softness and warmth of a woman's body.

He curled his right arm under her neck and shoulders, drawing her more tightly to him. His left hand explored her body, sliding down to the hem of her light dress. Slowly his hand roved over her thighs, caressing and fondling, rising tenderly to her crotch.

Her lips searched his with increasing frenzy. Her hands burrowed beneath his shirt, exploring his chest, rubbing his nipples. She drew his shirt over his head and tucked it beneath them. Her hands traveled down and caressed the muscles of his abdomen, tracing tiny circles with her fingers around his navel.

His fingers found her cleft, and he explored and fondled. Then he raised her skirt over her buttocks and loins bringing it higher and higher over her body, which writhed and twisted beneath his hands; each movement invited and encouraged him. He drew the dress over her breasts. His lips left her mouth to explore the valley between her warm breasts. A slight salty taste ringed his lips as he found the dusky nipple. His lips teased, his tongue taunted, and the dark nipple hardened and peaked. A sweet, syrupy liquid replaced the salty taste. The woman beneath him moaned.

He freed the garment from her shoulders and flung it aside. He raised himself and looked down on her naked body. Her dusky skin gleamed in the sunlight; a sheen of moisture covered her. Her eyes remained closed as she drew his mouth to hers. He lips roved over his face, down his neck, along his chest to his navel. His trousers were in the way so she pulled them down over his lower body and legs and placed them under her. She opened her eyes and gazed at his blood-engorged organ. Her hand took it and steered it to her opening.

He entered her. Pleasure enveloped him. The warmth and moistness stimulated him, his movements matching hers. Their energy flowed together, moving in rhythm, slowly, faster, building. Their bodies moved in unison. He could feel the explosion coming. Her body convulsed uncontrolled; her breathing came in great gasps; she flung her head wildly. Moans and whines emitted from her lips, and the sounds kept building until all her muscles spasmed, and she straightened in a final thrust.

At the same moment, his body erupted, and he fell limp atop her now relaxed body. For several minutes, they lay surfeit and exhausted. The power of their lust shocked him. He was never so satisfied in his life.

The next days were difficult for Pierre. Each time he looked at Françoise, guilt swept over him; he was sure she knew that he was unfaithful to her. Even worse, he found it difficult to keep his eyes off Debitkat Iskisy. Each time he looked at her, his mind returned to the short moments of pleasure that were his. Her passion stirred feelings he never experienced before. He still loved Françoise, but that love was shaken by the lust he felt for the Indian woman.

He threw himself into a frenzy of work. He re-organized his stock of trade goods; he prepared all his tools for the coming spring work; he inspected his fields and dikes; he did everything to be away from the house and the two women who were the source of his problem, but, even so, as he worked and planned, he could feel the pleasure that the young woman gave him.

The days lengthened, and the sun shone warmer and longer each day so he could spend more time outdoors. The entire colony was preparing for the planting season.

A small group of the oldest settlers decided to move to a new location east of Port Royal under the leadership of one of the wealthiest and most prosperous farmers, Jacques Bourgeois, a surgeon under the former governor of Acadia, d'Aulnay, who drowned when his canoe overturned in the Dauphin River in 1650.

Pierre was invited to join them, but Françoise's illness made such a move impossible. He could see the advantages of the new area—the choice of excellent lands, a less exacting seigneur who understood the problems of the habitant, distance from the governor and his officials that made it easier to trade with the Indians. The idea appealed to him, but he worked hard on his concession; he was proud of his accomplishments. As well, the governor, Grandfontaine, was his friend, who supported him in his dealings with the Indians; he gave Pierre a license. Pierre was careful to keep his trading activities as private as possible. Belleisle and many of the other colonists resented the favoritism the governor appeared to promote.

Pierre heard many complaints about Grandfontaine in this regard, especially his granting of licenses to the merchants and fishermen of Boston who traded in furs and fish. He knew that petitions were organized and sent to the minister in France; many rumors persisted that Grandfontaine would soon be replaced. Pierre hoped not. He prospered under Grandfontaine.

Although he was not part of the new settlement, he was interested in what went on. He was concerned about how it would affect trade with the Indians. Its location, on the main Indian route from the east, would intercept them as they came to Port Royal. Once during the winter, Jacques and he went to the new location; they were surprised at the amount of work that was done; the construction of dikes, homes, and fences impressed them.

Even though he kept busy and avoided Debitkat Iskisy as much as possible, he could see that the situation was becoming intolerable. She was open in her invitations for Pierre to pay attention to her; it would soon be apparent to Françoise the relationship between them was no longer a platonic one. The situation was trying on his nerves. He was committed to Françoise, and his duty lay with her. His standing in the colony would suffer greatly if his liaison with the Indian woman became common knowledge. His faith and religion forbade such behavior; each time he thought of the situation, feelings of guilt bothered him.

At every opportunity, Debitkat Iskisy tried to be alone with him. She flirted with her eyes and body, swinging her hips provocatively whenever she thought he was looking. Often she allowed her loose dress to slip from her shoulder revealing more of her breasts than was proper. She allowed the hem of her long skirt to ride up over her knees, even exposing her thighs and hips. She rubbed against him whenever she could, trying to arouse him. And he could feel the desire each time she encouraged him. He knew it was only a matter of time until he would succumb to her blandishments.

One morning she followed him to the barn, and flung her arms around his neck, clinging to him and trying to kiss him. He stiffened and tried to resist her aggressiveness, but her moist, warm lips against his weakened his resolve, and he found himself joining her passion. His hands roved over her body, feeling its pliancy and vibrancy as she pressed against him. The strength of his lust shocked him, but his mind cleared. He pushed her from him roughly, and whispered hoarsely, "I can't do this again. I love my wife and child. I can't make love to you."

She stared up into his face. "We're good for each other. It's right that you love me. I will ask Miskoo to let me stay with you. We are right for each other. You will be my man."

Pierre's eyes widened. What kind of mess was he in? This woman wanted to be his wife; she wanted to live with him. She would ask Miskoo to make her a gift to Pierre. He knew that was not uncommon among the Micmacs. What would he do? If he refused to accept her, Miskoo might be affronted. True, he enjoyed making love to her, but that was natural; he was without a woman for a long time, and she was available. He did not love her as he loved Françoise: it was lust. He did not want her as part of his household or his life. He did not want her to be the mother of his children: she was a pleasant roll in the grass, but that was all. What was he to do? How would Françoise react if she found out about his relationship with this attractive Indian girl?

He knew his life with Françoise would be finished. She would, without a doubt, return to France, and he would never see her again. She would take his son—his golden haired, blue-eyed boy—with her. He must do something or his whole life would be ruined.

Chapter Eighteen — Recovery

In the weeks that followed, Pierre was amazed at the change that took place in Françoise. The color returned to her cheeks; her appetite improved. Soon she spent little time in bed although, at first, she limited her activities to the easier chores about the house.

Pierre returned Debitkat Iskisy to Miskoo with the excuse that she was no longer needed in his house. Françoise was sufficiently recovered to care for most of his and little Louis needs; whatever else was needed he could manage himself. Miskoo accepted the explanation without comment although Pierre noticed an understanding look in his eyes. He reminded Pierre it would soon be time for little Louis to join his Indian family while Miskoo's sons would become part of Pierre's household. Pierre hoped the young chief forgot their deal, but he did not. So the arrangement was made that the exchange would take place when the Indians returned to their summer camp in three weeks time, after they finished trapping muskrats.

As Françoise recovered, Pierre returned to his bed. The boy now subsisted on goat's milk and solid food that Françoise prepared. Her breasts were dry; the child made the transition with little disruption.

Françoise made no comment about the disappearance of Debitkat Iskisy, and Pierre offered no explanation. The change seemed to help Françoise, and each day brought a brighter sparkle to her eyes and a jauntier bounce to her step.

April 16, a Sunday, Pierre, Françoise, and little Louis were invited after Mass for dinner at Jacques and Marguerite's. Although it was a dull, overcast day, it was the first time Françoise felt well enough to venture out. The congregation greeted her warmly, and she felt she was alive again. Pierre was happy to see the change in her, and he was particularly pleased at the effect the outing had on her. Her confinement to their tiny, gloomy house was not conducive to her recovery.

The ice was gone from the river, so boat travel was the order of the day. Many types of boats were drawn up on the shore before the well-built chapel, but most common was the birch bark canoe.

After the usual visiting and exchange of news after Mass, Pierre and his small family accompanied by the Bretons paddled to the Breton home. The youngest daughter, Angelique, was almost as big as the oldest, Geneviève, who was over two years old. She celebrated her second birthday on March 14, and Pierre and Françoise, who were her godparents, made a special effort to please the tiny girl. Pierre carved a doll for her so he made a special trip to give it to her. Her delight at the present sent a glow to his heart.

Once they were seated around the sturdy table Jacques constructed during the winter and that now Marguerite covered with bowls and dishes of steaming food, they bowed their heads and asked God's blessing. Solemnly, Jacques led the prayer and added at the end, “May God grant Françoise the strength to resume her duties as wife and mother, and give her the joy and happiness she has missed in the past months."

The group responded with a loud "Amen". Loudest of all was little Geneviève's tiny voice.

Françoise looked at Pierre and smiled. He reached out to clasp her hand. "My darling, I know you're on the road to recovery. Soon you will be as good as new."

"Yes, Pierre, spring has brought new hope. Soon I will be well and I can be you're wife once more."

The promise enlivened his desires. He pressed her hand in response; she returned the pressure. Pierre's gaze roved over her; she was an attractive woman; he could hardly wait for the day the promise would be fulfilled.

Both Jacques and Marguerite noticed the emotion that passed between them, and Jacques chuckled. "You two old married people shouldn't be behaving like two moonstruck youngsters, especially when you're visiting old friends."

Pierre grumbled, "It's been a long time since I've been able to behave like a moonstruck swain."

Françoise struck him with a clenched fist. "That's true, but we will make up for lost time. Louis needs a sister for company, and I need a little helper in the kitchen."

Pierre glanced from Louis to Angelique; the similarity of their appearance struck him: both were blond with fair skin; both were robust, sturdy children; both were able to sit and crawl about actively, although they were not walking yet. The older girl, Geneviève, although she could walk, was a quiet, pale child with her father's dark brown hair and complexion. While the two younger children gurgled and babbled with glee, she watched them with quiet curiosity.

Pierre felt a twinge of jealousy: Jacques and Marguerite did well. He glanced around their well built home; it was clean and comfortable—two large fireplaces, one at each end of the long building kept it warm and cozy. They were seated in the kitchen area that was at the left on entry through the door situated in the long wall that faced the river. To the right, was the sleeping area, and the center portion was the main living area. He felt pride also, as he had helped Jacques build the house; he knew that Françoise waited eagerly for the day when she would have a similar house. Perhaps, soon, he would be able to begin construction; then, maybe, she would forget about returning to France.

He heard Françoise say, "Geneviève is becoming a very pretty girl."

Marguerite smiled but said nothing. It was obvious she was pleased with Françoise's observation.

Jacques beamed and professed, "Some day she will break many hearts. All the boys will desire her, but she will probably enter a convent."

Pierre grinned. "That's true. Many nuns are pretty."

"How would you know? Where did you get your information about nuns?" Françoise teased.

"Ah, that's my secret." Then he looked at the child again.

Yes, she would be a beauty. Her dark hair was soft with highlights that reflected the light; her head was round and well shaped; her large dark eyes looked solemn, yet warm and loving. She had a pert nose and a small delicately formed mouth with rosy lips; her complexion, although dark, was even, and her skin was velvet smooth, without blemishes. Her delicate health and her small, dainty figure, though, might keep her from being an asset in an economy that required strong, robust women. Yet, if she retained her present aspect as she grew, she would be a beauty.

The day passed pleasantly, and it was late when they returned home. Pierre looked at his house with new insight; he could see why Françoise was depressed and hoped for a larger, more comfortable home. Their single room was cramped and cluttered although it was easy to keep warm and cozy. It was two years old, and the new home he promised her was still a desire.

As they lay side by side, Pierre mulled over the idea of building a new home. "Darling, I've come to a decision. This year, we must build. This room is too small and cramped. There's no room to turn around. We need more space."

He heard a gasp in the darkness, but she did not make a comment. For a moment he thought she might be asleep, but then she stirred and turned toward him. Her hand touched his face gently. She whispered, "You promised me that we'd go back to France."

He gasped. She had not forgotten. She still wanted to return to France. He raised himself on his elbow and tried to see her face in the darkness. "Yes, I did, and we will go for a visit. But not before we've made our home and fortune here."

She turned away from him; he could hear her sob quietly. The sound tore at him, his throat went dry, and tightness stiffened his muscles. "Darling, we will go back to France…in style, when we're wealthy, when we've achieved our goals, don't you remember? When we came here, we decided this would be our new home. And you agreed."

Her sniffling continued although it was apparent she was trying to control herself. The sobs lessened. She turned, sliding her arms about his neck. "Oh, Pierre, this country is too hard. One has to work day and night to earn a living. The winters are too long; the summers are too short. We will never make our fortune."

He held her close and patted her long loose hair with his right hand. She clung tightly to him, and he could feel her heart beating wildly. "Relax, my darling. You mustn't become so upset. You're working yourself up for nothing."

She clung to him for several minutes; her heartbeat slowly returned to normal, her sobs subsided, and she laughed, "I do take on so, don't I?"

He kissed her gently and murmured, "My poor sweet Françoise, this past year hasn't been a pleasant one. The future will be better, my darling." He kissed her again, and she responded.

Slowly and gently Pierre caressed and kissed her, and slowly she returned his careful questing. His tongue found her mouth and quivered tensely as it explored and entwined with hers. He moaned softly; it was so long since he felt her demand that the urgency of it surprised him. She drew him fiercely to her, and her hands massaged and clawed at his shoulders stirring him further. He slid his hands along her night-gowned body, found the hem, and slowly, languidly raised it over her knees, along her thighs, his hands exploring, searching, and caressing as he lifted it passed her hips. Françoise sighed deeply and writhed gently under his probing fingers. He drew the coarse nightgown along her stomach and lifted her hips to draw it past her waist. His hand slid along her stomach and gently patted her pubes, feeling the softness of her curly hair.

She moaned softly, sliding her hand along his chest to the taut muscles of his flat stomach. Its warmth was like a fire burning into his genitals, and his penis quivered with tension and excitement. His mouth explored her neck, and moistly, his lips roamed over her chin and neck. The opening of her gown obstructed him so he drew it quickly past her shoulders and over her head. Almost in one motion, he tugged his own heavy nightshirt over his head and flung it to the floor. His passion was building to a climax, and he forcibly restrained himself. He must make this a memorable event, not only for himself, but also for Françoise.

He nuzzled her ear and whispered huskily, "My darling, I love you with all my heart. You're my world. For so many months, I've been dead. I longed for you so strongly, yet I dared not think of this day. You were so sick I feared gravely I would lose you."

She said nothing, but drew his head toward her lips and smothered his face with passionate kisses. Pierre's left hand curled around her right breast, and the heat of it excited him; he searched carefully for the full nipple and squeezed it gently between his thumb and forefinger. It was firm and erect. Pierre slid his mouth to it and kissed the swollen protuberance gently, tasting it, sweet and syrupy. Françoise moaned softly as he fondled each nipple, first with his lips and then with his fingers. She clung to him and murmured quietly, though fiercely, "My Pierre, I love you. You're mine; you belong only to me."

Guilt flooded over Pierre as he recalled his unfaithfulness with Debitkat Iskisy. He stiffened momentarily, and the shock of it turned his passion to impotence. His mind swirled as he tried to banish from it the pleasure and guilt that his moment of weakness now burdened him.

Françoise inquired, startled, "What's the matter, Pierre? What happened?"

Pierre laid his head upon her bosom; a deep sigh escaped his quivering lips. His guilt tore at his inwards, and his passion subsided as quickly as it arose. He remained silent, trying to clarify his thoughts. Should he tell her of his indiscretion? If he did, would she forgive him and be his loving wife, or would she leave him and return to France with their child? Indecision and anxiety befuddled him so he remained silent.

"My poor Pierre, it's been so long since you've made love to me you've forgotten how." She laughed, and drew his face toward hers. "We must try again."

If she suspected he was unfaithful, she hid it well. Perhaps he should tell her, and then the heavy burden of guilt would be lessened. He knew he could not change what happened, but at least it would not be a barrier between them.

"Françoise, I've something very important to tell you."

He tried to see her face in the darkness. He listened for her reaction, but none occurred. Her breathing was even and quiet. "Did you hear me," he whispered.

She whispered back, "Yes, I heard you. I hope it isn't what I think." Her hands searched for his and found them. "I hope it's not what I think," she repeated. He noticed the anguish in her voice.

"I love you, Françoise, and I always will. You're my love, my life, and my wife."

"I love you too, Pierre, and I always will. When I married you, I vowed I'd loved you until death, no matter what happened. I took that vow seriously and with God as my witness. What you have to tell me sounds serious, but I promise you that no matter what it is, it won't change my love for you."

Pierre sighed with relief. Even if he was unfaithful, it sounded as if she was willing to forgive him. "It's nothing, my love. I will tell you another time. When it's more appropriate."

He bent to kiss her, and she clung to him, the warmth of her body flowing through him like lightning. Her passion revived him and coursed through him. She flung her legs around his thighs and squirmed atop him, her arms tightening about his neck as she squirmed upward so her firm, small breasts brushed his face. She moved from side to side so first one and then the other nipple slid to his mouth. He sucked at one until it was engorged and hard, and then he turned to the other. He could feel his erection returning; soon it was strong and vibrant, searching for her cleft. She reached down; her smooth hand enclosed it and traced a path along the lips of her vulva. Slowly she inserted it into her moist and slippery vagina. A raging fire engulfed their organs, and their pelvises moved in unison, the tempo increasing as their passion climaxed.

The next days were difficult for Pierre. Françoise became her usual happy self; it was pleasant to see her joyful and smiling again. Each day enlivened her, and her strength returned with renewed vigor. The months of neglected love seemed to inspire her to great levels of passion. Each night their lovemaking was wild and insatiable; Pierre never experienced such passion. On one occasion, she made love to him at noon when he came from his outdoor work for the midday meal.

Each time they made love, the specter of Debitkat Iskisy intruded, and guilt robbed him of the full pleasure of his wife's passion. The physical pleasure was satisfying, but his conscience gnawed at him and made him miserable.

He berated himself for not telling her about his infidelity when he had the chance. Now, each time they made love, he felt as if he was desecrating his wife's body with his sin. Although she did not seem to notice his anguish, he tried to find the appropriate opportunity to tell her about it and to beg her forgiveness. His desire to tell her became an obsession, and, even as he worked, he thought of nothing else. Twice his preoccupation caused her to ask about his pensiveness.

The first occasion was the morning after they made love for the first time. He sat staring at his plate of baked beans, fried pork, and coarse bread. Françoise noticed his distraction and murmured softly, "Pierre, what's the matter? You seem worried about something?"

He lifted his head and stared at her vibrant, smiling face. If she knew, would she still love me? he pondered. He returned her smile and mumbled, "It's nothing. I was just thinking of the work I must do today." The lie only added to his distress. One lie fosters another, he mused to himself. Why don't I tell her the truth and be done with it? He answered his own question. Because I'm a coward and I'm afraid my wife will hate me.

"It looks more serious than that, my love."

He did not reply and attacked his food.

The second occasion occurred as they were preparing for bed. Françoise climbed into their comfortable rush-filled mattress after she checked Louis Joseph for the night. Pierre, with a candle in a ceramic candleholder, checked the doors and windows carefully, taking an inordinate amount of time. He felt that she was anxious for him to join her, and the idea of making love to her repulsed him. His sense of impropriety stifled him; he hoped this night he could avoid his wife's passion.

She called, "Pierre, I'm waiting for you. Hurry. You never were slow to come to bed before my illness, but you seem to be avoiding me. Have you lost your strength?" She laughed.

Pierre blurted, "Darling, I must tell you something. It's very important."

She saw the pain in his face, and the smile left hers. The anxiety froze her and her face blanched. Pierre stared at her for several moments. Although she was recovering rapidly, she still appeared pale and fragile. Her lips whitened and her mouth tensed. He could see a strange glitter in her eyes as shock registered. The sudden change in her manner jolted Pierre; he wondered if she was strong enough to bear what he was to say. He knew this time he must go on; he must confess his sin to salve his conscience.

She remained tense, staring. Then she whispered hoarsely, "What must you tell me?"

Pierre set the candle carefully on the small table beside the bed and sat down on the bed beside her. "My darling, I love you and I always will."

She turned slowly and grasped his right hand in hers. She could see he was suffering. His eyes were dull and the lines around his mouth deepened with the mental strain. He looked away from her; he could not bear to look into her eyes. She clasped his hand more firmly, and he could feel the warmth and tenderness.

Why was I such a fool? How could I do that to my sweet Françoise? But I must tell her and beg her forgiveness.

Slowly he turned to face her. "What I have done is unforgivable, but…Françoise…you must forgive. Promise me…you will forgive me. Promise me."

She looked at him, perplexed. "How can I forgive you if I don't know what it is that you have done?"

He remained silent. His mouth worked, but no sound came from it.

She rubbed his hand gently. "Darling, you must tell me what's bothering you."

"Darling, I have sinned against you. I…I…" but he could not continue; his voice broke, and he bowed his head. His breath came in shallow gasps. He looked up at his wife. Her face was white, her eyes imploring, and her lips moved slowly.

He continued, "While you were so ill, I was weak. I let my animal instincts rule. My passion overcame me." He stopped momentarily and then rushed on. "I became an animal and behaved like one." He stammered, "I…made love…to…the Indian woman, Debitkat Iskisy."

Silence hung like a pall in the room. Pierre waited for Françoise to say something. She did not. She removed his hand from her grasp. She turned away from him. She twisted onto her side; he could see her shoulders shudder; he could hear her sob softly. He stared at her back. He wanted to reach out to touch her, but he dared not. It was not right to do so. He was the one who was unfaithful. He was the one who broke his marriage vows. He was the one who sinned.

The next two days were the most miserable that Pierre experienced. She treated him with contempt, as if he did not exist. She went about the house like an automaton, doing the household chores, tending to the needs of Pierre and Louis Joseph mechanically, silent and morose. Each time Pierre looked at her, his heart, already heavy with guilt, seemed squeezed with the pain of her sadness. Several times he tried to appeal to her, but she refused to listen to him and turned away or left the house to go outdoors and walk about the small yard.

Pierre was glad that neither Jacques nor any of his other friends and acquaintances came to interpose in their troubles, which he felt were private and personal. During these trying days, Pierre slept on the floor as while Françoise was ill. He tried to be patient and attentive, to draw her from her silence and hurt. No matter what he did, she ignored him.

The third morning, as she set his plate of fried pork, boiled gruel, and coarse bread before him, she looked at him fiercely and muttered hoarsely, "Pierre, I'm returning to France with Louis. I can't live with you anymore. You've destroyed our marriage and my love for you. I will be leaving as soon as I can make the necessary arrangements."

He was not surprised. He knew she never accepted the colony as her home although she agreed to come to the wilderness with him on the strength of his enthusiasm and glowing description of the land and its possibilities. He knew he was gambling since she was born and raised in the city. Port Royal was not the great seaport of Le Havre. But he was convinced that once she lived in the colony for a while, it would become her home.

It did not work: their home did not become established as quickly as he hoped, and he blamed himself for that. Instead of tending his land as Jacques did, he dabbled in the trade with the Indians and the merchants of Boston. Although he was reasonably successful and accumulated a credit with his Boston merchant friends, he did not develop his concession as he should. What could he say to convince her that he was sorry for his weakness and that he still loved her?

"Darling, I beg you. Give me one more chance. I will make it up to you. Please reconsider."

"I've thought about it carefully. I've tried to find in my heart the strength to forgive you, but I can't. You've hurt me too much. You've placed our love at the level of the savages. You've made our vows a mockery. You've reduced me to the level of a pagan barbarian."

"My love, you're right, and for that I'm truly sorry. I've already confessed my sin to the priest, and he's given me absolution. God has forgiven me, why can't you?" he pleaded.

A loud knock at the outer door sounded, and Pierre recognized Jacques's voice when he shouted, "Is anyone up in this house?"

Pierre shouted back. "Come in, my friend. Of course we're up. Do you think we're stay-a-beds like you?"

Jacques entered the dim lit room and bowed to Françoise as he took the chair Pierre proffered.

"What brings you here this fine morning, Jacques? Have you come to help me with my work?"

Jacques laughed heartily. "No, I've not finished my own, but the spring planting is coming along very well. I haven't seen either of you for several days so I thought I would see how you were. And give you some of the latest news. Lieutenant Richard tells me that Grandfontaine has been recalled to France. Soon we will have a new governor."

Pierre watched Jacques face. He was not surprised. He heard rumors the governor would be recalled. It seemed some of the important people of the colony felt their interests were ignored. One of these was his seigneur, Belleisle.

"I'm sorry to hear that. Grandfontaine was my friend and

benefactor. Do you know who will be the new governor?"

"No, Richard didn't give me that information. I don't think he knows, although I'm sure he had something to do with Grandfontaine's removal."

After Jacques left, Pierre said to Françoise. "Darling, you see, everything has a new beginning. Spring's in full bloom. The animals and plants have a new beginning. The birds have a new beginning; they're nesting and starting again with new nestlings. Even the colony will have a new beginning with a new governor. We must have a new beginning too."

He watched her intently. His heart went out to her. She looked so sad and forlorn. He waited patiently for her to speak. But she remained silent.

"Darling, I love you. I would do anything you want, but please don't go back to France with the boy. I love you both too much. I couldn't bear it if you were to leave me. I will build an new home for us...it will be a new beginning."

She raised her eyes to him. They were glassy with tears; her lower lip quivered slightly. She tried to speak, but her emotions interfered.

Pierre rose quickly and stepped toward her. He enclosed her in his arms, drawing her to him. He felt a shudder run through her body; the tenseness evaporated as she melted against him. He held her tenderly and slowly raised her face to his with his right hand. Tears accumulated at the inner corner of her eyes and slid down her cheeks. He kissed them tenderly savoring the salty taste.

"My darling, you mustn't leave me. I love you, and I believe you love me." He held her, and he could feel her heart beating strongly and quickly against his chest. She buried her head against his shoulder; quiet sobs shook her body. Silent, he held her, tenderly rocking her in his arms as a mother a hurt child. He knew he hurt her gravely. It would take time to heal such a wound.

He did not know how long he held her in his arms although he was happy at her closeness. Slowly her sobs subsided, and she clung to him for a long time. Pierre crooned to her and patted her head with loving strokes while his heart filled with joy. She still loves me, he thought. What a fool I've been. But I will make it up to her. I will never give her cause to doubt my love again.

Françoise lifted her tear-stained face to his and smiled softly. Her eyes glistened, and he could see the love shining in them.

"My darling," he whispered, "I love you. I will do anything you want."

Her face became serious, and the smile left her lips. "Would you leave this land and return to France?"

Numbed, he pondered her question. He never considered returning to France. He tried to visualize a life in France. He would be a poor peasant burdened with taxes. The taxes were staggering due to the continuing wars of King Louis XIV. Little opportunity existed for an ambitious person to improve himself; while here, in Acadia, the possibilities were unlimited. Farming, trading, commerce with Boston, and contracts with the military were all possibilities. A man could improve his position if he was not afraid to gamble a bit.

All these thoughts crowded into his mind and weighed heavily upon him. Françoise was asking him to give up much, particularly his dream of a better life for his family. If he returned to France, he would resume the life he had known—a poor coastal fisherman like his father who could barely provide for his family, or he might work for Françoise's father in the tavern. Neither of these possibilities appealed to him. Yet he promised her that he would do anything she wanted him to do. He loved her, and that was more important to him than anything else.

"Yes, my love. If you want, we will return to France. I would prefer to stay here, but my love for you is so great I will leave everything and go back for you."

Her face broke into a happy smile. She threw her arms around her neck, clasping him firmly. She kissed him on the cheek, and then she placed her hands on his shoulders and pushed herself from him to arm length.

"I'm so happy, Pierre. We will have a new beginning." She paused and smiled. "But, my darling, it will be here…in this land…that you love. We will make this land our home. We will make it better than France. We will make it a home that our children will be proud of. It will be our land."

Pierre stared at her. Did he hear right? Did he understand what she said?

She shook her head affirmatively. She smiled broadly.

Pierre's mouth dropped open in astonishment. He clasped her to him. His face beamed. She forgave him. Even more, she accepted this land as their home. All his hopes triumphed.

Printed in the United States
60568LVS00001B/4-21